THE COMPASSION OF FATHER DOWLING

THE COMPASSION OF FATHER DOWLING

RALPH MCINERNY

FIVE STAR

A part of Gale, Cengage Learning

GALE
CENGAGE Learning·

Detroit • New York • San Francisco • New Haven, Conn • Waterville, Maine • London

GALE
CENGAGE Learning·

Set in 11 pt. Plantin.

LIBRARY OF CONGRESS CATALOGING-IN-PUBLICATION DATA

McInerny, Ralph.
    The compassion of Father Dowling / Ralph McInerny. — 1st ed.
        p. cm.
    ISBN-13: 978-1-4328-2510-2 (hardcover)
    ISBN-10: 1-4328-2510-0 (hardcover)
    1. Dowling, Father (Fictitious character)—Fiction. 2. Catholics—Fiction. 3. Clergy—Fiction. 4. Detective and mystery stories, American. I. Title.
PS3563.A31166C66 2011
813'.54—dc23   2011033063

Published in 2011 in conjunction with Tekno Books and Ed Gorman.

Printed in Mexico
2 3 4 5 6 7 15 14 13 12 11

COPYRIGHT INFORMATION

Copyright Information

CONTENTS

OCCULT COMPENSATION

The suitcase full of money was left at the St. Hilary parish house early one morning. Marie noticed it lying on the back porch but left it alone—she knew all about bombs and the IRA. This was something with which the pastor could deal.

"There's a suitcase on the back porch," she said to Father Dowling when she brought his breakfast into the dining room. He was frowning over the sports page.

"Are you eloping?"

It would serve him right if she did just walk out and leave him to fend for himself. But the best response to such remarks was to ignore them.

"The Cubs walked in the winning run," he said sadly. "Bases loaded, bottom of the ninth, and they walked the opposing pitcher!"

"Maybe the suitcase belongs to him."

Father Dowling looked up.

"Who?"

"The Cubs pitcher. Maybe after that loss he's thinking of going into a monastery."

"Then he's come to the wrong door. Is there really a suitcase on the back porch?"

"There was the last time I looked."

He went on with his breakfast, taking his time about it, but Marie Murkin did not reveal her impatience. She was dying to know what was in the suitcase.

Eventually Father Dowling went out onto the back porch and looked at the suitcase. He studied it from various angles. He put his foot against it and pushed. It moved only with difficulty.

"What's in it?" Marie asked, trying to hurry him up.

"We'd have to open it to see."

"Bring it inside."

After another minute he did, laying it on the kitchen table.

"I suppose it's locked."

Marie pressed the clasps and they popped open. She lifted the top, stepping back warily as she did so. She gasped. The suitcase was packed full of money.

Marie bought lotto tickets regularly, not telling Father Dowling she did so, because he liked to explain how statistically impossible it was for her to win. But people won every day. For a crazy minute Marie imagined she had bought a lucky ticket and they had delivered her winnings during the night. This must be what winners felt like.

"How much is there?"

"Better not touch it, Marie. Why don't you call Phil Keegan?" Of course that is what he would suggest, and Marie could imagine the rest of it. He would turn over the money, the police would never find out who it belonged to, but they would never see it again.

"Don't you suppose the person who left that knew what he was doing, Father?"

"There must be hundreds of thousands of dollars here."

Marie had not seen many one-hundred-dollar bills in her lifetime, but here were stacks of them, none of them looking absolutely new.

"Someone meant for you to have this money, Father Dowling." It was a triumph of character that she had not said "us."

"Me? And left it on the back porch, near the kitchen door? More likely it was meant for you."

Thoughts of lotto returned. How often she had imagined what she would do if she won the big prize. Of course she would leave some money to St. Hilary's, several million. And she would help this person and that, make a large gift to the Poor Clares. But there would still be a huge amount left for her. It would transform her life. Exactly how remained vague, but it seemed to go without saying that Marie Murkin with millions would be different from Marie Murkin without them. Father Dowling had spoken of hundreds of thousands, quite a comedown when you have been dealing in imaginary millions, but Marie thought she could be a great benefactor with the contents of the suitcase.

"That's ridiculous," she managed to say. But then it was ridiculous for someone to just leave a suitcase full of one-hundred-dollar bills on the back porch.

"Well, if you don't want it, I guess we should call Phil."

Captain Phil Keegan, captain of detectives in the Fox River Police Department, came to the rectory, looked at the suitcase, opened it, and stared at the money.

"It looks real."

"It looks used anyway."

"Any idea who might have left it?"

The phrase that had come to mind when Father Dowling first looked at the money was "occult compensation." It was one of those phrases from moral theology that sticks in the mind. A penitent makes recompense for his sin secretly, this being justifiable under certain circumstances. He would have to check on those circumstances; he certainly didn't remember them after all these years. In the privacy of his own mind, he could ask if he had had a recent penitent whose forgiveness would have depended on his returning a large sum of money. But there had been no one.

Phil Keegan, once his judgment that the money was real had

been confirmed, assumed that it had been stolen.

"The problem is, as far as I know, there has been no recent theft involving a large sum of money in hundred-dollar bills."

"Maybe it was changed into hundred-dollar bills."

Phil looked at Marie. "All right, there has been no theft of this amount of money. But I'll check on it."

Actual thefts of money were usually in the hundreds of dollars, sometimes several thousand, depending on whether it was a gas station or a branch bank. Large thefts were now done in highly sophisticated ways, by transferring sums from one account to another via computer.

Two days later, when he came by to watch the Cubs, the team having returned from a disastrous West Coast road trip, Phil shook his head when Marie asked if anyone had reported the money missing.

"I'm glad you're being discreet about it, Phil."

"I don't want every professional beggar in Chicago descending on you."

"Maybe it wasn't stolen."

"Why would a benefactor just leave money on the back porch?"

"Bashful. Not wanting his right hand to know what his left hand was doing. Not wanting to be a Pharisee." Marie ticked off these reasons as if she had been giving the matter some thought.

"Anybody might have taken it."

"The fact is, there is no reason to think it was stolen or lost, Phil Keegan. I think it belongs to St. Hilary's and that you ought to return it."

"I'll leave it on the back porch some night."

"Phil Keegan, I am serious."

"That's up to the city attorney."

"The city attorney?"

"Fred Maxwell."

"Fred Maxwell! He's little more than a child. I remember when he was in the parish school . . ."

"He grew up. He is now the city attorney. He will decide where the money should go."

"I will call him."

Father Dowling shook his head. "Don't, Marie. If there is any chance the money was stolen, we couldn't use it anyway."

"What kind of thief would give what he stole away?"

"Robin Hood."

The following afternoon, Marie came to the door of Father Dowling's study, fixed her eyes on the far wall, and said, "Fred Maxwell is here to see you."

"Marie . . ."

"He just stopped by. I never called him." Marie said this in an angry whisper.

Maxwell was shorter than Marie and accentuated his baldness by shaving off what little hair nature had left on his head. His bright dark eyes behind thick glasses looked like Spanish olives in a jar. He was carrying the suitcase. Marie could have kissed him.

From the hallway she listened to Maxwell explain that so far as he could see this was found money and it was finders keepers.

"That's the law?"

"Well, not literally. But that's the idea."

"If it's lost, someone lost it. I'll run an ad."

Marie stopped herself from banging her head against the wall. Honestly. Put an ad in the paper and God knows who would show up at the parish house claiming all that money. But how could they prove it was theirs? The suitcase was a cheap and nondescript item, more new than old, with no initials or any other kind of identification on it. But what Marie feared was that they would be put in the position of disproving a claim.

Meanwhile in the study Father Dowling was actually trying to persuade Fred Maxwell to take the money away again.

"It doesn't belong to the city," Maxwell said. "I have no power to take it. That's why I brought it back."

"What would you do if someone left a suitcase of money on your back porch?"

"Don't ask."

Good man, Marie thought. And an honest one. Finders keepers was a rule most people would recognize as valid.

"Like flotsam and jetsam and sunken treasure?" Father Dowling asked her.

"Like a suitcase full of money left on the back porch of a parish house by a bashful donor."

"In *Huckleberry Finn,* whatever floats down the river is fair game for scavengers: lumber, houses, canoes . . ."

"Houses?"

"How long since you read *Huckleberry Finn?*"

"It's a children's book. A boy's book."

"You're very much mistaken about that, Marie."

Later, when Marie went up the walk to the shrine of the Blessed Mother to say a little prayer that the money would end up in the account of St. Hilary parish, she ran into Eleanor Pickerel. In her early sixties, Eleanor was a devout and pious widow and had become more so since the death of her only son. She was a bit of a pain in the neck, if the truth were told, but on this occasion Marie was delighted to see her. Not that she felt authorized to divulge the great secret.

"A glorious day," Eleanor sighed. Since it was chilly with the threat of rain in the air, Marie expressed surprise. "I mean it's Wednesday. The glorious mysteries." She flourished her rosary.

People like Eleanor could give religion a bad name. On the other hand, how could one discourage someone from praying?

"Remember my intention, Eleanor."

"What more could you want? Living right there in the rectory, busy all day with the Lord's work. You're almost as good as a priest."

"Don't say that!" Marie scolded, managing to suppress a smile of pleasure. "And don't think my life is all peaches and cream either."

"I know you have your crosses, Marie. We all do."

Eleanor's eyes rolled heavenward. There were those, and Marie was among them, who thought Eleanor Pickerel's life was smooth and uneventful, or at least it had been until the death of her unmarried son George, who had lived with her and, though he had no wife or family, had held a steady job at the bank for twenty years. All alone now, Eleanor seemed bewildered, almost like a girl again. Marie wondered what Eleanor's son the banker would have thought about a suitcase full of one-hundred-dollar bills showing up on the rectory porch.

Janice O'Grady came by that afternoon and Marie knew right away she spelled trouble.

"I'm from the *Tribune*."

"We already have a subscription."

She laughed a bell-like laugh. "I'm a reporter. This is Larry."

Larry wore jeans and an earring and had a tattoo on his forearm. Cameras were slung around his neck as he slouched a step or two behind the reporter, chewing gum and looking around the parish plant disinterestedly.

They had come to talk to the pastor about the fortune that had been left to the parish in such a curious way. So the news was out and the *Tribune* intended to broadcast it to the ends of the earth.

"Is Father Dowling in?"

It was a moment when Marie's moral fiber was tested to the ultimate. How easy it would be to convey without actually say-

17

ing it that Father Dowling was not available. She could say he was indisposed, whatever that meant. Of course Janice O'Grady would not believe her. Marie could not tell a convincing lie— that required a practice she did not have—but never had the impulse to lie been stronger.

Suddenly Larry sprang into life, lifting a camera and going into a crouch. Father Dowling had just appeared on the walk coming from the school, and the photographer shot half a roll of film as the priest approached.

"You're Father Dowling!" Janice cried, and Marie, saved from temptation, was now ignored.

That, of course, was the end of the suitcase of money as a secret. Pictures and story were splashed across the pages of the local paper, telling of the great bonanza that had come the way of the parish of St. Hilary. It was a media event when the suitcase was returned to the rectory. Fred Maxwell handed it to Father Dowling on the steps of the rectory, half turned toward the camera, the gleam of his bald head subdued by makeup. The cameraman moved slowly to the back of the rectory and Marie got inside just in time to avoid a cameo television appearance. She clumped upstairs to her room and it was all she could do not to cry.

Someone was certain to step forward and claim the money now.

Father Dowling would be eager to turn it over to the first plausible claimant.

There went a new roof for the rectory, so that the small stain on the ceiling of Marie's room would grow gradually larger.

There went a subsidy for Edna Hospers' work with the parish seniors.

And there, though she did not articulate the thought even in the privacy of her own mind, there went Marie Murkin's pilgrimage to Rome and an audience with the Holy Father. In her mind's eyes she saw herself wearing a mantilla, her chair pulled up next to the Holy Father's, while she gave him the benefit of her years of experience as housekeeper at St. Hilary's. Her job was after all a form of ministry. Now that consultation would never take place, and the Church would continue on its rocky course, unaided by her sage and prudent advice.

When the intruders were gone and she came downstairs, Father Dowling had stacked hundred-dollar bills all over the dining room table and was examining the empty suitcase.

"Are you going to leave that money just lying around?" she asked, shocked.

"Why don't you put it in the safe?"

He meant it. The safe was a little bread box affair behind one of the bookshelves in his study. Marie couldn't remember when it had last been opened.

"I don't know the combination."

"It's on a slip inside."

"Inside."

"It isn't locked, Marie."

It took her several trips and he brought in several bundles along with the suitcase.

"I wonder if Phil or Fred Maxwell noticed this, Marie."

He was pointing to a faded legend on the lid of the suitcase. The light had to strike it at a special angle for it to be visible at all. It looked like letters.

"Tripp," Father Dowling deciphered.

"As in going on a?"

"With two p's?"

"You think that's the name of the person who left the money?"

"I wonder if there is anyone by that name in the locality."

He would look it up, you could count on that. Marie went into the kitchen. Putting all that money in the safe had made it seem like theirs, but Father Dowling was obviously still intent on getting rid of it if he could.

"There are several Tripps," he called from the study.

"I never doubted it," she called back.

Tom Tripp was a plumber who snuffled as he talked and seemed reluctant to meet Father Dowling's eyes, but that was probably due to the convictions behind the evangelical slogans on his pickup's bumper stickers. "Call no man Father," he blurted out when Father Dowling identified himself.

"Have you read about the suitcase full of money that was left at my rectory?"

Tripp gave his head a little nod, as if one of his profoundest convictions had just been corroborated.

"The suitcase had the name Tripp on it."

"What?"

"I wondered if it belonged to you."

"You think I brought you a suitcase full of money?"

"Your name was on it."

He got out the suitcase and showed it to Tripp, having to angle it toward the light several times to get the letters to appear. Tripp stepped back as if he were drawn into some Romish liturgy.

"That's not mine."

"Isn't that your name?"

"The suitcase isn't mine."

"Do you know Myrtle Tripp?"

"My aunt? She died."

"I see she lived just a few blocks from here."

"She don't no more. The house is up for sale. We sold everything worthwhile and gave the rest to Goodwill."

"Could you have sold this suitcase?"

"You'd have to ask Louise."

"Don't mind Tom," Louise Tripp said. "He hates Catholics."

"I didn't think it was personal."

She looked at the suitcase, waited until he made the name visible for her, nodded. "That was Myrtle's."

"Did you sell it?"

She looked at him. "Would you buy it?"

"So it went to Goodwill?"

"Uh huh."

At Goodwill, Ainsworth the manager laughed when Father Dowling asked if they kept a record of their sales. It was a silly question. The Tripps had made their donation a month and a half before. The suitcase had been left on the back porch a week ago. Father Dowling went to the luggage section. Every suitcase there looked better than the one that had held the money.

Marie brightened as she listened to the account of the pastor's fruitless search to learn who had bought Myrtle Tripp's suitcase from Goodwill.

"All he wanted was something to put the money in. That's not much of a suitcase."

Marie sighed. "Well, we'll never know."

"It was someone in this locality who bought it during the month before the money was left here."

"I think you have exhausted the possibilities, Father. Finding the name Tripp on the lid seemed to promise a solution, but obviously we are no further along than we were."

"There would be no point in asking the one who bought the suitcase to come forward."

Of course he did not expect her to comment on that. With a light step, Marie went off to the grotto to say a little prayer of thanksgiving. She stopped to look back at the rectory roof. It was strange that it could look in such good shape. But then it only leaked over her room. Eleanor Pickerel was at the grotto,

21

saying her rosary. She turned. It was Friday. If she said, "It's a sorrowful day . . ."

"Marie, I am praying that Father Dowling will keep that money."

"He's doing everything he can to give it away."

"Why doesn't he just put it to good use?"

"He has been tracking down the suitcase in which it came."

"How could he do that?"

"He found a faded name on the lid and traced it to Goodwill."

Eleanor followed this with little birdlike movements of her head, hanging on Marie's every word. Marie was grateful to have so wholehearted an ally in her desire for that money to give a financial shot in the arm to St. Hilary's.

A man emerged from the bushes behind the grotto and cried, "Boo!" Eleanor let out a scream. It was Willie, the worthless maintenance man, armed with a hedge clippers, which he proceeded to snap at the now-giggling Eleanor.

"You frightened me to death," Eleanor said.

"I can't scare Marie."

Marie? How she wanted to tell this little Lothario to call her Mrs. Murkin if he presumed to call her anything. Eleanor turned toward Marie, covering her mouth with her hand, a giggling schoolgirl.

Willie went chuckling off down the walk toward the school. He had an apartment in the basement of the building. Having spent a good deal of his life in public institutions, he found life there very much to his liking. Watching him saunter off, Marie had an inspiration, one that she would have given anything not to have had.

The next twenty-four hours were agony. She could not sleep, she overcooked the vegetables, she thawed pork chops without realizing it was Friday and at the last minute substituted some sole from the freezer which tasted like its shoemaker counter-part. Of course the pastor did not notice, but he would have noticed being served meat on Friday. He kept to the old discipline as a reminder that one was expected to perform ascetic practices despite the doing away of Friday abstinence. Some, he thought, had taken that change to mean a repudiation of the grim asceticism of the preconciliar Church. Later in her room, Marie said the rosary again and again, if you could call slipping beads through your fingers and murmuring Hail Marys when your mind was a million miles away saying the rosary. She was haggard when she went down to her kitchen in the morning. No soldier going into battle had required more fortitude than she when she spoke to Father Dowling after he had finished breakfast.

"I have been thinking of that money, Father."

He looked reproachfully at her, but she ignored this.

"I think I know where it came from."

"Oh?"

She leaned across the table and said significantly, "Willie."

"Marie, I doubt that Willie had that much disposable cash."

"It's stolen!"

"But both the police and Fred Maxwell looked into that. There is no unaccounted-for stolen money in this amount."

"You mean lately."

"I don't understand you."

The explanation had leapt into her mind unbidden and she could not believe that he had not seen it right away, too. She spelled it out for him. Willie was an ex-convict. He had spent years and years in the company of men who were murderers and thieves. That money could have been stolen years ago and only now turned up.

"On our porch?"

"Father Dowling, I have heard Willie as much as tell people

23

that he lives right here in the rectory with you. You would not believe the way he describes his position in this parish."

"I still don't understand."

"The money was meant for Willie. One of his old cronies got out of prison, dug up the money he had stashed away, and left it with Willie for safekeeping."

He sat back and lit his pipe. He nodded through an aromatic cloud of smoke. "The best thing about your theory, Marie, is that it can be easily tested."

She was surprised. From skeptic he had become her ally. She was wary.

"What do you mean?"

"We talk to Willie and to the Joliet and find out who has been released from prison in the last six weeks. We get a picture of them and we take it to Goodwill and ask if this person bought a suitcase there."

Marie's heart sunk even further. Of course he would think of a surefire way to test her theory. He telephoned Chavez, his classmate who was prison chaplain at Joliet, and two hours later pictures of three recent parolees curled from the fax machine. Father Dowling asked Marie to mount them on cardboard. Meanwhile he went off to the school.

As they drove to Goodwill, Marie wondered aloud what they would really learn if the purchaser of the suitcase was identified.

"Well, if he is a thief we will find what he was imprisoned for stealing. If it is an amount of money as large as what was left on the porch, we can return it to its rightful owner."

Marie nodded, staring gloomily ahead.

At Goodwill, Ainsworth the manager came with them as they showed the clerks the pictures. Several seemed unsure whether they should admit it if they did recognize the man in any of these pictures. Ainsworth assured them that they should. Even so, all Father Dowling received was shaking heads. No, they hadn't seen any of those four men.

"Four?" Marie asked.

"I added one as a control."

But it was to the fourth picture that a fifty-year-old woman with coal black hair and orange lipstick pointed. "Sure, I remember him. He tried to get a date. What's he done?"

"Did he buy anything from you?"

She shifted her gum and shut her eyes. When she opened them, it took a second for the lashes to become unstuck. "A suitcase."

"You're certain of that, Maxine?" Ainsworth asked.

"What's wrong with buying a suitcase?"

"There's nothing wrong with it," Father Dowling assured her.

"The little rascal wanted my phone number He said that now that he had a suitcase we could run away together." Despite herself, she giggled.

Marie took the fourth picture to look at it. It was the face of Willie that smiled at her from it.

"Willie!"

"It's your theory, Marie."

But she was no longer sure what to make of her theory. If Willie had left the money on the back porch, that meant the parish would be forever indebted to the little ex-convict. A benefactor was a benefactor, but Marie was certain she could not survive such an elevation in Willie's status. He was pompous on the bottom rung. What would he be like on the top? She could not keep the thought to herself.

"If he be like this in the green wood, what would he be like in the dry?"

"He'll be impossible."

"Marie, if Willie left that money, he obviously wanted it to be a secret."

"And we have to respect that!"

"I wish we could!"

"What do you mean?"

"Marie, if it's stolen money . . ."

When Willie showed up in the doorway of Father Dowling's study, his expression was unsure. How many times in his life had he been called on the carpet with devastating consequences for himself? Before Father Dowling informed Phil Keegan of Willie's purchase, he wanted to give the maintenance man a chance to explain himself. There had been thefts in Willie's career on the far side of the law, but Father Dowling was certain there was no unaccounted-for money. If there had been, it is doubtful Willie would have been allowed out on parole.

"You wanted to see me, Father."

"Close the door, would you, Willie?"

In the kitchen, Marie cleared her throat, but then the door was closed and there was silence.

"I should have asked you this before, Willie, but what do you make of that money being left on the back porch."

Willie pretended that he had to remember. "What do I think about it?"

"Have you ever heard such a thing?"

"Father, since I came to work here, all kinds of things I never heard of happen. Meaning no disrespect."

"A suitcase of money would be a surprise anywhere, don't you think?"

"I guess it would."

"Any idea where it came from?"

"You're asking me?"

"The police tell me that there have been no recent thefts of that amount of money."

"They ought to know."

"But what if it isn't a recent theft?"

"I don't follow you."

"It's just a wild idea, you understand. But imagine that someone you came to know in Joliet had stolen money and hidden it away. Finally he gets out and he retrieves the money."

Willie closed his eyes and wrinkled his nose. "I'm trying to think if any of those who got out lately . . ."

"It wasn't any of them. At least it's not on their record."

Willie's eyes opened. "So what are we talking about?"

"The suitcase you bought at Goodwill."

Willie was obviously unprepared for that. He had been warming to the theory that Father Dowling had suggested, and his manner had become one of collaboration. Now he nearly fell off his chair.

"How'd you know that?"

"Tell me about it, Willie."

"They can't prove that I—"

"Maxine remembers you, Willie. Black hair, orange lipstick."

Willie made a face. "But what's the charge? What have I done wrong?"

"The suitcase you bought ended up on the back porch with a very large amount of money in it, all in one-hundred-dollar bills. How did that happen?"

"I take the fifth."

"Willie, this is just you and I talking. This isn't a court. It isn't police headquarters."

Willie squirmed at the mention of these institutions. But he said nothing.

"Tell me, Willie. I can't help you if I don't know what happened."

"I can't."

"Why?"

He shook his head. "I just can't."

"Are you afraid?"

"Of what?" His narrow shoulders firmed.

"I don't know. I can imagine that you might not want to tell me who you bought the suitcase for because you're afraid of what they'll do to you."

"I ain't afraid."

The silence grew. Finally, Father Dowling broke it. "Willie, think this over. Take until tomorrow. Then let's resume our conversation."

Willie scrambled to his feet. "I will. I'll think about it." At the door he turned, his chin lifted. "But I can't tell you, Father. Not ever."

Phil came and they watched a ballgame although only the White Sox were on. Neither of them had even been born when the infamous Sox threw the World Series, yet they thought of the Southside team as a new arrival, seeking to usurp the role of the venerable Cubs. Still, rooting for the other team went against the grain, and they were grateful when the skies opened and there was a rain delay.

"I don't want to listen to Popeye and Wimpy," Phil groused.

Roger turned off the set. He wanted very much to tell Phil about the suitcase, if only because he feared Phil would hear about it from someone else, but he had given Willie until tomorrow and he meant to keep his word. Did he think the postponement would make a difference? Willie had been so uncharacteristically firm when he repeated that he would never explain why he bought that suitcase. Father Dowling wished that he could believe that Willie out of loyalty was protecting a fellow parolee. Yet he had said he was not motivated by fear and Roger Dowling believed him. There seemed only one other explanation.

Whatever the provenance of the money, it made no sense that Willie would have put it in a suitcase and just left it on the back porch of the rectory, expecting it to be discovered safe and sound. What now occurred to Father Dowling was that only Willie might be involved. He alone was responsible for that money. And he had given it to the parish. At the outset he had thought it might be a case of occult compensation. Did that fit Willie?

"Phil, was Willie ever involved in a large robbery?"

"Large enough, I guess." Phil's eyes might have been scrolling down Willie's record on the computer of his mind.

"I suppose all the money stolen was accounted for."

Phil thought, then nodded. "I'm sure it was."

"Could you check?"

"Any reason?"

"I'll tell you, depending on your answer." Marie came in with popcorn then and wondered why the game wasn't on. If Phil had been inclined to pursue the matter, Marie's interruption distracted him. When she left, claiming she couldn't breathe with all that smoke, the conversation turned to different topics.

"It's Eleanor Pickerel," Marie said the next day. It was just after nine and Father Dowling had been about to go over to the school. Something in Marie's tone and expression caught his attention.

"Maybe I should see her in the front parlor."

Marie's nose wrinkled. "I would. Meanwhile I'll open the window."

"Don't." He shepherded her before him and closed the door of the study. That room was off limits to Marie and she knew it.

In the front parlor, Eleanor sat facing a window, staring straight ahead, seemingly in a trance. When the pastor greeted her, she lifted from the chair as if she might rise effortlessly to the ceiling. She ran to the door and pulled it shut.

"I have to talk to you, Father."

He sat behind a table, not reacting to her agitation, and

pointed to the chair she had been sitting in. She pulled it up to the table and faced him.

"Willie told me that you found out he bought that suitcase."

"He told you that?"

"Yes?"

"Why?"

"Because I asked him to buy it."

Marie had brought the pastor stories of Willie's flirting with Eleanor and of her schoolgirl reaction. Had Willie prevailed on the poor woman to sacrifice herself for him?

"What did you want it for?"

"To put the money in."

"I see."

"Willie didn't know what I wanted a suitcase for. I didn't really intend to ask him to buy it. But he said he was going shopping and wanted me to come along—imagine! Of course I said no and then he asked me if I needed anything, and I said yes, a carton or maybe a suitcase. That is why he bought it."

"But where did the money come from?"

She glanced over her shoulder at the closed door, then continued in a whisper. "You remember my son, George."

"Indeed I do." The young man's funeral had been from St. Hilary's of course and Father Dowling had presided. "I remember him in my Masses."

"Oh, thank you, Father. Thank you." Her eyes brimmed with tears. "I found the money when I was straightening out his room, afterward, decided what to keep, what not to keep. It was in the closet. There's a little dresser in there, wedged in, sort of for overflow, socks, shorts, that sort of thing."

"The money was there?"

"In the bottom drawer. Just as you found it in the suitcase. Oh, Father, think of it. All those years working in the bank, and he was a thief!"

She broke down completely then and Father Dowling tried to comfort her. He felt like a fool for suspecting Willie. There would have been something almost innocent about a professional thief possessing stolen money, but George Pickerel had been the picture of rectitude. Father Dowling had never seen the man except in a suit and tie. He seemed to belong behind his desk, visible to those who were doing business at the counters, in his element.

"You think he embezzled that money?"

"You saw the amount!"

"Had you thought of returning it to the bank?"

"And destroy George's reputation? They thought so highly of him at the bank. Of course I couldn't keep it. So I put it in that suitcase and left it on your back porch."

Having told her dread secret, Eleanor wanted to retell it, again and again, and Father Dowling felt he owed her the patience he eventually found difficult to summon. Of course it was a dreadful thing, to come upon a fortune hidden in her son's closet after his sudden death.

There was a tap on the door and Marie peeked in.

"Only ten minutes until your Mass."

"Thanks, Marie."

When the housekeeper closed the door again, Father Dowling said, "You could confide in Marie, Eleanor. She is discreet. It won't go beyond her. And you have to talk about this with someone."

She agreed. He took her to the kitchen and when he left for the church to say his noon Mass they were huddled over tea while Eleanor told her story one more time.

Emery Bouffant occupied the presidential offices of the Fox River First National Bank with authority. He was a Methodist and a Mason but tolerant of error and he welcomed Father

Dowling with edgy cordiality. The priest got right to the point.

"Has money been embezzled from this bank in the past half year?"

"I beg your pardon."

"Are there any unaccounted-for losses?"

Bouffant had grown red and placed his palms flat on his desk. "I resent these questions, Father Dowling. They have the tone of accusations. Are you making an accusation?"

"George Pickerel was my parishioner."

"So?"

"After his death, his mother found a large sum of money hidden in his closet."

Bouffant fell back in his chair, his eyes seemed to be following a tennis match just behind his visitor. He looked directly at the priest. "The money I've been reading about? The money left at your rectory?"

"Yes. If it the bank's, of course I want to return it. Hence my questions."

"They caught me by surprise."

"Is your answer still the same?"

"Father Dowling, I will have a special and very confidential audit conducted. I cannot believe that such an amount could have been embezzled from this bank. Still, over many years . . ." He shook away the unwelcome thought. "I will let you know." He stood. "Meanwhile, can this be kept out of the newspapers?"

"I was about to ask the same thing."

On a note of offsetting indignation, they parted.

Two weeks later a large expensive car drew up at the curb and Emery Bouffant emerged from the back seat. He strode toward the door of the rectory, and seeing him approach Marie could have wept. The banker had the look of a man come to claim his money.

Marie opened the door, showed him into the parlor, and went to fetch Father Dowling. She went on to her kitchen, closing the door, too dispirited even to eavesdrop. So much for the rectory roof. So much for Edna's program. So much for the private audience Marie had wanted to give the Pope. She poured a cup of tea, but it went cold in the cup, undrunk. Outside a squirrel scampered across the lawn, its tail flying. Birds sang. Sunlight threw moving shadows of branches on the grass. It was a picture of peace and contentment and Marie wanted to cry.

Half an hour later, Father Dowling looked in on her.

"Well?" she said.

"I sent the money off with him."

Marie, unable not to, let out a wail. Now all hope was gone.

"He will put it into the parish account. Is there a roofer among our parishioners?"

Whiplashed between emotions, Marie rose to her feet, demanding to know what he meant.

"Didn't George Pickerel steal that money?"

"Steal? A member of this parish embezzle money? Marie, please, get control of yourself."

And off he went, the dining room door swinging back and forth after him. Marie clamped a hand over her mouth. She felt another wail coming on and didn't know whether it was joy or anger or what.

Eleanor Pickerel's joy in the exoneration of her son was clouded by the fact that she had suspected him of stealing from his place of work. The truth was that each week, when he cashed his salary check, George had asked for a hundred-dollar bill. Cashiers over the years remembered this. Ten years ago he had asked for two one-hundred-dollar bills each week. If curiosity were permitted in cashiers they might have wondered about it, but they did not. Remember it they did, however, and that had been more decisive than the negative results of the audit.

"The money is yours, Eleanor," Father Dowling insisted.
She shook her head. "I gave it to you."

"But at the time you didn't think it was yours to keep."

"I owe it to George not to keep it."

It seemed an odd moral rule, yet Father Dowling thought he understood it. He told her he would take half and finally she agreed and Emery Bouffant transferred it to her account.

"Why didn't George keep his savings in the bank?" Phil wondered.

"Apparently he didn't trust banks."

It was a curious story. A man squirreling away those hundred-dollar bills over the years. His mother finding them after his death, assuming he had stolen them, and then packing them up and leaving them at St. Hilary's rectory.

"Occult compensation," Father Dowling said, and puffed on his pipe.

"Occult what?"

"Occult compensation," Marie repeated, looking at Phil as if he were the class dunce.

"What's it mean?" Phil demanded of her.

"Tell him," Father Dowling urged.

A wild look came into her eye. "You tell him."

"Its unemployment insurance for fortune tellers," the pastor of St. Hilary's said didactically. "That's right, isn't it, Marie?"

"If you say so."

And she retreated to her kitchen.

QUEEN BEE

1

Marie interrupted her counting of the collection and went impatiently down the hallway. The pastor of St. Hilary's, happy to have his housekeeper sort and count the offerings from the Sunday Masses, was in his study reading Aquinas.

"Another fifty-dollar bill?"

For answer Marie flourished an envelope. "Someone put this in the basket."

It was one of the small envelopes in which parishioners made their weekly offerings. Marie pulled from it a sheet of paper that had been folded several times so that it would fit.

"I thought it was a wad, even if they were only ones." Marie was disgusted with what she clearly considered a dirty trick.

Father Dowling unfolded the paper. After a moment, he looked up. "Did you read this?"

"What does it say?"

"I'm not sure."

"Let me see it."

She took the paper and frowned over it for several minutes. "Ooyay iliway eyeday?" She looked up and thought and then, "It's pig latin!" But triumph quickly gave way to alarm.

"What does it mean, Marie?"

"You will die." She spoke in a whisper.

"That's true enough."

"Father, it's a threat!"

"To whom?"

"You."

"I wonder."

Marie thought about it. She was not bashful about letting people know that she counted the collection each Sunday, immediately after the noon meal, before she went upstairs for a nap. Could this threat be directed at her? She didn't like that at all.

"Call Captain Keegan."

"He's coming over. I'm surprised he isn't here."

When the doorbell rang, Marie was down the hallway like a shot, and after admitting Phil Keegan she chattered to him all the way to the study. The Fox River captain of detectives came into the study, looked at the note, and raised his brows.

"This Polish or what?"

"It's pig latin. It says 'you will die.' "

"Who?"

"What difference does it make who? It's a threat. Someone put that in the collection basket this morning."

"What Mass?"

"I don't know!"

"Maybe it's a joke," Phil said. He had come for the second half of the first game and then for the Bears who played the Vikings at three.

"What are you going to do about it?"

"I'll take it with me," Phil said. He did not quite wink when he glanced at Father Dowling.

"Fingerprints?" Marie asked.

"If you haven't smudged them all."

It was when Phil was putting the folded sheet of paper into the envelope again that he stopped.

"You missing a pin, Marie?"

It was a common pin, of the kind found in great number in

new shirts. Phil shook it out onto Father Dowling's desk. The priest leaned forward.

"Better be careful of that, Phil."

"Why?"

"There seems to be something on its point."

The something, lab tests showed, was not a poison. The tip of the pin had been dipped in honey. Phil, feeling that someone was pulling his leg, was no longer disposed to take the matter lightly.

"Has anyone been threatening you, Roger?"

"No."

"Can you think of anyone who might have done this?"

"Syl-ves-ter," Marie said in a hissing whisper. "Sylvester!"

"Oh, Marie, come on," Father Dowling said.

"Who's Sylvester?"

Marie sat down in a chair whose back was snug against a bookshelf. "I want to hear this explanation myself."

"He's one of Marie's admirers."

Marie was on her feet immediately. In the doorway, she turned, searching for some devastating remark on which to leave, but finding none made a despairing sound and clumped off to her kitchen.

"Tell me about Sylvester."

The fact was that Roger Dowling knew very little of the man who had been a frequent presence at St. Hilary's over the past several weeks. Most seniors showed up at the parish center in casual clothes, but Sylvester Sloan always wore a suit. It lent him a prosperous air.

"It's always the same suit," Marie said, puncturing that balloon. "And his shoes need resoling."

"You should talk to him about it."

"Hmph."

For some weeks past, the collection had contained, along with envelopes and bills that were rarely higher than fives, a rather noteworthy fifty-dollar bill. Several times, Sylvester had sought unsuccessfully to engage Marie in the pointless conversation that signals the beginning of courtship. This came down to Marie's saying that he was becoming a pest. Her advice had been that, at his age, he should be thinking of the next world. Marie had formed the theory that Sylvester Sloan, doubtless rendered delirious by passion, was the generous giver, but now she had cast him for another role.

The following Sunday there was another note, but if Father Dowling had not asked Marie, he might never have known.

"It's a silly joke."

"What's the message this week?"

She fished a crumpled piece of paper from the wastebasket and handed it to him as if her right hand did not know what her left was doing. Father Dowling unfolded it.

"Ooyay ryay eetsway as oneyway." Having grasped the principle from the previous note, Father Dowling deciphered. "You are sweet as honey? You'll want to keep this one, Marie."

"I want you to speak to Sylvester Sloan. It's not right using the collection basket for messages."

"I suppose he's bashful."

"I don't want to talk about it."

"I understand."

Marie glared at him and he mentally struck his breast. He had resolved to stop teasing the housekeeper, but found it difficult to resist the opportunities afforded.

The following day, having finished saying his Mass at noon, Father Dowling was about to return to the rectory for lunch when he noticed a man sitting in a back pew. Had he been there during Mass? And then he recognized Sylvester Sloan. It seemed a golden opportunity to speak to him about his notes to Marie.

Father Dowling went down a side aisle toward the back of the church. From one of the open windows came the sound of buzzing of bees. Sylvester took no notice of the pastor's approach but sat staring straight ahead. Private prayer was usually engaged in with closed eyes, but Sylvester seemed to march to another drummer in many things.

Father Dowling came up behind the seated man, and said, "Mr. Sloan?"

No reaction at all. The pastor felt rebuffed. Of course, the man might be deep in prayer. But the prospect of returning to the rectory without availing himself of this opportunity decided Father Dowling.

"Sylvester," he said, quite loudly. After all, it might be deafness that explained the lack of response. Father Dowling put his hand on Sylvester Sloan's shoulder and immediately the man began to tip sideways. In a moment he was lying on his side, his body still in a seated posture. His expression did not change. That was when Father Dowling realized that Sylvester Sloan was not breathing.

2

It was some hours before anything like calm was restored to the parish plant of St. Hilary. The retired parishioners who spent their day in the senior center had been drawn outside by the arrival of ambulance and police cars. That one of their number had died was of course a matter of some interest to them, since they were all fast approaching that decisive moment themselves. But how might it happen, and when and where? There were those who seemed to be grudgingly envious of Sylvester Sloan, dying in church, the very vestibule of eternity.

"He had absolutely no identification on him," Phil Keegan

reported when he stopped by the rectory later. "In fact all his pockets were empty."

"He had a handkerchief in the breast pocket of his suit."

"With a phony fifty-dollar bill wrapped in it."

"Phony?"

"Why did you think his name was Sylvester Sloan?"

For this, Edna Hospers, who was director of the senior center, had to be consulted. Edna had a touch of flu and had to be called at home.

"That's the name he gave me when he signed up."

"Is that in your office?"

It was. Marie offered to go get Edna's records, but that would have been like giving Edna the freedom of Marie's kitchen. The uneasy truce that had been obtained between the two women must not be unduly tested. The pastor said that he and Captain Keegan needed the walk.

Edna had computerized her records. The entry for "Sloan, Sylvester" came up on the screen, along with an address. Phil immediately called it downtown where they were still looking for next of kin to notify. Cy called before they left Edna's office, alerted by Marie as to their whereabouts.

"That address is the McClough Building."

"I thought they tore that down."

"The tenants keep getting stays. That's where he has his office."

Keegan looked at Father Dowling and then at the receiver. "Thanks, Cy."

"You want me to talk to Tuttle?"

"I think I'll do that myself."

Back in the rectory it was Father Dowling who made the call to Tuttle the lawyer. After a dozen rings he was about to give up when a sleepy voice answered. It was now two in the afternoon. "Father Dowling!" Tuttle seemed to be fighting his way toward consciousness. "Just the man I want to talk to."

"Good."

"I have a theological question, Father Dowling. Does the televised Mass fulfill the Sunday obligation?"

"I didn't realize you were Catholic."

"I am asking on behalf of a client."

"That seems an odd question to put to you."

"You'd be surprised how our fields overlap, Father Dowling."

"Is the client Sylvester Sloan?"

"Describe him."

Father Dowling responded to this surprising question.

"That's my client."

"Your late client."

"He had no appointment today."

"Are you too busy to come by the rectory, Mr. Tuttle?"

There was the sound of pages turning, perhaps an engagement book. "Would an hour from now be all right?"

It was slightly more than an hour before the little lawyer bustled down the hall after Marie Murkin and appeared in the doorway of the study. If he was surprised at the presence of Phil Keegan, he did not show it."

"You say he was a client?"

Tuttle hesitated. "Informally. He hadn't a dime, but I offered to help him."

"He had a fifty-dollar bill in his lapel pocket when he died."

"I wouldn't try to spend it, Father. He tried to palm that off on me as a retainer."

"What did you offer to help him with, if that isn't too intrusive a question?"

"He chatted about it with Peanuts in the room, so it's not a confidence. He wants to change his name."

This was something he had already done at least twice without benefit of the legal system. An item on the evening news about the man found dead in the pews at St. Hilary prompted a little badinage among the news crew about the lethal effects of sermons, but it also alerted the relatives of the dead man.

"It is my brother Cecil," a burly man with a sad expression said to the camera the following day. He identified himself as Willis Beamer.

Cecil Beamer was described as a man suffering from losses of memory who sometimes wandered away from the house like this. How long had he been gone? That was difficult to say. Had he been reported missing? "Oh, he always came back. Or we found him. I suppose we should have worried more."

The event might have faded away if Dr. Pippen in the medical examiner's office had not announced that the cause of death was poisoning.

"Poison!"

"Of a sort. He died of a bee sting. Apparently he was allergic to bee stings and that's what killed him."

Sitting in church? Father Dowling remembered the sound of buzzing bees just before he discovered that Cecil, as he must now be called, was dead. It seemed a sign of the times that he wondered if his insurance covered such a thing. There was something impious about being insured against an act of God.

"Oh, bees are everywhere," Dr. Pippen said, as if responding to his unvoiced concern.

3

Willis Beamer came to Father Dowling to inquire about a funeral service for his late brother. His wife was with him, a dour woman whose eyes squinted skeptically whenever the priest spoke.

"Of course, we're not Catholics."

"Wasn't your brother?"

"Not that I know of. Why would you think so?"

"He did die in my church. And he had been a frequent presence in the parish in recent weeks. Senior citizens gather here, so that would have been a draw, but he also came to Mass. He put several fifty-dollar bills in the collection."

Willis Beamer laughed. It was not a happy laugh. "My wife and I have had a time of it, taking care of Cecil. He was not well, of course, in the sense that he had little notion of where he was, or who he was, for that matter."

"Is it Alzheimer's?"

"Perhaps it was. He had all the symptoms."

"That's what it was," said Mrs. Beamer with finality. "I have seen many cases."

"You're a doctor."

"I was in social work."

Roger Dowling did not like liturgical innovations, but there was latitude in what he might do to send Cecil Beamer into the next world with suitable prayers and readings. Mrs. Beamer murmured something about Tennyson but Father Dowling managed not to hear her. The church, while not full, had a respectable turnout, most of the mourners coming from the senior center. The old people in the pews were perhaps less sorrowing than curious, imagining themselves soon occupying the place of honor at a similarly somber occasion. Willis Beamer and his wife sat rigidly in a front pew, following the proceedings with wary interest. They seemed terrified that they might be called upon to use the kneeler.

At the cemetery, the final blessing given, Father Dowling bade goodbye to the Beamers and then to McDivitt, who had secured the undertaking business on Father Dowling's recommendation. Then the pastor started toward his dented dusty car, parked under a weeping willow whose branches swept across it as if they were suggesting a quick drive through a car wash, when his name was called.

Tuttle stepped from behind a tree and was followed by a short heavyset man whose brow had more thrust than his nose. This was the legendary Peanuts Pianone, member of the Fox River police and constant companion of Tuttle.

"They stand to make a bundle," Tuttle said, looking at the departing Beamers.

"How so?"

"All the money was in Cecil's name."

"In fifty-dollar bills?"

Tuttle accorded the remark the laugh it deserved. Marie Murkin was less inclined to find Cecil's tossing of phony fifty-dollar bills into the collection as amusing. But then, the pastor had told her to take those contributions for her kitchen fund.

"What if I had tried to spend one?"

"I would hire Tuttle to defend you."

"Tuttle!"

The unwitting object of this disdain turned to Father Dowling. Shadows ran across his face from the moving branches above him and the sun beyond. There was the buzz of a bee, and Peanuts began to circle nervously, looking around him, his hat in his hand, ready to defend himself.

"You're not allergic," Tuttle assured him.

Peanuts did not look convinced.

"The way Beamer died," Tuttle said, shaking his head. "You ever hear of a thing like that?"

"I can't say that I have."

"I wonder if Cecil knew of his allergy. Peanuts thinks he didn't."

"He couldn't have felt at risk in church."

"If he was stung there."

"What is this money you're talking about?"

"The question is, where is it? Willis Beamer has hired me to find it."

"And where does he suggest you look?"

Tuttle to his credit looked sheepish. "He wondered if Cecil had made a large bequest to the church."

"Not to St. Hilary's. Apart from several fifty-dollar bills, that is."

4

Tuttle was not professionally comfortable with an honest man, one who had no need to dissemble and had no ulterior demands of his own. A lawyer is used to dealing with people who, while not exactly crooked, come to him when their circumstances are not in every way as they should be. They are being sued or they want to sue someone else. They want help in gaining access to goods to which they have a questionable claim. Their statements to their lawyer tend to be at best incomplete and seldom simply mendacious. Tuttle found it hard not to contrast the ingenuous simplicity of the pastor of St. Hilary with the greed Willis Beamer had been helpless to hide.

"It is not simply the money," Mrs. Beamer said.

"It is the principle," Beamer agreed. "I have nothing against money going to the church. But if it is money that is rightly mine—"

"And you have not decided to give it away—"

Tuttle interrupted this spousal colloquy. "Why do you think your brother gave money to the church?"

"Do you have a better idea?"

"Most people had no idea your brother had any money."

"Thank God," breathed Mrs. Beamer.

"Where did he get his money?"

"How well did you know Cecil?"

"About as well as you can know someone you've talked with only once."

"He was your client?"

"Yes."

"That is why we have come to you."

"I thought that might be it."

"What was your estimate of Cecil's, well, mental capacity?"

"He's as smart as most of my friends." That, of course, would be Peanuts. But Tuttle realized he had formed no fixed estimate of Cecil Beamer's IQ. He was a simple man, no doubt of that, but it was not a serene simplicity. He seemed always to be trying to remember something he had forgotten.

"He was a genius," Willis said emphatically.

"A genius!"

"A boy genius. Before he was nineteen years old he had exhausted his intellectual capital, but by then he had patented inventions that brought him a fortune."

"What kind of inventions?"

Cecil's inspiration seemed to have been the kitchen. He had invented devices to whip cream by hand; the popcorn button on microwaves was a Cecil idea; he had devised a vegetable chopper, a fruit parer, a juice maker.

"He sold them?"

"But retained royalties. His royalty statements would give some inkling of his income."

"Have you seen them?"

Willis frowned and looked at his wife. How to put this? "Cecil always laughed away inquiries about money."

"Is that why he handed out phony fifty-dollar bills?"

"Exactly! He bought those at a novelty store. He affected to despise money."

"Maybe he did."

"No man despises money," said Willis Beamer with conviction. "Whatever money Cecil has should come to me. He had no other heirs."

"Perhaps there's a will."

Willis looked at him with narrowed eyes. "Did you draw up a will for him?"

"If I had, and of course I do not say one way or the other, it would be a matter of professional confidence."

"Because he was your client."

"Yes."

"Sealed with a fifty-dollar bill, I suppose."

That hurt. Tuttle had indeed agreed to become Cecil's lawyer on the basis of two fifty-dollar bills slapped down on his desk. He had given one to Peanuts to pay for the Chinese dinner that was to help them celebrate the acquisition of the new client. Peanuts came back with the food but a glum expression.

"That was phony money, Tuttle."

"No!"

"Charlie just laughed when I gave it to him."

"You sure it wasn't the size of the bill?"

"He tore it in half."

Tuttle got the other fifty from his drawer. Looking at it with a skeptical eye he felt like a fool for thinking it real. It now seemed an obvious fake. Then he realized that his new client had given the address of this building as his own. But he had returned the next day and willingly admitted that he had given Tuttle fake money and brought out some travelers checks and signed over five hundred dollars' worth. They were good.

Cecil Beamer had not asked Tuttle to draw up his will. But he had confided that, after years of single life and little or no interest in the opposite sex, he believed that he had fallen in love.

"My brother has married recently, after a lifetime as a bachelor."

"It's contagious."

"I feel like a schoolboy." He paused. "Perhaps because when I was a schoolboy I didn't feel like a schoolboy."

Tuttle had regarded him as an eccentric old man; the bogus money had been made good by the travelers' checks, but the ruse had made the client seem somewhat less than serious. Now, after the discussion with Willis Beamer, Tuttle became curious about the sealed manila envelope that the man he now knew was Cecil Beamer had given him to keep.

"Put it in your safe," he had suggested.

"I'll do better than that," Tuttle, who had no safe, replied. He tossed the envelope into the trunk of his car and slammed it shut. The trunk was the repository of the few valuable and confidential things to which he could lay claim. When he popped open the trunk now he looked around to see if perhaps Willis Beamer were watching. He got behind the wheel of his car and opened the envelope. Somehow he wasn't surprised that it contained a will, handwritten and signed "Cecil Beamer." In it Cecil had left the entirety of his fortune to Marie Murkin of St. Hilary parish.

5

Marie Murkin had been placed in a false position by the death of the man she had known as Sylvester Sloan. Like many widows of an age, Marie liked to think of her condition as chosen and nothing encouraged this more than the attention of eligible men. It was not that she encouraged such attention. The thought of leaving her settled existence as housekeeper of the St. Hilary rectory did not tempt her for a moment. Nonetheless, a woman did like to feel that she was still capable of making the male heart flutter. Sylvester Sloan's heart had fluttered.

"Are you a nun?" he had asked her and it was difficult to know if he were making a joke.

"Why would you think such a thing?"

"Well, living here." His long-fingered hand made a sweeping gesture meant to include the church, the rectory, the school.

"I am the housekeeper!"

"And the churchkeeper, too?" He had been waiting for her when she emerged from the side door of the church.

"You are being deliberately obtuse."

"I'm not a Catholic."

"Why not?"

He stepped back in surprise and then surprised her with his answer. "I don't know Latin."

"Latin! What has that to do with it?"

"I do know pig latin."

"I must get back to my kitchen."

"Can you marry a non-Catholic?"

The conversation did not make her think much of Sylvester Sloan's mind, but he was an attractive man. The fact that he always wore a suit was a commendation. Marie was weary of casual dress. It was easy to imagine standing beside him as their photograph was taken, her arm through his, holding a bouquet of flowers. She would be wearing her green suit . . .

"What nonsense you talk," she cried, and bustled off to the rectory. An hour later she found herself singing at her work.

He brought flowers, leaving them on the back porch if she pretended not to be in the kitchen and waited, holding her breath, to see what he would do. What a silly man, she told herself, but without conviction. She could hardly question his taste in women. Or in flowers.

"Where do you find them?"

"I grow them."

"Where is your garden?"

"Do you know Ben Jonson? 'I lately sent to thee a rose . . .' "

She chased him away, trying not to giggle with delight. The next day he brought her a mason jar in which there was some clover and a bee. He had punctured the lid to let in air. The years fled as she looked at it and she was a little girl again.

"You should let him go."

"At your command."

He twisted off the cap and placed the jar on the porch ledge. It was some time before the bee realized it was free to go and whirled away into the scented air.

"I used to capture bees when I was a kid."

"Everyone did!"

"They made me stop."

"Why?"

But he did not want to speak of that. He wanted to know if he should ask Father Dowling for her hand. That was when she put an end to the foolishness. She told him if he so much as breathed a word to the pastor, she would, well, she didn't know what she would do, but he would regret it until the day he died.

She was convinced that Father Dowling knew nothing of all this. She had grieved at the death of her awkward swain, a tinge of regret mingling with her sorrow. Now, a week later, Father Dowling called her into the study to tell her that she was an heiress.

Marie looked at Tuttle and at Phil Keegan, who were with the pastor. They seemed to have prior knowledge of what he was saying. Cecil Beamer, the man she had known as Sylvester Sloan, had left a will in which all his earthly possessions were left to Marie Murkin.

"Why would he have done that, Marie?"

"He must mean the parish."

"No, no. He is quite explicit."

He handed her the will and she recognized the hand that had put notes in pig latin in the collection basket.

"His brother has brought a serious charge, Marie," Phil Keegan said.

"What charge?" She had wanted to ask how much money was involved, but that would have sounded greedy. She was determined not to take a cent of Sylvester's money.

"He contends that his brother's death was not accidental."

"He was stung by a bee!"

Phil Keegan looked desolate. "Dr. Pippen made note of an odd circle enclosing the puncture that would have been made by the bee's stinger. She thinks it could have been the mark of an open bottle."

Marie slumped into a chair. She could see it all. Someone had caught a bee and held the open jar against Sylvester's neck. He had said that as a child he had been forbidden to catch bees. Of course. He was allergic. Marie looked at Father Dowling.

"I know how it was done."

She described the scene she had just viewed with the eye of imagination.

"That's just what Dr. Pippen imagined."

Father Dowling took his pipe from his mouth.

"Then it's obvious who killed him."

"Who?"

"Someone who knew he was allergic to bee stings."

"I nominate his brother, Willis."

"To what end?" Willis asked grandly when he came to the rectory and found himself confronted by the pastor and Captain Philip Keegan. "I am not mentioned in the will. I had nothing to gain." He paused. "And I have lost a beloved brother."

Even as they spoke, Cy Horvath was going through the Beamers' house on the strength of a search warrant. There was a beautiful garden at the back of the house, and a little potting shed. There, on a shelf, hidden behind a dozen vases and pots and bottles, Cy found a mason jar. Its opening suggested the scenario sketched independently by Dr. Pippen and Marie Murkin. He took it downtown to the lab.

Willis was still there, deflecting the suspicion cast upon him, when the call from Cy came. The fingerprints on the mason jar, and the fact that it had been hidden, suggested that it was the murder weapon. Willis rose in righteous indignation.

"This is fraudulent," he cried. "I was never in that shed. I never touched a mason jar!"

"Oh, the prints aren't yours, Mr. Beamer."

"What!"

"Where is Mrs. Beamer?"

6

"One of her husbands died of snakebite," Phil said to Father Dowling when they were alone. Marie Murkin, wrapped in mysteriousness, brought them snacks. She had formally renounced all claim to Cecil's money and it would go to Willis.

"He's eligible, Marie."

"You should have kept the money as a dowry."

She looked serenely at her tormentors. Was it any fault of hers that she made such an impression on susceptible men? The queen bee was attended by a host of drones. It seemed an unflattering way to think of the deceased.

"Oh, I saved some," she said.

And with some ceremony she presented each of them, the pastor and Captain Keegan, with a fifty-dollar bill.

THE BASE OF THE TRIANGLE

1

When Earl Haven showed up at the rectory door there was fire in his eyes, and his manner with Mrs. Murkin would normally have drawn a rebuke from the housekeeper, but she brought him to the pastor's study without complaint.

"Father, this is Earl Haven."

"I'm not a Catholic."

"I am. As doubtless the collar tells you."

"She's Catholic. Harriet."

"Ah."

"Harriet Dolan," Mrs. Murkin said, and her brows lifted in significance.

"The girl that's getting married?"

A groan escaped Earl and he collapsed into a chair. "She can't marry that idiot, she can't."

The reference would be to Leo Mulcahy, with whom Harriet had sat in the front parlor not an hour before, making arrangements for their wedding.

"If it's being Catholic she wants, I'll do it."

"Become a Catholic?"

The man's expression suggested inner anguish. "If she'll marry me, yes, I will."

Marie stood in the doorway wringing her apron but her expression was not in every way anguished. The housekeeper had a taste for other people's troubles and she found the vari-

53

ous permutations of the relations between man and woman irresistible.

"It will never happen," she had said an hour before, after Harriet Dolan and Leo Mulcahy had finished discussing with the pastor their impending nuptials and had left the rectory. Ahead of them lay months of preparation before the big day. Father Dowling conducted a weekly class for couples preparing themselves for marriage. Harriet and Leo would have to attend those classes.

"They seem very attached to one another."

"In love with love."

This was not like Marie, who was one of the last romantics, something she concealed beneath a crusty exterior. Father Dowling wondered if she were seeking to deflect trouble from Harriet and Leo by predicting it; there were depths to Marie's Irish superstitiousness that the pastor did not pretend to fathom. But Marie shook away this explanation, like a pitcher not getting the right signal from his catcher.

"She's taking him on the rebound."

"From what?"

"From whom?"

But Marie had intuited little more than this fact. She did not then know who the third party might be; it was simply something that Harriet had said. Now, with Earl Haven collapsed in a chair in the rectory study and unable to suppress his groans, Marie had clearly made an identification.

"Have you proposed to Harriet?" Marie asked.

"She knows."

"But have you asked her?"

"I was going to."

"Apparently Leo Mulcahy got there before you," Father Dowling said.

Marie glared at the pastor and Earl doubled over, as if in

pain. Suddenly, he looked up and his expression changed. "He can't afford to marry her!"

"Two can live as cheaply as one," Father Dowling said. Although this was an article in Marie's somewhat-plagiarized creed, the housekeeper again glared at him. But then she asked Earl in a soothing voice what he meant.

The question restored Earl to the land of the living. Once his attention had been diverted from his broken heart, he spoke with succinct authority of the business in which both he and Leo Mulcahy were engaged.

There are amazingly inventive ways for people to earn their daily bread, and one would have had to lack soul not to respond to the entrepreneurial creativity represented by Boxers, Inc. The idea had been Earl's and it involved cutting himself in on the thriving business of the package delivery systems that had proven to be such competition for the U. S. Postal Service. Usually these giants had their own depot, at or near the airport, where the client not large enough to be visited by one of the pickup trucks might go to send off his packages. Earl had opened a storefront in a mall, the first Boxers, Inc., which had served as a clearinghouse for the various national deliverers— UPS, Federal Express, two or three others—making their services convenient for the occasional noncommercial user. A birthday present, something for a son or daughter at school, the odd item that must be elsewhere in a finite period of time. Boxers provided packaging as well as a clearinghouse for package delivery. At intervals throughout the day, the packages were taken to the depots of the great delivery systems. Earl had declined the offer to have trucks pick up the packages. It was important for the client to see what Earl was doing for them, thus justifying the modest fee he charged which, added to the payments from the deliverers, made Boxers, Inc., a moneymaking enterprise. With success came the urge to expand. Earl set

Leo Mulcahy up in the business.

"He didn't have a nickel," Earl said, almost with contempt.

"I didn't either, when I started, but then I started from scratch. Leo's location in the Naperville mall would be the replica of the original Boxers, Inc."

"You lent him the money?"

"Twenty-five-thousand dollars."

The whistle came from Marie. "How much does he still owe you?"

"With interest, twenty-seven five. Only Leo could take such a simple idea and mess it up."

"He's in debt twenty-seven thousand, five hundred dollars?"

"My accountant could kill me." Earl stood, and there was an unattractive expression on his face. "I am going to collect that money now."

Father Dowling, at his desk, listened to Marie as she accompanied Earl down the hall to the front door. The housekeeper cajoled, threatened, pleaded, and, in the end, prophesied.

"Harriet will never forgive you!"

"She would never forgive herself if she married that idiot."

2

Life was full of mystery, Marie Murkin felt, and in this she was certainly not alone, but she took the common point to uncommon lengths. To identify the mystery was in some degree to have overcome it. But like everyone before her, she was utterly baffled by the men to whom some women were attracted and, of course, vice versa. The most improbable combinations formed before one's eyes, defying every law of probability. Father Dowling often cited a seminary definition of man as a rational animal and of course he did not have to explain to her that the phrase was meant to cover women as well as men. But the truth was that it applied to neither men nor women, not when it came to affairs of the heart. Marie was not being cruel when she thought of Harriet Dolan as, well, what she was, and how any man, let alone two of them, could make fools of themselves over the girl, Marie did not understand. Nor did she regard this as merely the limitations of her own abilities. She defied anyone to explain how a girl hardly more than five and a half feet high, with a round plain face, abundant if nondescript hair worn in the current hag lady style, a narrow little mouth, and the body of a boy could turn the heads of both Earl Haven and Leo Mulcahy. It made no sense, not even when you acknowledged Harriet's smile that transformed her face, crinkled her eyes behind the lenses of her glasses, and was admittedly infectious.

"I hope I'm doing the right thing," the girl had whispered to Marie, when Leo was alone with Father Dowling on the occasion of their first visit.

"How long have you known him?"

"All my life."

"That's good."

"And his whole family," she added significantly.

"Ah. And he is in business for himself?"

"It's his partner who knows things."

Of course a girl was nervous and said odd things when she was on the brink of marriage, but Marie found this particularly enigmatic. Until Earl Haven showed up at the rectory door. If Leo was a fine specimen of a man, and he was, Earl Haven was even more so, and his near despair at the thought of Harriet marrying Leo did nothing to detract from his attraction. One of the advantages of age was that Marie could deal with handsome men as she never could have when she was young and they were the same age. All the more did she marvel at the way Harriet had wrapped Leo and Earl around her finger, effortlessly manipulating them. She sent Leo to the rectory as soon as she learned that Earl had been there.

"It's none of his business," Leo almost shouted. His anger added to his imposing presence. He was a larger man than Earl, dark-haired, craggy—a term that was much used in the novels Marie read. Earl, on the other hand, was blonde—golden-locked, Marie's author might have said—slim and graceful with the clear blue eyes of a dreamer. Yet he apparently was the business whiz, and Leo, in looks the practical man of action, was inept, losing money running a business that, according to Earl, ran itself.

"I understand you and Earl are in business together."

"He leant me some money, Father. Now he wants it back. I don't have it. It's sunk in that lousy business I was talked into starting."

Talked into by whom, Marie wondered. But she did not have to wonder long. Leo's expression had softened

"I did it for Harriet. I was happy enough working for Midwest Power."

"Why not give up the business and go back to work for Midwest Power?"

Marie could have cheered this suggestion from Father Dowling. She found herself being tugged from side to side in this matter. On the one hand, she did not like to think that a couple would come talk to the priest about getting married, make arrangements for instructions, and then just drop it. On the other hand, if she were Harriet, her choice would certainly have been Earl Haven. But again she was mystified by the fact that little Harriet had her choice of these two paragons.

"I lost my seniority when I quit."

"That could not have been much at your age?" Marie said.

"They gave me a going-away party." It seemed clear that Leo had left Midwest Power in such a way that any return would be demeaning. "I can't pay Earl back, not now, I'm losing money."

"He's just bluffing," Marie assured Leo. "Besides, if you don't have it—"

"He could take over my business."

Leo's situation was not enviable. He was stuck with a business that was losing money, and his partner was demanding repayment of a loan and threatening to take over the business if Leo did not come up with the money. And all this out of spite because Leo had won the hand of the girl Earl loved. Father Dowling would not have thought of Harriet's as a face that would launch a thousand ships. But she was incentive enough for both Leo and Earl.

"I'll talk to Earl," Father Dowling said.

Hope leapt momentarily into Leo's eyes then faded away. "He won't listen to you."

"Let's find out."

3

Peanuts wanted to return some videos he had purchased from a catalog, and Tuttle took him to the Boxers, Inc., store in Naperville to send the merchandise back.

"You know the place?"

"It's just like the one in Fox River."

Peanuts didn't know it, but how often did he need someone to pack up and return merchandise for him? Tuttle assured him that Boxers, Inc., was reliable.

"What's wrong with the post office?"

"Don't get me started. What's wrong with the videos?"

"I've already seen them."

"You're returning them just because you watched them?"

"Not these. I've already seen these. They're not what I ordered."

Peanuts had ordered several dozen old episodes of *The Untouchables.*

"I like Frank Nitty."

"Who doesn't?"

Tuttle meant the actor. He wasn't sure what Peanuts meant. No matter, they were at the mall and Tuttle was searching for a parking spot as close as possible to Boxers, Inc.

"There's an ambulance," Peanuts observed.

"I noticed the light." Tuttle was also noticing that it seemed to be stopping traffic right in front of Boxers, Inc. This could mean anything, of course. It may or not concern Boxers directly; then again, it could be a customer fallen ill. Naperville was beyond the jurisdiction in which Peanuts was an officer of the law and a policeman out of his jurisdiction feels like an imposter. But then Peanuts felt like an imposter in Fox River. His sinecure in the local constabulary was due to the influence of his family. When he was on duty he was given tasks of minimal responsibility. This suited Peanuts fine. He was not an ambitious man and was not personally proud, though fiercely loyal to his dubious family.

"I don't have to send these back right now."

"As long as we're here," Tuttle said. He had maneuvered his car through the lot and now drew up to the curb behind the ambulance. "I wish we had a squad car."

If Peanuts had been driving they could have turned on the warning light and given a little goose to the siren, arriving in style and authority. As it was, an overweight cop signaled imperiously for Tuttle to drive on. Tuttle put the car in neutral and hopped out.

"I got here as quick as I could," he said to the cop, silencing the order he was about to bark.

"Who are you?"

Tuttle took off his tweed hat and extracted a calling card from the crown. While the cop was reading it, Tuttle circled him and saw that the commotion was indeed inside the Boxers.

"That's Officer Pianone in the passenger seat."

Tuttle breezed on past them and swept into the door of Boxers, Inc. He did not need any explanation of the scene before him. The store was alive with officers and plainclothesmen and paramedics. A young man in a white coat got up from a crouch and, looking at a cop, crossed his eyes and drew a finger across his throat. The paramedics were prepared to turn matters over to the medical examiner. Tuttle pressed on through to where the body lay on the floor. A man. Leo Mulcahy! Tuttle had the feeling that he had been brought providentially to this scene.

"His name is Leo Mulcahy," Tuttle said in a raised, authoritative voice.

Heads turned to look at him.

"The deceased is a friend of mine. What happened?" What happened to Tuttle was that he was collared by two officers and hustled outside and into a patrol car. He tried to wave to Peanuts as he was hustled across the walk to the car, but the reflection on the windshield made it impossible to see Peanuts. In the back seat of the Naperville squad car, Tuttle was bracketed by a uniformed officer and a plainclothesman.

"Who are you?"

"You're making a great mistake."

"You want to talk to a lawyer?"

"I am a lawyer."

The plainclothesman, who had a face still bearing the traces of teenage acne, narrowed his eyes. Outside the car, the cop to whom he had given his card tapped on the window. It was rolled down and Tuttle's calling card was passed in.

"This you?" the detective asked.

"Tuttle the lawyer."

"You say you know the dead guy?"

"What happened to him?"

Tuttle posed a problem for his captors. His manner disarmed

then and yet they were disinclined to admit to having made a mistake. It was easier to act as if they had pressed Tuttle into service as an informant.

"I was afraid something like this would happen," Tuttle said, letting out a little line, getting in deeper. He hoped Peanuts had enough sense to put his car in a parking space. Peanuts could catch a nap in the back seat then and derive some benefit from this failed effort to return the unwanted videos. As for Tuttle, he was asking himself what kind of bill he could send the Naperville police after they solved the murder of Leo Mulcahy.

4

Cy Horvath drove out to the Fox River mall and parked where he could look at the front entrance of Boxers, Inc., which was described in the write-up Cy had downloaded from the web page of the *Tribune* as the original store of Earl Haven's nascent franchise. The store in Naperville where the body of Leo Mulcahy had been found was a spin-off that had been jointly owned by Haven and the deceased.

Cy got out of the car and wound his way among parked vehicles, crossed the access road, and pulled open the door of Boxers, Inc. There were people waiting at the counter, there were customers availing themselves of the pack-it-yourself facilities; there was soothing music oozing through the place. All in all, a picture of pastel prosperity. Cy looked around and then decided that Haven's office would be down the hall past the computers and fax machines and copying facilities. A diminutive woman whose blonde hair seemed shaped like a helmet looked up in surprise. The nameplate on her desk said Rose Hanlon. Cy told her he wanted to see Earl Haven.

"Oh, he's over in Naperville."

"At the store there?"

"Can I help you?"

"I'm Lieutenant Horvath."

"Lieutenant?"

"Fox River police."

"Is anything wrong?"

"Do you know Leo Mulcahy?"

Her expression changed. "Why do you ask?"

"Isn't he Earl Haven's partner in the Naperville store?"

She looked at him with growing disapproval. "If that were so, why would it be of interest to the Fox River police? Or are you asking personally?"

"Leo Mulcahy was found dead in the Naperville store an hour ago." No need to tell her that he had been strangled to death with a scarf.

Her gasping intake of air set her chair in motion and she backed away from him. Her eyes were round as dollars and her lips trembled.

"Dead?"

"Yes."

"That's impossible. He was a young man. His health was good."

"How well did you know him?"

"How well did I know him?" she repeated.

"The Naperville police would like some help in their investigation. This looks like something that spans our jurisdictions. When did Mr. Haven go to Naperville?"

"He always went over there on Wednesdays."

"A regular visit."

"Yes."

"He hadn't heard of what happened to Mr. Mulcahy?"

"He must have been there already."

After she said it, she seemed to regret having said it.

"I understand that there had been a falling out between the two men."

"I'm not sure I should talk about such things."

"Rose, a man has been murdered."

"Murdered! Oh my God." Tears welled into her eyes and then she was sobbing helplessly. Cy took a chair and waited. He let her cry as long as she wanted to and that turned out to be a long time indeed.

"You did know Leo Mulcahy."

"Of course I knew him. We were engaged to be married. Some years ago."

"You and Leo Mulcahy?"

"Yes." Her chin lifted, as if he had doubted her word.

"You broke off with him?"

She thought for a minute. "It wouldn't have worked out."

Phil Keegan had called the St. Hilary rectory while Cy was checking out the *Tribune* web page. The call from Naperville reminded the captain of something he had heard from Father Dowling. But it was Marie Murkin he talked with. Leo Mulcahy? He was soon to marry Harriet Dolan. Now, talking with Rose Hanlon, Cy wondered if Leo's one-time fiancée knew of his marriage plans.

"Do you know Harriet Dolan?"

An angry expression formed on Rose Hanlon's lace. "Whatever happened to Leo Mulcahy is her fault."

5

Phil Keegan was in the study with Father Dowling, telling him what he knew of events in Naperville, and Marie was listening in. The picture seemed clear. Earl Haven had been driven half mad by the thought that the woman he loved intended to marry such an ass as Leo Mulcahy.

"The Wednesday visit to the Naperville store was apparently a regular event," he said.

"Have you talked with him yet?"

"Earl Haven? He can't be found."

"Who has looked for him?"

"Cy."

Phil as much as said that very little mystery remained as to what had happened to Leo Mulcahy. Not only was Earl Haven the prime suspect, he was the only suspect.

"He left a trail as wide as the interstate. Half a dozen people noticed him arrive at the Naperville store. Two people who were in the store have told us of a fierce argument between two men. The argument was the kind that would almost inevitably lead to blows."

"Did anyone witness a fight?"

"Haven told Mulcahy he was stupid. He told him he could not run a penny lemonade stand. He just threw insults at Mulcahy."

"What was Leo's reaction?"

"He laughed."

"Laughed."

That was when Haven cleared everyone out of the store. "Being laughed at got to him, that was obvious. Mulcahy was hit on the head, probably with a Scotch tape holder made of heavy metal. But it was the scarf that did it."

"Scarf."

"He was strangled with a scarf. It was not a pretty sight."

"Did anyone see Earl leave?"

Phil took the cigar from his mouth, studied it, then returned it to his mouth, clamping it between his teeth.

"Of course we're just assuming the man was Earl Haven."

Whatever the ostensible reason for the quarrel, it seemed obvious that Harriet Dolan was the real explanation. Earl's anger was more easily explained by the fact that he had lost Harriet than that he had lost money.

6

Harriet Dolan was unconvincing in the role of tragic woman. Surrounded by the sisters of Leo Mulcahy, she looked around her as if seeking a cue as to how she should behave. Her fiancée was dead and the man who killed him had professed his love for her and was now the object of a police search. Any of Leo's sisters was more attractive than Harriet but none of them had been the cause of such a romantic tragedy. It seemed assumed that Harriet would be brokenhearted by events and from time to time she dabbed at her dry eyes with a handkerchief. She might have been concealing the little smile that kept forming on her thin lips. Of course, perhaps it had not really dawned on her that Leo was dead and that Earl had killed him.

"She is in shock," one of the Mulcahy girls said to Marie Murkin.

"Who could blame her?" the housekeeper replied, but her eye was on Harriet and her tone was not as definite as her words. The chair next to Harriet was offered to Marie and she took it. She patted the girl's arm and sighed.

"You have lost them both."

Harriet looked at her.

"Leo and Earl."

"I didn't encourage him," Harriet protested, and rubbed the forming smile from her lips.

"It's not your fault."

But Harriet was distracted by the arrival of a young woman who turned out to be Rose Hanlon, accompanied by her brother. Their arrival created an awkwardness, and when Rose approached her, Harriet grew apprehensive, but Rose just took her hand and shook her head in silent disbelief at what had happened. Steve Hanlon stood unobtrusively against a wall. Everyone seemed to be waiting for Rose to say something, but she held her silence. Finally she drifted off to the side of the room and joined her brother.

"She is affected as much as Harriet," a Mulcahy girl whispered to Marie.

"Why would she be?"

"She and Leo were engaged, you know. Informally."

Marie Murkin looked at Rose with new interest. The young woman had begun to weep and was being comforted. The contrast with Harriet was eloquent.

7

Earl Haven was located in a cabin north of town overlooking the Fox River, a summer place that afforded relief from the midwestern heat. His car had been parked sideways on the narrow gravel drive and he had appeared in the picture window armed with a shotgun. Phil Keegan had prudently decided to address Earl by bullhorn from the road. It added to the drama that Earl replied through a bullhorn of his own, one he had made notorious as a fan of the local high school football team.

"Come on out, Earl. We don't want anyone else getting hurt."

"I haven't hurt anyone."

"No reason not to come out then, is there?" Phil looked around, obviously pretty proud of that retort.

When Father Dowling arrived, Phil and Earl were still exchanging one-liners. Roger Dowling stood beside Cy Horvath.

"What are they talking about, Cy?"

"Football."

"Football!"

"Earl played for the Fox River Reds. His touchdown pass record to Steve Hanlon, who played wide receiver, will never be broken."

"How long has this been going on?"

Cy thought twenty minutes. Phil and Earl were discussing a

game against Naperville played in the misty past when Earl had first become the toast of the town.

"Don't spoil it now, Earl. Face up to this."

"Do you think I killed Leo?"

"It doesn't matter what I think, Earl. We've got to straighten it out. Do you have a lawyer?"

Suddenly, through the no-man's-land between the police cars and the cabin door, a short figure, arms raised, one hand waving a grayish handkerchief, waddled toward the door of the cabin.

"It's Tuttle," Father Dowling said.

"Who else?"

8

A more successful lawyer can wait for clients to come to him. But Tuttle was always on the alert for poor devils in need of legal representation, and he had been riding in a squad car with Peanuts when he switched the radio dial from Rush Limbaugh and picked up the report of Earl Haven holed up in his riverside summer cottage. Immediately they were on their way to the scene. Tuttle had jumped out of the car, listened for a few minutes, and, when his opportunity came, seized it,

His breath came in rapid gasps and he had a stitch in his side before his hand closed over the knob of the front door. He panted for a moment and then lifted his free hand toward the knocker. In doing this, his hand turned the knob, the door opened, and he tumbled inside, literally sprawling across the uncarpeted floor of the cabin. The windows overlooking the river blinded him with their brightness and he got to his knees and looked blinking about.

"Who are you?"

"Can you pull those blinds?"

"Are you a reporter?"

"No!" Tuttle rose to his feet in indignation. He might be at the bottom rung of his chosen profession but he had not sunk to the level of those purchased pens who hung around the pressroom of the courthouse. "I am Tuttle the lawyer." He found his tweed hat and put it on his head. It was like resuming his true persona.

"Oh yeah."

"My advice is that you make no statement whatsoever. We will march out of here, they can book you, but I will do the talking."

"There's nothing to say."

"Exactly."

"I didn't hurt Leo."

Tuttle remembered the scene at the Naperville Boxers, Inc. He had not seen Earl there. He could not remember anyone else who had. Rose Hanlon, Earl's secretary, had unwisely told the police that Earl had gone to Naperville.

"That could work."

"What do you mean?"

"Look, I was at the store in Naperville when the cops were investigating. It couldn't have been long after—"

Something in Earl's eye caused Tuttle to stop. He did not want to antagonize a potential client.

"What time were you there?"

"I never got there. I got caught in traffic. A jackknifed semi blocked the road, and finally I just turned around and started back to Fox River. I heard about it on radio, and that I was being sought. I headed here."

"Why?"

"Look out there. I feel like a treed squirrel."

But why would an innocent man run? Tuttle did not ask this question. A lawyer can often represent his client better if he lets innocence remain a presumption.

Knowing too much can be a burden.

"Earl, we're going out there. We're going to open that door and march right out to the police, those cameras, everything. You can't stay here forever."

Earl looked as if he wanted to argue about it, but suddenly his shoulders slumped. "You're right. Let's go."

"Let me look at you first."

Tuttle stood in front of Earl and squinted his eyes, imagining what he would look like on television.

"Why don't you take off your cap?"

"You going to take off your hat?"

"Okay, leave it on." Tuttle took the door handle, inhaled, and pulled. Silence fell. Tuttle stepped outside first, his eyes shaded by the brim of his hat, and located the television cameras. When Earl came out, Tuttle took his elbow and they walked right at the cameras. Tuttle kept up a nonstop patter as they walked, a lawyer advising his client. Earl looked bewildered but that wasn't bad. It could be mistaken for innocence. All this was being taped. It would be like running a commercial on television. Tuttle moved even closer to his client. He didn't want to be focused out of the picture.

Phil Keegan and Cy Horvath came forward to meet them.

"Remember, Earl," Tuttle said, addressing the media. "You don't have to say a thing."

"I didn't do anything," Earl protested. "I'll say that."

There was an unbaptized part of Marie Murkin's soul that took mordant pleasure from the spectacle of Harriet Dolan being deprived of two men, either one of whom had been too good for her. But the fact—or alleged fact, as Tuttle always insisted in speaking to the press—that one of those men had killed the other out of insane desire for Harriet was something that was difficult to accept cheerfully. Harriet rose to her tragic role during the funeral of Leo Mulcahy, sitting in the front pew with the Mulcahy girls, for all the world as if she were a widow. But it soon became clear that Harriet had no intention of going into deep mourning.

"Does she intend to wait for Earl?"

"Ask Phil Keegan about that."

"Does she confide in Phil?"

"She hasn't even been to visit him in jail."

"Well, after all, he is accused of killing her fiancée." There was no point in trying to explain it to the pastor. One needed a woman's intuition to maneuver through the intricacies of the matter. It was Marie's fear that while she might ignore him while he languished in jail awaiting trial, Harriet would be all too prominent in the courtroom once proceedings began. What a magnet she would be for the press. The woman whose fiancée the accused had killed because she had spurned him. It was almost too much to bear.

Marie noticed that Harriet came regularly to Mass on Sunday and had to acknowledge that she did nothing to draw attention to herself, not coming late nor leaving early, dressing in a subdued way. Marie was on the verge of thinking that she had misjudged Harriet when she ran into her as she was leaving the mall.

"Hello," Harriet replied warily in response to Marie's greeting.

"I'm Marie Murkin, housekeeper at St. Hilary's."

"Of course I recognize you."

Marie would have liked to chat with the girl but the moment was not propitious. They parted and Marie started for her car. When she got in, she noticed that Harriet was still standing near the door, looking out over the lot. Had she forgotten where she had parked? But then her expression changed as a car drew up to the curb. Harriet, radiant, pulled open the door. Marie had started her engine and managed to drive forward to where she could get a good glimpse of the man behind the wheel of the car that had come for Harriet Dolan. At first she did not recognize him, but then she did. Steve Hanlon.

9

Earl Haven's trial proceeded with slow inevitability, and the apparent fate of the accused could not be ascribed simply to the want of skill on the part of his lawyer. Indeed, when Father Dowling asked Amos Cadbury what he thought of Tuttle's performance, the patrician lawyer, dean of Fox River attorneys, thought for a moment.

"I am only surprised that the prosecution has not called those who said they saw Haven at the Naperville store that morning."

Amos was right. At the time any number of people claimed to have been eyewitnesses to a quarrel between Earl and Leo.

"Maybe they don't need that evidence."

"You may be right."

"It looks bad for Earl."

"His chances of acquittal are not good."

"Poor fellow."

"Perhaps he is guilty."

"Perhaps?"

But apparently it was simply the caution of the lawyer. Father Dowling had spoken with Earl Haven, and while he was privy to no confidential matters so far as Earl's soul went—as a non-Catholic, Earl would not ask to confess his sins—he had the distinct feeling that he was speaking with an innocent man. Or at least with one innocent of the crime of which he was accused. Earl's story about never having gone to the Naperville store on that fateful morning had been difficult to sustain in court. The traffic jam Earl said had convinced him to return to Fox River could not be verified. Earl had spoken of a jackknifed semi, but no police report corroborating the incident had been discovered. Earl said he had never actually seen the semi, but a similar delay three weeks before had been caused by a jack-knifed semi. Tuttle was able to verify that, and he produced police reports, subpoenaed half a dozen drivers, proved it beyond the shadow of a doubt. But, as the prosecutor pointed out, that had nothing to do with the traffic on the day Leo was killed. Tuttle then turned to the undisputed negative fact that no one had seen Earl in Naperville that day. The prosecutor did not counter with eyewitnesses. It was soon clear why.

"Ah, but he left proof of his being there," the prosecutor said. A long gray scarf was introduced into evidence. It had been twisted around the neck of the hapless Leo Mulcahy. The scarf was definitely Earl's. It had his name in it.

"I lost that scarf," Earl cried. "I haven't seen it for years."

"Lost it? No, you didn't lose it. But you did leave it behind at the scene where you killed Leo Mulcahy!"

Earl was doomed. The jury withdrew to consider their verdict. Within an hour they were back. They found Earl Haven guilty of causing the death of Leo Mulcahy and with malice aforethought.

"He will be an old man when he gets out," Father Dowling observed to Marie Murkin.

"The poor man."

"There will be no point in the young lady waiting for him."

"There will be no danger of it either."

"Oh?"

Listening to Marie, Father Dowling sat very still. It was as if she had suddenly been given the key to recent events. It was unclear that Marie saw the full significance of what she was saying. He said nothing at the time, and the housekeeper eventually returned to her kitchen, a little embarrassed at having passed on such gossip. Father Dowling remained at his desk for half an hour, thinking. He got out a piece of paper and prepared to write on it, but did not. He did not need to make a list of what he knew in order to arrive at a conclusion.

He got up and put on a coat and said on his way through the kitchen, "I'm going out, Marie. Would you call Phil Keegan and Cy Horvath to come over tonight?"

"For supper?"

"What a wonderful idea."

The one-time wide receiver of the Fox River High School Reds had an office in the same mall in which Earl Haven had opened the original Boxers, Inc. Stephen Hanlon was an accountant, a bald man in a blue shirt and striped tie who sat coatless behind his desk, his unblinking eyes concentrating on figures and columns and the quantification of the romance of commerce. He greeted Father Dowling and asked him to be seated. His eyes never left his collar.

"How I marvel at anyone who can do that," Father Dowling exclaimed when Steve Hanlon answered his question as to what he did in this bare and orderly office.

"Who keeps the books at St. Hilary?"

"I keep one set."

The pale brows rose above pale eyes.

"No mortal knows enough to keep a complete account, does he, Steve?"

"There is no mystery about a good set of books."

"Income and outgo, plus and minus, add and subtract?"

Steve Hanlon nodded.

"What sort of balance can there be for taking another life?"

Perhaps if his life had gone differently Steve Hanlon might have become a Trappist. He seemed comfortable with silence. His eyes were all but expressionless as he looked across his neat desk at Father Dowling.

"Was it jealousy, Steve?"

Silence.

"Did it anger you that your old quarterback had teamed up with Leo Mulcahy?"

The fan of Hanlon's computer purred evenly. A digital clock on the wall measured time not quite noiselessly.

"Of course it wasn't that, was it? It was what Leo had done when he jilted Rose."

Steve rose as if he were managed by invisible wires. His hand closed on a large smooth stone that did service as a paperweight.

"You use what's at hand, don't you? How did you happen to be wearing Earl Haven's scarf?"

"You're guessing, I know. But if you can guess, so can others."

"That seems a reason for not compounding your troubles, doesn't it?"

Steve stood there, the rock gripped menacingly in his hand, but he was thinking. What Father Dowling had said was entered into one column; his mind went on to the next. After a moment, he sat down. He put the large stone where it had been and placed his hands on the arms of his chair.

"You're right. It was Rose. She loved him. She still does."

"Does she know?"

"Of course not." Another item was entered in the ledger in Steve's mind, and Father Dowling feared that he had put himself in danger by the question. But Steve simply looked at him. Finally he said, "What do you want me to do?"

"Come to dinner at the rectory?"

For the first time Steve Hanlon reacted to what Father Dowling had said. His mouth opened in surprise.

10

The drive to and from Joliet was not a long one and Father Dowling did not remain long at the prison. Steve Hanlon seemed to appreciate his visits, but he simply did not have the gift of conversation. Besides, his talents had been put to work in the business office and, while he was no longer a free man, he was free to engage in the accounting that had always made up a large part of his life. Only one thing had truly bothered him. He had kept the books for Boxers, Inc., and picked a quarrel with Leo Mulcahy over his terrible business sense when he heard that his sister's old fiancé was engaged to marry Harriet Dolan, sacking his old quarterback.

"Please explain to Rose, Father," he had said when, having dined with Phil Keegan and Cy Horvath at the rectory table, he had told the detectives what he had done in Naperville.

"You invited a murderer to dinner?" Phil asked, after Cy had taken Steve downtown.

"Is this a confession?"

"You know what Captain Keegan means," Marie said, coming in from the kitchen. "When I think that I was urging all that food on someone who had taken a human life."

"He did have a good appetite, didn't he?"

"Second helpings of everything."

"Perhaps he figured out how much he was saving."

But the personality of Steve Hanlon was not known to Marie or Phil Keegan. His matter-of-fact admission that he had strangled Leo Mulcahy, dabbing at his mouth with his napkin as he told of it, had not exactly promoted digestion. Nonetheless, Father Dowling was certain he had been right in following his instinct and asking Steve Hanlon back to the rectory for dinner. The police were already scheduled to be there.

"He ate a hearty meal before he was condemned," Phil said. He seemed to have decided to let Marie carry the complaint alone.

"Well, he certainly won't have to worry about where his next meal is coming from," Marie said.

Phil Keegan sighed. "I can still see him gathering in a pass from Earl Haven."

"That will doubtless be Harriet Dolan's game now," Marie said. She widened her eyes and then turned on her heel and went into her kitchen.

Earl Haven had always attracted Harriet. Nor had his attraction suffered from the accusation that he had strangled Leo Mulcahy rather than let him marry Harriet. When it seemed that this act of gallantry would cause Earl to spend most of the rest of his life in prison, it was only human that Harriet should become susceptible to the charms of Steve Hanlon. Of course she misread his interest. He had been motivated by anger that Leo had dropped his sister Rose for Harriet. But Harriet's fickleness had dissolved the charm she had for Earl.

As he drove back to Fox River from Joliet and his visit with Steve Hanlon, Father Dowling checked his watch. Earl Haven would be coming to the rectory for instructions that evening. He professed to be interested in becoming a Catholic.

"Rose has told me to make up my own mind, of course."

"Of course."

"We would like to be married at St. Hilary's."

Whether the ceremony came before or after Earl's entry into the Church was still undecided. He still seemed to think a Hail Mary was a pass rather than a prayer.

THE MISSING LEONARDO

The shrine to the Blessed Mother was visible from the rectory kitchen as well as from what had once been the parish school. Edna Hospers looked out of her office window but saw nothing unusual about the figure kneeling at the shrine—at least the first time she noticed him. As for Mrs. Murkin, she had altogether too clear a view of the shrine and the disgraceful condition it was in, weeds sprouting around it, the cut flowers going limp in their vases before they were replaced. Harry, the latest derelict employed by Father Dowling to work around the parish grounds, had proved to be as industrious as his predecessors.

"Derelict?" the pastor of St. Hilary's repeated. "Marie, he has been returned to society in as good standing as you or I."

"I have not spent time in prison."

"And you should thank God for it."

Marie was unsure how to respond. Was he suggesting that she had deserved to spend time in prison and had escaped the hand of justice? Or was he simply invoking the there-but-for-the-grace-of-God-go-I principle? Marie herself piously affirmed this truth from time to time, but on her own initiative. She had wisely let it go, but that did not improve her estimate of Harry.

"What do you mean?" Harry said when Marie asked him what he was.

"What religion?"

He just stared at her.

"Protestant? Catholic?"

"Neither."

"Mohammedan?"

He had a barking laugh she didn't like. She concluded that he was a pagan and not at all the kind she gave money to the missions for.

"Is Harry a Catholic?" she asked Father Dowling.

"He didn't say."

"Did you ask him?"

"Marie, he isn't going to do pastoral work. I hired him to take care of the lawn."

All the leaves had been raked and removed the previous autumn before Harry's arrival and now in early May the lawn had yet to revive. The flowering Judas had bloomed and the dogwood was glorious but there really wasn't any yard work to speak of. This seemed to suit Harry just fine. He spent most of the time in his apartment in the school basement listening to ball games.

"I hardly know he's here," Edna Hospers said when Marie asked how she could stand to have that drone around.

"He's supposed to be working."

If Edna was bothered by the inactivity of the supposed yard-man she gave no indication. On the way back to the rectory, Marie stopped to cut some lilacs and then went on to the shrine. A vase of limp lilies of the valley still stood before the statue where Marie had put it two days before.

At the time, she had told Harry to replace them once a day. He looked at her and then at the statue.

"What for?"

"To honor the mother of God."

"That's just a plaster statue."

"And the flag's a piece of colored cloth."

He stared at her. Obviously, he wasn't going to pay any reverence to what he took to be an idol.

"Where are you from?"

"Ask Father Dowling."

"I mean before Joliet."

"It's so long ago I can't remember."

"How long were you in prison?"

"I forget that too."

Well, Marie could take a hint. She ostentatiously knelt and said a Hail Mary for Harry whether he wanted it or not. "Now and at the hour of our death," she said aloud, rising.

"Aren't you feeling well?"

Well, who is not made uneasy by the reminder of mortality? Marie knew that she must die some day, but it still seemed extremely remote, even though she was in her seventies now. Sometimes she felt that the aging process had bypassed her, but at other times, making the painful arthritic climb to her room at the end of a day, she felt like an old woman. Harry must be very nearly her age. Had his life passed away while he was in prison?

On the next Wednesday, Edna noticed that a man had been kneeling at the shrine for some time and called Marie to tell her of Harry's change of heart, but from her window Marie had a better view.

"That's not Harry."

"Are you sure?"

"It looks like him but it isn't."

This man had his long gray hair pulled into a ponytail, something of which Marie disapproved. If Harry had tried such a hair-do she would have spoken to him about it. The man in the ponytail was still kneeling there half an hour later. Such devotion merited attention and Marie went outside and cut some lilacs and headed toward the shrine.

"Excuse me," she said, getting between the kneeling figure and the image of Mary while she exchanged today's lilacs for yesterday's. When she turned, she glanced at the kneeling figure. The eyes were fixed on Mary, wide open, but there was something funny in their expression. And they didn't blink. Marie put her hand on the man's shoulder and he tipped slowly sideways and fell on the ground beside the kneeler. Marie stooped to help him and finally saw that he was beyond any help of hers. He's dead, she told herself almost calmly. Then she stood and began to scream.

Father Dowling had traced a blessing over the dead man and was holding back the curious seniors who spent their day in the parish center. The center was housed in the school that was no longer practical now that most families with children had moved out of the once-prosperous parish. Marie Murkin was trying to look like the pastor's assistant in calming the old people but her expression was one of muted terror.

"He died at his prayers," she said to Captain Phil Keegan.

"Smell him. He was drunk as a lord."

The thought of the man being catapulted into eternity, ponytail flying, with the smell of liquor on his breath was not one Marie cared to dwell on.

"Was he a regular?" Keegan asked Father Dowling.

The pastor said he wasn't sure. "You'd better ask Edna Hospers."

"I never saw him before in my life," Marie said indignantly. The idea that aging hippies were likely to show up at the parish center!

Edna hadn't seen the man before either. Father Dowling pretended to be surprised at this.

The mobile medical examiner unit arrived with Dr. Pippen in charge. It was her habit to make cases more complicated than they were, so Keegan was not surprised when she lifted her brows skeptically when asked if it had been heart failure.

"Maybe he is still alive," Keegan said sarcastically and went over to Father Dowling.

"Any idea who he might be, Roger?"

"Just guesses."

"Do you know him?"

"Did he have identification on him?"

Lieutenant Cy Horvath had checked the man's billfold. "Bonaparte," he said as if it were Smith.

"You're kidding."

"Should I get it? I put it in the evidence safe in the trunk."

"Evidence!"

But Cy did not explain. "Just Bonaparte?" Keegan asked.

"N. Bonaparte."

"I think I will take a look at the billfold."

The two detectives went off to their car and Father Dowling helped Edna shepherd her wards back to the school. The reactions ran the gamut from fright to nervous laughter, but then with age these men and women could no longer think of death as a far-off rumor. It was not unusual for someone who had come regularly to the center to fall ill and never return. They were used to such winnowing of the ranks; they expected it. But it was rare that the event occurred before their eyes. It was even more eerie because it had been a stranger who wandered onto the parish grounds, visited the shrine, and met his death while he breathed his prayers.

"What's going on?" Harry called to Father Dowling. He stood on the basement stairway, one hand on the banister. But it was Dr. Crawford who answered Harry.

"Some vagrant died over at the shrine."

Father Dowling glanced at Crawford. Vagrant? Perhaps the silver-haired retired podiatrist was making a point about Harry. A week ago, he had headed a small delegation that had come to the pastor to ask whether he really thought it was wise to employ such a man as Harry at St. Hilary's.

"He doesn't want to start drawing his Social Security yet."

"That isn't what we mean, Father."

"I know, I know. But I assured Harry that the work would not be laborious and if it became so, you men would pitch in and help."

"Wasn't he in prison, Father?"

"Like Peter and Paul."

The delegation saw that their mission was futile and Crawford deftly turned the conversation to the topic of Father Dowling's library that lined the walls of his study.

"Do you have them in order, Father?"

"I know where things are."

"Mrs. Bingham was a librarian, you know."

The tips of Loretta Bingham's teeth rested on her lower lip, giving the impression of a constant smile. She showed more of her teeth in a deliberate smile. Father Dowling assured her that he liked his books just as they were.

"Marie wouldn't let anyone near them anyway."

Marie herself had standing orders not to rearrange, restack, or in any way alter the state of things in the study. In that sense, she would be furious if someone else were given access to the room.

"Was he a vagrant, Earl?" the priest asked the podiatrist now.

"I was just guessing, Father." But his tone seemed to suggest that the unsettling event had something to do with the pastor's carefree hiring policy.

"He had a ponytail," Loretta Bingham said. "He must have been sixty years old and he wore his hair in a ponytail."

"You say he's dead?" Earl Crawford asked.

"His name was Bonaparte," the priest answered. Puzzled by this, the old people went back to their various recreations.

"Bonaparte?" Harry had gone down a step on the stairway.

"That was on the identification they found on him."

"Funny name."

"Did you know him, Harry?"

"I don't know anyone named Bonaparte."

His original name had been Willard Sellars; after serving his sentence and his parole, he legally changed his name to Napoleon Bonaparte. The records of that name change enabled the police make the identification.

"Turning over a new leaf?"

Phil Keegan shrugged. "I stopped trying to figure out ex-cons long ago. They sit in those cells and convince themselves they're innocent and start reading the law."

"When did he get out of prison?"

"A couple years ago."

"How long was he in?"

"The last time? Ten years. Not that he served ten."

"What prison?"

"Joliet."

Roger Dowling had more questions but it was difficult to watch the Cubs and find all about a man who had changed his name from Willard Sellars to Napoleon Bonaparte at the same time.

"I'll send you everything we have."

It came the next morning, dropped off by Cy Horvath, his nostrils flaring at the aroma of baking coming from the kitchen. Marie peeked out and invited Cy back.

"Do you like pie crisps?"

Pie dough, sprinkled with sugar and cinnamon and baked like cookies. Cy reacted like a kid, even looking to Father Dowling for permission.

"If you don't eat them I'll have to, Cy."

He took the folder into the study and laid it on his desk. Before he opened it he looked out at the shrine where the body of Sellars/Bonaparte had been found kneeling before Our Lady. What was the significance of that?

The life of Willard Sellars made a sad story. He had been a teenage delinquent; his first offense was car theft, followed by holdups that had netted him less than a week's wages at the kind of job he could easily have had. His last offense had been different, for then he had been involved in a well-organized plan to burgle the Fox River museum. Father Dowling remembered that as a theft in which Harry had been a peripheral figure. The official list of missing items was supplemented by newspaper clippings that featured photographs of the museum and drawings indicating how the thieves had gained access to the medieval exhibit that was about to go on to another museum. There had been a censer from St. Denis, several worm-eaten wooden statues that had lost their color, and four drawings by Leonardo da Vinci. Everything had been recovered, except for one of the Leonardos.

"Was the missing drawing ever recovered?" he asked Cy when he looked into the study before leaving. His broad Hungarian face did not change expression. But then he saw the dossier open on the pastor's desk and understood.

"I don't think so."

"How could I find out?"

"I'll check it out."

"What was the cause of death?"

"Poison. Arsenic."

"Good Lord."

"Pippen thinks he might have died elsewhere and been brought here. That's because there is no evidence he was poisoned at the shrine."

"What kind of evidence?"

"Someone laced his booze with arsenic."

Cy did not ask for the dossier so Father Dowling put it into his desk drawer and then started for the school.

"It's only ten o'clock," Marie said when he went through the kitchen.

"That late?" Apparently she thought he was heading for the church and his noon Mass.

"Want a pie crisp?"

"Maybe for lunch. I'm going over to the school."

"You're having pie for lunch."

"No soup?"

The closing screen door and Marie's impatient reaction combined to set him off at a quick pace toward the school. But he slowed as he neared the shrine and then stopped to say a Memorare. The kneeler on which the dead body of Bonaparte had awaited discovery looked as it always had. There were fresh flowers before the statue. Marie. He said a prayer for the housekeeper, to make up for teasing her.

There were two serious tables of bridge in progress where silence reigned, and a competitive game of shuffleboard, but by and large people just visited at the parish center. Two grandmothers were trumping one another's photographs of grandchildren, last night's Cub game was being subjected to minute analysis, and some stared at the television as if in disbelief of the story unwinding there. Father Dowling acknowledged greetings but kept on going. He went down the stairs to the basement where Harry's apartment was and knocked on the door.

There was silence on the other side and he tapped again. "Harry?"

"Who is it?"

"Father Dowling."

A key turned, a chain was removed, and Harry looked out. He seemed relieved that the priest was alone.

"What can I do for you, Father?"

He could imagine Marie's reply to an opening like that. "Can I come in?"

Harry stepped aside. The room was neat as a pin, bed made, no clothes strewn around. Not everyone who had occupied this apartment had been so orderly. Father Dowling sat in a chair whose plastic upholstery crackled under him. Harry settled into a La-Z-Boy and tipped it to a comfortable angle.

"You said you didn't know Bonaparte."

"That's right."

"How about Willard Sellars?"

"You didn't ask me that."

"They're the same man."

Harry nodded. "He came to see me."

"You knew him at Joliet?"

"Funny guy. He wanted to talk about Joliet as if it were the good old days."

On the wall beside Harry's chair a picture was taped to the wall. Father Dowling rose and went to it.

"Where did you get this?"

"Sellars."

"Leonardo," Father Dowling said, as he studied the drawing.

"What?"

"Leonardo da Vinci."

Harry shook his head. "That's Castle."

"Castle?"

"Sellars' buddy. Sellars was Bonaparte, Castle was Leonardo."

"Do you know who Leonardo da Vinci was? The real one?"

Harry turned and looked at the drawing taped to the wall. "That his picture?"

"I believe it is."

"He looks sad."

"He was the artist, not the subject."

"You want it, you can take it."

It was a way to make sure the priceless drawing got into the hands of the police. But Father Dowling preferred to have Harry tell his own story.

"You're going to have to tell this to the police, Harry."

Harry hit a lever and the lounge chair snapped upright, nearly spilling him onto the floor. He shook his head. "I can't do that."

"Harry, a man has been killed. That drawing is stolen property."

"You want me to get killed?"

"The police will keep you out of it."

Harry gave a barking laugh. "My friends the police."

Harry came to see he had no choice, and Father Dowling called Phil Keegan, who said he'd come by for Harry.

"Is that necessary?"

"He can identify Napoleon's body. We haven't been able to reach Josephine."

Phil put it off until afternoon and Father Dowling went along with his employee. The first stop was the morgue. When the sheet was pulled back, Harry hit his forehead.

"That's Castle!"

"It's not Napoleon?"

"Castle was da Vinci."

"This isn't Willard Sellars?"

"What in hell are you talking about?" Phil Keegan exploded.

It took some time to straighten it out. Father Dowling summed up for Keegan that Castle and Sellars had been involved in the Fox River museum theft of some years ago.

"Weren't you involved in that?" Keegan asked Harry, the details coming back.

"Could we get out of here? I'm freezing." But Harry looked

at the lifeless body of Castle as if he feared he could hear him chatting with the police. When they were in the warmer outer room Harry said, "I drove. That's all. I didn't even know what was planned. The prosecutor accepted that."

"You made a deal."

Harry winced. Father Dowling opened his briefcase and took out the drawing Harry had taped to his wall. "Sellars gave Harry this."

Keegan wrinkled his nose as he studied the drawing. "I don't blame him. It's not finished."

"It may be one of the missing art works."

"Accepting stolen property," Keegan muttered.

"How was I to know?"

"You were just driving. When did he give you this?"

Harry thought. "A week ago?"

"Be exact."

Exactness took them to the day that the body of the pony-tailed stranger had been found dead at the grotto at St. Hilary's.

"You're saying that Sellars came to see you the same day Castle was killed at St. Hilary's?"

"I guess so."

"And he gave you this stolen picture to put on your wall?"

"He asked me to keep it."

Harry was not arrested but he was subjected to hours of questioning. An APB went out for Willard Sellars. The theory that emerged was this: The thieves had managed to sequester one extremely valuable item from their museum theft. Through thick and thin they had denied they knew where the missing drawing might be. The rest of what they had stolen was in the trunk of the car they were driving when they were arrested. Now, years later, the dust settled, the indemnity on the exhibit having paid a huge amount to the Milan museum from which the exhibit had come, the two thieves, paroled at last, were free to profit from the Leonardo drawing.

"They must have had a falling out. Why split when the whole could be had?"

"So Sellars planted the drawing with Harry."

"And was followed by Castle. Pippen never did think he had died while kneeling. His partner must have propped him up there after killing him."

"After putting his own billfold into his pocket," Father Dowling murmured.

Phil looked at him.

"Castle was Leonardo, not Bonaparte."

This was answered with an impatient noise. "They sound like a bunch of kids."

The puzzle could be solved when Sellars was arrested. There was no way he could escape the dragnet that had been thrown out to catch him. Roger Dowling found the switched billfold the least of the puzzle. What nagged at his mind was that these men had planned so sophisticated a theft. So far as he could see, their cultural level was roughly that of Harpo. Medieval and Renaissance artworks were unlikely to have danced like sugarplums in the heads of Castle and Sellars as they dreamed on their bunks in Joliet.

The Fox River museum was a bit of a museum piece itself: one of the original Carnegie libraries, which after its original purpose had been outgrown became the headquarters of an insurance agency, then a restaurant, and ultimately the Fox River museum. The permanent collection boasted two paintings by minor impressionists, a fourteenth-century lectionary, and some studies by Mary Cassatt. Other even lesser things.

"We have an extensive slide collection as well," Mr. Bassett said. He was the director and he looked more like a football player than an art custodian.

"How long have you worked here?"

"Ever since the injury that put me out of football."

Father Dowling stepped back and looked at the director. "Moose Bassett?"

A crooked grin revealed unnaturally straight teeth. "I'm surprised you remember."

"Forget someone who played for Halas?"

"Not even two seasons. You must be quite a fan."

Bassett invited Roger Dowling into his office and offered him a cup of coffee and they talked for a time of Bassett's aborted career in pro football.

"I went back to Champagne and finished my degree."

"How long have you been here?"

"Since graduation. I worked up through the ranks." Although the staff was only half a dozen, Bassett's pride seemed understandable.

"Were you here when the Nectarini collection was robbed?"

"I became director shortly afterward. Ciapi, my predecessor, could never live it down. He was a broken man."

"I understand that the missing Leonardo drawing has been recovered."

"What!"

"The police haven't contacted you?"

Bassett was excited and impatient. Roger Dowling told him what he knew. He gave him Phil Keegan's number. He listened while Bassett demanded to see the recovered drawing. An impatient pause and then he said, "Father Dowling told me. He is sitting right here in my office."

Phil wore a reproachful look when he and Cy arrived with the drawing. Bassett took it with reverence and carried it to the window to study it.

"I thought it was public knowledge, Phil."

"It is now."

Bassett seemed to be muttering to himself. He turned to his visitors, holding the drawing in one hand as he might a Frisbee.

"This is a copy."

"What do you mean?"

"It's not bad but it is not the original."

"Are you sure?"

Bassett thrust the drawing at Phil Keegan. "Ask any art historian."

Phil asked two, and they confirmed Bassett's judgment. It seemed that Sellars had played a trick on Harry as well as on his old partner in crime.

"God knows where he might be now," Phil groused.

"What about your dragnet?"

"Yeah."

As it happened, Sellars had not gone far. He was found behind the wheel of a junked sedan that had been stripped of everything valuable and was rusting in a back row of what was called all-too-appropriately Sumski's Car Cemetery. The rising temperature and the laws of nature had drawn attention to the body.

Harry was arrested. It was a desperation move but Phil Keegan could hardly be blamed. The St. Hilary yardman seemed the only living link to the two dead ex-convicts, the long-ago art theft, and the copy of the missing Leonardo drawing. Harry professed his innocence with tears in his eyes, but he obviously regarded the attendant publicity as ruinous. No crook would ever trust him again.

"Why did you leave the arsenic in the maintenance shed?" Cy asked.

"Arsenic? What are you talking about?"

"Your old partner was killed with arsenic."

"I don't know anything about it. I don't even know where the maintenance shed is."

"You can't harm Castle and Sellars, Harry," Father Dowling told him. "They are beyond the reach of that."

"I'm worried about me."

"What can they do to you?"

"They have friends."

"They must have had a friend who knew the value of art."

Phil Keegan shrugged off the suggestion. "The papers at the time must have been full of that exhibit. Anyone would have figured out the stuff was worth a lot."

Sure enough, the Fox River paper had run several stories on the visiting exhibit, stressing the value of the items on display. But why would ex-convicts notice such a story?

Joe Stoner had been chaplain at Joliet since before anyone could remember, and he had overcome the hostility of even the most hardened criminals and ended as their friend, sometimes the only one they had. Not that he was deceived by this.

"I'm not here to make friends, Roger."

"Did you know Castle and Sellars?"

"God rest their souls."

Stoner knew that Harry was working at St. Hilary's. He had recommended him to Father Dowling, suggesting he hire him for a few months, as a transition. "It will make it easier to get the next job."

"Did either Castle or Sellars know anything about art?"

Stoner laughed.

"Isn't it odd that they would rob a museum?"

"They would have robbed the zoo if they had a chance."

Harry was released, and that made Marie Murkin grumpy. She thought now might be a good time for Harry to move on. As if in response, Harry was suddenly very visibly at work around the grounds, trimming, mowing, fertilizing. He seemed to have a knack for gardening. Phil Keegan was not much better company than Marie. He had two dead ex-convicts and no explanation of how they had died and no one cared. There was no media crusade demanding that justice be done. Chief Robertson told him to close the case. Instead they arrested Harry.

"Harry!"

"Think about it, Roger. He knew Castle and Sellars and they knew him. Sellars was here and gave him a drawing on the very day Castle is found dead at your grotto."

"The drawing was only a copy."

"A copy of a stolen drawing."

"Roger, there's something else."

"What?"

"The arsenic. It came from the maintenance shed. Pippen is sure the stuff that killed Castle came from here."

"I didn't even know we had any arsenic in that shed."

"We got a call."

To his credit, Phil seemed a little shamefaced about this solution. On paper Harry seemed a plausible suspect but no one who knew him could think him capable of these crimes. For one thing, the expenditure of energy that would have been required seemed uncharacteristic of the lethargic yardman.

"I suppose you have a motive, Phil."

"Who knows about convicts?"

"But Harry gains nothing and loses everything."

Marie observed an almost Trappistine silence, afraid perhaps of saying aloud that she had after all warned the pastor. Earl Crawford, on the other hand, seemed amazed at this turn of events, although Loretta Bingham smiled vacantly and clutched the podiatrist's hand.

"Ask him, Earl."

"This isn't the time." But he squeezed her hand.

"Father, we want to get married."

"Without any fuss," Earl said quickly. "Can it be private?"

"Up to a point."

Well, well. But Father Dowling was becoming almost used to the way romance bloomed as the shadows of life lengthened. Edna thought it was loneliness, but Marie took notice of the dismay of the prospective heirs and wondered if venality played as much of a role as Venus in these belated liaisons. But both Earl and Loretta were alone in the world, except for a nephew of Loretta's.

"We think Harry knows where the original drawing is, Roger."

"Bassett tells me that most works of art end up being stolen. He wanted to tell me all about Napoleon."

"Sellars?"

"No, the other one. He carted whole museums back to Paris."

"Hitler."

"He mentioned him too."

A week later Joe Stoner called from Joliet. "I been thinking, Roger."

"Yes."

"You wondered how a couple of convicts would know enough about art to steal it? I think I may have found the answer. We had a lecture here a few months before they were released on their previous convictions. Art history. It was really popular. You never know with convicts."

"They liked it?"

"I suppose it was because the speaker had played profes-sional football."

"Bassett?"

"You know him?"

"We've met."

Bassett seemed to be waiting for him. He hurried toward Father Dowling and led him into his office, where he carefully shut the door. "I was afraid of this," he said.

"Of my coming here?"

"No, no. Father, there's something I didn't tell you. I knew those men, Castle and Sellars. I gave a talk at the prison when they were there and there was such interest I went back several times. Sellars began reading art history and was full of questions, and I corresponded with him." Bassett shook his head and his dewlaps swayed. "They even hung around here after they got out. I couldn't offer them a job, although the chaplain, a man named Stoner, urged me to. They were volunteers."

"How long did that last?"

"Not long. A couple weeks, at most three."

"Was the exhibit here at that time?"

"No. This was months before that."

"And now you think that they were just casing the place."

"I thought that right away. And I wasn't the only one. After the theft, Ciapi told the police about them. That's why they were arrested so quickly. But their connection with the museum was kept quiet. What a fool I was. I don't think it can be kept quiet any longer."

"Did you know Harry, too?"

"He drove the car when the things were stolen. I know that. But I never met him."

"Why should any of this become known then? It is Harry they've arrested."

"Because someone returned the drawing."

"The missing Leonardo?"

Bassett went to the door and locked it. Then he opened a

cabinet and reverently removed a wooden case which he placed on his desk. Father Dowling was standing beside him when the case was opened. It was empty.

"It's gone," Bassett cried. "It's gone."

When a man the size of the director becomes hysterical it is a difficult situation. Bassett emptied the cabinet from which he had taken the case, spilling things onto the floor. He looked under his desk. He looked wildly at Father Dowling.

"When was the drawing returned?"

Bassett seemed relieved that his story was accepted. He dropped into the chair behind his desk and closed his eyes. He recounted the facts as if he were reading them off his closed eyelids. A messenger had delivered the crate, saying it was to go to the director's office.

"Frieda said she would put it there. She did. She had no idea of its importance. I found it on my desk, opened it and let out such a shout that the whole staff assembled. You can imagine our joy."

"When was this?"

"At ten o'clock this morning." He looked at his watch. "Three and a half hours ago."

What a temptation that drawing must have represented for the underpaid staff of the Fox River museum. They had all known where it was, they would all have been able to go into Bassett's office. The director grew angry as Father Dowling intimated what might have happened.

"No. Never. None of them would do such a thing."

Father Dowling found himself certain that Bassett himself would not have made off with the returned drawing. Not after making such an event over its return. But his anger subsided into sadness.

"The worst thing of all is that I called the archivist who was here at the time of the theft. I took her to lunch and told her the drawing was back. She had felt as responsible as poor Ciapi when it was stolen."

"Where is she now?"

"She's retired, has been for four or five years. Not that you ever really leave a job like this."

When Bassett put through the call to the police, Roger Dowling left the director to his agonizing duty. But it was with a sense of bafflement that he drove back to St. Hilary's. It was not at all clear that this new development would help Harry.

Carl Hospers came along the walk on his bicycle and gave the pastor a hearty wave. Marie Murkin's mood was considerably different when he came in the kitchen door.

"The nerve of some people," Marie muttered.

"Anything wrong?"

"No! Not while I have breath in my body."

"What happened?"

"A little delegation came by, wanting me to persuade you to change your mind about their earlier offer."

Father Dowling sat at the kitchen table, almost glad to be diverted by Marie's doubtless petty grievance. "A delegation?"

"The foot-in-his-mouth doctor."

Father Dowling laughed at the description. "You mean Dr. Crawford?"

"Is a foot doctor a real doctor?"

"It depends on the condition of your feet."

"At least his trusty companion had sense enough to stay away."

"And who is his trusty companion?"

"Loretta Bingham!"

He had almost forgotten the suggestion that she rearrange the books in Father Dowling's rectory study. "I wonder what it would cost?"

"That woman is not going to mess up your books. She's not a real librarian anyway. Both of them are quacks."

"I think she said she was a librarian. Or was it Crawford?"

"She worked in the museum. Probably mopping and dusting."

"The Fox River museum?"

"I told them you were not interested." Marie paused. "I told them you wouldn't even let me touch those books."

"But you don't have library experience."

Marie looked on the verge of tears and he hastened to assure her he had no intention of unleashing Loretta Bingham on his study. Settled behind the desk in his study his thoughts began to come together. He telephoned Bassett.

"How did it go with the police?"

"They're still here. I've closed the museum. They are swarming all over the place."

"Was Loretta Bingham the museum archivist?"

"Yes." A pause. "She is also a kind of relative of mine."

"Have you told her yet?"

"I dread the thought."

The lilacs lining the walk to the school filled the spring air with their perfume. Father Dowling stopped at the grotto but it was difficult to pray with all the commotion in his head. At the school, he looked into the former gym and saw that Loretta was there, with Dr. Crawford.

"Hello, Father."

He turned to Edna Hospers. "I saw Carl a while ago."

"Wearing a big grin?"

"He did seem pretty happy."

"He was given ten dollars for delivering a package."

"At the museum?"

"How did you know that?"

He tapped his forehead. "ESP."

"What's that?"

"Empty, *s'il vous plait.*"

He moved on and found Harry, who was out on bond, brooding in his apartment. Harry groaned when he realized that Father Dowling wanted to talk about the events that had led to Harry's arrest.

"Why did Sellars come to see you that day?"

"It was both of them."

"Castle, too?"

"And they didn't come to see me. They came to see one of the old ladies."

"Loretta Bingham."

"They brought her along. She brought the bottle."

"And Castle had a drink."

"Sellars doesn't drink. Neither do I."

"Did Loretta?"

Harry thought. "I don't think so."

"Did she take her bottle when she left?"

"It's in the kitchen."

Father Dowling found it there and then took it up to Edna, carrying it carefully, where he put it in her closet. After he called Phil, he went downstairs and found Loretta and Earl holding hands, deep in conversation. Earl at least seemed grateful for the interruption.

"I'm sorry I wasn't in when you stopped by, Earl." He turned to Loretta. "Just what do you propose to do with my study?"

"Father, I have the distinct impression that Mrs. Murkin would murder me if I set foot in that study."

"With arsenic?"

Loretta paused. "With her bare hands most likely."

"Moose Bassett tells me you had lunch together today."

"He is so excited. A stolen picture has been recovered."

"He wouldn't be deceived by a copy, would he?"

Loretta's teeth pressed into her lower lip and she peered at Father Dowling. "I am not sure I follow the drift of your question, Father."

Phil and Cy arrived then and Father Dowling was sure that Loretta would get the drift of their questions.

"What a wicked woman," Marie said.

"Maybe she saw it as her dowry," Father Dowling said. "She wouldn't come to Earl empty-handed."

Loretta and the podiatrist had been an item for some time, even when Earl's wife was still alive, brought together by a malformation in Loretta's big toe. When her nephew Bassett befriended Sellars and Castle, Loretta had seen an opportunity to pad her retirement income. She was the insider who enabled the theft to go so smoothly. Her own theft of one of the Leonardos seemed covered by the arrest of Sellars and Castle.

"It is odd they didn't tell the police about her."

The contemplative quiet of Joliet had apparently brought insight. One of the thieves must have guessed why they were accused of stealing one more drawing than they had. They looked forward to release so that they could cash in on the missing Leonardo. Once again they were outwitted by the wily archivist. Castle had accepted a lethal drink. Stopping at the shrine had been his own idea.

"Mary never fails," Marie said with enigmatic fervor.

Earl Crawford had been Loretta's accomplice with Sellars. Sellars had seen the advantages of no longer having a partner and had gone on with Loretta to her home. She had served him arsenic with his coffee. The automobile junkyard had been Earl's suggestion. The podiatrist had burst into tears when he was arrested, blaming it all on Loretta. She had, he said, pursued him relentlessly for years. She had ruined his life. He claimed not even to know who Leonardo was.

"He can read up on him in Joliet," Phil said.

"She was an aunt by marriage," Moose Bassett explained. "But I can't believe she did this."

"Why did she send the drawing back to you?"

"To keep it away from her partners, I guess. She had given them a copy and they thought they had the real thing."

"And asked Harry to keep it?"

"He knows less about Leonardo than Earl Crawford does."

"It could be a toss-up," Marie said.

It was arguably the nicest thing she had said about Harry.

Some weeks later, Moose Bassett sent a card from Milan where he had gone to return the missing Leonardo to the Nectarini collection. It was a picture of the Last Supper before the efforts at restoration.

"The one at the end of the table is either Loretta or Earl Crawford," he wrote. "At least I got this trip out of it."

INTO THIN AIR

When Marie Murkin opened the rectory door Sandro Manzoni took her by the arm and marched her down the hall to the pastor's study. Father Dowling looked up, almost as surprised as Marie herself.

"What's this?"

"This woman ruined a sale for me, Father, that's what. We were ready to close and now it's all off. Because of her!"

He let go of Marie's arm as if he feared continued contact with the housekeeper would sully him.

"I don't know what he's talking about," Marie said, addressing the pastor in an effort to regain her dignity.

"I'll tell you what I'm talking about. Did you or did you not tell the Webers the Bradley house is haunted?"

Marie took a step away from Manzoni. Guilt was written all over her face. There was a moment when morality hung in the balance, when she looked about to lie, but she conquered the temptation.

"Well, it's true."

"Father Dowling, are you going to let your housekeeper spread superstition around the parish?"

The pastor of St. Hilary's was in a delicate position. On the one hand, Marie was undoubtedly prone to assume a role that did not fit the job description of parish housekeeper. There were those who thought her a busybody. It seemed clear that she had said something to some prospective buyers that had cost Manzoni a sale, not a negligible fact. Sandro Manzoni was a parishioner and the son of parishioners and could reasonably expect that the parish house would be, if not a business partner, then certainly a well-wisher as he went about the earning of his daily bread. On the other hand, Marie was a parish institution, her seniority considerably greater than Father Dowling's. She was loyal to him, and he would be loyal to her. But a Solomonian decision was called for.

"Where is the Bradley place?"

"On Wintheiser Avenue."

"Big frame house?"

"Brick, Father. A magnificent family house. The Webers wouldn't look at another house after they saw it. And then she butted-in."

"Sandro Manzoni, you know perfectly well what happened in that house."

"What?"

Marie turned impatiently from the realtor. Father Dowling looked at her, waiting.

"Well, what happened?"

Marie made a line of her mouth and squeezed her eyes shut. It was bad enough to be on the carpet, but to have a witness was worse.

"It was before your time."

"Tell me about it."

"Catherine Ryan." She said the name and looked at Manzoni. His expression was blank. Marie grew impatient. "You know what I'm talking about. Your parents must have told you."

"Told me what?"

"Father Dowling, years ago, not long after I became a housekeeper, Catherine Ryan just disappeared. Into thin air." She hesitated and then went on. "As if she had been snatched into heaven."

"That's what she's been telling the Webers, Father."

"Catherine Ryan? I thought it was the Bradley house."

"They bought when old Mr. Ryan sold it. Brokenhearted, he was, too. And his son with him."

"Has anyone else disappeared from the house, Marie?"

"How many do there have to be?"

"There hasn't been any, Father. That woman ran away."

"So you do remember!"

Half an hour more was required to arrive at a resolution of the problem. Marie was to talk to the Webers, show them around the Bradley place, and make crystal clear that there were no supernatural impediments to their buying the house and settling into St. Hilary parish.

"It would be nice to have them back," Marie said.

"Back?"

"Her grandparents lived here."

"Ah."

"Should I have the Webers call you, Father, or will you call them?"

"Oh, Marie will take it from here, Sandro."

Father Dowling showed Manzoni out, relieving Marie of that humiliating experience. When he came back she had slumped into a chair in his study and was staring moodily out the window.

"Marie . . ."

She looked up at Father Dowling as if her mind was a million miles away.

"Into thin air, Father Dowling. As if she had been snatched into heaven."

"I thought you were warning us away from that house," a somewhat-puzzled Meg Weber said when Marie called to suggest that the two of them go through the Bradley house.

"That lovely brick house?"

"You said it was haunted."

"All houses are haunted, Meg, with good and bad memories of those who lived in them. I think of all the good memories that house must hold."

"You said a woman had been kidnapped from there."

How bitter it was to remember the zest with which she had told Meg of the disappearance of Catherine Ryan. But it had all been true. Marie's only recourse was to cover that truth over with other reassuring and pleasant truths about the Bradley house. She just ignored the period when the Ryans had lived there.

Meg was in her early thirties, mother of two, her brunette hair worn at half length so that it swirled freely with every movement of her head. Marie had been watching from the kitchen window when Meg drove up. From that vantage point, it was difficult to see if there were any children in the back of the station wagon. Or dogs! But Marie steeled herself and marched out to the car. It helped if she thought of this errand as simply a favor to a young couple trying to get settled in the parish. Sandro Manzoni had nothing to do with it.

"I'm so glad I misunderstood what you said, Mrs. Murkin," Meg said when they got out of the station wagon and looked up at the Bradley house. It was indeed an impressive house. Marie ignored the remark about having been misunderstood. The prospect of going through a house she had never been in before quickened her step.

Meg marveled at the front porch, at the fireplace in the living room, at the sunroom facing west; the kitchen gave pause and they considered ways in which it could be modernized. Upstairs there were five bedrooms, enough for all the actual and possible Weber children.

And then they took a look at the backyard. The potting shed was attached to the garage and was entered from inside the garage. Marie went down the three steps to the sunken floor of the greenhouse. The lawn outside seemed a continuation of the U-shaped table that bordered the inside of the greenhouse. Stacks of pots, planters, plastic flats that once had held young plants. The floor was of brick, laid in a pattern. Marie was about to call Meg's attention to it when she looked beneath the table and saw how imperfectly the pattern had been kept. Whoever had laid those bricks might have been careless because he thought his artistry would never be seen. Or he had simply worked in haste. There was something else about the floor beneath the table. And then she had it. The area of oddly laid bricks made a rectangle of suggestive size.

"It looks like a grave," Marie said half aloud, then clamped a hand over her mouth. But Meg was not behind her.

Marie resolved to say nothing now, mindful of the wrath of Sandro Manzoni.

"I just love this place," Meg Weber said when Marie came out of the garage.

The lawn stretched before them, coming to an end at a stand of trees. There was no sense at all that there were other houses close by or possible observers of whatever was done here. Marie's mind was filled with the grave-sized rectangle of imperfectly laid brick beneath the table in the greenhouse.

"What do you mean it looked like a grave?" Cy Horvath asked. He was enjoying a quarter of a lemon meringue pie that Marie had put before him.

"It was its size."

"You mention this to anyone?"

"I wanted to tell you, Lieutenant. You could check it out, discreetly."

"You want me to go over there and dig up the floor of the Bradley greenhouse?"

"Is there an easier way to find out if a body is buried there?"

107

Cy looked at the pie on his plate. To finish it would be to agree to do what Marie was in effect asking. He brought a forkful to his mouth, hesitated, then devoured it.

"Whose body you think it is?"

"Why don't we let that go until we see if there is a body there?"

The body buried under the floor of the greenhouse at the Bradley house was that of a woman. Catherine Ryan, as Cy was able to determine by consulting the identifying traits that had been recorded years ago during the search for the woman and then been entered into the comprehensive computerized database of the Fox River Police Department. It was the sort of information that might reasonably have been excluded from that database. What possible future value could information about a woman who had disappeared all those years ago have?

"She would have been eighty-one," Cy said to Father Dowling when he and Marie told the pastor what had been discovered in the Bradley house.

"So she wasn't snatched up into heaven," the pastor mused.

"No wonder I thought the house is haunted."

Father Dowling did not like to think what Sandro Manzoni's reaction to this development would be. One thing was certain, he had now lost the Webers for good, at least so far as the Bradley house went. What the realtor would doubtless characterize as Marie's nosiness had turned up a body and turned away the Webers.

"I don't suppose Mr. Ryan is still alive," the pastor said.

"He would be eighty-three."

Would be and was. Larry Ryan was a resident in the Good Shepherd Retirement Home right there in Fox River. When Father Dowling went to see him, accepting the task of informing the man of the discovery of his wife's body, the old man listened with exaggerated attentiveness.

"I got most of that, Father. Could you say it again?"

The common room in which they were talking made Father Dowling reluctant to raise his voice sufficiently to overcome Larry Ryan's defective hearing. The old man's eyes were weak, his hearing all but gone, and his mouth empty of teeth. As if remembering, he fetched a denture from his shirt pocket and put it into his mouth. The result was not an improvement.

"Do you have a hearing aid?"

"It doesn't work."

"Would you like me to get it fixed?"

"I mean it doesn't do any good. It works as well as it can."

"I will conduct a funeral service for Mrs. Ryan."

"I never wanted to do that before. It would have said she was never coming home."

"She left you?"

"She could have been kidnapped," Ryan said edgily. "Or developed insomnia."

"Amnesia?"

"Maybe. It made no sense that she just walked out the door and never came back. I don't like to think of all the things that might have happened to her."

"Apparently she never left home at all."

"Where'd you find her?"

"I haven't seen the site myself. I am told there is a greenhouse attached to the garage."

Ryan had been listening before but his attention seemed to move into another gear. He sat back as if thinking of the house in which he had lived with his wife and son. How must he feel to learn that the woman he had reported missing had been lying under the brick floor of the greenhouse all those years?

"Where is your son, Mr. Ryan? Shouldn't he be told?"

"Basil? Yes, yes, of course."

Again the old man's mind seemed to slip away; in a minute he sat forward.

"I want to make a confession, Father."

Father Dowling looked around at the old people near them. Like most deaf people Ryan spoke very loudly but the others seemed to pay no attention to him. But then they were speaking pretty loudly themselves.

"Why don't we go to your room, Mr. Ryan? I'll hear your confession there."

"I don't want to confess to you. I want to talk to the police."

"Why don't you tell me first?"

But he confessed to the whole room and it was what Father Dowling had feared.

"I did it, Father. I killed Catherine and buried her there in the greenhouse."

"You're not serious."

"Of course I'm serious!"

"But you thought she was missing, that any number of awful things might have happened to her."

"I was lying. I killed her." And then he heaved a sob and tears began to leak from his eyes.

"How did you kill her?"

"I'll save that for the police."

"Where can I get in touch with your son?"

"I want to confess first. To the police."

The old man's confession presented first Phil Keegan and Cy Horvath and then the prosecutor with a problem. Ron Senski shook his head.

"I'm overloaded now. Say the case got on the docket, what am I going to ask for, life imprisonment of a man eighty-three years old? It's a waste of time."

"Can you outlive the time when killing someone is murder?"

Father Dowling asked.

"People outlive it every day. What evidence do we have that he did it?"

"Why would he confess if he didn't?"

"His saying so isn't enough, Keegan, and you know it. How did he say he did it?"

That was a problem. Ryan was vague about what had happened. But there had been a quarrel and he hit her and she hit her head and when he saw that she was dead he did what he did and reported her missing.

He wasn't any help in finding his son, either. But somehow the media got hold of the story. They descended on the Good Shepherd Retirement Home and soon the TV screens, first in Chicago, then throughout the nation, were filled with pictures of the octogenarian who had gotten away with murder all these years.

"I deserve the chair," Ryan said, glowering at the camera's eye.

"Did she have a terminal disease?"

"She was fit as a fiddle."

"Did she ask you to . . ." The reporter's voice delicately dropped away.

"Kill her? Are you crazy?"

Clearly Larry Ryan did not provide the media an opportunity to befuddle the moral sense of the nation. They seemed to think that if his wife had given him permission, killing her should elicit the sympathy of the audience. The publicity raised once more the question of what was to be done to the self-confessed murderer. The police and prosecutor could no longer keep secret any decision not to pursue Larry Ryan's claim that he had killed his wife and buried her in the greenhouse attached to his garage.

★ ★ ★ ★ ★

Vindication was sweet but Marie Murkin kept her counsel. No need to say "I told you so," whether by word or deed. The warm feeling of having her intuition confirmed was reward enough. But her privacy, too, was soon invaded by the press, when word got out that it was she who had first noticed the odd configuration of the bricks on the floor of the greenhouse at the Bradley house.

"Did you know the dead woman?"

The question was put by a young woman wearing jeans and a blouse who had said, "I'm Judy, this is Hiram."

They had matching ponytails, though Hiram's started from rather far back on his head because of his receding hair line. He wore some sort of denim vest and was draped with cameras.

"Don't take my picture," Marie cried too late.

"Catherine Ryan," Judy said, consulting her notes.

"I knew of her."

"That was what, fifty years ago?"

Marie stepped back at the mathematical implications of the question. How old did this child think the housekeeper of St. Hilary's was? Marie emphasized that she had been a very young woman when she first came to work at St. Hilary's.

"Not as old as you are now, my dear."

Her memories of the dead woman not proving to be a fertile topic, they went on to the discovery of the grave.

"Were you looking for it?"

"Let's say, I wasn't surprised."

"You thought there was a body buried there?"

"Catherine Ryan disappeared into thin air," Marie said, then paused. "It was as if she had been snatched up into heaven. Ordinary mortals do not just vanish in that way."

"The family filed a missing person's report."

"Well, she was certainly missing."

"And now we know why."

Marie lifted her eyes and opened her hands.

"The husband had done it all along."

"That's what he says."

"Did you know him?"

There were few people who could now know whether or not she had known the Ryans, except for Mr. Ryan of course. They might have been parishioners but Marie had had no knowledge of them before tragedy struck the family. It would have been nice to help Judy out with a portrait of the Ryans of long ago. But she decided to quit while she was ahead.

"They had a son, didn't they?"

"Yes."

"What was he like?"

"No one has heard anything from him in years."

"Not even the father?"

"That is a question you will have to put to him."

The address for Basil Ryan that the Good Shepherd Nursing Home had was no longer valid. Basil had moved from the apartment in Encino four years ago. Keegan put in a request to the Encino police.

"What's up?"

"The body of his mother has been found."

"So it's urgent?"

"Not really. She had been buried in her garage for the past thirty years."

"The kid do it?"

Basil would be in his mid-forties at least. "The father has confessed."

"This will be a nice homecoming for what's his name?"

"Basil."

"I knew his brother Herb."

It seemed to be a joke. Well, you expected California police to be a little strange.

Two days later Basil Ryan showed up at the St. Hilary rectory. He was prematurely bald and might have been his father's younger brother. Marie would have loved to have a little chat with him before taking him to the pastor, but the door of the study was open and Father Dowling would have heard her go by to answer the front door.

"I'm so sorry," Marie said mournfully.

Basil looked at her as if he didn't understand English. Later, when listening from the hallway, she heard him tell Father Dowling that he had been living in Mexico in recent years, Marie wondered if he just hadn't gotten his ear for English back yet.

"You work there?" Father Dowling asked.

"I'm retired."

"You don't seem old enough for that."

"I'm not. But I can afford not to work, at least if I live in Mexico, so I don't."

There was silence in the rectory. What in the name of heaven could justify a man still in his vigor to simply drop out of the human race and live in a foreign country doing nothing at all?

"I do a little painting," Basil said, as if sensing the inquisitive character of the silence. "As a hobby. I'm no good at it."

"It must have been a shock, hearing about your mother."

Basil looked around the study. "This room doesn't look the same. The parish seems different."

"Oh, it's the same."

"I went to school here."

"It's no longer a school. There aren't enough children in the parish for that. Now it's a parish center. For retired people."

"The policeman who got in touch with me said your

housekeeper discovered the body."

"Marie! Could you come in here?"

She hesitated, stepped toward the dining room and pushed the door, let it swing back and forth, then turned and went to the study.

"Did you call me, Father?"

Marie kept her eyes on the pastor lest she betray any curiosity about their guest.

"This is Basil Ryan."

"Well, for heaven's sake." He hadn't seemed to understand her in the hall so she would just start from scratch.

"I was told you found my mother's body?"

"Oh I wouldn't say that. I just noticed something strange about the floor. The police did the rest."

Basil Ryan looked at Marie. "Why would you call the police about a thing like that?"

Marie could not tell whether the question was motivated by anger or mere curiosity. It was difficult to explain the click that had gone off in her head when she looked down at that brick floor in the greenhouse. After being scolded by Manzoni in front of Father Dowling and having to volunteer to take Meg Weber to the house and pretend that it was not haunted by the awful mystery of Catherine Ryan's disappearance, it was as if God wanted her to go to the house and discover the spot where Catherine Ryan had been buried. But she couldn't say that. Basil Ryan was a pathetic figure of a man, overweight, prematurely aged, his bald head knobby and pale. He must not sit out in the sun much in Mexico.

"It was just a hunch."

"I guess I always knew it would be discovered."

"You knew your mother was buried there?"

Basil looked at the pastor, a confused expression on his face. "Yes."

"Did your father tell you?"

Basil seemed to slump into himself, but once more he looked around the study.

"The last time I was here, Father Polycarp was pastor."

"A Franciscan."

"I guess so. He wore a white rope."

"He was a Franciscan," Marie said and her tone suggested she could say a lot more if she wanted to.

"Tell me about your mother's disappearance."

Basil looked bewildered. "She just left. That day, I asked Dad where she was and he said somewhere in the house and later I began to look for her and she wasn't there, not anywhere. Not that we were worried at first. You don't think that your own mother will just vanish."

"Into thin air," Marie murmured.

"After a while we got worried but it was several hours before we called the police. It wasn't like her, but my mother could have gone shopping or something without leaving a note or telling us. Finally we called the police. They thought we were panicking and we thought so, too. Of course they asked lots of questions."

"What kind of questions?"

"You know. Had my parents had a fight, that sort of thing."

"Had they?"

"Fight? My parents?" Basil shook his head slowly back and forth. "They were that close." He entwined two of his pudgy fingers. "They were both so good to me but I always felt like an intruder."

"Was she ill?"

Father Dowling knew from Phil Keegan that Catherine Ryan's health had not been robust. Several months before her disappearance she had had a hysterectomy, but there was no reason to think that her recovery was not normal.

"She was in good health," Basil said. "And good spirits."

"You know that your father says he killed her."

"That's nonsense."

"That could not have happened?"

"It's impossible."

"Why would he say he did it?"

Basil shrugged. "Age. Feelings of guilt all these years. I know I felt half-responsible for my mother's disappearance."

"How do you suppose she ended up beneath the floor of the greenhouse?"

"God only knows."

"Oh, not only God."

Not only was the body of the woman missing all these years found buried under the floor of the greenhouse behind the house where she had lived, the tools used to dig the grave and to replace the bricks, however hastily, were found in the garage, undisturbed by the Bradleys during their tenure of the house.

"I hired a crew to do the yard," Hank Bradley said.

"If I look at a flower it wilts," Isabel Bradley said. "I never gardened."

"I wish we'd sold the house before they began to dig up bodies around the place."

"Bodies!" Isabel Bradley made a face to complement her tone.

"One's enough."

"The poor woman. Lying there like that."

"She didn't feel a thing."

"Hank!"

The Bradleys carried on their lighthearted love-match in the confines of the Good Shepherd Retirement Home.

"Do you know Larry Ryan?"

"How can you talk to a man that's deaf as a post."

"He did it, didn't he?" Isabel eased forward on her deck chair.

"He says he did."

"Get him a jury of husbands and he'll get off."

"Hank, be serious."

"I was serious once and look what it got me."

Isabel threw a look of despair at Father Dowling but clearly such badinage was the coin of their marriage.

It wasn't only the son Basil who described the Ryan marriage as idyllic. Willis Pope, shuffleboard champ of the St. Hilary Center, had known the Ryans well.

"They were still on their first date. Like kids. I can't imagine them raising their voices. Unreal."

"You don't think it was genuine?"

"Oh, I didn't mean that, Father. Unreal as in rare, unheard of, seldom seen, It was genuine enough all right." He looked around. "It was almost holy, you know?"

Of course it was wrong to wonder how a frail old man like Larry Ryan had managed to kill his wife and then dig a grave and bury her. He would have been in vigorous middle age at the time. It was the description of the Ryans' affection for one another that made the old man's improbable confession less probable still. Nor was it without significance that the confession had been made to the police. A devout Catholic like Larry Ryan would have attached more importance to seeking the mercy of God in the Sacrament of Penance than to squaring the scales of justice. Had he confessed the murder long ago to a priest? Father Dowling hoped there was no confessor who would react to that with a simple "Go and sin no more." The scales of justice would have had to figure in any adequate penance assigned by a priest.

"That's all taken care of," Larry said, removing his hearing aid and fiddling with a dial on it.

Father Dowling discarded once and for all the possibility that the man had killed his wife. For years he had lived with the thought that she was mysteriously missing. Now when the body had been found, he insisted that he had killed her. Why? Father Dowling picked up the phone.

Basil came to the rectory in response to the call and pulled the door shut behind him when he came into the study.

"A man from the prosecutor's office told me they are seriously thinking of indicting my father."

"His confession puts them in a difficult position."

"They don't have a case."

"Maybe they would rather try and fail than suggest that it isn't a public matter when a man claims to have killed his wife."

"He didn't do it."

"He says he did."

"He's lying."

"Why?"

"To protect me."

"From what?"

"I did it, Father. I killed my mother."

From outside came the syncopated complaint of a lawn mower; the ticking of the clock became audible as Basil looked across the chasm of years of presumed guilt directly into Father Dowling's eyes.

"You killed her."

"You already guessed that, didn't you?"

"It's not the kind of thing I care to guess about. But I can't believe your father did it."

He sat up straightly. "I poisoned her."

"Are you going to tell the police this?"

"I wanted to tell you first, Father. I have not been frank with you. When I returned to Fox River I did not think that my father's absurd claim would be taken seriously or, if it were, that anything would come of it. I hid behind that possibility. It is clear now that I no longer have a shield. Yes, I want to talk to the police!"

"Your father confessed in order to protect you?"

"He knows I did it. He saw right away there was no other explanation."

"He knew your mother was dead?"

"He had to suspect it. He knew her far better than I did and would never have accepted the theory that she just wandered off. Kidnapping? Why? No ransom was ever demanded. No, he knew what had happened. If he ever thought of it he must have dreaded the discovery of the body."

"Have you ever talked about it?"

Basil looked away and his lower lip trembled. "He won't talk to me. He pretends to be addled or that he can't hear. He keeps asking me what my name is." The lip was brought under control by being drawn between Basil's teeth. He cried silently for a minute and then regained his composure.

"I am ready to talk to the police, Father."

"What kind of poison did you use?"

"It was right there in the garage. She used it for gardening. It might have been set out for me."

"Why did you kill her?"

"None of the reasons I had then make sense now. I was young . . ."

The arsenic of which Basil spoke had already been found, along with the tools used to dig the grave and to relay the bricks, but no significance had been attached to it. It was a poison once commonly used by gardeners. Father Dowling went back to the Good Shepherd Retirement Home to talk with Larry Ryan. He wheeled the old man into a room where they could have some privacy. Larry Ryan got the message the first time, although Father Dowling had spoken in an ordinary voice. "That's nonsense. Basil could never do a thing like that."

"That's what he says of you."

The old man waved this away as an irrelevance. "I did it. The police know I did it. They mustn't listen to that boy."

"All they know is that you say you did it."

"I did!"

"How?"

He seemed not to have thought of that before. Finally he had the answer. "I struck her. Hard." He winced as he said it.

The choice between father or son as the killer of Catherine Ryan would have to be made by the autopsy. Dr. Pippen, the lovely young assistant medical examiner, made her determination known in an almost formal meeting attended by the prosecutor, Phil Keegan, and Cy Horvath. Father Dowling was brought along to the meeting by Phil.

Dr. Pippen began as if her intention was to acquaint them with every aspect of her findings. Keegan stirred and the prosecutor began to hum.

Cy said, "Before you go into all that, could you tell us what the cause of death was?"

Pippen's eyes rounded with disappointment. "That's all you want to know?"

"How was she killed?" Keegan growled.

"She wasn't killed."

The prosecutor and Phil Keegan rose to their feet and said in unison, "She wasn't killed!"

"I am almost certain it was a heart attack."

"Were there any signs she had been struck?"

"No."

"Poisoned?"

"No. The poison you found would have been easy to find if that had been used. But I tested for others as well. No, she died of natural causes."

Cy Horvath asked the question. "Then who buried her in the greenhouse?"

"And why?"

"The husband did it," Marie decided. "That son couldn't hurt a fly."

"Dr. Pippen says that Catherine Ryan died of natural causes."

Marie made an impatient noise. "Isn't she the one Phil Keegan is always complaining about, because of her wild theories?"

"She doesn't have a theory this time."

"How can she tell after all these years?"

"It's rather a question of what she ruled out. Larry Ryan said he beat her to death and there is no sign of that; Basil says he poisoned her but no traces can be found."

"Maybe he did it some other way."

"He?"

"The husband!"

"It's too late to make up another story."

"Imagine, getting away with murder."

"There has to be a murder first, Marie."

The next day Basil came into the sacristy after Father Dowling had finished saying his noon Mass.

"I'm back in the parish, Father. I decided to come home."

"Where will you be living?"

"I bought our house back, the one I grew up in."

"The Bradley house?"

He thought a moment. "They bought it from us. For me, it's the Ryan house."

Outside the early afternoon air was sweet with the smell of the roses Willie the gardener had planted beside the church.

"My mother's roses were a thing to see."

They came to a bench halfway to the rectory and Father Dowling suggested they sit.

"Tell me what happened to your mother, Basil."

His chest rose and fell as he looked out over the lawn. His eyes when he turned toward the priest had a new serenity.

"I can't tell you what a relief the coroner's report was, Father."

"Learning that your mother had died of natural causes?"

"Yes."

"Now you don't have to protect your father."

"Oh, he had nothing to do with it. I found her." He continued to look out over the lawn as he described the scene he had come upon so many years ago when he had found his mother lying in the greenhouse.

"She had fallen forward off the camp stool she sat in when she was potting things. Her coffee cup was on the bench. The box of poison had tipped over and trailed over the bench and onto the floor. The coffee cup was empty." He looked at Father Dowling.

"You thought she had killed herself?"

"Yes!"

"Why?"

"She had been sick, she . . . I don't know why. The thought hit me and it was as if I had watched her do it. My next thought was what the scandal would do to my father. They were so close . . ."

Basil had gone to the house to tell his father he had been unable to find his mother. Then he returned to the greenhouse and began removing bricks, intent on saving his mother from the judgment that tortured him. She had committed the unforgivable sin. She had despaired and taken her own life. The punishment must be eternal damnation. So he had buried her and provided his father the ambiguous consolation of mysteri-

123

ous disappearance.

"That is something you could never have known, Basil. The condition of her soul."

"It was a thought I couldn't get rid of. Thank God that isn't what happened."

The interment of Catherine Ryan could have been done with quiet discretion, just Basil and his father, no need to publicize. Perhaps, unsurprisingly, Basil wanted a parish funeral. He and his father sat side by side in the front pew, and behind them were nearly a hundred parishioners, the dozen or so who never missed a wedding or funeral but also many elderly people who had known the Ryans. Sandro Manzoni was there, and the Bradleys, he informing everyone that his wife was getting in practice for you-know-who's final rites. Father Dowling said Mass, blessed the body, and reminded himself and the congregation of their common mortality, making the barest of allusions to the unusual circumstances that had led to the exhumation of the body. What he did not have to tell Basil was that it is always presumptuous to imagine the ultimate fate of this soul or that. In the end it is mercy we all require, not justice.

From her front pew on the left side Marie Murkin looked around from time to time as if to remind the others of the special role she had played in the providential discovery of the remains of Catherine Ryan. Sandro Manzoni avoided her gaze, as well he might. It is a foolhardy man who questions the intuitions of the housekeeper of St. Hilary's rectory.

BINGO NEXT TIME

1

The idea to raffle off a car to raise money for the St. Hilary parish center had come from Manfred Schell. Schell was familiar to far more people than knew him because for years he had done his own television ads for the automotive agency he operated in Fox River. "Mannie the Maniac" was the way he styled himself in these ads. He adopted the persona of a dealer who was out of control, offering prices that threatened his own financial well-being. Em, his wife, played a prominent role in these commercials, although she never appeared. Her efforts to stop Mannie the Maniac from giving away automobiles always failed, to the benefit of the customer. Em, it turned out, was a fictional character. This became clear when, having retired on the advice of his doctors, Mannie began to show up at the St. Hilary parish center, the former parish school that had been remodeled as a place for seniors to congregate.

"No offense, Father Dowling, but what you have here is a bush league operation."

"People like it."

"That's because they don't know any better."

"You seem to like it yourself."

"I think I can help."

Help took the form of a brand new automobile to be raffled off on Easter Sunday.

"Where would we get an automobile?"

"I'll get it wholesale. We'll raise enough money to cover the cost and make more beside."

"You're sure."

"Leave it to me."

Marie Murkin warned Father Dowling that Manfred might not be someone he should leave the matter to. "Make him bring his wife Em into it."

That's when they found out there was no Em. Mannie had never married. "I was too busy making money. Now I have a pile of money, a bad heart, and nothing to do."

"At your age, you should be saying your prayers," Marie said.

"When I have you praying for me? I'm in good hands."

"What makes you think I pray for you?"

"You say the Hail Mary, don't you? 'Pray for us sinners.' That includes me."

"You're not the only sinner in the world," Marie said huffily.

"You can say that again."

Mannie developed a television ad for the raffle and suddenly St. Hilary's parish was the talk of the greater Chicago area. There were two kinds of clerical callers. Those who teased Roger and those who wanted to know if they could hire Mannie next.

"He's a volunteer."

"How much do you expect to clear?"

"First we have to cover the cost of the car."

"Roger, you'll be able to buy a fleet of cars."

He didn't want a fleet of cars. What he wanted was what Edith Hospers called a Wellness Room with the latest equipment so that the seniors could keep in good shape as they whiled away the hours at the center. "How are tickets going?" he asked Edith.

"We're having more printed."

"Good Lord. How many have you sold?"

The answer was breathtaking. The cost of the car had long since been covered and the Wellness Center, too. What in the world would they do with the surplus?

When the car arrived, it caused a sensation. Mannie drove it in wearing the grin he had worn on television when he confided he was defying Em and letting the customer have a vehicle slightly above cost. The car was huge, maroon, expensive. He parked it on the lot behind the school, sideways across several places, to set it off. In the trunk were plastic pots filled with artificial flowers. Mannie crawled in and brought them out. He placed these at the four corners of the space consecrated to the automobile that would become the possession of the one who bought the lucky ticket.

"What would I do with a car like that?" Marie Murkin cried, but her voice was that of a schoolgirl.

"Sell it," Mannie said. "You know what you could get for that car?"

"I might keep it if I won it."

"And I thought you were going to ride with me." Mannie nudged her in the ribs and Marie danced away, trying unsuccessfully to look indignant. She must have been aware of the envious eyes of other ladies at the attention Mannie paid to her.

Alas, Mannie was a bumblebee so far as the flower of womanhood was concerned. He was an irrepressible flirt, a mindless flatterer, who seemed unaware of the stir his attentions caused. The women giggled and the men growled.

But the actual car gave a further spurt to sales, and this posed a moral problem.

"How many chances can you sell on a car?" Phil Keegan asked.

"We're not violating the gambling laws, are we?"

"What gambling laws? What I mean is, the odds get longer

the more you sell."

"No problem," Mannie said. "We gave a date when the car is raffled, that's all. We didn't say there would be a limited number of tickets."

"It will be as long a shot as the lottery."

"Don't you believe it, Captain. You like that car?"

"Yeah."

"You lose, I can get you a deal on a similar car."

"Get out of here."

"I'm serious," Mannie called, waving as he went out the door.

"What a guy," Phil said, shaking his head.

"Well, he's done a lot for the parish and for the center," Marie said.

"When's the wedding, Marie?"

She glared at Phil Keegan but she was so mad she didn't say anything. She just turned, tilted her nose, and sailed back into the kitchen.

Tuttle the lawyer bought a twenty-dollar book of raffle tickets and thought he had covered the odds pretty well, but then he heard how many tickets were being sold.

"I might just as well throw my money away at a casino," he groused to Peanuts Pianone, the Fox River police officer with whom he was polishing off a Chinese meal that had been delivered to Tuttle's office.

"They ought to try bingo."

"Don't say it. He might do it."

"How often can you raffle a car? Bingo you can have every week."

Bingo was a passion with Peanuts. On or off duty, he made a practice of dropping in on this parish or that on bingo night and playing two cards at a time.

"You ever win?"

"Sure. But I just like to play."

Neither of them went near the state-run casinos that had proliferated in recent years. Pianone's family considered this unfair competition, since they had controlled local gambling for years. But now it was getting out of hand.

"First the lottery," Peanuts said. He seemed to be expressing the official family line. "Then the casinos—boats, wharfs, you name it. Everybody is squeezing the working stiff, taking his money from him."

"Stick with bingo, Peanuts."

"Don't worry."

"You buy any raffle tickets?"

"A hundred."

Tuttle's heart sank. What were his ten against so many?

"Why don't you swing by St. Hilary's," he suggested when he and Peanuts were driving around in a patrol car. Tuttle considered such transportation a benefit from the taxes he would pay when his law practice got better.

"What for?"

"I want to take another look at that car."

Peanuts did not object. No one could see that car and not fall in love with it. Tuttle would never have put that much money into a car, even if he could have afforded it, but if it just fell into his lap, well, it could really impress prospective clients. They were surprised to find Mannie there, showing three women the merits of the automobile. They seemed more interested in Mannie than the car. But the dealer directed his spiel at the new arrivals with renewed enthusiasm.

"You sure you aren't taking orders, Mannie?"

"This is a giveaway."

"These ladies probably will want one whether they win or not."

"I wouldn't be surprised. This car sells itself. They wanted me to leave it in the showroom until the raffle, just so customers could drool over this model."

Peanuts asked if it was just left out all night, in the weather and all. But Mannie reassured him. At nightfall, the car was put in the large maintenance shed at the end of the parking lot.

"We don't want anything to happen to this finish."

Mannie himself took the car out of the shed each morning—weather permitting—and parked it where parishioners could indulge the fantasy that one day soon that vehicle would be theirs.

2

"It's just his manner," Edna Hospers said to Wallace Molson. "He doesn't mean a thing."

"If he talks that way to Mabel again, I'm going to give him a fat lip."

Wallace Molson had a metabolism that had kept his weight slightly over a hundred pounds, and a lifetime sitting in an office working as an accountant had not built up the muscles he did have, but there was fire in his eye when he complained about the way Mannie Schell was flirting with Mabel.

"It's not as if Mabel were your wife, Wallace."

"Well, she's not his either. Besides, for all you know, I've been thinking about it."

"For all I know? Mabel's the one you should be telling."

"Maybe I will! Right after I give Mannie Schell a knuckle sandwich."

Edna kept a straight face. The little accountant's way of speaking had little to do with what he was physically capable of. Perhaps in his imagination he had developed another persona during the years he sat at his desk, arranging numbers on a columned page. It was an oddity of the parish center that the seniors who came there—widows, widowers, lifelong maids and bachelors—developed crushes on one another so that there was forever some rivalry going on that Edna had to adjudicate. She was not surprised when Wallace asked her to speak for him to Mabel. She shook her head.

"That is something a woman wants to hear directly from a man."

"But what will she say?"

"You'll have to ask to find out."

What Wallace wanted Edna to do was to see if Mabel was really interested in him before he popped the question.

"How did you get married the first time, Wallace?"

"That was different."

There were other men who were obviously annoyed by Mannie's way with the ladies. A delegation appointed themselves and confronted Mannie in the corridor outside Edna's office, so she was a secret sharer whether she wanted to be or not.

"I'm just pushing the raffle," Mannie said, attempting to laugh off the complaints.

"I'll push your raffle if you don't cut it out." Edna recognized the voice of Wallace Molson. Why did she imagine that he was addressing Mannie over the shoulders of intervening complainers?

"Cut what out?"

"You know what!"

"No, I don't. Help me."

It was obviously a difficult charge to articulate, and Mannie's taunting tone did not help. There was a menacing murmur and then Wallace piped up.

"Take this as a warning, Schell."

Mannie's laughter followed the delegation down the hall and a moment later he looked in at Edna. He came to a stop in the doorway and lifted his hands, forming a frame in which to picture her.

"I should have made movies, Edna. What a picture."

"What was the argument about?"

"You overheard that? You tell me."

"I think Wallace Molson is seriously interested in Mabel."

"Mabel?"

"The redhead." Edna said it with a straight face. God had given Mabel red hair but in recent decades art had come to the aid of nature, perhaps too much so. It was difficult to believe that Mabel's hair had ever looked so carroty before she took to dying it.

"Ah yes," Mannie said. "I don't blame him."

Edna regretted passing the information onto Mannie. The little car dealer immediately began an intense campaign with Mabel. Whenever Edna looked into the old gym, the two of them seemed to be together. Mannie would be helping Mabel master the intricacies of shuffleboard, his arm about her waist; he would be hovering over her chair as she fanned her cards, eager to tell her what to bid. And in the background, glowering, would be Wallace Molson. Edna would have been amused by these romantic antics among the elderly, but the expression on Wallace's face made it clear it was no laughing matter. Mabel was laughing, of course, in the giddy manner of a woman getting the attention she knows she deserves. But what game was Mannie Schell playing?

Marie Murkin answered the phone the following morning when the security guard at Mannie Schell's condo called to ask about the retired auto dealer's whereabouts. Marie hadn't seen him that morning but transferred the call to Edna. Father Dowling's eyebrows lifted in inquiry when she looked into his study.

"Someone looking for Mannie."

"I see the car isn't parked in its usual place."

Marie went to the window to verify the absence from the

parking lot of the car on which hundreds of raffle tickets had been sold. It had become a morning ritual, Mannie opening the maintenance shed and driving the car onto the parking lot. Usually he made several wide circuits before pulling into the usual spaces and placing the plastic plants precisely at the corners of the imagined square containing the car.

Marie went off to her kitchen and Father Dowling returned to his book. Half an hour later, Edna called. Marie took it in the kitchen and then came down the hall to the study.

"Edna wants to talk with you."

"Father Dowling? The guard from Mannie's condo called. Apparently he wasn't home all night."

"Well, he's too old for the curfew."

"It's silly to worry, I suppose."

"Was the guard worried?"

"I am."

Edna had not seen Mannie leave the night before. "But he put the car away in the maintenance shed, and that's always the last thing he does before leaving."

"Maybe he's romantically involved."

"Then you've heard?"

"Heard what?" Father Dowling backed away from the phone. His had been an idle, facetious remark.

"He is quite a ladies' man."

Father Dowling remembered the way Mannie had of reducing Marie Murkin to the status of a giggling school girl. On the other hand, Mannie must be seventy years old, not the golden age of a Lothario. Edna had told him in the past of the alliances formed and dissolved among the seniors who spent the day at the parish center. Sometimes it had been a genuine case of a serious interest. There had even been a wedding or two as a result. But by and large, the interactions among the elderly men and women were prelapsarian in their innocence, reminiscent of the time before puberty more than anything else.

"In the plural?"

"Until recently, yes. He has flirted indiscriminately with us all. I'm afraid I'm responsible for his concentrating on Mabel."

Father Dowling listened to what Edna had to say. It was difficult to know how to react.

"Do you have the keys to the raffle car, Edna?"

"I have a set. Mannie left them with me."

"Why don't we meet at the shed? I'd like to put car on display."

Where do ideas come from? Father Dowling probably felt that once the car was parked where Mannie usually parked it, the mystery of his whereabouts would be solved. Not that he thought there was much of a mystery. The guard at Mannie's condo, when Father Dowling called, seemed eager to downplay the importance of his inquiry.

"For all I know he's asleep in bed."

"Did you call him?"

"Sure. No answer. They're all deaf as posts, though, so what does it prove?"

Edna was waiting for him when he arrived at the maintenance shed. Her hands were plunged into pockets of her coat and her breath was visible in frosty air. She handed Father Dowling the keys.

Having raised the door of the maintenance shed, Father Dowling went into the musty interior with odors of oil and exhausted fumes. The car gleamed in the dim light and not for the first time Father Dowling felt grateful to Mannie for coming up with the idea of the raffle. The motor purred into life at the turn of key and Father Dowling eased the car out of the shed. Edna stood aside as if to direct him to the appointed spot where Mannie always parked the car. Before getting out, Father Dowling popped the trunk, wanting to set out the plastic pots with which Mannie always marked off the space for the car, and which were kept in the trunk. Edna nodded, as if she understood why the trunk lid was lifting. Father Dowling had stepped out of the car when Edna screamed.

She was backing away from the trunk, her hand lifted protectively, a horrified expression on her face. No wonder. When Father Dowling hurried back and looked into the trunk, his eyes met the sightless gaze of Mannie Schell. The little fellow was on his hands and knees and his head was tipped at an angle. He was stiff as a board.

"Is he . . . ?" Edna said, getting as close as she dared.

"Call nine-one-one, Edna."

Tuttle and Peanuts were driving off a huge breakfast—a four-by-four, with waffles and hash browns on the side—when the news of the death of Mannie Schell came over the police radio.

"St. Hilary's," Tuttle said.

"A dead guy in the trunk of a car?"

"Mannie the Maniac."

Peanuts just looked at Tuttle. It was like hearing that the weatherman was dead. Everyone in Fox River had grown up listening to Mannie yap like an idiot on television, trying to get you to buy one of his cars.

"Let's go."

But Peanuts had already made up his mind. He made a great U-turn, causing a general squealing of tires and honking of horns, but then he turned on the siren of the patrol car and clamped down on the gas, silencing his critics. But even reacting as quickly as that, they were not the first ones at the scene.

The flashing lights of the 911 ambulance sent pulses of color into the misty morning air. Peanuts pushed the nose of the patrol car gently through the crowd of old people who had gathered on the parking lot behind what had once been St. Hilary's school but now functioned as a center for seniors to pass the day playing cards and shuffleboard and whatever else. Tuttle had checked the center out more than once, thinking how much his paternal parent would have enjoyed going there. Tuttle's father was commemorated in the name of Tuttle's law firm, Tuttle & Tuttle, because he had backed his son through thick and thin, the years and years it had taken him to get through law school, taking every course as often as he had to in order to pass it. Just remembering the pride in his father's face the day he got that diploma never failed to bring a tear to Tuttle's eye. Passing the bar exams had been another long-distance trek and by the time Tuttle succeeded his father was dead. But his father was his partner, no doubt about that, and Tuttle took the death of Manfred Schell on the grounds of St. Hilary's as almost a personal affront.

The initial on-site judgment of the cause of death was asphyxiation. Tuttle just looked at Dr. Pippen. It was like being told that a drowned man had died of water in his lungs when the point was, who had held him under?

"Any sign of a blow?"

"Nothing obvious."

"He didn't just crawl in there and shut the door on himself, did he?" Tuttle looked around at the others crowding about the assistant coroner and his eyes met Father Dowling's. Tuttle snatched off his tweed hat as a sign of respect and got pushed out of place for his pains. He ended up shoulder to shoulder with the priest.

"A terrible thing, Father."

The priest nodded. Of course this sort of thing was his line of work, but when Tuttle learned that Father Dowling had found the body, he urged him away from the nosy reporters.

"Actually Edna Hospers was the first to see him."

Tuttle had built his career around the ability to recognize the significance of such apparently throwaway remarks. Five minutes later he was going down the corridor in the school toward the old principal's office from which Edna Hospers directed the center. Tuttle walked right in and sailed a card onto her desk, then took a chair.

"Have you been questioned by the police yet?"

"Questioned by the police! No."

"Good. I will be at your side when you are. You have a right to legal representation."

"But they're not going to question me. Father Dowling knows as much as I do."

Tuttle took off his hat and put it on the knee of his crossed leg. "I just came from him."

Tuttle had no wish to alarm Edna. On the other hand, what he was telling her about her right to representation was true. It was also true that he could use a client. Not that Edna could afford him. But just being in the eye of the storm, moving in and out of the courthouse when something big was afoot, was better than a month's worth of ads on television.

"Of course I will represent you pro bono."

"What does that mean?"

"No charge."

She laughed unhappily. "Well, you wouldn't make much money from me."

Tuttle uncrossed his legs and sat forward. "Now tell me everything. From the beginning."

Who is able to resist a chance to talk about himself? Nobody, in Tuttle's experience. But when Edna got to the part about Mabel and Mannie and Wallace Molson, Tuttle felt that he was really on to something now. Offering to represent Edna pro bono left him free to see what sort of legal representation Wallace Molson could pay for.

★ ★ ★ ★ ★

"No one is going to want that car now," Marie Murkin said. "Not after a dead body was found in its trunk."

There was that in Marie's voice that suggested she was miffed that it had been Edna and not Marie Murkin who had been the first to look into the trunk of the car and see Manfred Schell.

"We'll see what you do when your number is drawn."

Marie had an impatient sound. "I have never won anything in my life and I don't plan to start now."

Nonetheless she had invested twenty dollars in raffle tickets. She had just brought in the paper and was standing in the doorway of the study, slapping the rolled-up *Tribune* against her leg. Now she opened it and let out a gasp.

"Murder! Honest to Pete, look at that."

The paper she laid upon the pastor's desk had a teaser on the front page, advertising a murder at St. Hilary's parish, with the story to be found within. The pastor did not bite.

"You have to stop them, Father. They have no right printing sensational nonsense like that. A murder at St. Hilary's! What will people think?"

"Oh, I suppose the damage is already done, Marie."

"Are you going to let them get away with that?"

The truth was that Dr. Pippen no longer classified the death as anything other than by violence. A contusion had been found on the back of the head, suggesting that Mannie had been struck from behind and put into the trunk of the car. Dr. Pippen had gone on with somewhat ghoulish relish to speculate that Mannie had regained consciousness in the trunk and had spent his last hours fighting for air. It was a death that reminded Father Dowling of the most lurid rotogravure sections of his youth. Man buried alive. What had happened to Mannie Schell was worthy of Edgar Allan Poe. "The Cask of Amontillado," wasn't it? He decided not to ask Marie if she remembered.

Later Cy Horvath, Phil Keegan's right-hand man, stopped by. He had spent several hours questioning senior citizens in the parish center.

"The women all loved him," Cy said, and Marie made a little noise.

"And the men?"

"What do you know of Wallace Molson?"

"Wallace Molson!" It was Marie who reacted, and her expression was an odd mixture of disdain and tenderness.

"Wasn't he sweet on you, Marie?" Father Dowling asked.

"That is not for me to say."

"He sent Marie a ten-pound box of chocolates last Valentine's Day."

"Ten pounds!" But Marie clearly liked the hyperbole. "Anyway that was last Valentine's Day."

Cy said, "Edna said he was in pursuit of Mabel Hoyle."

"Mabel Hoyle," Marie repeated, her smile condescending.

"And Mannie was trying to steal her away."

"I hope you don't think Wallace Molson capable of harming a fly, let alone Mannie Schell?"

"He's as good as confessed, Marie."

Marie just stared at the detective lieutenant. If she were assigning marks for intelligence, Cy would have been in trouble.

Father Dowling went back to the center with Cy. Wallace Molson was in Edna's office and when Father Dowling was about to enter, a hand closed on his arm.

He looked down into the flaming red hair of Mabel Hoyle. Her eyes were red, too.

"It's all my fault, Father. I wanted to tease him."

He nodded, aware that the mysterious relations between man and woman were being alluded to. It had been Cy's suggestion that a romantic triangle lay behind the tragic death of Mannie Schell.

Wallace looked up when the priest came in, and there was an odd expression on his face, as if he had succeeded in surprising himself.

"I did it, Father."

"Did what, Wallace?"

"I killed Mannie Schell. And I'd do it again. I did it for Mabel."

"For Mabel."

"He had turned her head. She had no experience with such a man. She was helpless."

"So you killed him."

Phil Keegan was sitting at Edna's desk, his face propped up with both hands. His eyes went back and forth from Wallace to Father Dowling.

"I killed him."

"How?"

Wallace turned toward Phil, startled by the tone of the captain of detectives' voice. Did he expect to be congratulated for killing another human being?

"You know how."

"Tell me."

But Wallace turned back to Father Dowling. "I mean I am responsible for his death."

"Tell me how it happened."

"I should be making this a confession, Father."

"After you tell Captain Keegan what happened."

A conscience trained at a later time might have let Wallace off the hook entirely. His story of what had happened the previous night was complicated. His rage with Mannie had reached fever pitch, he said, his tone somewhat rehearsed. He had held back when the others left, knowing that Mannie put the raffle car away as the last thing before leaving.

"I saw him go out to the car, I watched him circle around the playground a couple of times as if millions were watching, and then he backed it into the shed. I went out there."

Wallace closed his eyes as if to evoke the scene more vividly. Phil was growing impatient.

"When I went into the shed, he wasn't there. The car was there and the door was still open, I hadn't seen him come out, but he wasn't there. I looked around. I thought he had seen me approach and had taken the coward's way out. I closed the door and went to report to Mabel."

Phil made an angry noise. "I thought you said you killed him."

"I did. This morning, when I heard what had happened, it all became clear to me. When I called out for him in the shed, I heard something, I'm not sure what. Now I know."

It was Wallace's story that he was responsible for not hearing Mannie cry out from the trunk of the car. His anger blinded him and made him deafer than he already was.

"I could have saved his life, and I didn't. I knifed him, Father."

"There's only one difficulty," Phil said.

"What's that?"

"We have to find the one who dumped him into the trunk."

That remained the question in the following days. Mannie was waked and buried in style. A suggestion that he be buried in the car in which he had been found dead was vetoed by Father Dowling, who threatened to withdraw if any such thing was contemplated. Short of that, the funeral left little to be desired and it was lovingly covered by most of the newspapers in the region, but by none so thoroughly as the *Fox River Tribune*. When it was over and Mannie appropriately buried, the question of who had stuffed him into the trunk of the raffle car was once more on the table.

Tuttle seemed to think some sort of charge should be brought against his client. "Wallace admits negligence," he insisted.

"Tuttle, with his hearing, he wouldn't have heard a brass band in that shed."

The contusion Dr. Pippen had found on the back of Mannie's head made it impossible to rule out foul play. Had one of the other old men at the center bopped Mannie on the head and dumped him into the trunk? If so, the miscreant was not as eager as Wallace Molson to thrust himself into a starring role.

"How heavy a blow was it?" Father Dowling asked Dr. Pippen.

"It broke the skin; the hair had dried blood in it."

"A knock-out blow?"

"Apparently."

This made for an uneasy atmosphere at St. Hilary's. Marie wondered aloud if there was a homicidal maniac loose among the elders in the center. Father Dowling, seated in his study, looked out toward the center and the parking lot and the maintenance shed and pondered what had happened.

In his mind's eye he could see Mannie scampering around the car after he had parked it. Up went the trunk and out came the potted plants, to be placed precisely at the corners . . . He stopped the train of thought, and backed up, recalling how Mannie's feet had left the ground as he reached in for the pots. Once, he had actually crawled in . . .

Father Dowling's hand went to his telephone. A minute later, he dialed. There were several rings before Dr. Pippen answered.

"Doctor, do me a favor. Would you see if there is any blood from Mannie's head wound up on the trunk door."

"There is. I noticed it before."

"How do you suppose it got there?"

"I don't know. There are many ways, I suppose. You realize

that he regained consciousness and spent a dreadful time in the trunk before he ran out of air."

"And you think blood might have rubbed off his head on to the trunk door?"

There was a long silence and then she said, "Let me call you back."

He hung up and waited. What exactly should he be praying for? The main thing was to be relieved of the suspicion that there was someone about the place who had struck Mannie on the head and dumped him into the trunk of that car and left him there to die. It was twenty minutes later when Dr. Pippen called back.

"Father, I think he hit his head on the trunk door. That's how he was wounded."

"And I think I know what happened."

He had to give the explanation several times over the next few hours and even days. He described the way Mannie had sometimes climbed into the trunk to retrieve the plastic potted plants with artificial flowers that he had used to demarcate the parking spot of the raffle car. He must have climbed into the trunk that fatal night, to put the pots in it, and the trunk door fell on him, trapping him. Dr. Pippen compared the sharp metal corner inside the trunk door and the photograph of Mannie's head wound. A perfect match. The blood on the door had not simply rubbed off an already-existent head wound.

"So it was an accident," Edna cried with relief.

"What a dreadful way to go," Marie said.

But both were relieved to learn that there was no murderer among them. Wallace Molson showed the smallest trace of disappointment, but that soon evaporated. He and Mabel came to the rectory and announced that they intended to marry. Nor was this the full extent of Wallace's good luck. When the raffle was held, he held the winning ticket. He had won the car.

"I'll sell it," he said.

"I'll buy it," Tuttle cried.

But Peanuts Pianone only looked glum. "With bingo I have a chance. I don't like raffles."

"Our next fund raiser will be bingo," Father Dowling assured him. But he assured himself that in fact there would be no more fund raisers at St. Hilary's parish.

THE DUTIFUL SON

1

When Roger Dowling came out of the church after saying the noon Mass, he stopped to inhale the odor of lilacs that filled the air. The sun on his face, that wonderful smell, and the prospect of the lunch Mrs. Murkin would have ready for him added an animal contentedness to his spiritual peace.

"Father Dowling?"

He opened his eyes and, in the sunlight, had only the impression of a person, a silhouette. He stepped back, out of the sun.

"I didn't mean to startle you, Father. Could I talk with you?"

It was tempting to tell the man to come back in an hour. He did not like the prospect of being cheated out of a peaceful lunch. But that was temptation.

"Have you eaten lunch?"

"I attended your Mass."

"Come along. We can talk while we eat."

His name was Francis Stendall; he had come from Oakland, California, specifically to talk with Father Dowling about a most important matter. A matter, as it turned out, not wholly apt as a luncheon topic.

"I had no idea I was known in Oakland."

Stendall did not smile. Perhaps he thought Roger Dowling was serious. It seemed best not to assume a sense of humor in this short, stocky, bald-headed man.

"I came to see whoever was the pastor of St. Hilary's."

145

Marie Murkin, reconciled to this stranger consuming half the lunch she had prepared for the pastor, began to apportion it between them.

"My parents lived in this parish many years ago."

"Stendall?" Marie said, giving it some thought. The guest looked surprised that the housekeeper should enter into the conversation.

"How long ago was that?" Roger Dowling asked.

"It was during the Depression. Nineteen thirty-one, perhaps thirty-two."

"That was before your time, wasn't it, Marie?"

She glared at him and huffed off to the kitchen with a serving bowl.

"I have the address. Before coming to you, I found the house."

"I see."

"I want an exhumation."

"An exhumation?" This seemed an abrupt change of subject. Father Dowling had thought they were talking of the house in which Stendall's parents had lived.

It emerged that the two topics were one. Francis had the story from his mother, who told it to him in great detail during her final days. "She died of cancer two months ago. She exacted a promise from me, and I am here to keep it." Francis Stendall had the look of a man who did not make promises easily and kept the ones he made.

Roger Dowling was forming the somewhat grotesque idea that Stendall's mother had made her son promise to exhume her body, ship it from California, and bury it in the yard of the house in which they had lived all those years ago. Not wholly off the mark, as it turned out.

"My mother gave birth to a baby while they lived in that house. The baby died almost immediately. The doctor, who was a Catholic, baptized the baby and helped my father bury the

146

body in the backyard." He waited for a shocked reaction from Roger Dowling, and when he did not get one, went on.

"I, of course, was shocked by this. My first thought was that it was illegal. But that was the least of my mother's concerns. Everyone was poor then, as she told it, and burial expenses for a dead infant would have been a luxury. They buried the baby in the yard to save money."

"Is that what bothered your mother?"

"Oh no. Not at all. It was the thought of her child lying in unconsecrated ground, perhaps liable to be dug up accidentally. It always weighed on her mind that new construction might take place, that perhaps a high-rise building might be put up over that grave site. What then would happen to the remains? She could not be at peace until she knew her child would be exhumed and reburied in consecrated ground. I assured her it would be done."

"Well."

"I have come to you for two reasons. I would like you to be there when the digging is done. And you will know how to go about doing this."

"Well, I know whom to call anyway."

He called Phil Keegan, captain of detectives on the Fox River police force, an old friend, and after a number of other calls suggested by Phil, got in touch with McDivitt, the undertaker, as well. All problems but one were swiftly solved.

"Have you talked with the present owner?" Father Dowling asked.

"My hope is that it will be a parishioner of yours."

Roger Dowling had the feeling that he was the one keeping Stendall's promise to his mother. Well, why not?

"What is the address?"

"It's a house on Macon. Thirty-three oh six."

While Roger Dowling tried to visualize the neighborhood, a

Ralph McInerny

voice was heard from the kitchen.

"Whelans," Mrs. Murkin called. "The Whelans live there.
Have for years. I don't envy you asking Jennings Whelan if you
can drop by and dig a hole in his yard."

Francis Stendall cocked an ear as Marie spoke, then said to
Roger Dowling, "I'm sorry. I didn't hear all that. My hearing is
going, just as my mother's did."

"Mrs. Murkin thinks I had better contact the present owner
right away."

"Is it a parishioner?"

Fortunately Stendall did not hear the laugh from the kitchen.

Jennings Whelan had been on the books of the parish for
years, but two years ago he informed Roger Dowling that he no
longer recognized in the Catholic Church the faith of his fathers.

"Mr. Whelan, I assure you that nothing that takes place at St.
Hilary's—"

"St. Hilary's has nothing to do with it. It's been my parish,
yes. But as part of a diocese, part of a global Church. I used to
know where the Church stands. Now every paper I read seems
to have some crazy nun or priest denying the Creed. I give up."

It had been the start of a long and eventually unsuccessful
argument. Roger Dowling had been unable to convince Whelan
that, whatever he might hear on the news, there was more clar-
ity about Catholic teaching now than there had ever been. But
every time he had made headway, some other outrage would
make Whelan's anger return, more virulent each time.

"This isn't personal, Father Dowling. I have nothing against
you."

"Come to Mass, Jennings. Say your prayers. Don't let things
upset you so."

"I'll say my prayers. Don't worry about that. But I'll support
the Church again when it gets its act together."

What would Jennings Whelan make of the request Father

Dowling must convey to him on Stendall's behalf?

"I'll come with you," Stendall said.

"I think I'd better go alone."

"Whatever you say." He seemed relieved. "I am staying at the Holiday Inn just outside Elgin. I'll call you tonight."

He had rented a car and now drove away in it. Marie Murkin cleaned up with a little smile on her face.

"You should have taken him with you," Mrs. Murkin said.

Father Dowling decided not to give her a chance to repeat her condemnation of Jennings Whelan. The man's decision to stop coming to Mass had prompted good old-fashioned anathemas from the housekeeper.

"What if everyone did that?" she wanted to know.

"I couldn't afford to keep you on."

"Hmph. No Jennings Whelan is driving me out of here."

Now he said how admirable it was of Francis Stendall to fulfill his mother's dying wish.

"I don't wonder it bothered her. Burying a baby in the backyard. What did Captain Keegan think of that?"

"You mean rather than the front yard?"

"You know what I mean."

"They won't prosecute."

Suddenly there was a glint in her eye. "Maybe they can prosecute Jennings Whelan."

Marie didn't care what the charge or pretext; she wanted Whelan punished for failing to come to Mass.

2

Roger Dowling decided to stop by Whelan's without telephoning first. This no longer seemed like quite such a good idea as he stood at the Whelan door, pressing the doorbell for the fourth time.

Still no answer. Roger Dowling walked around the house,

and there was Whelan in a lawn chair. He wore swimming trunks and a sun hat, but his large body, white as the belly of a beached fish, was exposed to the sun.

"Mr. Whelan?"

He came sputtering awake, looked up, and tried to get to his feet. He lost his balance and began to trip across the lawn until Roger Dowling caught his arm and steadied him. His hat askew on his head, Whelan regarded the priest.

"You have me at a disadvantage, Father Dowling."

"I am truly sorry. I rang the bell several times and then took the chance of coming round to the backyard."

"I was catching some of this sun."

Roger Dowling looked out over the quarter acre that made up a yard surrounded by a high hedge, which provided Whelan with privacy for his sunbathing. The edges of the lawn were lined with flower beds, and there was another bed halfway to the back, a circular plot alive with spring blossoms.

"I see you are quite a gardener."

"I am not. That is Imelda."

Mrs. Whelan. "She does a splendid job." Imelda Whelan slipped away to Mass without her husband knowing it.

"She wouldn't have heard the bell," Whelan explained. "She is taking a nap. As I was."

"You must forgive me."

"I hope you don't think you can change my mind about you know what."

"I never lose that hope. But that is not why I'm here."

"I watched a talk show last night, local. Some woman on it claimed she was a nun. She looked like a weight lifter. All about how terrible her life was, everyone telling her what to do just because she took a vow of obedience."

"A man whose parents once lived in this house came to see me today."

Whelan looked confused.

"His parents lived here in the early thirties."

"I bought it in forty-two," Whelan said.

"He has a most unusual request to make."

Whelan smiled indulgently. "Not unusual at all, I know just how he feels. Drove into South Chicago a few years ago and stopped at the house where I grew up. Asked if I could take a look at the inside again. Nostalgia. They let me. A colored family."

"This is more than nostalgia. In fact it isn't nostalgia at all. I don't think this man ever lived here."

"Stendall?"

"He lives in California. His mother died recently and he promised her to exhume the body of an infant and have it reburied in consecrated ground."

Whelan looked at Father Dowling as he must look at talk shows. "I don't follow you."

"His mother had the baby in this house. It died almost immediately."

"Yes."

"They buried the baby in the yard."

"In the yard? Good God!"

"The idea is to rebury the child."

"You want to dig up the yard?"

"I'm afraid that's the idea."

"You say they buried a baby here." Whelan looked out over the carefully kept lawn, at the flower beds that ringed it. He had the air of a man whose home has just become an unfamiliar place.

"You'll have to talk to Imelda about that, Father."

Imelda had even more difficulty grasping the nature of the request than her husband. Jennings had put on clothes now and sat listening to Father Dowling explain it to Imelda. This might have been one more proof that the world was coming unglued.

"Dig up the yard? But where will they dig?"

"His mother gave him very explicit instructions which he will pass on to McDivitt."

"McDivitt?"

"The undertaker."

He kept at it, not losing his patience. After all, this was not an ordinary request. Imelda Whelan did not like the thought of her yard being dug up, but that was not the worst of it.

"You mean all these years there has been a body buried out there?"

"We've been living in a cemetery," Jennings said with mordant satisfaction. He was not a lot of help.

Eventually Imelda and then Jennings Whelan gave their permission. He had assured them that the legal aspects had been looked into and that McDivitt knew his business. Neither Whelan looked happy to be reminded of McDivitt's trade; they were all too likely to provide business for him in the near future. But perhaps what swung it was that they wanted any corpse in the backyard removed. Jennings said he didn't think he could sunbathe out there until the matter had been taken care of.

It was a somewhat weary but satisfied Roger Dowling who returned to his rectory. He said his office and then read a few cantos of the *Purgatorio*—Dante was one of his two favorite authors, St. Thomas Aquinas being the other—smoked a pipe, drank coffee, and was well disposed when Phil Keegan called to suggest they watch the Cubs tonight. He meant at the rectory, of course, and he was inviting himself for dinner as well. There was never an objection from Marie when Phil Keegan joined Father Dowling at table.

"Good," Marie said. "I want to ask him about this business of burying people in your backyard."

"I wouldn't advise it, Marie. This was during the Depression, and unusual things were permitted then."

"You mean they asked permission?"

"Oh, I doubt that."

It must have been a sad scene, a man whose infant had not survived, out in his backyard with the doctor consigning it to the ground. How that must have haunted the parents over the years.

Francis Stendall called while Phil was there, and Roger Dowling told him that everything was set for the following day.

"So soon?"

"There's no point in delay."

"I hadn't expected it would be tomorrow, Father. I'm not sure I can be there."

"Well, that isn't necessary, of course. The reburial won't be tomorrow in any case. There are legal delays."

"Could I call you at this time tomorrow?"

"Of course."

He and Phil talked a bit about the strange case, but the conversation wandered, both because the Cubs made an unexpected rally in the late innings and because Phil was inclined to want to pursue Jennings Whelan's grievances.

"He's right, Roger. Look at the Church now and from when we were kids."

"Look at us."

"The Church is supposed to stay the same."

"It is supposed to last until the end of time. That's not the same as not changing."

He was glad to get off the subject when the fortunes of the game changed, and the Cubs snatched defeat from the jaws of victory.

After Phil had gone, Roger Dowling sat up in the study, having a final pipeful, thinking again of that long-ago scene: a father and the doctor digging a grave in the backyard of a home in

Fox River to bury a newborn infant who had not survived. Despite the mother's fear, the infant had lain undiscovered all these years. Maybe it would have been best to let well enough alone.

3

McDivitt, with the instructions he had been given by Stendall, made short work of it. Unfortunately, the digging had to be done where it disturbed a round flower bed in the middle of the lawn, and Imelda had to be persuaded again.

"Thank God you're here, Father," McDivitt whispered. Pink complexion, hair like cotton, McDivitt did not look like a man who made a living burying the dead.

The body was found ten minutes later. But it was the body of an adult, not of a child. Also found was a valise containing stocks and bonds. McDivitt stopped the operation at once.

"The police must be called," he announced. He obviously thought he had been deceived, and he did not like it. But his surprise was as nothing compared with Father Dowling's.

"I'll call them," he said.

The Whelans were in the house, preferring not to witness what was happening in the backyard.

"Are they done?"

"The police are going to have to be called."

"Doesn't McDivitt have a license?"

"The body that has been found is that of an adult, not a child."

Imelda Whelan had not understood, and her husband repeated it to her. Her mouth fell open as if she were going to cry out, but no sound came. Perhaps the old do not need to make noise.

"Some money has been found, too," Roger Dowling said, as he dialed Phil Keegan's number.

"I'd better go out there," Jennings Whelan said.

Phil arrived, and he had brought Cy Horvath and another officer, Agnes Lamb, with him, as well as a mobile lab unit. The Whelans looked more and more like guests in their own home.

"Get a hold of this guy Stendall," Phil told Cy Horvath.

"He's staying at the Holiday Inn in Elgin," Roger Dowling said. "I'll call him."

"Wait," Phil said, "I want to think a minute." But in less than a minute, he said, "Call him but don't tell him what happened."

"Are they going to keep digging until they find the baby?" Jennings Whelan wanted to know.

"If there is a baby," Keegan growled.

There was no Francis Stendall registered at the Holiday Inn in Elgin. Nor had there been in recent days. It was a confused Roger Dowling who put down the phone and thought about his conversations with Stendall.

"I checked the plat book," Whelan said. "If they lived here, they were renters. No Stengels ever owned this house."

"Stendalls."

"No one with a name anything like that."

Roger Dowling went out into the backyard, where the mobile lab unit had put the body on a large rubbery sheet and was peeling back the burlap in which it was rolled. It was like seeing a mummy unwrapped.

The crew, after some preliminary examination, put the corpse in a body bag and sent it downtown. The valise went into another car. Two experts remained to examine the burial site.

"I feel like a fool," Roger Dowling said to Phil Keegan.

"He must have made up the story just to get that body dug up."

"And the stocks?"

"I'll bet he didn't know about that."

"Whoever he is."

"Don't worry, Roger. We'll find him."

Roger Dowling walked back to the rectory, wishing he could share Phil's confidence.

From half a block away he saw the car parked in front of the house. His step quickened. He was certain that was the car Francis Stendall had been driving the day before.

Caution overcame him as he neared the house, and he cut through the playground of the school in order to approach the rectory from the church. This brought him to the kitchen door.

He went up the three steps to the back porch, then stopped, frozen in place. Voices. From the kitchen. Marie Murkin's and Francis Stendall's!

The voices went back and forth, antiphon and response, seemingly just an ordinary conversation, a passing back and forth of words to make the time go. After what had happened in the Whelans' backyard, Father Dowling felt no compunction at all about eavesdropping. Marie seemed to be reassuring the man.

"It's perfectly understandable," she said.

"No, it is cowardly. It's not as if it were a brother I had known."

"Were you born in Fox River?"

"No. My parents moved west before I was born."

Roger Dowling tried to detect duplicity in the man's voice but could not. What a consummate actor he was. The priest backed silently off the porch, to make another audible approach to the door, and nearly bumped into an old man. Erickson. If Erickson had not put out a hand to stop him, Roger Dowling would have toppled the ancient parishioner.

"Mr. Erickson, I'm sorry."

The old man looked warily at the pastor. Erickson had reached an age where everyone treated him like a child, an idiot child. Confused by the way Roger Dowling had come off the porch, he seemed on the verge of thinking that his mind really had gone.

"Oh, it's you," Marie said from the doorway. She meant Roger Dowling.

"Hello, Mr. Erickson." Her voice changed as she addressed the old man.

"Thanks," Roger Dowling said to Erickson, in a normal voice. "I might have fallen."

"When I was a kid we used to do that, walk backward." Erickson's face, though lined, had a peaches-and-cream look about it; little wisps of white hair stood up on his head. He looked newborn.

"How did everything go?" Stendall said, coming out on the porch.

He seemed the same as he had the day before. There was no apprehension in his voice or manner; no indication that he knew what had been dug up in that yard.

"Not quite as expected."

"How do you mean?"

"Let's go inside." He turned. "Good-bye, Mr. Erickson. Thanks again. Are you going back to the school?"

A little delay and then Erickson nodded. Roger Dowling waited until he started back to the school, which had been turned into a center for senior parishioners.

"How about lemon meringue pie?" Marie said brightly. There were two plates on the kitchen table. When in Doubt, Serve Food was Marie's motto.

"We better talk in the study," Roger Dowling said to Stendall, avoiding Marie's look of disappointment. Clearly she wanted all the gory details.

Roger Dowling shut the door of the study after Stendall was seated and then went around the desk and got settled.

"I tried to call you from the Whelans' house."

"I was probably already here."

"The Holiday Inn in Elgin said you weren't staying there."

"Did I say Holiday Inn? I'm at the Howard Johnson."

Roger Dowling opened the telephone directory to the yellow pages, found the number, and dialed it. Stendall looked puzzled. A voice said, "Howard Johnson."

"Mr. Stendall's room, please."

"One moment."

Roger Dowling listened to the phone ring, looking across his desk at Francis Stendall.

"Why are you doing that?" Stendall said, genuinely puzzled. Roger Dowling put down the phone.

"It was not an infant who was buried in that yard. It was an adult."

Francis Stendall watched him as if waiting for a clue that the priest did not mean what he was saying. "An adult?"

"The body was wrapped in burlap sacks. A man apparently. The remains were taken away."

"My God." Francis Stendall sat back in his chair as if he had been pushed.

"Is there anything you want to change in what you have told me thus far, Mr. Stendall?"

But Stendall was staring at a bookshelf, not seeing it.

"Did your parents own that house?"

He looked at Roger Dowling, there and not there. "No. No, they rented it. They were poor."

"Do you have any idea who that man is?"

"No. Of course not."

"Your mother gave you instructions on where to dig."

"Yes, yes."

"Then she must have known what was buried there."

"She told me it was a child, her child." He looked at Roger Dowling. "Was she lying?"

That was not a question on which Roger Dowling could be of any help to the man. He lit his pipe while his visitor was clearly reviewing those moving scenes he had described the day before, his mother's deathbed, the anguished tale of the stillborn infant, extracting the promise that he would have her child exhumed and buried in consecrated ground.

"Was your mother prepared to die?"

"She knew for months it was inevitable. I used to think that would be an advantage. Now I don't know."

"In what way an advantage?"

He looked at the priest as if he should not have to explain. "You could prepare."

"Did your mother see a priest?"

He nodded slowly, as if not quite trusting his memory.

"Before or after she told you this story?"

"Both. She saw the priest frequently. Father, I still can't believe that she lied."

"What we know is that where she told you an infant was buried the body of an adult was found." He still did not want to mention the valise.

"I wonder whose body it is," Francis Stendall said.

"I should tell you that when the body was found, the police asked me to contact you. I called the Holiday Inn and you were not there. They—I—assumed your story about the infant was merely a device to have the adult body found."

"But I didn't know!"

Roger Dowling believed him now. "They will want to talk with you, I'm afraid."

"Of course." He rubbed his forehead as if it ached.

"There's something else."

"What?" He seemed ready for a further blow.

"A valise was found with the body. It contained stocks and bonds."

He actually sighed. "My parents were poor."

He almost cheered up. Whatever dark speculation had been going through his mind was eradicated by the news of the stock certificates. He pushed back his chair. "I'll go see the police now."

"Why don't we have them come here? Captain Keegan often comes to my Mass at noon. We can all have lunch together."

"I'll go to Mass too."

4

The body was that of a male adult of perhaps thirty years of age. It had been lying in the yard for nearly half a century. It was going to be very difficult to make an identification.

"It's more a research problem than anything," Phil said, laying into Marie's lasagna. "Checking old newspapers."

"How did the man die?" Francis Stendall asked.

"Oh, there's no difficulty there. He was shot." Phil wiped his mouth with his napkin and called to the kitchen, "Marie, this is marvelous!"

"Would you like more?"

"As long as you're up."

Francis Stendall had reached a numbed point where further information simply registered without reaction on his part.

"What about the money?"

"That should be easier."

"How much is there?" Roger Dowling asked.

"It's difficult to say. Some of the companies may be extinct, or they may have been absorbed by others. But it will amount to a large sum."

"Who does it belong to?"

Keegan shrugged. "All I know is that Whelan said he was going to talk to his lawyer. He thinks if it was found in his yard it ought to be his."

"Does he want the corpse too?"

Phil was watching Marie refill his plate. He smiled at Roger Dowling, "I'll ask him."

"More lasagna, Francis?" Marie asked their other guest.

"No. No, thanks. It's good."

"You should eat."

This nostrum held little appeal for him, and Roger Dowling felt sorry for the man. He had come on a pious mission, keeping a promise to his mother, and was caught up in a mystifying business.

Over the next several days, some things became clear. Or rather, things became more obscure when the conclusion became unavoidable that the man who had been dug up in the Whelans' backyard was Stendall's father. Roger Dowling had asked Stendall if he would like to stay in a guest room at the rectory while this baffling matter was being investigated, and he accepted with relief.

"I'll turn in my rented car, too. It's costing me a fortune." As a teacher, Stendall did not have money to throw around, and Roger Dowling was happy to help him cut down on his expenses. When Phil called the rectory to reveal the startling turn of events, Stendall was upstairs reading.

"The damnedest thing, Roger. The dental records match those of a man who served in the First World War whose name was Philip Stendall."

"And he was about thirty when he died?"

"Do me a favor, Roger. Ask him what his father's name was."

"Philip," Francis Stendall answered. "Why?"

"What kind of man was he?"

"We didn't have many photographs of him, and my mother was reluctant to talk about him. I do have a diary he kept in France."

"France?"

"He was in the AEF in World War I. He was gassed and sickly, and I guess that's why he died so young. He was a delayed casualty of the war."

"Did he die in California?"

Stendall nodded. "Why all the questions?"

"Francis, there is a possibility that the buried body is that of your father."

There was no way to cushion the blow, so he didn't try. Poor Stendall had been absorbing so much psychic punishment that this added horror brought no visible reaction. His cigarette had hesitated as he brought it to his lips, but he dragged on it and then let smoke slip from his mouth.

"My father."

"Is it possible he never went to California?"

"I have only my mother's word." He smiled sadly. "I asked her where he was buried, and she said a military cemetery. That was one of the things I always wanted to do, find out where he was buried, visit his grave. The tomb of the unknown father."

He fell silent. Neither of them said anything of the fact that the body of a dead stranger was now Stendall's father. The big question remained: Who had killed him?

Stendall excused himself, saying he wanted some air, some time to think of all this. From the window, Roger Dowling watched the man pace back and forth on triangular walkway that ran between rectory, school, and church. He disappeared into the church for a time and then emerged. Roger Dowling had gone back to his desk, and when he looked out again he saw Stendall talking with Erickson. He tried to get away, but Erickson stayed with him. Finally they parted, and Stendall came inside.

"I see you met Erickson, the old fellow."

"He didn't say what his name was. That's a good idea, using the school for old people."

"It's a place for them to come."

"Are they all parishioners?"

"Mostly. We don't turn anyone away. Erickson has lived in the parish forever, I guess."

"He wanted to know if I did. I said no, and he asked my name. I really must look woebegone."

"Why?"

"I had the impression he was trying to cheer me up." He sighed. "I guess there's no escaping the fact that my mother killed my father."

Roger Dowling said nothing.

"It's the only way it makes sense. The guilt she felt was real enough, but she couldn't tell me the source of it, not even when she was dying. I guess I'm not surprised. But she had made up her mind she wanted me to know what she had done."

"Why?"

"The stocks? I don't know. Where did they come from?"

That was the other clarification that did not clarify. No report of missing stocks had shown up. No robbery, no misappropriation of funds. Stendall had thought his father was an invalid, that he had received a pension until he died. But there was no record of his having been gassed or wounded in any way. He had not received a pension.

The Stendalls had had a phone, a forty-call number, as it was classified, a special low rate unless the number of their calls exceeded forty a month.

Cy Horvath paused and looked across the desk at Father Dowling. "That's the kind of thing they've filled computers with."

"Where did Stendall work?"

"He was a bank guard."

Roger Dowling's brows lifted. "Is that where the money came from?"

Horvath shook his head. "There is still no indication on that. We've got people inheriting money, that sort of thing, but no big theft. Twenty-five dollars would have counted as a major haul in the early thirties."

Who would get it? Jennings Whelan called to ask Father Dowling to stop by. An urgent matter. Dowling went over, wondering if the odd events of recent days had prompted a change of heart in Whelan, but the urgent matter did not concern the recalcitrant parishioner's soul.

"Imelda is mad as blazes because I say that money is ours. Can you imagine that?"

"Mr. Whelan, right now I can imagine almost anything."

"Would you talk with her?"

"To what purpose?"

"Talk some sense into her."

"You mean, persuade her you should initiate lengthy, costly legal proceedings of dubious outcome?"

Whelan threw back his shoulders. "You've been talking with Amos Cadbury."

"Is he your lawyer?"

"Not on this matter. He doesn't think the court would go my way, necessarily. Do you know why?"

Roger Dowling shook his head. "I haven't discussed it with Amos."

"I'll tell you why. Because I'm not an heir or consignor of the poor devil they dug up. Does he think they're going to find a relative when they don't know who he is?"

"They've identified him, Mr. Whelan. And he does have an heir."

Whelan's face went blank and he sat down. "You're not just saying that?"

Imelda Whelan, who must have been listening from another room, came and put her arm about her husband.

"Who was he, Father?"

"A man named Stendall."

"No. I meant the corpse."

"That's what I mean. It appears that the body is that of the father of the man who asked it to be dug up."

"Telling us it was a baby!" Whelan shook his head at the baseness of mankind. "He knew it was his father, and he knew there was money."

"How did he die?" Imelda asked.

"He was shot."

"Killed himself and tried to take it with him?" But even Whelan saw the silliness of that remark. He said, "I have been assuming they wouldn't be able to identify him."

Imelda patted her husband's shoulder. The remark was equivalent to a statement of a complete change of heart. He was going to reject his dreams of avarice.

5

Amos Cadbury was more than willing to represent Francis Stendall in any claim he wished to make for the money. "If it isn't stolen and it was found with him and the man is his son, I should think the decision would go in his favor. Of course there will be taxes. And my fee. Both exorbitant, needless to say." Amos paused. The silence indicated he had made a joke. "That will still leave a considerable sum."

"I will suggest that he contact you."

But Francis Stendall shook his head. "No, Father. I don't want it. I don't know where it came from or how it got into the grave with him, but it doesn't interest me."

"You might want to think about it more before you decide."

"I won't change my mind. It would be ghoulish. Do you know what I thought of when you first mentioned the money? *Treasure Island.* I would bet there is some story of greed and treachery that explains the money. Dear God, I wish my mother were still alive so I could ask her some questions. Why did she want to put me through this?"

"When you first talked to me it was with the intention of reburying an infant in consecrated ground."

He nodded. "Of course. Could we do that for my father?"

"Certainly."

"A funeral Mass too?" He shook his head. "After all these years I'll be able to attend my father's funeral. And only weeks after attending my mother's."

"Maybe that is what she really wanted, not to put you through an agonizing experience."

"She should have told me."

"It is not easy for us to admit to having done something so wrong."

"Murder?"

"We don't know that."

"That is what is hard. Not knowing."

Agnes Lamb continued the routine search, trying to locate anyone who had been a neighbor of the Stendalls all those years ago. And she came up with two people, a man and a woman, unrelated, who had lived as children in the neighborhood. They were both in their sixties and, somewhat to Agnes' surprise, seemed to consider it perfectly normal to be asked about a neighborhood as it had been well over half a century ago.

"They talk about it as if nothing had changed. The man, Peters, can close his eyes and name every family on the block, both sides of the street. Of course he still lives there."

"In the same house?"

"When he married he brought his wife home and they stayed there when his parents died. The woman's memory is much more selective."

"How so?" Roger Dowling noticed that Keegan looked on

with approval as the black officer showed how good she was. He had come downtown to Phil's office to hear what Agnes had found.

"She remembers her mother talking about the Stendalls. One or the other was being unfaithful; she doesn't remember which, if she ever did know. Anyway, the move to California was meant to solve that problem."

"Remove one or the other from temptation?"

"That's right. Rose says her mother always thought it was someone who lived right there on the block."

"Well, well."

Phil said. "Tell him your theory, Agnes."

She made a little bow. "I say he was the one fooling around and that mama put him in the cold cold ground. The California move was meant to cover that. Or maybe they decided to go, and he started acting up again, a last fling."

"Why the money?" Roger Dowling asked.

"That is the fly in the ointment, Father," Agnes said. "But I don't know any theory that's going to make burying that much money and just leaving it there make much sense."

"Maybe leaving it there wasn't part of the plan."

"Well, then the plan fell through."

Of course it could have been buried by mistake, but such explanations were considered the last refuge of the scoundrel in Phil Keegan's department. He urged his people to live in a completely determined universe; every event had a cause. It was just that sometimes they weren't able to find it. But that is what they must believe, not that something just happened one way as opposed to a million others.

Agnes handed him a printout of her findings. They were counting on him to keep Stendall informed, figuring he had a right to know whatever they learned. But how much more bad news about his parents could the poor fellow take?

On the way back to St. Hilary's, Roger Dowling decided that the remarks by the woman Agnes called Rose could be regarded as mere gossip and there was no need to pass it on to Francis Stendall. If something further came to light, maybe, but for the nonce he would not add further to Stendall's load.

The memorial Mass and burial service for Stendall Senior went off with some pomp and circumstance. Marie urged the stalwarts of the parish to be there; Mrs. Hospers suggested to the oldsters at the school that they might want to attend, and Erickson of all people volunteered to line them up and march them over.

It was difficult to know whether Erickson knew anything about Stendall's situation, but he at least guessed the younger man had received bad news of some kind and required moral support. More than once Roger Dowling looked out to see Stendall and Erickson pacing back and forth on the parish sidewalks.

"What does he say?" Roger Dowling asked.

Stendall laughed. "He doesn't get a chance to say much. I have to keep reminding myself to put questions to him. So far I've told him a lot about Mother. There isn't much I want to say about my father just now."

"I hope you haven't decided we know how your father died."

Stendall started to say something, then stopped. "Oh, it doesn't matter. I talk about growing up in California. I guess I'm looking for clues in those years for what is coming to light now. My mother was a good woman, Father. As you say, we don't know how my father died, but the fact remains that she was a good mother to me."

Aside from a few lies and deceptions. Well, Erickson might be an ideal sounding board for a man who was trying to salvage as much of his past as he could.

Merlin of the *Fox River Tribune* got wind of what had been happening and wanted to interview Stendall.

"Why are you calling me?" Roger Dowling said, crossing his fingers.

"Peanuts Pianone says Stendall's been staying with you. Is that right?"

"He has been through a lot, Merlin. I really don't think he should be put through any more. Whatever story there is is over half a century old."

"That's the story!"

"Are things that slow?"

"Father, I understand what you're saying. Reacting just personally, I might feel exactly the way you do. But I have a duty to my readers. And those readers have a right to know."

A right to know what Merlin and others like him decided people should know. "Why don't you talk with Mr. Stendall about it?"

"That's why I'm calling."

"He is out of the house at the moment. Where should he call you?"

"I'll call him," Merlin said, his voice heavy with skepticism. But Stendall had left the house, if only to go over to the school and give Edna Hospers a hand. "It occurred to me that most of them are the age of my parents. The men are the age my father would have been."

It was remembering that remark that led Roger Dowling reluctantly to pick up the phone and call Phil Keegan.

"Phil, did Agnes check on births during those years?"

"Whose?"

"Was Stendall born here or in California?"

"Does it make a difference?"

"I'm just curious."

"What was he told?"

"California."

"He must have a birth certificate."

"Would you ask Agnes and have her call me?"

"What are policemen for? What did he think of the story Agnes dug up about his parents?"

"I didn't tell him. How do we know it's true?"

"Maybe you're right."

Agnes dropped off a photocopy of the birth announcements, and Roger Dowling read that a son had been born to the Stendalls of 3306 Macon Street on April twentieth, at home. Perhaps being born at home was not all that unusual at the time, but the memory of Stendall's original story when he came to the rectory gave the priest an odd feeling.

He put the copied page in his desk drawer, along with the papers Agnes had given him a few days before.

"Jennings Whelan is here." Marie Murkin whispered this, stagily, as she stood in the door of his study.

"Show him in."

"Not here in the rectory." She gave him a look. "At the school. With the other old people. Maybe it's a first step."

And maybe not. Should he drop by the school and accidentally run into Whelan? A tempting idea, but first he wanted to have a talk with his houseguest. Francis Stendall had said the night before he would be heading back to California soon. He hadn't done what he had come to do, but no doubt he had accomplished what his mother had in mind when she gave him those instructions. He had stood at his father's new grave the previous day, a lonely figure, staring down at the rather sumptuous casket that contained what was left of his father after more than half a century moldering in the backyard of the house on Macon Street. To think of a man Stendall's age as an orphan is odd—who isn't an orphan when he nears sixty?—but he had the look of a man who had been abandoned by both his parents. No wonder he wanted to go back to his own life now and escape the haunting presence of his mother and father. But Roger Dowling thought he should stay on at least for a few days more.

"What's the point, Father? I feel like a parasite as it is, camping in your rectory."

"Nonsense. Marie appreciates someone with a better appetite than I have."

"I can't understand why you're not overweight. She is a wonderful cook."

And so she was. He had decided early in his tenure as pastor that he would have to hide behind the excuse of an inadequate appetite or he would balloon up like a monsignor.

"They sent over the notice of your birth in the local paper if you'd like to see it."

He shook his head. "That's one thing I am sure of, that I was born."

Roger Dowling did not push the matter. But it was agreed that Stendall would stay several more days at least.

"It sounds morbid, but if I do stay, I'd like to see that house."

"The Whelans? I'll see if I can arrange it."

Equipped with an excuse, Roger Dowling sauntered over to the school. He dropped by Mrs. Hospers' office, and they talked a bit about the program she had developed. What he liked about it was that it left the old people to figure out many of the activities themselves. How awful it would be to fall into the hands of some breathless enthusiast who would insist they must keep busy, do this and that, whatever their inclinations.

When he went to what had been the auditorium, there were card games in process, three checkers matches, one game of chess, and of course shuffleboard. The one game all the old people seemed to like was shuffleboard. And there indeed was Jennings Whelan playing a game with Erickson. Roger Dowling stopped at a checkers game not far from the shuffleboard area, kibitzing a while, giving Whelan a chance to notice him and disappear if he liked. But the game continued, and Roger Dowling went over just as Erickson, with a practiced push, managed to remove all Whelan's markers from the target area.

"Damn it!" shouted Whelan and turned to Roger Dowling. "Did you see what that burglar did?"

"It's part of the game," Erickson said, clearly enjoying himself.

"I was counting on beginner's luck," Whelan moaned as they trudged to the other end of the playing area.

It soon became clear to Whelan that he was no match for Erickson, and he returned his pole to the rack.

"I'm going to quit while I still have my house."

"Speaking of which," Roger Dowling said, and Whelan's eyebrows went up.

"Oh, no. Not another archeological dig in my backyard."

"Only metaphorically. Young Stendall wondered if you'd let him come visit the house."

"Why not? He managed to get the backyard ruined. He never did see the result of that, did he? Sure, send him over."

"When would be a good time?"

"Well, Carl and I are moseying back home now. He can come along now, if he wants."

"Carl's going too?"

"To his own house, of course. He's given up trying to buy mine."

"You're neighbors?"

"For my sins," Whelan said. "For my sins."

"We must talk about those someday."

"You never quit, do you, Father? You're as bad as Imelda."

"Thank God for Imelda."

Whelan puffed out his lips, then nodded vigorously. "I do. I do. The very words that got me into it, and I'd do it again tomorrow. I'm not sure she would though. Being married to a lapsed Catholic is hard on her."

"It's harder on you."

"Where is this young Stendall? We've got to get going. Right, Carl?"

"I think I'll stay," Erickson said. "You have someone to walk with now. You don't need me."

"Were you just going to do me a favor?"

Erickson didn't answer.

6

After Stendall and Whelan had gone, Roger Dowling sat at the desk in his study, smoking his pipe, looking straight ahead but not seeing anything.

After a few minutes, he opened the drawer of his desk and took out the first papers Agnes Lamb had given him. The list of residents of Macon Street when Stendall's parents had lived there. Was he really surprised to find the name of Carl Erickson on the list? And what did it mean? One thing it explained was Erickson's interest in Francis Stendall; he had known his parents, though apparently he had not admitted this to Agnes Lamb. Might he even have seen Francis as an infant? Not impossible. But Roger Dowling had the feeling that there was more.

He called Mrs. Hospers. "Edna, would you ask Carl Erickson if he would like to join me for lunch? After the noon Mass. Tell him I would particularly like him to come."

One of the advantages of saying Mass facing the people—a change that had followed on Vatican II—was that he knew who was in church. Carl Erickson was not there, and he wondered if he would show up for lunch.

"You have a guest," Marie Murkin said when he came in the kitchen door. Another answered prayer. "He's in the study."

"How glad I am you could come," Roger Dowling said when he joined Erickson.

"I don't have that busy a schedule, Father. Not anymore."

"Lucky man. Come, let's have our lunch."

Where had he gotten the impression that Carl Erickson was a doddering old imbecile? He was an enjoyable table companion, with many amusing observations about growing old, and much praise for what Mrs. Hospers was doing in the school.

"I was surprised to see Jennings Whelan here this morning," Father Dowling said.

"I suggested he come."

"Are you friends?"

"I think of him as one of the new boys on the block."

"Ah, the block. I want to talk with you about that when we go back to the study."

"I noticed you have a complete set of St. Augustine."

"Oh, yes. I've been reading him for years."

"I know only the *Confessions.*"

"Have you read it?"

"It has become a favorite. A good book for old sinners."

When they had adjourned to the study, it was easy to continue the conversation along those lines. "You seem struck by the story of Francis Stendall."

For the first time, Erickson seemed ill at ease. "It is a fairly incredible happening."

"Did you know his parents?"

There are gestures, looks, remarks that prove to be the open sesames, and that question sufficed to open Erickson's heart.

"I had wondered if that would become known. The police called and asked about the Stendalls—they knew I had lived on the block in those days—and I am afraid I lied to them. But in many ways I have been living a lie for all these years."

Roger Dowling knew that all he need do was wait, be silent,

be receptive, and the story would be told. And what a story it was. Carl Erickson had been Mrs. Stendall's lover. He used that term, not without irony. "That makes it sound much more romantic than it was. Those were gray days, Father. Impoverished days. A movie was an event. Her husband worked nights as a bank guard, my wife was tending to her sister's children. I asked Rosemary to go to the movie. It was one of those frothy Depression pictures. They plied us with tales of the idle rich at a time when a square meal was rare for many. That is how it started."

It ended with Rosemary getting pregnant. Her husband was upset. He lived almost like a monk just so she wouldn't have children, not yet, and here she was pregnant.

"Both Rosemary and I formed the idea that the child was mine."

"Was it?"

Erickson looked at Roger Dowling in anguish. "I don't know. She didn't know. There was no way of knowing for sure. But she said she was sure. The child was mine. I felt as much terror as joy. I had a wife. Rosemary had a husband. It was an impossible situation. And they quarreled constantly about her pregnancy. He decided they would move to California. Like so many others he had the notion you could live in California on nothing. There was sun, there was fruit. It sounded like paradise. She thought it a crazy idea. We decided to run away. I had no money, but I had lots of worthless stock as it then was, but stock in which I never lost hope. I put all the certificates in a valise; they would go with us. Other bags were packed and waiting. I was ready to desert my wife." He said this as if even now after all these years he could not believe his intended perfidy. "But I had already been unfaithful. I seemed caught up in something that deprived me of my freedom.

"And then came an awful night, a weekend when her husband

was home, just days before the planned flight. They argued and she told him her child was not his. He became enraged. She telephoned me and I went over."

He paused, "There are moments in life when everything is settled. They do not announce themselves as so significant, but in the event they are the great hinges on which everything turns.

"When I showed up, not knowing what she had told him, he immediately drew the appropriate inference. He lunged at me. We fought. He was much stronger than I. I thought he would kill me until there was a shot. She had killed him with his own revolver."

The dead body of the husband had purged them both. Any thought of running away together was now repugnant. It was one thing to be joined by a child, but to have a killing link them was too much. And so they had decided to do what they had done. In the still of the night, when there was no moon, Erickson dug the grave. Meanwhile, she got gunny sacks from the basement and wrapped him. "She seemed to want to make him warm." And then Erickson carried him out into the backyard and buried him. Before he covered the body, in a fit of disgust, as a symbol that he was rejecting his plan to flee, he pitched the valise into the grave and covered it and the body.

"I could hardly believe afterward what labor I had engaged in. Yet I did it swiftly and effortlessly, carried along by panic. When I was done, we decided she would say her husband had left for California. She would follow after her baby was born. I would let it be known that they had impetuously decided to put his romantic plan into effect."

After she left, there was complete silence. She did not write. Erickson did not know where she was or even if she had actually gone to California.

"The house was sold, then sold again to Jennings Whelan, and from time to time I would dread that the body would somehow be discovered. But I had dug deep, at least six feet, that seemed important, and there was little danger."

"Whelan said you tried to buy the house."

Erickson looked away. "I was motivated by greed rather than fear. Those worthless stocks are far from worthless now. The companies revived; shares split and split again. I do not dare guess what they are worth. I used to dream of ways of digging up that valise, but nothing feasible ever occurred to me. And then a year ago I heard from Rosemary."

He held his hands in a praying position and brought the tips of his fingers to his lips.

"She was dying. She was determined to tell her son what had happened."

"She wrote you?"

"Yes, and I telephoned her, many times. Her voice sounded unchanged, and it was like talking to the half-hysterical woman I had parted from that awful night. I begged her to keep the secret. What difference did it all make now? Her answer was that her conscience bothered her. Not the murder, she had long since confessed that, but the thought of him lying there wrapped in gunny sacks in unconsecrated ground. I was still trying to dissuade her when she died. You can imagine what it has been like for me during these past days."

Roger Dowling let silence settle, a not-uncomfortable silence. It was clear that Erickson was relieved finally to have told what had happened.

Roger Dowling said softly, "I doubt very much that anyone will guess what happened."

"But you must tell the police?"

The priest shook his head. "No, I don't think so. If a crime was committed, it was not by you. Unless the burial was a crime, and that has been rectified now."

7

After Francis Stendall had left for California, his strange visit over, Father Dowling missed him. Even Marie lamented not having another mouth to feed. Amos Cadbury had convinced Stendall not to disclaim the stocks until he had given it more thought.

"I won't change my mind," Stendall told Roger Dowling.

"You can give it to charity. Think of something you would like to support."

"Thank you for your hospitality, Father."

Erickson drove Stendall to the airport with who knew what emotions. Was he saying farewell to a son or not? Phil Keegan had problems of his own.

"I hate a crime where there is no criminal to indict," Phil said. It was received opinion that the wife had killed the husband.

"Well, no one profited from the crime anyway."

"I would like to know why that valise was buried with the body, Roger. There must be a perfectly logical explanation of that."

"Remorse?"

Phil laughed. It seemed to cheer him up. Marie, drawn by the laughter, brought Phil a beer, and they settled down to watch the Cubs. Perhaps there was a logical explanation of that, too, but Roger Dowling did not know it.

WHERE THERE'S SMOKE

1

It was unusual for men and women of the age reached by those who frequented the senior center at St. Hilary's to object to the smell of tobacco, but there were several who had been tainted by the lopsided morality of the age. Most notable among them was Marvin Smith, who always wore a coat and tie, and, when he came to the rectory with his proposal, sat down with Father Dowling in the study with a confident man-to-man air about him. Also in the air about him were the last clouds of smoke from the pipe the pastor had been smoking. Marvin diplomatically ignored this and went directly to the point. He wanted Father Dowling to impose restrictions on smoking in the parish center for seniors.

"Many office buildings now require employees to go outside if they want to smoke."

From the study window the ribbed remains of sooty snow were visible on the parish lawns, and a stiff March breeze periodically rattled the doors and windows of the rectory.

"I've noticed that," Father Dowling said. He might have been warming his fingers on the bowl of his pipe. "It reminds me of high school."

Marvin sighed. "I suppose that's where they got hooked on cigarettes." He stressed cigarettes, as if he were issuing a *nihil obstat* to the pastoral pipe. "But times have changed."

"In what way?"

"The attitude toward tobacco has completely altered in American society, Father. We see now that it was all a conspiracy by Big Tobacco. They knew the stuff was lethal and they concealed what they knew. The advertising was insistent."

"LSMFT," Father Dowling murmured.

Marvin Smith cocked his head. "Again?"

"Lucky Strike Means Fine Tobacco. That was a kind of mantra of their commercials. People walked a mile for a Camel, but then nine out of ten doctors preferred them. Not a cough in a carload."

Marvin Smith nodded vigorously at this recital of the tobacco commercials of yesteryear. It provided him with a firm basis on which to remind Father Dowling of the restrictions that had been placed on tobacco advertisement since the surgeon general's report. Not that there weren't constant efforts to get around these restrictions.

"I would like to take up a petition, Father, but more of that later."

"A petition?"

"Gathering signatures expressing support for banning tobacco advertisement on billboards in the greater Fox River metropolitan area."

"Does that include Chicago?"

"Others are working on the matter there, Father. But that is not why I am here. I wish to propose that a separate room be set aside in the center for those who want to smoke. If it is adequately ventilated, the rest of us will be protected from the effects of secondary smoke."

Father Dowling scratched his chin and looked beyond Marvin at the wintry scene visible from the window. The restrictions on smoking when he was in the seminary years ago had been tied to discipline and ascetics, not health. Roger Dowling could remember many a pleasant afternoon walk around the grounds at Mundelein, everyone smoking up a storm, arguing about some point raised in class. Marvin Smith represented a new moral zealotry that concentrated on governing the acts of others.

"Did you ever smoke, Marvin?"

"Oh yes. I had my share. And I drank, too. They went together for me; to stop the one was to stop the other."

"When was that?"

"Twenty-two years ago." He had not hesitated before he answered.

"That long ago?"

"My wife made me do it, Father. She wouldn't let me smoke in the house or in the car either, not if she was going to ride in it with me. For a year I would slip out to the garage whenever I wanted a smoke. If the weather was clement, I would raise the garage doors and unfold a lawn chair and get a little sun as well. But it was more a nuisance than a pleasure."

"You owe your wife a good deal."

"God rest her soul."

"I don't believe I knew her."

"Oh, she's been dead for years."

"How long?"

"Twenty-two years."

There was a sound in the hallway and then the quite audible tiptoeing of Marie Murkin back to her kitchen. Apparently she had been eavesdropping on this conversation. His wife's death had affected Marvin strongly. "My first impulse was to smoke and drink myself to death. But I couldn't. Every time I took out a cigarette in the house I could hear Agnes telling me to go out to the garage. It was the same with drink. Even beer. So I quit."

Now Marvin wanted to play the role of Agnes for the other old people who spent their days at the parish center, what had once been the parish school. Father Dowling told Marvin he would look into the matter.

"There may be opposition, Father." Marvin stood on his stubby legs, straightened his jacket, and gave a tug to his necktie.

"Do you think so?"

"But it's for their own good."

"To smoke outside?"

"That will discourage at least some of them and they will quit."

"Ah."

After he had shown Marvin to the door and returned to his desk in the study, he was relighting his pipe when Marie Murkin stood in the door.

"You're lucky he didn't lecture you about your smoking."

"It would only be for my own good."

Marie Murkin studied him with narrowed eyes. "Now don't think I don't know what you think of that man."

"All right."

"All right what?"

"I'm not thinking."

"You certainly aren't." Marie sat down. "Sitting there and letting that Johnny-come-lately tell us how to run a senior center. Can you imagine expecting Kenneth and Sibyl to go out in the parking lot whenever they wanted a smoke? That's nonsense. Let him go out and freeze if he wants fresh air."

"This is unexpected, Marie. I thought you were a foe of tobacco."

"I never smoked myself, no. But live and let live, I say."

2

From her office on the second floor of the school, Edna Hospers, director of the parish center, saw Marvin Smith marching back from his visit to the rectory. Had he told Father Dowling that she had sent him over there, wanting to get the pest out of her hair? Marvin Smith had been a regular at the center for the past several months, and almost from Day One he had been giving Edna advice on how to do her job. He had raised his eyebrows and then his voice when he saw that people were playing bridge for a penny a point.

"They're gambling."

"Wednesdays we have Bingo," Edna told him.

"I was going to mention that."

Edna had been patient. In her position, she had come to see how difficult it was for men and women to acknowledge that they had indeed entered their twilight years and to find an appropriate *modus vivendi* in this new status. New arrivals at the center had to decompress. At first they resisted thinking of themselves as one of the group, one of these old people, and they sought to carry over the role and status they had known in their active years. With time, people tended to mellow, realizing that there is at least one thing worse than being old. Edna had watched serenity come over even the most pugnacious and frenetic types. She was willing to give Marvin Smith time.

But time did not dim his censorious attitude as he wandered about the center, looking in on others playing bridge, standing behind the group watching television, clearly disapproving of what enthralled them on the screen, checking the window sills for dust.

"What did you do, Marvin?"

He looked at Edna as if he did not understand the question.

"Before you retired."

"I do not think of myself as retired. Anyway, that's what I did for a living."

Edna stared at him. And then she got it. "Smith's Tires? Are you that Smith?"

He nodded, not expressing surprise that she had made the connection so soon. He was in the process of selling out, his

183

name and goodwill going with the property and inventory. He might spend his days at the St. Hilary senior center, but Smith's Tires would continue to roll along without him. On that occasion, he became confiding, and although there was an edginess in his voice as he spoke of handing his business over to another, Edna was certain he was turning the corner into acceptance of his new life.

"I'm beginning to feel like a spare, Mrs. Hospers. Not another full tire, but one of those temporary things that will only take a car to the garage. You know what I mean?"

"I've driven on them."

"Fifth wheel," he mused. "A familiar phrase. But a fifth wheel that's not really like the other four . . ."

His voice drifted off as he got lost in the intricacies of the comparison.

"There are no fifth wheels here, Marvin."

He winced and she realized that among his grievances was this practice of addressing everyone by his or her first name. Maybe that was part of the pain for the elderly, to be treated like preschoolers or like anyone in a dentist's office. Edna got to her feet and came around her desk.

"It is always a pleasure to talk with you, Mr. Smith."

He stood. "I understand. You're busy. I'll go."

"That isn't what I meant."

But of course it had been. A little bit of Marvin Smith went a long way, and Edna did have other things to do than help the former tire dealer grow old gracefully. As he left her office, shoulders back, chin tucked in, she remembered his advertising slogan, If You Must Retire, See Smith.

It was Smith's crusade against smoking that became the real problem. It began with his theatrical coughing as he staggered out of range whenever someone lit up a cigarette in the recreation room. He tried to enlist the presumably sympathetic women, but they shunned him, even those who had never smoked in their lives, all save little Meg Sullivan, who smiled agreement, but then she was deaf as a post and her assent was equivocal. Kenneth and Sibyl O'Brien, whizzes at the bridge table, were chain smokers. They objected to Smith's kibitzing as much as he did to their smoking. Smith's next move was unilaterally to declare one corner of the room out of bounds for smokers.

"Since when?" Gerald Sandeen wanted to know. A thick cigar jutted from the corner of his mouth and he held a massive kitchen match with which he was about to light it.

"As a consideration to others."

"You want to borrow a cigar?"

"I don't smoke."

"Well, no one can make you smoke. It's a free country, Smith. Enjoy it."

"How can I breathe if you're going to be filling the air with that!" He indicated the cigar with an extended, disdainful finger.

For answer, Sandeen brought his thumbnail across the tip of the match and it flared into flame. He seemed to take an inordinate number of preliminary puffs, as if he were sending up warning signals to other members of the tribe of smokers. *There is an enemy in our midst.* That had precipitated Smith's resolution that something had to be done about smoking in the parish center. It was clear as could be that he would allow himself—and others—no rest until he had driven all users of tobacco into the out of doors where God's good fresh air might convert them and turn them from the wickedness of their ways.

"You will have to talk with Father Dowling, Marvin. I would not presume to introduce such a restriction myself."

3

Marvin Smith knew that they considered him a crank, first Edna Hospers, then Father Dowling. He gave no weight at all to the opposition of Kenneth and Sibyl or of Gerald Sandeen. Mrs. Hospers' authority was delegated and therefore limited. Marvin accepted her claim that she simply could not introduce such a change on her own. For years he had been in charge of his environment, and what he said was law. After the death of Agnes, God rest her soul, he resolved never again to let anyone else get him under their thumb. He saw himself as a forceful man of action. And so he had gone off to the rectory and bearded the lion in his den. He had been prepared for the smoke-filled air and made no allusion to it. If a man chose to harm his health in the privacy of his own study, that was between him and God. Unless, of course, Mrs. Murkin the housekeeper objected. Marvin made a mental note to pursue that possibility later. But first things first. The priority item was to have smoking banned from the parish center.

He accepted Father Dowling's promise to do something about it and returned along the path to the school with the pleasant sense that he had made some progress toward bringing order into the environment of the senior center. Inside the school, he roamed around the great recreation room that had once been the school gymnasium, and felt godlike watching men and woman smoke, knowing as he did that their days were numbered. But Marvin was pleasantly surprised when, only ten minutes after his return, Father Dowling appeared and asked for everyone's attention. This was fast action indeed.

"A suggestion has been made that we provide some relief for those who do not smoke," Father Dowling said.

There was grumbling from the direction of Gerald Sandeen, who was thoughtfully puffing on his cigar. Sibyl emitted a nervous little laugh and looked around, but the eyes of all had searched out and found Marvin Smith. They knew from whom the suggestion had come.

"I didn't hear what you said, Father," Meg called out. "Could you repeat it?"

Someone whispered first into one ear and then went around to the other and finally Meg got it. Father Dowling then asked for a show of hands of those who smoked, and then for a show of hands of those who did not. There were one or two more smokers than nonsmokers.

"How many nonsmokers are troubled by others smoking?"

Marvin's hand shot up and Meg's, but she gradually lowered hers again when she sensed the feeling in the room.

"Very well, we have one person opposed to others smoking."

"May I say something, Father Dowling?" Marvin asked.

"Of course."

"Something like this cannot be decided simply by majority vote. In such a matter, it is sufficient that one person finds smoke offensive. I am that person and I find it offensive because it exposes me to the same dangers as those who smoke even though I do not. That is unjust."

"So what do you propose?"

But Gerald Sandeen wanted to speak. "He wants minority rule, Father. That's saying one guy can veto what everyone else wants."

Sibyl spoke up, too, and Kenneth as well. He wanted to know what we had fought the war for if this is the way we were going to treat veterans. Everybody smoked in the service. They practically gave away cigarettes. Whatever his point, it was obscured by the agitation with which he spoke. Father Dowling let him finish, then held up his hand and obtained silence and the attention of those before him.

"This is what I propose. It is reasonable enough for Marvin not to want to breathe in other people's smoke. What we need is a restriction on smoking. I propose that the library be off limits to smokers. We will call it our no-smoking zone. There Marvin, and others, can be safe from the effects of secondary smoke, whatever those might be."

This met with general approval, even applause, but a dark cloud settled over Marvin Smith's face. His disposition was not helped by the triumphalist reaction of Sibyl and Kenneth O'Brien. Edna thought the decision worthy of Solomon. Having adjourned the impromptu meeting, Father Dowling went to Marvin Smith.

"That was a cruel trick, Father,"

"Well, it provides a solution anyway."

"Does it? Every time I don't want a smoke, I go to the library? Meanwhile, others are polluting the air with tobacco. That's not my idea of a solution, Father Dowling."

"Marvin, I can't drive all these people away just to please you."

"They should quit smoking!"

"Perhaps. But let's leave that up to them, should we?"

"Father, I'm not going to give up. I was in business for myself for over a quarter of a century and no one ever got the better of me in a deal."

"I believe that. Do you have time to do me a favor?"

"A favor?"

"Could you take a look at the tires on my car? I think I should replace them."

They went off to the garage, and Marvin became very professional, walking around the car, checking the depth of the tread, noting the way the tires were worn.

"You could use new tires, all right. But you need your wheels aligned even more."

"Are you free now, Marvin? I'd feel more confident buying tires if you were with me."

"I know just the place."

And so they drove away to Smith's Tires, where Father Dowling's car got retired. He also met Branwell, the man who was in the process of buying the business. Smith and Branwell withdrew into a corner where their lively exchange grew audible from time to time. Branwell seemed to regard Smith in somewhat the same way as the smokers at the senior center did. For the nonce, the retired Marvin Smith was able to occupy at least momentarily the position of authority that twenty-five years in the tire game had conferred on him.

Smith's Tires was a gigantic operation: a showroom, an office wing, a garage where tires were mounted, a warehouse where tires, purchased in bulk, were stored. Marvin was particularly happy with the showroom and office wing.

"Do I detect the smell of tobacco?"

Smith frowned. "One must tolerate a lot from potential customers. Still, you shouldn't be bothered by secondhand smoke. I spent a lot of money insuring that would not happen." He smiled grimly. "Not as much money as I might have, but a lot."

"Well this is quite an operation you've built up, Marvin."

"But how long will it last under that idiot? If he can manage the financing. All of a sudden, he wants to renegotiate our agreement."

"Is that what you were arguing about?"

"An argument takes two sides. He has no case."

"You mean the deal could fall through?"

Marvin Smith brightened considerably. "I may have to come out of retirement."

It was indeed, as it turned out, his last day of retirement.

4

The library was one of the few rooms in the school that had retained its original purpose, serving the senior parishioners in somewhat the same way that it had served the school's pupils in earlier times. Of course the books on the shelves differed, though not entirely. There were volumes by Robert Hugh Benson and many titles by Francis Finn, S. J., wholesome novels which had stirred the imaginations of generations of children. Gerald Sandeen had made it a personal project to read systematically through the entire Finn canon. The stories, he pronounced, were every bit as good now as when he had read them as a boy. His favorite was *Tom Playfair.*

"What kind of stories are they?" Phil Keegan asked. He and Father Dowling were ensconced in the study with the radio broadcast of a spring training game of the Cubs as background. Marie Murkin had delivered a dramatic account of the way in which the pastor had dealt with a potential pest that afternoon. Phil, enjoying a cigar, liked the idea of a no-smoking zone for those who chose not to smoke. Father Dowling pointed out that his solution had its limitations. It would be difficult to ask office workers who did not want to smoke to go outside to not do it.

"Since they don't smoke all the time, if they have to go outside not to smoke, they would spend the whole day away from their work."

"They could take up smoking and stay inside," Phil chortled.

"My hope is that others will be more considerate of Marvin now when they smoke. I have a man coming to see if there isn't a way to ventilate the recreation room better. Do you know what a smoke eater is?"

"An ashtray?"

"One that traps and neutralizes smoke. There must be some way to provide that on a larger scale."

This made Marie indignant. Father Dowling was retreating

from hard-won ground. It was as if Marvin Smith had lost a battle but stood to win the war. "The next thing you'll be saying that the smokers have to go to the library!"

"What is this library?"

Phil's question led on to the mention of the books of Benson and Finn and his wondering what sort of novels the Jesuit author had written.

"Not unlike Horatio Alger novels, Phil. With a dash of Stover at Yale."

"I would really like to read *Treasure Island* again," Phil said with sudden fervor. "What a story."

"There is a copy of that in the school library."

"Could I borrow it?"

"We could go get it now."

"What inning is it?"

But the game was over. The two men put on coats for the short walk; it was a cold night and their breath puffed visibly before them as they went along the walk to the school. Father Dowling got out a key to unlock the outer door. Inside, the quiet corridors seemed haunted with the movements of all the children who had passed along them to their classrooms or on their way outside for recess. Phil stopped and listened as if the past were speaking to him.

"Doesn't this bring it all back?"

Father Dowling did not reply, but he understood. They went on to the library, which was at the far end of the corridor. Father Dowling reached inside and flipped the switch. He did not see the body until he almost tripped over it. The frowning, lifeless face of Marvin Smith stared unseeing at the ceiling.

5

After Father Dowling had knelt to give absolution to the fallen former tire dealer, although Marvin Smith's soul had most likely already left his body, Phil Keegan took over. He had first stepped into Edna Hospers' office, which was next to the library, to make a call, and when he returned and made a preliminary investigation of the body, several patrol cars pulled into the parish parking lot, convoying an ambulance. But Marvin Smith proved to be beyond the help of the paramedics.

"Cause of death?" Phil asked one of the paramedics, a young woman of pale complexion, red hair, and large circular eyes. She shrugged.

Her companion, a male with hair longer than hers, pulled into a ponytail, was kneeling beside the body. "This could have been it." He turned the head to expose the nasty wound just below the crown. The hair was damp with blood and moving the head revealed that blood had accumulated on the rug beneath. The medical examiner arrived some time later, photographs were taken, an onsite examination of the body was made, and then they prepared to take Marvin Smith's body away.

"Anyone know the deceased?"

Father Dowling explained that Smith had been coming regularly to the parish's senior center.

"You open nights?"

"No. And the building was locked."

But this was a spoor to be pursued by Phil Keegan and the police. When Phil asked Father Dowling if he would notify the next of kin, the pastor realized he did not know who that might be. Call Edna? He went into her office to see if there were some way in which he might find out who Smith's survivors might be without calling Edna. But there was nothing immediately evident on the desk. Father Dowling reached for the phone but stopped. A muffled sound came from the closet to the right of the desk. Father Dowling approached it quietly and stood, head cocked, listening.

"Something wrong, Roger?" Phil asked from the doorway.

Father Dowling beckoned him in, but kept a hand raised. Once more the moaning sound came from behind the closet door; Father Dowling gripped the handle and tried to open the door, but it was locked. The key was in the lock however. He turned it, opened the door. Edna Hospers, bound and gagged and tied to a chair, looked out at her rescuers with wide unfocused eyes.

6

The following morning, when Marie Murkin learned of all the excitement she had missed the previous night, she was at once furious and curious.

"Marvin Smith dead!" In her voice was the suggestion that although she had not thought highly of the man alive, she would mourn for him dead. But it was Edna Hospers' starring role that made the morning difficult for Marie Murkin.

Untied, the gag removed from her mouth, Edna, normally a pillar of strength, cried helplessly for some time. Then she called home, to make sure her children were all right. All she told them was that she was staying late and had been unable to call them earlier.

"Did you call here?"

They had. One of the more agonizing aspects of Edna's ordeal was to be shut into her closet, listening to her telephone ring, certain it was her children wondering where she was. Of course they could fend for themselves over the short haul, and had. Wieners and beans and potato chips had been their supper menu. Edna told them she would be home as soon as possible, but in any case they were to go to their rooms at regular bedtimes. That done, fully in control again, physically no worse for her ordeal, she told Phil and Father Dowling what had happened.

She had been getting ready to leave for the day when she heard a commotion in the library. It never occurred to her to seek assistance before marching out of her office to see what was going on. She was bowled over just as she stepped into the corridor and was sent sprawling face down across the recently waxed floor. Almost immediately the man who had run into her jumped on top of her. Her expression indicated that she had feared the worst, and neither Phil nor Father Dowling would have pursued the matter then, but the assault was only physical. She was pulled to her feet, her hands jerked up behind her back, and she was forced back into her office. Once her hands were tied, the gag was inserted, obviously only after a struggle. Then she was bound in the chair and put in the closet.

"At first, when the door closed, the darkness was almost welcome."

"He pushed the chair into the closet?" Father Dowling asked.

She looked at him, then slowly shook her head. "He carried it and me in."

"Did you recognize him?"

"How could I? He had a stocking pulled over his face. He looked like something from Toys R Us. What was he after?"

The consensus eventually arrived at was that the man had killed Marvin Smith in the library and as he ran from the scene collided with Edna. After what he had done to Marvin, what might he not have done to her? What he had done suggested that what he mainly wanted was time to get free of the scene of his crime. He did not want Edna sounding the alarm, as she would have if she had come upon the body of Marvin Smith. Edna's face fell when she was told what had taken place in the library.

"The poor man."

"I suppose he had gone there not to smoke," Father Dowling said ruefully. In the light of what had happened to Smith, the pastor felt ambiguous about the way he had resolved Marvin Smith's demand that smoking be prohibited in the senior center.

"Don't blame yourself, Father," Edna said, but that only underscored how silly the little triumph over Marvin had been. On the other hand, he could not have let Smith come in here and dictate how everyone else must behave.

Now the search for Marvin Smith's murderer began. Phil and Cy Horvath would wait until morning to talk with the regulars at the center, but in the meanwhile they would have a word with Gerald Sandeen and Kenneth and Sibyl O'Brien. Phil drew the O'Briens; Cy Horvath was sent to talk to Gerald.

7

Cy's wife Muriel had developed a passion for Scrabble now that the game was discontinued, and she was a lot better at it than Cy. Accordingly, he was not sad to be called away from the domestic hearth to speak to Gerald Sandeen. Phil gave him some of the details of what had happened and then Father Dowling came on to provide more.

"He had made a nuisance of himself in the center over smoking."

"What did he smoke?"

"Nothing. He was against it. He didn't want anyone else smoking."

Gerald Sandeen was a defiant cigar smoker. He was wearing a car coat when he let Cy in after the lieutenant explained that he wanted to ask a few questions about Marvin Smith.

"Yeah?" Sandeen seemed delighted. "What's he done?"

"I heard about his antismoking campaign."

"The guy's a damned fascist. What has he done?"

"It's what's been done to him."

Sandeen was in process of taking off his coat. He stared at Cy. "What's that mean?"

"Someone killed him."

"Naw. Where?"

"In the library at St. Hilary's school."

After a moment, Sandeen continued to remove his coat.

"You been out for a smoke?"

The little apartment reeked of stale cigar smoke. "I've been down at Fuzzy's watching the Cubs."

"Fuzzy's?"

"A sports bar."

Suddenly Sandeen flung his coat in Cy's face and by the time Cy got free of it the door was slamming. But when he came out of the apartment, Sandeen was in the firm custody of Peanuts Pianone, who looked at Cy the way a retriever with a mallard looks at his master.

"Don't break his ribs, Peanuts."

They took Sandeen downtown. A little checking showed that he had not been at Fuzzy's that night and he refused to say where he had been. But under pressure he did say, "A gentleman never tells."

Sandeen looked like what he was, a man who had spent his life installing poles for the telephone company. You could imagine him toting around by himself a fifty-foot pole. It had been humiliating for him to be so quickly subdued by Peanuts.

"You were with a lady?"

Sandeen twisted an imaginary key at his lips, then flung it away. Cy smiled. Obviously Sandeen was affected by hanging around the senior center all day. The reminder of school days must be powerful. It was his connection with the center that was the focus of interest, obviously. Others were not sure if they had noticed Sandeen leave the school that day. Could he have stayed on after others left? It was possible. The question was, had he been angry enough at Marvin Smith to clobber him over the head? The weapon apparently had been a large globe in the library. It was not the great globe itself that had done Smith in—there was a new dent in the South American continent, but it was the heavy, pointed, octagonal base that had delivered the lethal blow.

"You better get a lawyer, Sandeen."

Father Dowling was obviously dubious that Gerald Sandeen had killed Marvin.

"Well, it wasn't the O'Briens, Roger. They were playing duplicate bridge from six until ten."

With some reluctance the pastor then told them of his visit to Smith's Tires with the deceased. "He seems to have had a falling out with the man who was buying his business. A man named Branwell."

Phil talked to Branwell first, and before he had a chance to let the man know what had happened to Smith, he got an earful on what a monster the founder of Smith's Tires was.

"This place looks pretty good to me."

"It is. At least I think so. Our deal looked good to me, too, but now . . ."

Branwell checked himself. It seemed an indication of his chagrin that he would say even this much to a stranger.

"What do you want to know about Smith?"

"When did you last see him?"

"Is he missing?"

"That depends on how long since he was last seen."

"He was in here this afternoon. With some priest. Imagine, a guy like that coming in here with a priest and then telling me he might take the whole business back!"

"The priest heard him say that?"

But it occurred to Branwell again that he was babbling. "Why are you looking for Smith?"

"Oh, we've found him. The problem is, he's dead."

Branwell stared across the desk at Phil. After a moment, he

reached for his phone and deliberately dialed a number. "Mr. Cadbury? Joe Branwell."

Calling his lawyer before he was arrested seemed to make taking him into custody inevitable. Everything they subsequently learned about Branwell made him a far more plausible suspect than Gerald Sandeen. In any case, Sandeen's gallantry had been overcome sufficiently to enable him to say where he had been at the time of the killing of Marvin Smith.

"I took Meg Sullivan home. You have to speak right into her ear or she can't hear."

This process had an air of intimacy about it and romantic memories had been stirred in Gerald as he spoke into Meg's pretty little ear. His lips came into contact with it. He nibbled on its lobe. She turned to him with a receptive smile.

"That's enough," Cy told him.

"Now don't get the wrong impression!"

"Quit while you're ahead, Sandeen."

The case against Branwell swiftly became dark indeed. His outburst to Phil was not unique. Everyone within earshot had heard his angry estimate of the man from whom he was buying the business, or thought he was, but the deal was beginning to come apart.

"I warned you to move slowly," Amos Cadbury told his client.

"I didn't think the man was a crook."

"Original sin is everywhere," Amos said softly.

"I'm not surprised someone killed him," Branwell said. His lawyer did not of course directly ask him if that someone was him, but those who knew Amos Cadbury would have noticed that he wore the sad certainty that he was representing a guilty man. Not that he himself would represent him in court. Murder trials were not his forte. But someone in the firm would be at Branwell's side when the increasingly convincing case against him was made by the prosecutor.

Did Branwell look to Edna like the man who had accosted her, tied and gagged her, and locked her in the closet? She hesitated, but then nodded. "He could be."

But then earlier she'd had to admit that Gerald Sandeen was of the build of the man she had struggled with. And indeed Branwell and Sandeen were quite similar physical types.

8

Father Dowling followed the investigation closely and was kept privy to the police investigation by Phil Keegan, who stopped by the rectory on regular social visits.

"Did you hear Smith and Branwell arguing, Roger?"

"I couldn't hear what they said."

"But they were arguing?"

"I hope you don't expect me to testify against Branwell."

"We won't need you, Roger. It's strong enough without you. There are all kinds of witnesses to his wrath."

Branwell had left his office soon after Smith had been there with Father Dowling. The theory was that he had followed the two of them back to St. Hilary's, stalking his tormentor.

"Had anyone seen Branwell in the school?"

"Well, you know what Edna Hospers said."

There were no fingerprints on the globe. The recently waxed floor of the corridor provided no clues. Father Dowling was glad to get away from thoughts of the death of Marvin Smith and the impending ordeal of Joe Branwell and go over to the school to talk with Van Orman the air-conditioning man.

The Van Orman van—this legend was painted on its side— was parked in the lot by the school, and Van Orman himself was in the recreation room, checking the size of the place, getting a sense of the problem from the smoke-wreathed atmosphere.

"Do you think something can be done?" Father Dowling

asked after receiving a firm handshake from Van Orman.

"Oh sure." The man's eyes traveled around the room as he said this, as if he were envisaging ways to clear the room quickly of smoke.

"This will be a kind of memorial to Marvin Smith."

"Marvin Smith!" Van Orman literally jumped.

"You probably read what happened to him."

"Oh, I did a job for him." Van Orman's face clouded, then cleared. "And I think I can solve your problem here too."

"You ventilated his showroom and office wing?"

Van Orman nodded, but his attention was once more on the prospective job.

"How was he to work for?"

Van Orman thought about it and obviously decided to say nothing. He shrugged.

Father Dowling left him to his task. Van Orman would come up with an estimate for the work to clear the recreation room quickly of tobacco smoke. Halfway back to the rectory, the priest stopped. He stood for a moment looking at the miniature grotto a few yards from the walk, saying a prayer perhaps. When he returned to the school, he went to Edna Hospers' office. She wore a scarf around her throat to conceal a bruise. But no one would have suspected the ordeal she had recently been through.

"Edna, can you come with me for a moment?"

"What is it?"

"I'm not sure. I want your advice."

He took her down the corridor and down the flight of steps to the level of the recreation room. He led her quickly across the room to where Van Orman was measuring an expanse of wall. When the man turned, Edna gasped and stepped back. Van Orman's expression was eloquent. He looked as if he wanted to spring at Edna, but her instinctive step backward made Father Dowling a target of opportunity. The air conditioner man grabbed Father Dowling by the arm and began to hurry him toward the door of the room. He might have made it, too, if Gerald Sandeen hadn't sprung into action. In a quince, Van Orman was subdued, with Sandeen's knee pressed firmly into the small of his back.

"Should I tie him up, Father?"

"I don't think that will be necessary, Gerald. Edna, would you call Phil Keegan?"

9

The war that had been waged between Van Orman and Smith over the work Van Orman had done at Smith Tires was remembered by many. The Van Orman van had been seen near the St. Hilary school on the day Smith was killed. The man had come to gather information for the bid he intended to make and once inside the school he had spotted Smith and all the latent rage of months boiled to the surface. He decided to act at last. His chance came when Smith went off to the library at the end of the day. Van Orman followed him and did the foul deed. It was his luck to run into Edna when he left the scene of his dreadful crime.

"I didn't even feel good about it," he said to Father Dowling. "Before I had a chance to take any satisfaction in killing that bastard, I ran into the woman."

"Revenge is mine, says the Lord."

"He can have it," Van Orman said morosely. He had taken up smoking in jail and had suggested to the sheriff that he ought to do something about the ventilation. "I'd do it for nothing. It would give me something to do."

He wanted to plead guilty, but his lawyer vetoed that.

The purchase of Smith's Tires proceeded without a wrinkle, now that Smith himself was no longer in the picture. Father Dowling was reading in his study when Marie came to tell him someone wished to see him. She was wearing one of her expressions.

"Send him in."

"Them. I put them in the front parlor."

Father Dowling went to see his callers. It was Gerald Sandeen and Meg Sullivan.

"We want to get married," Gerald said.

And so the arrangements were made. Marie seemed as delighted as Meg.

"I'm surprised she heard the question," Father Dowling said.

"There are many ways to ask a question."

"Ah."

The question Father Dowling did not want to hear when he asked Meg if she took Gerald for her husband.

THE LOTTERY OF LIFE

1

Summer in the Fox River Valley is not a season for all men—
taking the term generically so as to include Marie Murkin, the
housekeeper of St. Hilary's rectory in the little town west of
Chicago that takes its name from the river. The waterways of
the nation were once the principal avenues of commerce and
they became punctuated with settlements that originally took
their *raison d'etre* from their proximity to the rivers. Some
became great cities served by railways and roads which, if they
did not eclipse the role of rivers, made them secondary to these
swifter and more supple means of communication.

Smaller communities like Fox River, Illinois, retained the
centrality of the waterways that had given them birth but that,
with the passage of time and what was generally accounted
progress, altered to become mere scenic attractions. Bridges
spanned the rivers and dams made passage up and down them
difficult but controlled flooding. Eventually, the banks were
lined with summer residences. Picturesque little boats whose
paddle wheels were less functional than ornamental went up-
and downstream filled with sightseers and tourists. The *River
Queen* was such a craft. It offered excursions north to one dam
then downstream again to the dock, where passengers disem-
barked to eat and revel and then get into their cars and return
whence they had come. Smaller boats carried sportsmen to
coves and inlets where fish were to be found. And there were

other boats whose principal point was the noise and speed with which, creating great chevrons in their wakes, they roared up and down between the cottages and wooded banks to the equivocal reaction of those in search of peace and quiet.

Marie Murkin's ears were keen enough to hear the racket of the river craft, which, for her at least, was never drowned out by the interstates that triangulated the town, let alone the chirp of birds and the lazy drone of bees and other insects in the flower beds around the rectory.

"There ought to be a law," the housekeeper said one Sunday afternoon when she was returning from the church to the rectory with Father Dowling.

"Laws are oughts in themselves," the pastor replied. "Or ought-nots."

"Can you imagine what it must be like living right on the river?"

Only then did the priest realize that Marie referred to the all-but-inaudible noise of motor boats on the Fox River.

"Ah well," he said with the philosophical air of one unbothered by the far-off noise.

But it was the summer season as a whole that was the cause of Marie's discontent. The midwestern heat was her chief motive for wanting to avoid the possible pains of the next world. Father Dowling had an air conditioner installed in a window of her quarters and its incessant hum had come to symbolize the summer for him far more than the pleasure boats on the Fox River. As the temperature rose in the outer world, it fell in the housekeeper's apartment, where she sat sweatered and sniffling, shielded from external annoyances by her own drafty and clacketing air conditioner. Since the rest of the rectory was cooled only by electric fans, it was Marie's practice to spend more time than usual in her chilly quarters.

"No need to help count the collection today, Marie."

"Nonsense. Of course I'll help."

And so, half an hour later, the table cleared of the luncheon dishes, Father Dowling and Marie sat down to sort and record the Sunday offerings that would be taken to the bank the following day. There was a machine to count the coins, whose racket did not seem to bother the housekeeper. Bills were bundled into different denominations and checks put into a separate pile. When the coins were accounted for, they settled down to open the envelopes and extract the currency and checks. Although the amount was written on the envelope, Marie never recorded a contribution until she had compared the contents of an envelope with that stated amount.

"Look at this," she cried.

She had opened an envelope and taken from it a colorful piece of pasteboard.

"What is it?"

"A lottery ticket." She frowned at it. "At least it's for next Wednesday's drawing."

From time to time, surprising items showed up in the collection, but this was the first time a worshiper had slipped a lottery ticket into one of the envelopes to be found in the pews.

"Who put it in?"

"Oh, there's nothing on the envelope."

"Perhaps it's the winning ticket."

"Oh, sure."

"You keep it."

She put it into her apron pocket and they went on with their work. Soon Father Dowling had settled down in his study, Marie had gone to her apartment, which was reached by a stairway in her kitchen, and a summer peace descended over the rectory. The whirr of Marie's air conditioner accentuated rather than disturbed the tranquility.

The languid summer Sunday mood extended into the week that followed. On Monday, the former parish school that had become a center for seniors attracted its usual contingent. Edna Hospers, who was in charge of the center, presided like a housemother over the games of bridge, the fierce rivalry at shuffleboard and darts, and the many conversations devoted to memories of more active days. Father Dowling said his weekday Mass at noon and attended to the undemanding business of the parish. There were times when he felt almost guilty about his uneventful life, but this week was not one of them. There were not many Chicago priests who envied him his assignment in a parish they considered moribund, a lonely outpost of one of the most populous archdioceses in Christendom, but for Father Dowling it was a welcome port to have come to in a sometimes stormy clerical career.

2

On Tuesday, a newcomer to the senior center, Ronald Phillips, stood athwart the walkway as Father Dowling was on his way to look in on Edna and her wards. Phillips' outfit made no concessions to the temperature, which had risen into the eighties. He wore a dress shirt and florid tie beneath his tweed coat; the crease in his tan trousers was sharp; his loafers were polished to a high sheen. He pulled out his watch and touched its stem, causing its lid to pop open. He looked from the timepiece to the priest.

"I could set my watch by you, Father Dowling."

"How so?"

"Two-ten. You always visit the center at this time."

"Am I that predictable?"

"Don't apologize. A man must have a schedule. It does not do to fritter away the day aimlessly."

To someone else Father Dowling might have mentioned Emmanuel Kant, of whom the citizens of Konigsberg had said what Phillips had just said to him. But Phillips had been a dispatcher for a trucking firm and was unlikely to find a reference to the German philosopher apropos.

"What is your own schedule like?"

Phillips told him in detail. He rose at five-thirty, he exercised according to a system that had once known a great vogue, he breakfasted for exactly twenty minutes and only afterward devoted an hour to the local paper. Then he came to the senior center.

"I am glad you find it attractive."

"My options are few," said Mr. Phillips equivocally.

"Do you play cards?"

"One game of solitaire before retiring."

"And Mrs. Phillips?" He was sorry he had asked the question when Phillips' frowning face became a tragic mask.

"I lost Hilda last March," he said slowly. "That's when I gave up the apartment in the city and turned our river cottage into my permanent home."

"That must be pleasant."

"I hope it will become so. Hilda always enjoyed it."

Portrait of a lonely widower? Father Dowling's heart went out to the elderly gentleman. He suggested that they walk to the center together. He would discreetly ask Edna to make sure that Phillips kept occupied. But when he had left Phillips kibitzing at a bridge table, where four women studied their cards like fortune-tellers, to mention him to Edna, she sighed.

"He is finding retirement difficult."

"Let us hope he will make friends."

He was almost surprised, given Phillips' reference to Hilda, but loneliness had turned more than one parish senior into a swain again.

"Florence Sparrow, to be specific."

Florence was one of the most popular frequenters of the parish center. Other women sought her out as a partner in bridge; her sweet disposition and somehow still-girlish manner made her a magnet to the men, not all of them widowers. But she had spent her long life as the target of attention and managed it with finesse and grace.

"He could do worse."

"Not if his hopes are high."

When Father Dowling passed through the game room, Phillips hailed him again.

"I am not registered in the parish."

"Would you like to be?"

"Of course. I am a permanent resident now." His gaze drifted in the direction of Florence Sparrow, whose trilling laughter had caught his attention.

"Have you met everyone?"

"I intend to learn bridge."

How much time would he allot to cards in his scheduled life?

Phillips returned to the rectory with him and Father Dowling duly registered him as a parishioner.

"I will want a supply of collection envelopes."

"Good."

"My income is fixed now, of course, but I want to pay my way."

"Don't think that you must contribute."

Phillips sat upright in his chair. "I intend to be an active parishioner."

Marie looked into the study and Father Dowling introduced him to the housekeeper.

"Our most eligible widow," he said and Marie harumphed. "Mr. Phillips lost his wife in March."

"I'm sorry to hear that."

"What are your duties?" Phillips asked her.

"Why don't you show Mr. Phillips around, Marie," the priest suggested.

She took him off to her kitchen, where he remained for forty-five minutes, accepting a cup of coffee and eyeing a chocolate cake until Marie gave him a slice.

"He wolfed it down. I wonder if he is eating sensibly!" Marie regarded all males, clerical or lay, as helpless boys who needed a firm feminine hand to keep them from going to seed. This did not seem a proximate danger to the scheduled Mr. Phillips, but Father Dowling was glad that Marie seemed willing to take him under her wing. The result was that he spent afternoons from three o'clock to three-forty-five in her kitchen.

"I won't say that he is a pest, Father. But he is regular."

"You will be pleased to know that you are preferred to Florence Sparrow!"

"Lucky me." But she did not seem to find the remark unwelcome.

3

Before the week was out, Phillips had signed up as usher; he had offered his automobile as transportation for those wishing to go to the mall; he hovered in a supervisory manner over Waldo when he did his work around the parish grounds; he picked up bridge with surprising ease and became the preferred partner of Florence Sparrow; and he continued his afternoon visits to Marie's kitchen, where he was fed by the suddenly maternal housekeeper.

"He has made the friend of his choice," Edna observed as they watched Phillips playing bridge with the concentration favored by Florence.

"He has made another in Marie."

"The other men are jealous," Edna said, and added, "because

of Florence."

"All the other men?"

"Particularly Henry Shea."

Henry was an old bachelor who had belatedly found in retirement the charms of feminine company, and he and Florence had been, in Edna's phrase, an item. But all that seemed ended now. When he was not sitting across the bridge table from Florence, Phillips enthroned her in the passenger seat of his car when he drove shoppers to the mall. There, they wandered the wide aisles and sat by the fountain. Then Phillips gathered up the shoppers and returned them to the parish center. It was on one such occasion that Phillips offered Florence a lottery ticket as another might have offered her flowers or candy and she showed it off with delight on their return.

"The last of the big spenders," Henry growled at Father Dowling's elbow. "You'd think he had handed her a fortune."

It was a turning point. Henry decided to contest his rival for Florence's attention. The two men were overheard exchanging sharp words. Or rather, Henry spoke sharp words and Phillips responded with the haughty confidence of one whose star was in the ascendancy.

"They're like boys," Edna commented, which seemed unfair to the manner in which Phillips handled the poor loser.

"He must be the one who put the lottery ticket in the collection," Marie remarked.

"Did you win?"

"How would I know?"

On Friday, Edna called to ask the pastor to come to the center at once. He hurried down the walk to the school and came into the game room to find everyone encircling Henry and Phillips. The ostensible cause of the dispute was Phillips coming too far forward on the shuffleboard squares when he pushed his marker with gusto, sending Henry's marker flying off a significant square. The two men were armed with shuffleboard cues as they faced one another.

"You don't understand the game!" Henry cried, flourishing his cue.

Whereupon Phillips lifted his and took up the stance of a swordsman. Challenged, Henry began to circle his rival. Suddenly with a deft motion, Phillips sent Henry's cue flying. The disarmed Henry then rushed at him, his fisted hands coming down like pistons on Phillips' chest. Screams, cheers, pandemonium. Father Dowling managed to separate the two men, which he did without any suggestion that something unusual was happening. He stooped and picked up Henry's cue.

"Let's play shuffleboard."

Henry, still fuming, saw in the invitation an honorable way out. "All right. At least you know the rules."

Father Dowling had never been particularly good at shuffleboard and he made certain that his game did not improve on this occasion. A triumphant Henry, unlucky in love and war, but still king of the hill in shuffleboard, rejoined the other men with his chin up and was warmly welcomed back. Although he had been bested, it looked as if Henry had acted as the paladin of all the males at the center except Phillips.

4

Some days later Edna called the rectory to tell Father Dowling of the wonderful idea that Mr. Phillips had come up with.

"An excursion on the river, taking the *River Queen* up to the dam and then back again for dinner at The Wharf."

"Wouldn't that be too expensive for some?"

"Mr. Phillips says he will foot the bill!"

"Good Lord. How much will it be?"

"He just said not to worry; he'd take care of it."

"Well, I suppose we shouldn't look a gift horse in the mouth."

"Another thing. He doesn't want it known that he is paying for it."

"Well, well."

The announcement met with great enthusiasm from the seniors and a date was decided on that would be most convenient for all. Phillips had arranged for a chartered bus to take them to the dock where they would board the *River Queen*, and it was a festive group, colorfully and informally clothed for the occasion. Florence Sparrow was a vision in a billowing light blue dress, long billed yachting cap, and great round sunglasses that gave her even more the look of an ingénue. A few women had incurred Marie's lifted eyebrows by wearing slacks that emphasized that their center of gravity had descended. The men in slacks and summer shirts, deck shoes, and a wide variety of headgear, milled around the women like peacocks. Father Dowling noticed that Phillips sought to lose himself in the crowd. No one would have guessed that he was their benefactor for this occasion.

On board, the men inspected the little ship, going up and down from deck to deck before deciding where they would settle. The woman came aboard in a cloud of laughter and perfume and settled where they might. Florence Sparrow went above, where from seats along the side one had an untrammeled view of the shore. Many men followed her up, including Phillips, but unlike on most recent occasions he made no effort to sit beside her. A somewhat-astounded Henry Shea found himself seated next to Florence.

"What a wonderful idea," she cried.

"Ever been on one of these?"

"No! Isn't that awful? All my life I've said that one day I would and yet I never did and now here we all are."

Henry sought to inform her of the nautical niceties of the craft and of the route they would be taking, but she merely smiled mindlessly at him.

"You've been on this excursion before?" she asked.

Henry hesitated, perhaps wanting to lie, then admitted that he too was on his first excursion on the *River Queen*. Just so there are natives of Manhattan who have never been to the top of the Empire State Building.

All were aboard, the gangplank was taken away, the whistle blew, and the paddle wheel began slowly to move, but it was the propellers beneath it that gave movement to the *River Queen*. There was great squealing and nervous laughter as the gap between the boat and the dock widened, but soon they were headed upriver and the passengers had front-row seats to observe the banks from the river's point of view.

It would be difficult to decide whether the excursion was more diverting for those on the *River Queen* than for those who lived along the Fox River and came out on decks and porches or into their front yards to wave at the passing seniors. American flags snapped proudly from poles in front lawns, kids ran along the bank for a while, as if they meant to accompany the *River Queen* to her ultimate destination, and dogs barked. On deck, the happy excursioners waved back and from time to time the captain would pull the whistle chain to salute those on shore. Some kids came out onto docks that jutted into the river for a closer look.

"Look at that," Edna said, pointing to one of the docks. A sign bearing the legend "The Phillips" was prominent on it.

"He makes his home here," Father Dowling said, remembering his first conversation with Ronald Phillips.

"Why does he bother to come into the center? If I had a place like that . . ."

It was one of the more attractive homes along the river and certainly did not have the look of a temporary summer residence. Great oaks sheltered it and there was a large flagged patio on one side of the house.

Edna murmured, "No wonder he can afford to pay for this excursion." But she quickly added, "Not that I'm ungrateful,"

On the upper deck, Henry Shea ceded the seat beside Florence Sparrow to one of his friends and decided to explore the lower deck. There he found Ronald Phillips, gripping the railing and looking downstream. Time had passed since his altercation with Phillips and his easy triumph with Florence on the upper deck had mellowed Henry Shea.

"How'd you like to live in one of those places?" Henry asked expansively.

Phillips looked at him and spoke softly.

"What?" Henry asked, cupping his ear.

"I said I do."

Henry stepped back, his face clouded with anger. He was sure that Phillips was ridiculing him. Phillips turned away and looked downstream as he had been doing. This apparent snub, ignited Henry's short fuse and he started away, bumping against Phillips, perhaps deliberately, and lost his balance. He reeled down the deck, stumbled, fell, and then, incredibly, rolled under the lowest railing and into the chill waters of the river.

"Man overboard!" Phillips cried, even as he was freeing a lifesaver from its perch. With a single motion he sent the lifesaver sailing through the air. It slapped into the water, just behind Henry, and almost accidentally one of his churning arms slipped through it. Then he was hugging it to him desperately and Ronald Phillips was reeling him in. Two members of the crew beat the crowd to the scene and Phillips stepped back as they brought the drenched and dumbfounded Henry Shea aboard. Henry had lost his glasses and the world had consequently lost its sharpness. The punch he threw at one of his rescuers was meant for Ronald Phillips.

Henry was taken below to be dried off and thus was spared

the scene on deck where the fast thinking of Ronald Phillips was universally applauded. Florence Sparrow swept off her long billed cap and stood on tiptoes to kiss the hero, but Phillips offered her only his check. This was greeted with playful jeers and Florence tried again, but an almost-flustered Ronald Phillips declined the ultimate accolade.

At the dam, the *River Queen* made a wide and graceful turn and started downstream. A glowering Henry Shea had tried unsuccessfully to convince others that Phillips had tripped him and more or less threw him overboard. But with both Phillips and Henry out of the running, the seat next to Florence was occupied by a succession of males who now considered Henry a vanquished rival.

As they neared home port and the restaurant where they would dine, Father Dowling joined Ronald Phillips on the upper deck. As they stood there in silence, the riverside home with "The Phillips" on its dock came into view. On the patio stood a thin elderly woman in a dark dress; her silver-gray hair was pulled into a bun behind her head. She stared vacantly at the passing boat, until another woman came out of the house, took her arm, and led her back inside. Phillips said nothing.

5

Father Dowling pondered what had happened on the excursion, particularly the glimpse of the wraithlike woman who had appeared on the patio of the Phillips riverside home. He had no doubt that Phillips had described himself as a widower, a man who had lost his wife in March and then decided to move out of the city and live permanently in what had hitherto been the summer home on the banks of the Fox River. But he had not said he lived alone, and of course there were many possible explanations of the frail gray-haired woman who looked as if she had wandered out of a Brontë novel . . . It could be a sister, a relative of some sort . . . There was no reason to think that Phillips had deceived him.

Marie wanted to hear all about the excursion and got a big kick out of the episode of Henry Shea tumbling into the river.

"And Ronald Phillips rescued him!"

"That might have been more humiliating than falling in."

Father Dowling had not told Marie that Phillips had sponsored the river excursion and the dinner afterward. But she did notice that in the days immediately following the excursion Phillips did not make his regular afternoon call to her kitchen.

"I wonder if he's ill, Father?"

But a call to Edna disproved that.

"Playing bridge?"

"No." Edna was unusually brief. Then she whispered, "He's helping me here today."

This seemed to be the new pattern of Ronald Phillips' involvement in the St. Hilary senior center. He concentrated on being chauffeur, on helping Edna with her accounts, on giving a hand to Waldo in the flower beds. Phillips had taken to dressing much less formally than he had when he first started coming to the center. Now that he had apparently lost interest in Florence Sparrow he was accepted by the other men, but he had less time for them because of volunteering for so many things.

"Ronald Phillips is in your study," Marie whispered one afternoon three days after the river excursion. Father Dowling found his visitor dressed as he had been at the first: shirt and tie, unseasonal jacket, highly polished shoes. He rose when Father Dowling came in, and when he sat, carefully lifted one creased trouser leg over the other.

"I suppose you have been waiting for me to come to you, Father."

"Well, I'm happy to see you, of course."

Phillips gave a little shake of his head, a pitcher rejecting the catcher's signal. "I should have told you then and there."

"I'm not sure I follow you."

"When we stood at the rail of the *River Queen* as it passed my place and you saw her standing on the patio."

"The tall thin woman with silver hair."

"Hilda."

"Your wife?"

Phillips' head went down and he studied the floor before snapping to attention and looking Father Dowling in the eye. "I misrepresented myself."

"I thought you had said you'd lost your wife."

"Oh, that was true. The decline was gradual but in March it became definitive. She no longer even knows who I am." His voice quavered but did not break.

"Alzheimer's?"

"Yes. I foolishly thought that moving out here permanently would matter, that a place she had so loved would . . ." He shook his head angrily. "Of course it didn't."

He wanted to talk about it, and the pastor wanted to hear. Hilda was gentle and usually silent, drifting ghostlike through the riverside home without any indication that she recognized anything in it. Mrs. Solomon and other nurses provided round-the-clock care.

"I didn't realize how much I missed having her to talk with. Talking with a woman, with one's wife . . ." He had thought to regain something of that with the women at the center. But he had found them superficial. "Mrs. Murkin of course is quite another matter."

"Indeed she is."

"When I told you I had lost my wife, I saw how you understood it, and I decided to leave it like that."

"Thank God you have the means to provide for her as you do."

Ronald Phillips fell back in his chair. "That is the most ironic thing of all."

"How so?"

"Hilda had a weakness for the lottery. For years she bought tickets to no avail. Last February, when she was declining so swiftly, I tried to stop it with a lottery ticket. I took her out and we bought one and I imagined that she was excited about the prospects but it was only imagination. When the drawing was made she had no idea what was happening."

"And you won?"

"A huge amount. That is what enabled me to retire."

"And pay for the river excursion."

"Father, I would give it all back if Hilda . . ." Tears welled in his eyes.

6

"Did he go?" Marie asked, peeking into the study.

"Yes."

"I thought he might stop by the kitchen."

"He says you're the only woman around here he can talk to."

"Oh, pooh."

Some days later Ronald Phillips took Father Dowling out to meet his wife, and the priest and Hilda enjoyed a silent visit in a pleasant room filled with dozens of plants. The serenity of her eyes, the mystery of a person seemingly unmoored in her own past, finding the world around her as novel as the first day of creation, was food for thought. Mrs. Solomon was grateful for a little time away from her ward so Father Dowling read his office and then said the rosary, aloud. Hilda listened but without comprehension. How tempting it must be to imagine a response, to think that once more the past is at the service of the present. He blessed her when he left, and she sat immobile through it, but then she was usually immobile.

Marie too visited Mrs. Phillips, but not regularly, she found it simply too difficult; but now Phillips could talk about Hilda with both the pastor and the housekeeper and that seemed to help.

"Let me ask you something," Marie said one day to Phillips. "Did you ever put a lottery ticket in the collection?"

He actually blushed. He said he had thought again that a lottery ticket might awake memories in Hilda and when it hadn't he had impulsively put it into an envelope and dropped it in the basket.

"My luck had run out," he said in an odd voice. But when Marie said she had no idea what numbers had won on the day of the drawing, he had her fetch the ticket and then called up the state lottery information number. Minutes later, Marie ran into the study with the expression Madame Curie had worn when she discovered radium.

"I won! I won! The ticket is good."

Ronald Phillips had followed her into the study and his expression suggested caution.

"How much has Marie won?" asked Father Dowling.

Phillips cleared his throat. "Ten dollars."

Marie looked as if she had been struck. She sank into a chair.

"That will have to go into the collection, Marie."

The housekeeper stared at the pastor, but years of discipline and experience with the clergy enabled her not to say what a lesser person might have said when thus provoked.

Ex Libris

1

Three days after her husband's funeral, Mabel Leahy came by the rectory to see Father Dowling. Mrs. Murkin wore one of her expressions when she brought this message to the pastor's study. Perhaps she thought that the new widow would become too frequent a visitor.

"Of course I'll see her."

Marie went off, and when she had brought Mrs. Leahy she stood in the doorway as the visitor settled comfortably into a chair. The housekeeper's eyebrows lifted another notch before she went off to her kitchen.

"What a lovely room, Father," Mrs. Leahy said, looking about.

"I hope the smell of tobacco doesn't bother you."

"Oh, poof. Walt smoked like a chimney." She looked directly at Father Dowling. "And that wasn't what killed him either."

Walter Leahy had been bitten by ticks at his lake place and had never fully recovered from the effects of Lyme disease.

"It's the books that make the room," Mabel said.

"They represent a lifetime of collecting."

"That's what I came to talk about."

Walter, it seemed, had loved books and had amassed quite a collection. Mabel was planning to move out of the house and into an apartment. "I can't possibly take the books with me."

"How many are there?"

"Ten thousand?"

"Good heavens."

"Walter had them all catalogued. And everything is in order." Her voice wavered and drifted away. She bit her lip and gained control of herself.

"My books are in completely random order."

"Father, I would like to give Walter's books to the parish."

Although she had come right to the point, it was clear that Mabel Leahy's decision was a major one. Selling the house and moving to an apartment was another, and connected, major decision. The occasion clearly called for a leisurely examination of all aspects of this generous offer.

"It will be like moving out of a library," Mabel said, with a wistful smile. "Every room has books in it. Walter had shelves built everywhere. If he liked a book he wanted to own it."

"Was he a professor?"

"Oh, no. A financial advisor. But we ourselves were his only clients for years now. He did lecture from time to time at the local campus, about book collecting." She frowned. "Book dealers are already contacting me, but I don't want to have Walter's books dispersed all over creation. I want them kept together."

Eventually, they walked over to the school that had been transformed into a senior center and consulted Edna Hospers, the director. There were rooms on the first floor of the building, former classrooms, that could become a parish library.

"Of course I will donate the shelving, too. I can't imagine anyone wanting to buy a house with that many bookshelves in it."

Later that day, Amos Cadbury, the patrician lawyer, was brought into the discussion.

"Of course I knew Walter," Amos said. Father Dowling recalled that the lawyer had been in the church during the funeral Mass for Walter Leahy. "I'm surprised he didn't make provisions for his collection."

221

"He thought he would get well," Mabel said with anguish. "I thought he would get well. Imagine, being bitten by a tick . . ."

They observed a moment of silence at this reminder of the contingency and seeming absurdity of life.

"I can draw up a document of transfer," Amos suggested.

"Yes," Mabel agreed. "I want it to be very official." She glanced at Father Dowling. "You have no idea what pests book dealers can be."

"They've called you already?" Amos asked, a little shocked.

"Roderick Liberati has been to the house twice. The second time I pretended to be out and didn't answer the door."

"Are the books that valuable?" Edna asked.

"All books interest dealers," Mabel said.

They made a little ceremony of the transfer, meeting in Amos Cadbury's office and signing the document he had prepared. Mabel, as if aware of the solemnity of the event, hesitated before signing.

"I hope Walter understands," she said. It seemed best to let the remark go uncommented upon.

2

Marie Murkin kept informed of the remodeling of the class-rooms to accommodate the parish library that had arrived in one fell swoop thanks to the generosity of Mabel Leahy. The books had been carefully crated and shipped to the school and were stacked in the lower corridor awaiting the installation of the shelving, which was next brought from the Leahy home.

"The rooms all look so large now," Mabel said "I couldn't live there with the books and I certainly couldn't live there without them."

Mabel came by the school after the shelves and books had been installed, transforming two erstwhile classrooms into a most impressive parish library. "They look so different here."

That fact made it easier for her to bid them farewell. Edna walked out to Mabel's car while Father Dowling made an inspection of the parish's new acquisition.

Parish libraries were not rare, but it was doubtful that any such collection as this had ever graced the shelves of a parochial school. Walter Leahy had been catholic in his interests, but the history and literature sections were the heart of the collection. Father Dowling took out what proved to be a first edition of F. Marion Crawford's first novel. Suddenly it dawned on him that many of the books on the shelves were not merely copies of important books, but rare editions. This troubled him enough to consult Amos Cadbury.

"Does she realize the value of these books, Amos?"

"She could hardly be unaware of it. She managed the business side of the collection for her husband."

The correspondence of the late Walter Leahy was part of the gift, seven metal file cabinets containing the records of purchases, bids, and searches that lay behind the magnificent collection. These file cabinets were stored in a dry empty room in the basement of the school.

Father Dowling found himself drawn back to the school again and again to admire the books in the new parish library. The seniors who frequented the parish center had come to inspect the new gift but by and large they merely marveled at the number of volumes and then returned to bridge and shuffleboard and television in the gym. Maurice Patrick was an exception. He stood in the middle of the room, eyes closed, breathing through his nose.

"There is nothing like the aroma of seasoned books," he declared, opening his eyes.

"Does it bring back your working days?" Patrick had been head librarian at one of the branches of the public library.

"Not at all. Our emphasis was on turnover. As soon as a

book was no longer in demand, we got rid of it. We were not repositories of learning, but transmitters of the evanescent."

He pronounced this last phrase carefully, as if it were one he had devised to describe his daily work. Father Dowling murmured appreciatively.

"Who will be librarian?" Maurice asked.

Now that Father Dowling had a better sense of the value of the collection Mabel had given the parish, the thought of it simply being here, accessible to all and sundry, made him nervous.

"I will need a volunteer," Father Dowling said. "I couldn't afford a salary."

Maurice Patrick had raised his hand when Father Dowling said "volunteer."

"Salary! Father, I'd pay for the privilege of looking after these magnificent books."

And so it was arranged. When he informed Edna, she breathed a sigh of gratitude, but Marie Murkin's reaction was guarded. Her expression suggested a classic question: *quis custodit custodes?* Who will keep an eye on the watchman? But Marie's reaction brought home to Father Dowling the responsibility he had taken on in accepting so valuable a gift. With possession comes the fear of loss—of moth and rust and thief. These uneasy thoughts were reinforced a few days later when Roderick Liberati stepped into the sacristy after Father Dowling's noon Mass.

3

Liberati was olive-skinned, silver-haired, slightly stooped, and nearsighted, but there was the deference of a long-practicing Catholic in his manner. He spoke in a whisper; after all, the sacristy was in the church, and this made it difficult for Father Dowling to hear him.

"Why don't we talk over lunch in the rectory?"

"Oh, I don't wish to impose on you."

"You won't be. We will both be imposing on Mrs. Murkin."

If Marie had been wary of Maurice Patrick, whom she knew, she was immediately and obviously taken by Roderick Liberati. When Father Dowling introduced Marie, Liberati was all attention. He asked how long she had been the housekeeper, he made a reference to the Franciscans of long ago who had preceded Father Dowling with just a suggestion of condescension, he apologized for burdening her. Marie all but giggled. If Liberati threw a ladder up to her window that night he could have stolen her away forever. At table, she served the guest first, which was a first for her. By then the pastor and guest were deep in conversation, Father Dowling having matched his guest with the book dealer Mabel Leahy said had sought to buy her late husband's collection. Father Dowling was intrigued by the motto on the book dealer's card: *Laqueus contritus est et liberati sumus.* Ps. 123.

"That is the old version, of course," Liberati said, as if anticipating the pastor's objection. "The new Vulgate has: *Laqueus contritus est, et nos erepti sumus.* I do not plan to change my name to Erepti."

Such erudition set the tone of the conversation, and Father Dowling took Liberati into his study after lunch—somewhat to Marie's dismay; she had been more in the dining room than out of it during lunch—because he was loath to end the conversation. He was almost surprised when Liberati mentioned his reason for coming by. The conversation had seemed reason enough.

"I congratulate you on the magnificent gift you have received from Mrs. Leahy."

"We must go over and look at the books. Everything is installed now."

"I would like that." But he remained settled in his chair. His expression was one of concern. "You do realize the value of the collection?"

"In the used book market?"

"Rare book market, Father. More than half the books Leahy owned were true collector's items. Estimates vary in such cases, but I would put the average value at between three hundred and five hundred dollars. Round it off at four hundred."

If half the books could command such sums, that meant that five thousand times four hundred . . . Father Dowling could not continue the figuring.

"It doesn't matter. I accepted the books as a gift to the parish as a library for the parishioners."

"People will just browse around?"

"Yes."

"And take things home?"

Father Dowling smiled. "I can't expect people to read entire books on the premises."

Liberati's complexion was now ashen. He lay back in his chair and his breathing was audible.

"I do have a librarian," Father Dowling said, to reassure the dealer.

"Ah."

"Maurice Patrick."

"Oh my God!"

"Do you know him?"

"The question, Father, is do you know him?"

Liberati refused to explain his reaction, and when they walked over to the school—where Patrick was showing him around what was now the St. Hilary's parish library—there was nothing in Liberati's manner to suggest his reaction in the rectory to Patrick's name.

4

Cy Horvath called back with the information Father Dowling had requested of Captain Phil Keegan.

"He learned his trade in Joliet," Cy said. "He worked in the library there and when he got out earned a degree and became a librarian."

"What was he in for?"

"Why don't I fax it to you?"

"I don't have a fax machine."

"I'll drop it off."

He left the papers with Marie, who brought them to the pastor when he returned from a visit to the hospital. Marie's expression made it clear that she had read the papers already. No wonder she looked smug.

Maurice Patrick had been involved in the theft of rare books from the collections of several midwestern universities. It was when his cohort offered Liberati a facsimile of Petrarch's commentaries on Dante that the ring had been broken. Maurice ended up in Joliet and metamorphosed into a librarian. By agreeing to be the St. Hilary librarian, he might have been inserting himself into a proximate occasion of sin. But apparently there had been no repetition of the crime that had sent him to prison. Of course there were no rare books in the branch library Patrick had administered. But now Father Dowling had set him down in the midst of tantalizing treasures.

Marie was very peripatetic that afternoon, going by the door of the study again and again, humming an enigmatic tune. Father Dowling fled to the school and, lest he seemed to be checking up on Maurice Patrick, stopped by Edna Hospers' office. When he asked her what was new she told him of the difficulties being created by Richard Fleischaecker's infatuation with Amy Meehan. Amy's husband, Fred, was not amused. Richard had been spiriting Amy away to the library, where they whispered over a large green book of Chesterton, *The Father Brown Omnibus.*

"Both of them read just that edition when they were kids."

"They're great stories."

"It's just an excuse. I think it was Amy who read that edition and Richard just pretends that he did!"

"How old are they?"

"The dangerous age. Seventy-nine."

"Good Lord."

"Oh, it's harmless enough, I suppose."

"How is the library going?"

Edna shrugged. "Fine."

"I just learned that Maurice Patrick spent time in Joliet!"

Edna bristled. Her husband was in Joliet and unlikely to emerge before they were both beyond what she had called "the dangerous age." "I didn't know that."

"Of course not!" Desperately he tried to change the subject back to the septuagenarian triangle, but Edna could not easily slough off the reminder of her imprisoned husband. After some minutes, Father Dowling found a note on which to rise and go. Any effort to solace Edna would only make matters worse. He was in a pensive mood when he had descended to the first floor and then decided to look in at the library.

Maurice Patrick was not in evidence behind his desk and Father Dowling went to the history shelves. Two days before, when he and Patrick were discussing how the library would work, Maurice drew his attention to the first editions of Francis Parkman. Patrick had taken *The Oregon Trail* from the shelf and Father Dowling had expressed his delight in the book.

"Have you read it, Father?"

"I intend to read it again as soon as I can."

It was for that volume that he had come to the school. With it in hand, he called out Patrick's name, but there was no response. Perhaps the librarian had decided to spend some time with the others in the gym. It was when Father Dowling went to the desk to leave a note indicating he was taking the volume to the rectory that something caught his eye. It seemed to be a shoe. It was. It was on the right foot of Maurice Patrick, who lay facedown in an alcove of shelves, He had tipped over a chair when he fell. Father Dowling knelt beside the fallen librarian and something in the stillness of the body decided him. He gave conditional absolution first, and sought a pulse later. He found none. And then he noticed the blood-matted hair. When he rose to his feet and turned, Edna was in the doorway.

"Father, about earlier—" But then she stopped, her eyes drawn to the body on the floor. "My God."

"Call nine-one-one, Edna."

"Who is it?"

"Maurice Patrick."

"But what happened?"

His expression brought back her usual efficient self. She reached for the phone on Patrick's desk, but Father Dowling stopped her. "Better not use that one."

5

It was perhaps inevitable that Phil Keegan would concentrate on Maurice Patrick's prison record when they talked about the librarian in the rectory after the paramedics and coroner and medical examiner had completed their tasks, the body had been removed, and the library sealed with a uniformed officer guarding the murder scene. Marie didn't help matters when she recalled her own misgivings at the appointment as librarian of a man who had been convicted of trying to steal rare books.

"Marie, the man was attacked. He was struck a terrible blow on the head from which he died. He is the victim, not the perpetrator."

But Marie just looked wise and assumed a smug silence. And then Cy called from Patrick's apartment, where he had gone in search of clues as to what had happened to the librarian.

"There are three very old books here," he reported. "They have the *Ex libris* sticker of Walter Leahy in them."

"Could Cy bring them here?" Father Dowling asked Phil.

"Here is where they belong, isn't it?"

While they waited, Father Dowling dismissed the notion that there was any dark import in the fact that Maurice Patrick had taken home several volumes from the library of which he was custodian. True, they had not yet worked out any provisions for the borrowing of books, but Maurice was the librarian.

"When I discovered the body, I was in the process of leaving a note telling Patrick I was taking a book to the rectory."

"Where is it?"

Father Dowling had to think. "I laid it on the desk."

When Cy arrived, things looked suddenly black for Maurice Patrick's reputation. Not only were there three extremely rare books in his apartment, there were also papers from the file cabinets. They were the records of Leahy's purchase of the volumes.

"With those papers missing, there would be no way to prove these books had been part of the collection, right?"

Father Dowling looked at Phil. It was a rhetorical question, of course. Still, Phil and Cy and Marie waited for him to say something.

"He didn't hit himself over the head."

"That's true."

"Whoever killed him had a motive. What was it?"

"Maybe other books are missing."

That Maurice Patrick had met his death by violence did little to offset the incriminating effect of the three volumes from the collection with the accompanying proof that they were indeed part of the Leahy bequest. But Father Dowling found it impossible to think that Patrick would do such a thing, and so soon after assuming the job of parish librarian. Phil countered that by saying the sooner the better. As time went on, Father Dowling and others would become familiar with the items in the collection and would be more certain to notice the absence of a volume.

Theft seemed the best explanation of what had happened to Patrick, and Father Dowling found it impossible not to think of the charming Roderick Liberati. The book dealer's interest in the Leahy collection was no secret. But then, he just happened to have met Liberati; doubtless there were other dealers just as interested as he. But Mabel Leahy took him aside at the wake, which was held at McDivitt's Funeral Home, and reminded him of Liberati's visits to her soon after her husband's death.

"I think he thought he could shove me around, a new widow and all. But I knew his type."

"He stopped by the rectory."

Mabel looked at him. "I wonder if he didn't stop by the school, too."

Marie overheard Father Dowling passing on to Phil Mabel Leahy's suspicion of Liberati.

"Oh, that's nonsense. He wouldn't hurt a flea!"

The police had been put onto the trail of a stranger who had been hanging around the school in the days before the murder of Maurice Patrick. Edna had noticed him before some of the old people asked who he was. There was evidence that someone had been using the furnace room in the school as an improvised bedroom and the theory grew that some vagrant had done away with Maurice Patrick.

"But why?"

"We can ask him when we find him," Phil said. "If there was any reason."

6

McDivitt, assured that the parish would cover the expenses for its murdered employee, gave Maurice Patrick a tasteful but impressive send-off. There was almost one-hundred-percent attendance at the funeral Mass on the part of the seniors of the parish, and many were transported to the cemetery in the shuttle buses whose normal destination was the shopping mall.

That afternoon, Father Dowling fell asleep over a book in his study and was awakened by Marie's stage whisper.

"Come into the kitchen," she urged someone. This was followed by the sound of muffled footsteps and then the diminishing swish of the kitchen door as it came to a stop. The voices from the kitchen were audible, and after a minute, Father Dowling recognized the voice of Marie's interlocutor. Marie's affected twitterings were answered by the rumblings of Roderick Liberati. Father Dowling decided to wait for Marie to bring the visitor to him. Apparently they had looked in on him and found him asleep.

"I didn't want to disturb your honest slumber," Liberati said when eventually Marie brought him in from the kitchen.

"You have had a very busy day," Marie said, and he did not care for the condescension in her voice. She sounded more like a nurse than a housekeeper. "I'll bring your tea here," she said to Liberati in a somewhat simpering tone. "Father?"

"No, thank you."

Eventually Marie closed the door and Liberati sat forward. "I came to the Mass for Patrick."

"It was a fine turnout."

"I also went to the cemetery."

"How well did you know him?"

"I am afraid my motive was not to mourn him, Father. I wondered if any of his old cohorts would show up."

Liberati meant those with whom Patrick had teamed up to

steal rare books from college libraries. He waited. Something in Liberati's manner suggested triumph.

"Williams was at the Mass and he went out to the cemetery, too, in one of the parish shuttle buses."

"Williams?"

"Bruce Williams. A wiry little fellow, you might not have noticed him."

"He went out to the cemetery in a parish shuttle bus?"

"I wondered if he had begun to frequent the senior center."

It was clear enough what Liberati wondered.

Obligingly, he had brought with him a photograph of Williams. "I thought I would give this to you rather than the police. My hope is that they will have noticed Williams on their own."

"That would take you off the hook."

Liberati thought about it. "That's one way of putting it."

Half an hour later, Father Dowling went over to Edna's office. Without preliminary, he put the photograph of Bruce Williams on her desk.

"Where did you get that?"

"Is that anyone you've seen?"

She picked up the photograph and frowned at it, but he sensed she was merely postponing her identification.

"That's the man who has been hanging around and making the old people nervous."

Bruce Williams was found in the homeless center downtown and ten minutes later was being questioned by the police. Later Cy Horvath passed on the preliminary results to the pastor of St. Hilary's. Williams had been hanging around the school; he had slept on several occasions on a cardboard bed in the furnace room. Since his release from prison, he had been making up for years of enforced abstinence and had developed a severe drinking problem.

"He admits talking with Patrick. Cadging off him."

"For drink?"

"There were bottles in the furnace room." Cy hesitated. "Dr. Pippen says that the blow that killed Patrick could have been made with a liquor bottle."

"A full one?"

"I suppose."

This suggested a sad scenario. Two ex-convicts, one reformed and employed, the other enslaved by alcohol. Patrick might have given Williams money out of a misguided sense of friendship. Had he known that Williams used the furnace room for sleeping quarters?

"Thank God for Roderick Liberati," Marie exclaimed. When the pastor did not take up the anthem of praise, Marie added, "You don't imagine that the police would have found Williams without Mr. Liberati's help, do you?"

"I'll ask Phil Keegan."

"Don't you dare."

Father Dowling told himself that it was merely a general inability to take pleasure in the fall of another, but the truth was he felt a quite special, and perhaps not completely praiseworthy, sadness at what had befallen Bruce Williams. Sobriety returned once he was in custody, and Williams made no ringing claim of innocence. He had no memory of what he was accused of, but neither could he dismiss it as impossible.

7

Bruce Williams was indicted and bound over for trial and the matter seemed settled. As if in search of distraction, Father Dowling returned to the parish library, now locked, for the book he had sought on the day he found the body of Maurice Patrick. But Parkman's *The Oregon Trail* was not to be found. It was not on the shelf where it belonged. If it had been put just anywhere, it would be a long and distracting search before he located it. He found he was not in the mood at the moment. He was sitting at Patrick's desk when the phone rang.

"Cy Horvath is here," Marie said.

"Tell him I'm in the school."

"I did. He's on his way."

Five minutes later, Cy was seated across from Father Dowling. He placed a plastic bag on the desk. In it was a book: Francis Parkman's *The Oregon Trail*.

"It was taken downtown with other things that seemed relevant to what had happened. That was on this desk."

Father Dowling took the book from the plastic bag and held it in his left hand, enjoying the heft of the volume and the texture of its cover. He spread his palm and the book opened. There was an envelope inside. He looked at Cy.

"I told them not to open that. It's addressed to you."

"To me!"

It was, and the hand was that of Maurice Patrick. Inside were two sheets, covered with script. Father Dowling read the letter once and then again.

"I wish you had opened this, Cy."

"What does it say?"

Father Dowling handed the letter to Cy Horvath and for the first time in days felt cheerful.

"Now that I think of it, he must have been sure I would eventually come for that book."

Maurice Patrick had written as if from beyond the grave, his message meant to exonerate him for crimes of which he would be made to look guilty. And it did exonerate him.

"Roderick Liberati!" Marie cried, when the book dealer was taken in for questioning. "Are they mad?"

"The police?"

"Yes."

"I'll ask Phil."

Marie spun on her heel and marched off to her kitchen. It was too much to expect that she would rejoice to see justice done, and she avoided the subject during subsequent weeks when Bruce Williams was released and Roderick Liberati became the prime suspect in the murder of Maurice Patrick. The weapon apparently had been a bottle of liquor Maurice had bought for Williams. A court order to search Liberati's office and home was hard fought by his lawyer, and in the end turned up nothing. It was Mabel Leahy who asked if they had searched Liberati's car. The dealer had a strong box in the trunk of his car in which he had transported particularly precious books. When opened, it contained ten items from the Leahy collection, along with the papers recording their purchase, which had been taken from Walter Leahy's records. The written statement found in Parkman's book related the pressure that Liberati had exerted on Patrick. The librarian had written prior to a visit from Liberati in which the dealer would force the compromised Williams to collude with him in the theft of some of the most valuable items in the Leahy collection.

Liberati remained silent throughout, taking the fifth amendment at preliminary hearings and in the trial itself. But there was no need for him to incriminate himself. The stolen books in his car and the statement of the murdered librarian were almost sufficient for that. But it was one of the bottles found in the furnace room that tipped the scales. On it were Liberati's fingerprints as well as hair and blood of Maurice Patrick.

"Bludgeoned with an empty bottle?"

The only explanation was that Bruce Williams had found the bottle, not seen, or ignored, his fallen friend, and repaired to the furnace room where he emptied the murder weapon.

"I'll never drink again," he said.

This time he meant it. Father Dowling installed Williams in the parish library as successor to Maurice Patrick, much to Marie Murkin's indignation. Edna was silent at first, but finally she accepted Bruce Williams.

"After all, you took me in, Father. I can't forget that."

"It's not the same thing, Edna."

"It certainly isn't," Marie said.

"I might hire Liberati too, Marie—when he gets out."

The housekeeper's hearing was perfect but there were things she seemed not to hear. She sailed off.

LIGHT FOOTED

1

What had once been the St. Hilary's parish school had for some years been used as a center where senior members of the parish could spend their days. The facilities were modest and few diversions beyond shuffleboard, pool, and bridge were available, but it was companionship the old people wanted. The turnover among the clientele was constant, largely due to the impersonal operation of the actuarial table. When debility or illness struck, the old men and women went on to places where care increased as autonomy decreased, and eventually they went to God. Scarcely a week went by when there wasn't a funeral, a good portion for people who had spent more or less time in the parish center. But new arrivals were likewise constant. It had been only a few weeks ago that Peter Scuderi first showed up at the center and stood tentatively in the doorway until Edna Hospers noticed him and went over to welcome him.

"He once lived in Fox River," Edna told Father Dowling later. "Years and years ago, and now he's moved back."

That pastor's eyes rounded. Few people thought of retiring in Fox River unless they were already there. Perhaps Peter Scuderi had come back in pursuit of the locale of fond memories.

Among the old people in the center, only Chet Williams had known Peter when he lived in Fox River, and Chet was one of the youngest frequenters of the center. He had retired early on reduced Social Security, but considered the penalty a small price to pay for no longer working.

"I had three companies leave town," he complained cheerfully. "Three strikes and I'm out. The first one Peter worked for, too."

"What was that?"

"Fox River Pipe."

Peter stood by as Chet told all this to Father Dowling, not adding anything to the story.

"Is that when you left town, Peter?"

"I hadn't heard the company folded."

"Folded. They moved to Mississippi, then to Mexico."

If this was news to Peter Scuderi, he showed no sign of surprise. Or perhaps he simply wasn't interested.

"He acts like he wants to come in," Marie said from the window.

Father Dowling lay a ribbon aslant the page of the breviary he was trying to read. But Marie's curiosity took precedence over all else. Her nosiness was a pastoral virtue, in her estimation, and she often wished aloud that Father Dowling had more of it.

"More nose?"

"Oh!" He turned and went back.

The object of her attention was Peter Scuderi, who to any eyes but Marie's was simply strolling back and forth on the walk between the rectory and center. But the housekeeper had invested his stroll with great significance.

She was certain that his pace slowed as he neared the rectory, that there was a moment of hesitation before he turned and started back.

Eventually Marie returned to her kitchen, allowing Father Dowling to finish reading his office. After he was finished, he settled at his desk to read, but on the edges of his mind he heard the unvoiced rebuke of Marie Murkin. Was she right that

Peter Scuderi wanted to see him? Father Dowling put down his pipe, rose, and went silently down the hall to the front door. No need to tempt Marie to pride at her victory. When he opened the door, Peter Scuderi stood there.

"Father Dowling, could I see . . ."

For an ignoble moment, he thought of stepping outside and talking to Peter somewhere out of Marie's sight. He took a deep breath.

"Do come in, Mr. Scuderi."

2

Edna Hospers had taken the job as director of the St. Hilary's Center half a dozen years ago. It was absorbing and interesting and from time to time amusing, and it did not keep her from her family. As often as not, she ended her day at three and was home before her children returned from school. She was what has come to be called a single mother, but only because her husband was in Joliet prison, unlikely to emerge before the two of them were older than her wards at the center. The tact shown by Father Dowling during the awful days before Gene was convicted and sentenced, and his offer of a job, had won her undying loyalty. She didn't realize at the time that he had created the job then and there. But it had turned out to be an inspiration. There were few young families in the parish, although from time to time a young couple would buy one of the magnificent homes whose value had plunged when the interstates triangulated the parish, making it a little island of peace in a constant roar of background noise.

"Aha," cried a voice behind her. "Caught you goofing off."

Edna turned from the window to face Chet Williams. He came toward her, beaming, and Edna scooted behind her desk. Amorous attachments flared up from time to time among the old people, but Chet was the first senior who seemed to have

Edna in his sights.

"What can I do for you?"

Chet considered the question with a significant expression on his face. Oh, for heaven's sake. Chet dressed as young as he acted: denim trousers, running shoes with little lights in the heels that went on and off as he walked, black turtleneck sweater. His magnificent silver hair was combed into elaborate waves, apparently held in place with spray. And he wore dark glasses inside and out, in dark or sunny weather. If he weren't so obnoxious, his good looks might have made him a threat. He slid into a chair, his legs thrust out before him, hands half plunged into his hip pockets.

"Do you have any aspirin?"

Edna was relieved by the question. His insinuating manner made her feel vulnerable as she had not in years.

"Get a divorce. Everybody here's wife has divorced him. Marry again."

"Gene, we're Catholic."

"Ha. Don't tell me you still buy all that?"

How depressing that he should have lost his faith as well as his freedom. Of course he had stories of the feigned religiosity of inmates, a ploy to be freed from the routine of the prison. Edna had prayed that he would not despair at the prospect of the endless stretch of time before him, but she had never dreamed he would turn against his faith. He had convinced himself that he was not really guilty and was the victim of massive injustice.

"For better or worse, till death do us part," she murmured.

She had meant it at the time and she meant it still. She was not going to spend her life feeling sorry for herself.

She took aspirin from her purse and placed the bottle on the table. "There's a fountain in the hall."

"As a matter of fact, I was looking for old Scuderi."

"That's right," she said. "You knew him before."

"Before." He nodded, then rested his chin on chest. "I think he has gone over to the rectory."

"Sometimes I think he's avoiding me."

"You must be imagining it." But her voice refused to repress the sarcasm she had intended.

To her relief, Chet heaved to his feet to get aspirin, and let out an involuntary groan. He looked at her, as if to see if she had noticed. His step was not spry as he crossed to the desk. He avoided her eyes as he opened the bottle and shook several aspirin into hand. He thanked her and, as he crossed the room, walked like any other old man in the center. No wonder he wore those silly shoes.

"Arthritis?"

"A little headache!" He glared at her, and left.

3

In the study, Father Dowling picked up his pipe and settled behind his desk. Peter Scuderi's eyes traveled around the room, noting the walls lined with books, but he said nothing.

"Do you mind if I smoke?"

"Of course not." Peter watched the priest apply a match to his pipe. "I never smoked, myself."

Scuderi's manner suggested that Marie's hunch had been right. He wanted to talk about something. But clearly it was going to be difficult for him. So they talked about the years Peter had spent in St. Louis.

"I left Fox River after my wife died."

"Did you have children?"

"A boy." Again, hesitation, as if there was a story there, too.

"What does Fox River look like after all these years?"

Peter Scuderi sat forward, as if he had not heard the question. "Father, I want to exhume the body of my wife."

A priest learns never to show surprise at what is said to him in confidence or in the confessional, but Father Dowling had to puff quietly on his pipe for a time to suppress the surprise he felt.

"I see."

"I know it sounds crazy."

"You must have a reason."

"Can it be done?"

"If your reason is important enough . . ."

"I hid something in her casket when she was buried." Now that he had said it, Scuderi fell back in his chair, looking at Father Dowling with a wild look.

"Something?"

"It's hard to explain!"

God knows what Scuderi had buried with his wife and now wanted back. "How long ago was this?"

"Thirty years ago."

Father Dowling puffed on his pipe, nodding, as if this were a perfectly ordinary conversation.

"I want you to bless her grave again. Afterward. Can it be done?"

"The blessing? Of course. Peter, let me look into it." Scuderi was on his feet, enclosing Father Dowling's hands in his. He would have kissed the priest's hand if Father Dowling had not risen. "Let's see what I find out before we start celebrating."

4

Francis McDivitt had cotton-white hair, a pink cherubic face, and eyes that seemed brimming with consolation when he dealt with the bereaved. His sympathy was quite sincere. Time had not dulled the pain he felt when a widow or the children of the departed came to him in their grief. Other undertakers might, more or less consciously, take advantage of the vulnerability of survivors, but McDivitt guarded against this temptation by identifying with the client's suffering. As often as not, he had known the deceased, and it was easy to occupy the role of one who had lost someone dearly beloved.

Colleagues might twit him about the monopoly he had on St. Hilary parish, but this was not due to cunning.

Like his father before him, he was a member of the parish; he supplied the church with calendars every December, religious calendars but tastefully done, featuring Renaissance art. And of course information about McDivitt's Funeral Home.

His late wife had shivered at the thought of what he did for a living. Perhaps she had a premonition of her own early death. Whenever McDivitt found it difficult to get into the proper mood, all he need do was imagine that the funeral at hand was Delores' and he wept real tears as he went about his work.

Father Dowling's arrival had surprised him; there was no funeral scheduled, but perhaps there had been a death that had not yet appeared in the obituary notices.

"What is the procedure for an exhumation, Francis?" McDivitt brought the pink tips of his fingers together and lowered his nose to touch them. From time to time, a family wanted a body exhumed and transferred to another city, near where they had settled.

"Who is it?"

"A Mrs. Scuderi."

McDivitt twirled his mental Rolodex, but no Scuderi came to mind.

"It was thirty years ago."

"Good Lord." Exhumations were seldom requested so long after burial.

"It's a special case."

McDivitt listened, surprised that Father Dowling was taking such a request seriously. The funeral would have been handled by McDivitt's father, before Francis had settled into the business, so of course he had no personal memory of the case. But the records of McDivitt Funeral Home were meticulously kept, and recently had been transferred to the computer. As Father Dowling spoke, McDivitt brought up the archives, tapped in Scuderi, and there it was.

"Not quite thirty years ago," he said. "Twenty-nine."

"Reburial will be in the same grave. He just wants the casket opened and the body blessed again before reburial."

"What on earth could he have put into the casket?"

McDivitt could not exclude the possibility that a mourner might do such a thing, and this troubled him. It suggested some professional delinquency on the part of McDivitt's. He found himself less amenable than Father Dowling to accommodating the widower.

"Why did he wait so long?"

"He has been away from Fox River since his wife died."

McDivitt let silence establish itself. Did Father Dowling find that an explanation? But it was clear that the pastor of St. Hilary's was intent on helping Peter Scuderi recover whatever valuables he had hidden in his wife's casket. McDivitt put his hands flat on the desk and outlined the procedure Scuderi must follow. In the end, he wrote it out so that things would go smoothly.

"How long will it take?"

"Not long. If 'twere done 'twere well 'twere done quickly!"

"Ah."

"I love Keats," McDivitt said, and regretted it when he saw Father Dowling's expression change. "It isn't Keats?"

"I think Shakespeare."

"Of course." He should have quit while he was ahead.

5

They gathered by the grave of Theresa Scuderi on a bright November day with sun streaming through the trees and igniting gold and copper leaves, those still clinging to branches and those that lay like abandoned treasure among the headstones of St. Mary's Cemetery. A crew had removed the dirt from the gravesite and there remained only to take the lid from the vault and then lift the casket from it. Father Dowling wondered if any lines from Hamlet were occurring to McDivitt as they watched the diggers emerge from the grave. One looked around like a muddy Lazarus, only his capped head visible, before being helped out by his companion. Peter Scuderi stood to the right of the pile of dirt that had once covered his wife and looked into the hole with a tragic expression. And then a handle was turned and the casket began its slow ascent to a world to which it had bade adieu some thirty years before.

Before the lid was opened, McDivitt donned a mask and looked a warning at Peter Scuderi. He had hoped they could do this without the widower being present. All he need do is tell them what to look for. But Scuderi had been adamant.

"I must be there."

Father Dowling turned away when the lid was opened. McDivitt had offered him a mask, but he had refused it. Once monks had kept skulls on their desk to remind them that they were mortal. Father Dowling's imagination could suffice on this occasion. He watched a squirrel scamper among the leaves and spring to a tree, clutching its bole and looking around as if conscious that this was an unusual scene.

"Where is it?" McDivitt asked, his voice filtered through the mask.

"Under her head."

Father Dowling turned. Scuderi, maskless, was at McDivitt's side, staring into the open casket. Suddenly he reeled, and

McDivitt steadied him. Scuderi's hand went to the edge of the opened lid. Father Dowling moved to be of help when McDivitt turned to him. But as the priest approached he saw Scuderi's hand move under the lid. When he withdrew it, his hand was closed. He allowed McDivitt and now Father Dowling to lead him away.

"There is nothing there," McDivitt assured him.

"It doesn't matter, it doesn't matter." He shuddered. And then he looked at the undertaker. "Let me have her rosary."

McDivitt drove Father Dowling and the somber Peter Scuderi to St. Hilary's, and after the old man had left them, McDivitt said, "I think it was the rosary he wanted all along."

"Perhaps you're right."

6

"Scuderi?" Phil Keegan said and gave it a little thought. "Doesn't ring a bell."

Nonetheless, he said he would have Cy Horvath look into it. The results were surprising. Thirty years ago, Peter Scuderi, accountant, had been accused of embezzling two hundred thousand dollars from Fox River Pipe, the company for which he worked, He was tried but found innocent. His wife had died during this ordeal, and shortly after his acquittal, having nothing but his son left in Fox River, Scuderi decided to leave.

"The son worked there, too. At Fox River Pipe."

"Where is he now?"

"Dead and buried in Aurora."

"How long ago?"

"Three months ago."

The marvels of modern information retrieval. Perhaps Peter had come back for his son's funeral and it was then that he decided to settle again in Fox River. Father Dowling did not mention that he thought that Peter Scuderi had found what he was seeking in his wife's casket. And it wasn't her rosary. He had taken something from inside the lid. Father Dowling had watched him slip it into his pocket when he and McDivitt had helped Scuderi to a granite bench, overcome by the experience of having his wife exhumed.

But he had stood next to Father Dowling when he blessed the closed casket and together they had watched it being returned to the earth.

"Peter Scuderi," Marie said two days later, popping her head into the doorway of the pastor's study "He'd like to see you if you're not busy."

"Have him come in."

After Scuderi came into the study and closed the door, he sat and looked at Father Dowling a moment. "I want to talk to you, Father."

"About what you took from your wife's casket?"

"You saw me?"

"Something inside the lid."

Scuderi reached into his pocket and held up a small flat key. "This."

"What does it open?"

"A safe deposit box."

Father Dowling lit his pipe, taking his time about it. Had Peter Scuderi been guilty after all, put the money in a safe deposit box, hidden the key in his wife's casket, and now, after all these years, made Father Dowling his ally in retrieving what he had stolen?

"I want to make a gift to the parish. To the center, I think, but you can use it for whatever you want."

"That's very good of you. Did you mean something in your will?"

"No, no. Right now. Cash." He inhaled deeply, then said, "Two hundred thousand dollars."

The amount that had been embezzled from Fox River Pipe. "That is a very large amount of money."

"It's all right. I don't need it."

"I am surprised you could have saved so much."

Silence fell. Scuderi looked to his right, then to his left, then at Father Dowling. He had the look of a penitent who could not quite bring himself to confess what he had done.

"I know about your trial, Peter."

The old man's shoulders slumped. "I had hoped . . ."

"Thirty years is a long time, but everything is recorded. I must tell you that I asked someone to get me any information they could. Your request for an exhumation piqued my curiosity. But you were acquitted."

"I was innocent."

"Then where did you get two hundred thousand dollars?"

Scuderi turned the little key in his fingers. "When I used this I found it."

"Found it?"

"It is a long story."

Indeed it was. He had been called to Aurora when his son Sandro lay mortally ill, and on his deathbed the son told his father that he had impulsively wedged the key into the satin that lined the lid of his mother's coffin.

"He was overcome by remorse for what he had done. He had stolen the money. He told me he would have confessed if I had been convicted but when I was found innocent he remained silent. He had been silent all these years."

"He embezzled the money?"

"He was the youngest employee in accounting. I think I was the only one who thought that he had done it. And done it in such a way that it appeared that I had. I was so shocked by this that I said nothing. You can imagine my relief when I was found innocent. My house had been ransacked, my bank interrogated;

there was no sign of the money anywhere. To the jury, it was simply testimony about figures on a page."

"Your son confessed this to you?"

"As he lay dying. He died a good death, Father."

"Whatever his life had been, he had the last rites."

"God is merciful."

"I don't want the money!"

"Perhaps you can return it to the company . . ."

But Fox River Pipe had long since been defunct, gone to wherever companies go when they die. Its assets had been bought, its local plant closed; there were no survivors of the events of thirty years ago.

"I want to give it to charity. To St. Hilary's."

Stolen money? But to whom could it be returned? He told Peter Scuderi that he must give it some thought.

"But yours is a generous impulse, Peter. I appreciate that."

"I just want to get rid of that money."

He had gone to his son's bank, the First Bank of Aurora, and gained admission to the safe deposit box. In it was the two hundred thousand dollars. It had lain there, presumably out of range of rust and moth, inaccessible for thirty years.

Alessandro Scuderi had indeed died in Aurora several months ago. Father Dowling spoke to the priest who had given him the last sacraments.

"First time I ever saw him," the chaplain said. "And no wonder. He led a pretty wild life. Gambling, drink, women."

"The father has returned to Fox River."

"That's right. Sandro had lived in Fox River."

7

Peter Scuderi did not come to the parish center for several days and Edna began to worry. He did not answer his phone, and when she went by his apartment, her ring was not answered.

"I know I'm a fussbudget, Father. But I always worry when a regular stops coming."

Father Dowling asked Cy Horvath if he could check it out. And so it was that the body of Peter Scuderi was found. Cy called the rectory and Father Dowling immediately left for Scuderi's apartment.

The old man lay on the kitchen floor. Dowling knelt and whispered the appropriate prayers. The gash on the side of his head might have been caused when he fell, ostensibly while cooking. The blackened pot on the stove had apparently been aboil for spaghetti—there were uncooked noodles on the counter, ready to be added—but it had boiled away and the flame beneath the pot burned on.

"I turned it off," Cy said.

Dr. Pippen had arrived with her crew and was examining the fallen body.

"Why the smell of gas?" Father Dowling asked.

"The oven." The oven door was open and, although Cy had turned off the gas, the smell of it was still heavy in the room.

"Have you looked around?"

"I was waiting for you to get here."

Whatever Cy was looking for, Father Dowling had his eye out for the safe deposit key that Peter Scuderi had shown him. It was nowhere to be found. Nor was it on the body. Father Dowling debated whether he should reveal Peter Scuderi's great secret, but the absence of the key decided him.

"Pippen says he was hit on the side of the head and then held in the open oven until he was dead. His chest was pressed into the garlic bread he was going to heat up."

"Going to?"

"He never got around to it." Phil Keegan shook his head and studied the label on the bottle of beer Marie Murkin had brought him. "And nothing seems to be missing."

"Just a key."

"A key?"

Father Dowling told Keegan the story then. Before he finished, Phil had called out to Marie for another beer.

"You know what I think, Roger?"

What Phil Keegan thought was that Peter had stolen that money, hidden the key, and disappeared. The story about his son was just that, a story.

"But he wanted to get rid of the money."

"Guilt." Phil spoke as one to whom the secrets of the heart were an open book.

"He was killed for that key, Phil."

"Roger, I don't even know there was a key. The fact that we didn't find one doesn't prove it's missing."

"It will be easy to find out."

"How?"

"Keep an eye on the safe deposit boxes in the First Bank of Aurora."

8

It had become the custom, after a funeral for one of the seniors, to have a meal in the center afterward. The turnout for Peter Scuderi was very likely due to the manner of his going rather than the affection in which he had been held, since he was a relative newcomer.

"I guess I knew him as well as anybody," Chet Williams said, following Father Dowling to the podium. "Actually, I knew his son better, we were closer in age. That was at the old Fox River Pipe." From there Chet drifted off into an account of his erratic employment over the years, but he did at the end come back to Peter Scuderi. "He will be greatly missed," he said, lifting his glass of water in a toast.

"I was afraid you might mention his trial," Father Dowling

said to Chet afterward.

"You know about that?"

"He told me."

Chet pondered this. Then he grinned. "He was found innocent."

Chet was wearing a shirt and tie and jacket for the occasion, but he was still in denim trousers and on his feet were the trademark gym shoes with lights in their heels that flashed on and off as he walked.

"Any other shoes kill me, Father."

It was those gym shoes and the winking lights that drew Cy's attention as he sat in the parking lot of the First Aurora Bank. He remembered seeing a pair like that at St. Hilary's Center. He got out of his car and followed Chet into the bank. After he had been admitted to the area where the safe deposit boxes were kept, Cy asked to see how he had signed. A. Scuderi. Cy decided to wait for him outside.

Chet Williams had the two hundred thousand dollars in the plastic bag he had brought to the bank when Cy arrested him in the lot.

"What's the charge?"

"The lights in your shoes."

9

Edna Hospers wasn't a bit surprised, though she wouldn't say why, when Chet Williams was arraigned. He tried to take his bail from the two hundred thousand but of course that wasn't permitted. He was awaiting trial in jail. To Father Dowling, if not to his lawyer Tuttle, he was willing to tell all.

"Sandy and I set it up together."

"Were you an accountant, too?"

"I was in payroll. That's how we worked it."

Chet would have liked to go on and on, but the details of the theft interested Father Dowling less than in finding out what happened next.

"Sandy became unglued when his father was accused of the crime. I told him the old man was safe—after all, he was innocent. But Sandy found out that I made it look as if his father had squirreled away the money. That's why he double-crossed me."

"How so?"

"His mother died during the trial. He was convinced it was the shame that killed her. He only told me about the key after the funeral was over.

"He had put it in her casket. What a dumb thing to do. I tried to think of ways to get it, but how are you going to dig up a grave?" Chet's voice was petulant, the tone of a man who had been unjustly dealt with.

"I'll come back," Father Dowling said.

"I like talking to you. Father, would you do me a favor?"

"What is it?"

"You see these shoes? Nice, huh? I need new batteries. Triple A, the small ones. They're supposed to flash on and off."

GIVING NO QUARTER

1

In her active years she had been the receptionist in the office of her brother the doctor, long since gone to God, but Jennifer Breen had survived to the age of ninety-nine and was likely to see the hundredth anniversary of her birth coincide with the beginning of the new millennium. The one impressed her as little as the other. St. Peter's was the second retirement home she had been in since her early eighties. The transfer six years ago had led to a significant change in what would be called her lifestyle. There were few other residents as old as she and yet she thought of herself as living among the old, among whom she emphatically did not include herself. It amazed her that so many seemed almost to welcome inaction, the waning of the faculties, the imminent and almost awaited fact of death. Jennifer had never quite thought of herself as mortal.

Because she had never married, she had made a point of remembering the birthdays and anniversaries of her nieces and nephews, and then of their children, and of theirs, even unto the fourth generation. Her memory might be unreliable in lesser things but dates of birth were inscribed indelibly in her soul. And of course she had a vast necrology as well, people for whom she prayed each day when she said her rosary, seated in her wheelchair in the front hall, monitoring the coming and going of guests. Visits from all those generations she remembered so assiduously were not as frequent as they might be, but Jennifer did not repine. Today, however, was different. An aged nephew had called to say he would come by that afternoon.

Teddie had been a roly-poly little boy on his seventh birthday when she had taken him downtown for lunch at Marshall Field's and, when she delivered him home, pressed a quarter into his hand. Such a trip and such a coin were standard for such occasions.

When Teddie came, Jennifer was almost surprised at how old he looked. He had the slight stoop of the aged; he walked slowly and in apparent pain. And he was not yet eighty. She wheeled toward him as he came through the doors that slid open automatically.

"Teddie!"

His smile was rueful as he bent to kiss her. "Nobody else calls me Teddie."

"Everyone calls you Teddie."

"That was long ago, Aunt Jen."

She tutted away such thoughts. She had no intention of listening to her nephew or anyone else go on about the way everything had changed, nothing was the same. It never had been, as far as she knew.

Teddie affected to push her chair as she took him away to the parlor. The gesture was unnecessary—the cart was powered by a battery—but she knew how people liked to fuss. In the parlor, coffee was brought and Jennifer began to ask about Teddie's children and grandchildren.

"How do you remember them all?" he marveled.

"I just do. It is not an effort."

"I could not give the birthdays of half my grandchildren. There are eighteen of them, you know."

"Of course I know. Tell me about yourself. It's been over a year since I saw you."

"I've meant to come, but at my age . . ."

"Pooh. You have years ahead of you."

Teddie affected to groan at the prospect. But soon the conversation turned to the senior center at St. Hilary's parish, and Teddie seemed to shed his years. He took his keys from his pocket and showed them to her.

"I still have this."

A quarter through which a hole had been drilled was held by the same chain that held his keys.

"You'd be better off wearing the Miraculous Medal."

"Oh, I do. This is my good luck piece."

"The best of both worlds?"

"I've met someone."

"Aha."

"I considered bringing her but thought I should tell you about her first."

Dear God, was he considering remarrying at his age? Jennifer did not show her surprise and dismay. Teddie's wife Catherine was almost as real a presence to her as Teddie himself. But Teddie became almost eloquent on the subject of Yolande.

Yolande. No one in the family had ever borne such a name.

"Yolande Murphy."

The Murphy eased the shock of Yolande. She was of course a widow. At his age, and at Yolande's, Teddie did not go on about her beauty, of course, but he was comfortable with her.

"I don't think her husband left her much."

"So you will pool your resources."

Teddie smiled. "You could say that." But of course Teddie had often told her of the wealth he had accumulated in his career as a wholesale supplier of food.

"All of my children make more money than I ever did. The same is true of theirs. And all along I thought I was providing for them. They don't need it."

"And now you will find a use for it."

"Aunt Jen, I intend to marry Yolande."

"So I surmised."

He sipped his coffee and looked around. "It must be very expensive to stay here."

"I can afford it, Teddie. Thank God."

"That's really what I wanted to know."

"Are you asking my permission to marry?"

"If you approve of the idea."

Jennifer hesitated. A marriage at any time of life is a great adventure that might bring many surprises happy and unhappy. But Teddie's anxious expression decided her.

"I think it is a wonderful idea. You must bring Yolande to see me."

2

Marie Murkin and Edna Hospers had established a *modus vivendi* based on mutual distrust. The housekeeper had never accepted the view that Edna did not fall under her authority and Edna, the director of the senior center at St. Hilary's, considered Mrs. Murkin to be a meddling busybody. It could be said, therefore, that they understood one another. There was the usual electricity in the air when Marie showed up in Edna's office, which had once been the office of the principal of the parish school.

"Tell me about Teddie Doyle," Marie said without preamble.

"What would you like to know?"

"Everything."

"That's a large order."

"His daughter Maureen has been at the parish house with a story that a widow here has set her cap for Teddie."

"Yolande."

"So you know about it." Marie's tone suggested that Edna

had withheld vital information from one who had a right to know.

"Did Father Dowling send you?"

Marie was capable of many things but not of an outright lie. She sat. "I have come to make sure that Father Dowling is well informed."

"Perhaps I should talk to him."

"And leave your wards?"

The old people who spent their days in the parish center would not have appreciated being referred to in this way. Nor did Edna appreciate it.

"Is Father in the rectory?"

"Edna, if there is anything he should know I can pass it on to him."

"I prefer to talk to him myself."

A small victory, but in the arena of St. Hilary's parish, not a negligible one. Edna stood and marched off to the rectory, leaving Marie to her own devices in the school.

Unwilling to acknowledge that she had been bested, Marie went downstairs to what had been the gymnasium and, redesigned, was now the principal gathering place of the seniors of the parish. Savage games of bridge were being played at four tables, shuffleboard engaged couples who held their sticks as if they were weapons. Dozens were gathered around the television, where a cable station was playing a tape of last Saturday's Notre Dame game. And there were men and women, formed into couples, speaking with doddering intensity to one another. Marie's expression wavered between sympathy and pain. December romances were a feature of the center. And then she spotted Teddie Doyle.

The woman with whom he was engrossed in conversation had to be the Yolande Murphy that Maureen Wilson had told her about over tea in the rectory kitchen. Marie, in her constant

259

campaign to keep irrelevant problems from the pastor, had waylaid Maureen before Father Dowling knew she had called. Maureen was concerned about her father's apparent plan to marry again in the twilight of his years.

Widows of an age can be very determined, Marie had said, to coax from Maureen the story. She had nodded through the narrative as if she knew all about it. The geriatric pairings that occurred in the senior center rarely went beyond a speculative exploration of what might be. But Maureen spoke of Yolande as a scheming female who had an eye on her father's money.

"I suppose he did well."

"Well? He is rolling in it."

Marie liked the image of the arthritic Teddie Doyle writhing in a tub filled with bills of large denomination.

"Hasn't he made a will?"

"He says he has made a new will."

"Ah."

"Mrs. Murkin, Father Dowling has to stop it."

Marie laid a hand on Maureen's arm. "I will take care of it."

"Would you?"

"I said I would. More tea?"

"No. Thank you." A sheepish smile. "I hate tea."

Now, in the gymnasium, Marie made a beeline toward Teddie and Yolande. They turned to her with the smirking expression one associates with lovesick teenagers. Marie noticed that they were holding hands. Obviously Maureen's fears were not unfounded. Another man joined them, as if Marie's presence licensed his.

"How about a game of shuffleboard, Yolande?"

Yolande looked at Teddie and then lifted her eyes. The newcomer, Bud Sullivan, was not to be put off. "Our record is being threatened."

"She doesn't want to play shuffleboard," Teddie said.

"I'm talking to Yolande. She's always been my partner."

"Please, Bud," Yolande said, and the remark was heavy with significance.

"Oh, go ahead, Yolande," Marie said. "I want to talk to Teddie."

Yolande hesitated but there was that in Marie's tone that made what she said an order. Yolande went off with Bud, and Teddie looked after the departing couple with mild alarm.

"Why doesn't he leave her alone?"

"Have you been monopolizing Yolande?"

"You heard her. She doesn't want to play shuffleboard."

"Your daughter Maureen stopped by the rectory."

Teddie was suddenly transformed. "Did she talk to Father Dowling?"

"Has she any reason for concern?"

"Concern. It's none of her damned business. And it's none of yours either."

And Teddie turned on his heel and shuffled off in his loafers. Marie looked after him as the Good Samaritan would have looked at the man he helped if he had been dismissed after taking such pains.

3

Father Dowling, puffing on his pipe, listened to Edna Hospers with a Solomonian mien. He had no wish to take the part of Edna against Marie or vice versa. Each woman was vital to the smooth operations of the parish, however impossible they found sharing a common harness.

"I know nothing about it, Edna. Tell me about Teddie and Yolande."

"It's an old story."

The oldest in the world, as it happened. Why the attraction of one eighty-year-old for another should precipitate a parish crisis he did not see.

"What do you think of it, Edna?"

"As little as possible. They're both of an age."

"Indeed. Nothing to worry about?"

"Not that I know of."

"Then we won't worry about it."

"Will you please call off Marie?"

"I don't know what I would do without the two of you."

"Edna has been to see me," Father Dowling said when Marie returned to the rectory. Marie said nothing, holding her tongue from uncharitable criticism, but her expression was eloquent. "She said you had been over there out of concern for a budding romance."

"Maureen Wilson said something to me."

"Did she? I thought you were motivated by anger because some other woman had been poaching on your new boyfriend."

Marie's earlier feigned long-suffering became genuine. Sometimes she feared that Father Dowling half expected her to go off with an affluent widower and end her days under the southern sun. Of course he knew the impediment of her long-gone-but-presumably-still-alive husband, a sailor who had been too much affected by such southern suns. In any case, she intended to be carried out of the rectory feet first. Not for her the living mausoleum of a retirement home.

"I wonder what Jennifer Breen would make of these shenanigans."

"What have they to do with her?"

"Ted Doyle is her nephew."

"Sometimes I think half the city is related to her."

4

If Jennifer had any misgivings about the place in which she was spending her last days, it was that there was not a resident chaplain. The previous retirement home had been cared for by two retired monsignors who had apartments there and said Mass every day for the residents. At St. Peter's she must be content with a weekly visit when Father Dowling brought her Communion and usually stayed to pass the time of day. On the following Wednesday he came, punctual as a train, and Jennifer received the Body and Blood of Our Lord and Savior Jesus Christ with a piety quickened by the rarity of her reception of the Eucharist. Before joining her hands to make her thanksgiving she indicated to Father Dowling that she wished him to remain. It seemed that had been his intention all along. He took a chair and began leafing through a photograph album on the dresser.

Jennifer's prayers after Communion were those she had been saying since she was a girl. Those done, she sat and hummed "Star of the Sea." Then she was ready for Father Dowling.

"My nephew Teddie speaks highly of the senior center at St. Hilary's."

"I wish you could come yourself."

She cocked an eye at him. "I get my fill of old people here. Teddie tells me he intends to marry a widow he met there. Yolande Murphy. Tell me about her."

Father Dowling told Jennifer what he knew of Yolande. A lovely woman, a childless widow. This touched Jennifer. Not having children when one had never married was one thing, but what a trial it must be to have a husband and no children. There were one or two instances of this in her extended family, and some younger grandnieces had only one or two, but however meager the number of children, their marriages were fruitful.

"Teddie has a great deal of money."

"I'm told that can't be said of Yolande Murphy."

"I suppose he has boasted to her of his wealth."

"Ted's daughter Maureen seems to think Yolande is a gold digger."

"Every woman wants security. It is our nature."

"You're a good deal more understanding than Maureen."

Jennifer shook her head. "Maureen is very well fixed herself. Her husband holds a patent on something used in satellites. Has Maureen talked to you?"

"She said something to Marie Murkin."

"There's a pair for you."

"Neither Ted nor Yolande has said anything to me."

"They will. Teddie is quite intent on marrying again."

"And you approve?"

Jennifer straightened in her chair. "He asked for my blessing and I gave it."

They talked of other things then. Jennifer found Father Dowling a sound spiritual director. Every other Wednesday he heard her confession and did not dismiss as peccadillos the venial sins that gave her so much sorrow. There had been priests who advised her to examine her conscience to discover her virtues and how wonderful she was, as if confession were an occasion for self-congratulation. Jennifer would have none of that. She might be ninety-nine but this is still a vale of tears and until she went shriven to God her fate was in the balance. Now they discussed the spirituality of Therese of Lisieux, a saint to whom Jennifer had a lifelong devotion and who recently had been declared a Doctor of the Church. The Little Way, offering up the slights and annoyances of the day to God, not seeking dramatic deeds. It was marvelous how aggravating people seemed suddenly loveable when Jennifer remembered, as alas she did not always do, to look on them as the Little Flower would.

"Perhaps you can come and give Ted away at the wedding," Father Dowling said when he rose to go.

"Let Maureen do it. Given away would have a sinister meaning for her apparently." Jennifer bit her tongue. After receiving Communion, after their conversation, the first thing she did was make a spiteful remark. She bowed her head for the priest's blessing, pained by her sinfulness yet trusting in God's mercy.

Some hours later, Jennifer was told that Teddie was coming to see her at three, bringing someone for her to meet. But at two o'clock, Maureen breezed in unannounced. The perfumes of Araby surrounded her like a cloud as she advanced on her aged relative and gave her a half kiss on the cheek. She sat and stared at Jennifer, her lipsticked mouth a straight line.

"Aunt Jennifer, my father has gotten it into his head to marry again."

"So he tells me."

"What did you tell him?" The fur wrap fell from Maureen's shoulders in her agitation. What a lovely dress she wore, and there were ropes of pearls cascading down its front.

"Old people get lonely, Maureen."

"Lonely! He's got all of us."

"A grown man cannot be prevented from marrying."

"I think he has gone senile."

"Nonsense. His mind is clear as a bell."

"Ha. The Liberty Bell. You know how he tells everyone how much money he has."

"His concern when he last visited me was that I might need his help."

"Do you?"

"I do not."

"I wish you had told him you did. That might have made him think again about what he is doing."

"Maureen, if it is your mother you are thinking of, don't. Catherine would, I think, approve."

"That isn't it at all."

265

"Surely you're not in need of your father's money."

Maureen looked sharply at her. "Why do you say that?"

"Because I can't imagine it is true." Maureen stirred and once more the scent of her perfume wafted toward Jennifer.

"That isn't the point."

"Besides, I don't think two old people are going to throw away a lifetime accumulation of money."

Maureen was still there when Teddie arrived with Yolande Murphy. The couple showed no surprise at Maureen's presence, but Teddie's daughter was taken aback. She stared in an appraising way at Yolande.

"Aunt Jen, I told you I would bring her. This is Yolande Murphy."

"The bride-to-be," Jennifer said extending her hands. Yolande took them in her own and looked with sheepish affection at Jennifer.

"I suppose you think we're being foolish."

"Because of your age? Not at all. Think of Abraham and Sarah."

"Abraham and Sarah," Yolande repeated, not following.

"Look it up. And notice when Sarah laughs."

"Yolande, this is my daughter Maureen."

Yolande turned and met an unsmiling face. She had started to put out her hand but she stopped the gesture.

"I've heard about you," Maureen said.

Yolande looked at Teddie, who shook his head as if to say "not from me."

Maureen said to her father, "You must come and see George and me. Soon."

"We'd be glad to," Teddie said, taking Yolande's hand.

"I was thinking of just yourself."

Shortly after, Maureen left. Yolande's expression was sad and

Jennifer sought to cheer her up. "There are always these little frictions."

Teddie said angrily, "She thinks you are a gold digger."

"To dig I am not able, to beg I am ashamed." And Yolande looked at Jennifer. But there was no need to identify the passage.

5

Maureen and her husband, George Wilson, came by the senior center and climbed the broad stairs to the floor where Edna Hospers' office was, following the signs. It was not a pleasant visit. George undertook to explain to Edna that she could be held liable if she encouraged the unsuitable match between Ted and Yolande.

"I have not encouraged it."

"Have you discouraged it?"

"Certainly not."

George Wilson looked as if he had established his point. He explained to her about old people and their weakened sense of responsibility.

"I have worked among people that age for many years," Edna replied.

"And how many marriages have you failed to discourage?"

"What exactly have you come here for?"

"To explain your legal vulnerability."

As soon as she got rid of the obnoxious couple, Edna went to the rectory to speak of the visit with Father Dowling.

"I wonder what their concern is."

"They speak a lot of Ted's money."

"Does he have any?"

"That's what he says."

"And Yolande?"

267

"She seemed to have enough. I haven't heard her mention it."

Father Dowling came back with her and spoke to the two old people, alone and separately.

"What's that all about?" Bud Sullivan asked Edna.

"Would you like to speak to Father?"

"What for?" Bud said, suddenly skittish. When Bud first came to the center he had been wary. He didn't want anyone forcing religion on him. When nothing of the sort was done, he seemed as disappointed as relieved.

"Father Dowling is always available for spiritual direction."

Bud went hastily away, but as he crossed the gym his eyes were on the priest talking to Yolande and Ted. Not watching where he was going, he walked right through a shuffleboard game in progress and was threatened by the irate players.

"The way you play, you're lucky I broke it up," Bud said, and continued outside.

"Well?" Edna asked when Father Dowling rejoined her.

"We set the date of the wedding."

"Good!"

"Be careful. We'll be accused of running a marriage bureau."

The following day, when Edna descended to the first floor, she looked over the staircase railing. She stopped, leaning over to make sure she could believe her eyes. Then she went swiftly down, turning and descending the stairs into the basement as well. The body lay crumpled and lifeless on the second stair from the bottom. It was Ted Doyle.

6

The rest of the day was filled with activities unfamiliar in the setting of the senior center. It became quickly apparent that Ted had not succumbed to natural causes, something that was confirmed by the autopsy. He had not had a stroke. There was no evidence that age or any ailment had brought on his death. But it was the great bruise on the back of his head that brought Captain Keegan and Lieutenant Horvath to the center.

Testimony of varying degrees of coherence was taken from the stunned old people. Edna looked around for Yolande and did not see her. This sent her on a somber search of the building and grounds, fearful that another body might be found. But Yolande had a doctor's appointment that day and received the news of Ted's death from Father Dowling later.

The poor woman was stricken, of course, but her first words were, "God rest his soul."

"I think I always knew it would never happen," she confided to Marie. "He was such a good man. I almost feel I have become a widow twice."

Captain Keegan listened to Edna's account of the visit of Maureen and her husband.

"That wasn't today?"

"Oh, no. They came yesterday."

"Maybe they came back."

Edna did not respond. Terrible as the death of Ted Doyle was, she had no wish to cast suspicion on anyone. But her suspicions were not needed. Lieutenant Horvath, armed with a newspaper photograph of George Wilson, was told by several old people that they had seen him in the center that day.

"Not the day before?"

"Oh, no. It was today. Is it important?"

When George himself was eventually questioned, he claimed to have been at his office at the time Ted had been assaulted and pushed down the basement stairway. His loyal secretary tried to lie for him but then broke down and said he had not been in that day. George was taken in for questioning. He was still being held, not yet indicted, three days later when the funeral was held.

Maureen, all in black, defiantly took her post in the front pew, and four pews on either side of the aisle were filled with the children and grandchildren of the deceased. It was thought inadvisable to bring Aunt Jennifer for the somber occasion. Yolande knelt unobtrusively among the mourners with Bud Sullivan seated uncomfortably beside her.

Theodore Doyle was duly consigned to the earth, his son-in-law George was arraigned and indicted for his murder. The financial affairs of George proved to be parlous. He had sold the copyright to his invention and made a sweeping and dramatic entry into the stock market that seemed to be climbing like one of the missiles that carried his device into space. His confidence in his shrewdness as an investor was misplaced.

"No wonder they were concerned about Ted's money," Marie Murkin said, shaking her head. "I felt uneasy about her questions as soon as she began."

"I thought you were uneasy about Yolande."

"Concerned, Father. Not uneasy in the other sense. A woman's heart is so easily broken."

7

Some of the old people became fascinated with the trial of George Wilson, and the parish shuttle bus took them off to the courthouse day after day. Yolande dismissed with a shudder Bud Sullivan's suggestion that she join the group.

"If you like I'll stay and we can play shuffleboard."

"Go along, Bud. You know you want to."

"When all this is over . . ." Bud said, getting into the shuttle bus.

Maureen came to the rectory and begged Father Dowling to intervene. She seemed certain that at his word, the case would be dismissed. He consoled her as best he could. Adversity had turned her into a more likeable person. Father Dowling did consult with Amos Cadbury, but his old friend could not provide him with any legal reason for hope that he could pass on to Maureen. The trial proceeded quickly and George was found guilty of the murder of his father-in-law. Sentencing would take place in a few days.

"Someone to see you, Father," Marie said, looking into the study.

Father Dowling rose, expecting that it would be Maureen. But it was Bud Sullivan who appeared in the doorway, hesitated, and looked around the room. "Go in," Marie urged.

Bud took a chair and turned as if startled at the sound of the door closing. He looked wildly at Father Dowling.

"I haven't been to the sacraments in thirty years!"

"That's a long time."

"I couldn't face the thought of confession."

"It's not meant to be an enjoyable experience. But it does take a load off one."

"Father, I've got a real load."

"We all do, Bud."

"I did it, Father. It was me."

"It?"

"I hit him on the back of the head with a shuffleboard stick and he went down those stairs ass over teakettle. I killed him."

Father Dowling nodded, suppressing his surprise. Whatever load of guilt Bud had carried for thirty years, it was what he had done a short while ago that had brought him penitent to Father Dowling. But they went over those thirty years, the high points, or rather the low. Had Bud thought God would be surprised by what he had done, or withhold His mercy? But he could not give absolution until they talked more of the deed Bud had blurted out when he first entered the study.

"Absolution will rid you of your sins. All of them. But you have a duty to tell the police about what you did to Ted. Another

271

man will be punished for your act if you do not."

"I'll tell them," Bud said. "I want to unload it all."

After he gave Bud absolution, Father Dowling asked if he'd mind if he gave Captain Keegan a ring so he could come and hear what Bud had to say.

"Bring him on. I'm ready."

8

"There's never been a criminal in the family," Jennifer said. "I'm not surprised."

George had emerged from detention exonerated. He had been provided with an experience that would become a staple of his conversation for the rest of his life. Only Father Dowling knew that at the time his father-in-law was killed, George had been parked by the Fox River seriously considering drowning himself. He had become a wealthy man because of his knowledge and skill and he had plunged into the stock market and plunged with it into penury. Only this happened not to be true. To his astonishment and Maureen's delight, the stocks that had seemingly lost all their value recovered and once more shot upward. George's poverty had been only an episode. His first move was to get out of the market and into something safe and dull.

His rebound was a good thing. When Ted's will was read, his fortune was revealed as modest indeed. His house was his main asset and the neighborhood in which it stood had not been kind to its resale value. Maureen was elated that the family would not profit from her father's death. And she was reconciled with her great-aunt Jennifer.

"I've thought of giving Yolande Murphy some little token of remembrance," she said.

"What did you have in mind?"

Maureen took from her purse a little chain of keys. "I suppose it's a silly idea. But they are personal."

Jennifer shook her head. "I'd give her something else."

The quarter she had given Teddie on his seventh birthday, the chain drawn through a hole drilled in it, was still there with the keys. After Yolande's visit, Jennifer was glad to have had the chance of stopping the proposed gift.

"How I envy you all those nieces and nephews and grand-nieces and grandnephews," Yolande had said.

"They are a consolation. They have all done well in the world and I think they have kept the faith. That is my main prayer for them all."

Yolande smiled ruefully. "Ted was always talking about how successful he had been."

"Somewhat of an exaggeration, it seems."

"Yes. And it kept me from telling him my own situation."

"Which is?"

"I won't say the amounts. But I am far better off than Ted imagined he was."

"Men are strange about money. It is a sin of virility, I think."

Yolande nodded. "He did leave some money with me."

"Oh."

She had it in her pocket and she took it out as if it were a relic. She held up a quarter. "I wonder if you remember where he got this?"

"Tell me."

Yolande's account of Teddie's seventh birthday when she had taken him to lunch at Marshall Field's was accurate enough.

"That was when you gave him this quarter. He had kept it all those years. And I shall keep it, too. I was very moved that he should give me something so precious."

When she was alone, Jennifer tried to persuade herself that Teddie had given Yolande a quarter she had given him on another birthday. Poor Teddie. He had bragged about an imaginary fortune, and, when he fell in love with Yolande, gave her a bogus memento. A strange man. Well, he had been a strange boy. Traits he had acquired from his father's side, Jennifer was sure. But she remembered the little boy tucked up to the luncheon table at Marshall Field's and her eyes were moist. God rest his soul, she prayed. God rest his soul.

The Dead Weight Lifter

The old man was found lying on the steps of the school when Edna Hospers arrived to open up. One or two senior parishioners huddled some distance from the door, in a little patch of sunlight, keeping warm. Perhaps they thought their distance was a way of showing respect, on the assumption that it was a vagrant who had spent the night there and must soon wake and slink away ashamed. That the man was dead occurred to no one, so it fell to Edna to make the discovery.

Her scream, the way she scrambled back down the stairs, brought the others rushing to her side.

"Someone go for Father Dowling," she said, over her first shock, mindful that these elderly people were more or less her wards. But death was more fascinating than her wishes. Jaws slack, a wondering look in their eyes, they stared down at the man. How long before they themselves would go?

In the end, Edna Hospers went for the pastor herself.

"Are you sure he's dead?" Father Dowling asked, rising from the table. In the kitchen door Marie Murkin, the housekeeper, twisted her hands in her apron.

"I think so."

"I'll bring the oils anyway."

"I'll call nine-one-one," Marie said.

Edna ran back to the school, where a larger crowed had gathered. Austin Beatty, one of the old people, was kneeling beside the body, and several others, thinking he was praying, lowered themselves arthritically to their knees. But Austin rose in a minute and turned away. "He's dead," he said to Mrs. Hospers.

"Father Dowling is coming. Mrs. Murkin called an ambulance."

"He's still dead," Austin said and shambled back into the sunlight.

It was a nerve-wracking way to start a day—and a week, Edna reflected, after Father Dowling had given the last rites and the paramedics had decided there was nothing they could do. There was no identification on the body.

Father Dowling did not accept Edna's offer to sit when he stopped by her office.

"Edna, last month there was a man who spent the night curled against the wall of the boiler room. Now this. We can't have it. We're going to have to provide sleeping quarters for poor devils like that."

"Two is not a trend, Father."

"But how many would there be if we provided shelter?"

"We're not on the beaten path for that sort of thing, Father. The man a month ago was lost. Who knows why this man chose to come to St. Hilary's to die?"

"I wonder who he was."

Since he knew that question would pester him until he had an answer to it, Roger Dowling checked the hospital to see if any identification had turned up there. The body had already been sent on to the morgue. Such efficiency suddenly seemed ghoulish, though the reaction was unfair. The morgue was awaiting instructions, but an autopsy would be performed. Roger Dowling put in a call to Phil Keegan, and his old friend, the Fox River captain of detectives, was not particularly moved by the story.

"Was there any evidence of foul play, Roger?"

"He looked as if he died in his sleep. But of course I don't know."

"Who was he?"

"That's the eerie thing. There was no identification on the body. It doesn't seem right that a person should leave this life so anonymously."

"It happens all the time."

"Not on the steps of St. Hilary's school, it doesn't."

"You sure he isn't someone who's been coming there?"

Because of the changes wrought by several interstates and the general flow to the more pleasant suburbs, St. Hilary's parish in Fox River, Illinois, no longer had a need for its parish school. An attractive building, in good repair, it seemed a shame simply to shut it up. So Father Dowling had turned it into a center where senior parishioners could spend the day, under the general tutelage of Edna Hospers and various volunteers, but not overly organized. If they wanted to spend the day just talking, that was all right.

"He would have been recognized, Phil."

"I suppose they've sent the body on to the morgue by now."

"They have. Would you look into it, Phil?"

Phil said he would, but he could not keep from his voice the feeling that Roger Dowling was overreacting.

It would have been presumptuous to have a religious ceremony for the stranger, but that did not prevent Father Dowling from saying a prayer for the repose of the unknown's soul. There was some consolation in realizing that he was not unknown to God.

Marie tapped on the door, leaned into the study, and whispered, "One of the seniors wants to talk with you."

How relative age is. The presence of the elderly men and women had done a world of good for Marie Murkin. Suddenly, in her sixties, she was, relatively speaking, a spring chicken.

"Who is it?"

"Austin Beatty," a man behind Marie said, and she turned to give him a look. No one got to the pastor except through Marie Murkin if she could help it.

"Come in, Austin."

Middle height, a bit overweight, iron gray hair still thick and wavy, he tipped his head and found the lens he wanted. Marie's tone had suggested that his visitor would be someone upset by the events of the morning, but Austin Beatty did not look like a man easily upset.

"That man found dead this morning?"

Father Dowling nodded. "I still haven't found out who he was."

"His name is Potter. Fielding Potter. He lives right here in Fox River."

"Sit down, Austin. Do you drink coffee?"

"Is it decaf?"

"That's against my religion, I'm afraid."

"Mine, too. Can't stand it. You got the real thing, I'll have a cup."

Roger Dowling filled a mug from the Mister Coffee that was always going in his study. "Now then, you say his name was Fielding Potter."

"That's right." Austin sipped the coffee, approved, and sipped some more. "Don't know what he was doing on those steps. He's not a Catholic. Moreover, he is a wealthy man."

"How come you recognized him?"

"I worked for him for thirty years."

Roger Dowling got out the phone book and looked up Potter. There were two listings in Fox River, Fielding and Regis.

"Regis is the nephew."

"I suppose I should call him. Or is there someone at the house?"

"There is unless his daughter Emily finally got married and moved away, but I haven't heard of it."

The priest dialed the number of Fielding Potter and listened as the phone rang and rang. He was just about to hang up when a sepulchral feminine voice said hello.

"Is this the home of Fielding Potter?"

A long pause. "Yes."

"Is he there?"

"If you are selling something, we are not interested. Goodbye."

"Wait! This is Father Roger Dowling, pastor of St. Hilary's church."

The phone had not been hung up. After a very long pause, the woman said, "I beg your pardon."

"Is your father there?"

"Why do you ask?"

Father Dowling fought his impatience. "Because an elderly man was found dead on the steps of the parish school this morning, and someone thinks it is your father."

A shorter pause. "What is your address?"

"He's no longer here. We called an ambulance. I am very sorry to be telling you these terrible things."

"You say someone thought it is my father." There was no change in her voice, but then it had been mournful from the beginning.

"There was no identification on the body."

"It cannot be my father."

"Why?"

"My father is in Florida."

"If I'm mistaken, I am very sorry . . ." But across the desk, Austin Beatty shook his head from side to side.

"It's Potter," he said.

"Miss Potter, the man who thinks it is your father tells me he

279

has no doubt of it."

"What should I do?"

"Someone should go to the morgue and identify the body. That is not a pleasant task."

"I will do so at once."

"If you would like someone to go with you . . ."

A pause. "If you have a car, that would make it less inconvenient."

"I'll come by for you in half an hour."

"Could we say an hour?"

"Of course."

When Father Dowling hung up, Austin Beatty expressed surprise that Emily Potter herself would go. "She almost never leaves the house. Likes being by herself. What kind of a wreck do you call a person like that?"

"A recluse?"

"That's it."

"Did you ever see her?"

"Twice. I took something to the house for Mr. Potter and when she realized I wasn't leaving until the door was answered, she came down. What I saw was one arm and the tip of her nose."

"Tell me about Fielding Potter."

From Austin Beatty's remarks, and later inquiries, the picture of Fielding Potter that emerged was this: He had broken with his family in Mobile when he was a young man and came north to make his fortune. So far as formal education went, he had been to grade school and three years of high school, but in the college of experience he earned an advanced degree. He found work with a printer, went on to newspaper work, ending in classified ads, when, at twenty-nine, he left to begin the first of the shopper guides that would make his fortune.

The paper was distributed free at every door in town, and

that guaranteed circulation enabled Potter to attract advertising revenue from the most modest to the full-page variety. His rates were better than the newspapers, and his paper was read, chiefly for two reasons. Personal ads were run gratis, and Potter himself, under the pen name Jeff Davis, wrote a gossip column that was ninety percent fiction but no less avidly read for that. Potter was the first to admit that it was the personals that explained why his paper was read. These notices were not as candid as such ads have subsequently become, but when they began to appear, they were daring enough for the time. Potter was sued early and often by irate husbands claiming his paper had aided in alienating the affection of their wives. Some matron wistfully responding to a plea for friendship in a personal ad ran off with the grocery money and the man. The publicity far outweighed the nuisance, and it was said that Potter came to hope for litigation.

From Fox River he had branched out to other communities, and in every case, the Jeff Davis column and the free personals led to success. At the peak of his career, Fielding Potter owned a chain of such shopping guides, which blanketed the towns that were to become the western suburbs of Chicago.

Fielding Potter was eighty-two when he retired. He kept an office in the building he had put up near a cloverleaf of interstates, a squat block of a building, all copper-colored glass. He continued to go to his office at least once a week, keeping the reins of power as he had kept his business a family corporation, with his nephew Regis as heir apparent.

The Potter property was surrounded by a wrought-iron fence marked at intervals of twenty feet by brick columns of striking and elaborate design. The gate was closed, but when Roger Dowling turned in, a voice seemed to speak to him from the heavens.

"Is that Reverend Dowling?"

"Yes, it is."

The gate swung slowly open and the voice spoke again. "Please drive in."

It would have been a good walk to the house. The grounds were striking because of the Spanish moss hanging from some of the trees and the terraced formal garden that seemed embraced by the wings of the mansion. Although it was built of brick, there was a *soupçon* of the South in its high-columned porch. As he drew to a stop beneath the *porte cochere*, a woman emerged from the house.

She wore a lavender turban, her face was powdered chalk white, her sunglasses were opaque, and, although it was April, she had on a fur coat that fell to her ankles. Father Dowling leaned over to open the door, and she extended a gloved hand.

"I am Emily Potter."

"Father Dowling."

She slid in beside him, wrapping her coat about her, and immediately the car was filled with her perfume.

"I still do not think the man you spoke of is my father."

"Did you try reaching him in Florida?"

"He might not have heard the phone. His hearing is bad. It is an inherited defect." She pulled back her turban to display a hearing aid. "Both sides," she added. "My father doesn't always wear his. I understand. The world of silence is preferable. You are a Catholic priest?"

"Yes."

"We are not Catholics."

"What are you?"

He could sense her eyes, or at least her dark glasses, on him. "Just non-Catholics, I guess."

"If your father had a church . . ."

"He avoided them. They did not avoid him, of course. He

was besieged by requests for money."

Father Dowling smiled. "Was he generous?"

"He is a stingy and avaricious man. He made a fortune unaided. He believes anyone else can do the same."

The attendant at the morgue led them to a room, pointed out the TV set, and left.

"I never watch television," Emily said. But when the face of the man who had been found on the steps of St. Hilary's school came on the screen, she went closer to the screen. She took off her glasses, but her back was to him, so Father Dowling did not see her eyes. She began to nod slowly. She put on her glasses.

"That is my father," she said.

Then she sank slowly to the floor, and for the second time that morning, Roger Dowling was bending over the body of a member of the Potter family.

It was after midnight when Emily Potter called. "Regis will be furious, but I want you to conduct a service for my father. I have never known a Catholic priest, and I doubt that he did. But he had no other clerical friends either." She paused. "He did not have a gift for friendship. But it's not just because there's no one else. You befriended him in death. And I would like prayers said for him. I myself do not believe in God."

"Did your father?"

"We never discussed it. But if there is a God, my father would need prayers all the more."

So it was that on Wednesday morning Father Dowling arrived at the Chadwick mortuary at ten in the morning and was ushered by Chadwick Junior to the parlor where the ashes of Fielding Potter were enshrined in a modest urn of burnished bronze, surrounded by flowers.

"We haven't seen much of you, Father," Chadwick purred as

they walked.

"Healthy parishioners."

There were seven people in the room, and one turned out to be a Chadwick employee. Of the others, Roger knew only Emily. She wore a black velvet turban for the occasion but otherwise looked as she had on Monday. Her gloved hand detained his for a moment. "How good of you to do this."

She introduced him to two men, Folwell and Earl, who were high in the Potter hierarchy, and their wives, all four looking a bit embarrassed to acknowledge mortality, and then, with seeming reluctance, to her cousin Regis. She immediately drifted away.

"We don't get along," Regis said with a smile. He seemed to have more than the usual number of teeth. "Thanks for what you did for my uncle, Father. And thanks for coming here. Fielding Potter was an old heathen, but he knew the Bible like the back of his hand. I think he would appreciate the humor of a Catholic priest praying over his ashes. No offense."

He put a hand on Father Dowling's arm and exposed several more teeth. Roger Dowling knew a good deal about Regis Potter because of the efforts of Detectives Horvath and Lamb, passed on to him over the phone by Phil.

Regis had majored in drama at Northwestern and had appeared in several movies as well as on television, and at sixty still had the manner of a man who was sure a camera was focused on him. Twenty years ago, recognizing that his acting was at best competent, he petitioned his uncle for a job and was taken on. Regis had had the notion he would be a great help to his uncle, being fresh from the wider world, but he soon learned that in his chosen field no one knew more than Fielding Potter. Regis, come to patronize, stayed to praise. His admiration for his uncle was sincere, but there were those, and Emily was among them, who considered his constant praise of Fielding

Potter to be purposed. More surprising, perhaps, was the obvious pleasure the old man took in hearing what a truly remarkable man he was. Regis rose like cream in the company and, if his uncle had ever really retired, would have been undisputed boss long ago. As it was, any decision of his was subject to Fielding's veto, and the old man used it with the gusto of a lame duck president vetoing Congress.

And so, in Chadwick's mortuary, when Regis' smile was conferring importance on him, Father Dowling tried unsuccessfully to pierce the facade. Had this man, out of patience at last, smothered his uncle and then put the body in a wholly unpredictable place to divert attention from himself?

"Why remove all identification?" Phil had asked when that question was put to him.

"Just to mystify."

"But why? The old man was found dead. Not so far from his home that he might not have walked."

"At eighty-two?"

"He could do it. Roger, this guy ran two miles every morning. He had his own masseur and physical trainer living right in the house."

Father Dowling read from the Book of Wisdom. He read from Acts the account of Christ's resurrection. He read a few verses of Paul. And then—why not, this wasn't a liturgy—he read some Tennyson. Finally he asked God to have mercy on the soul of Fielding Potter and welcome him into eternal happiness.

When he turned, tears were leaking from under Emily's glasses, making little arroyos down her powdered cheeks. Again she gripped his hand.

"I particularly liked the Tennyson," she said in her sepulchral voice. Regis joined them.

"And now for the reading of the will." He leered at Emily

and she spun away. Regis winked at Father Dowling. "Not that there will be any surprises."

"Who was his lawyer?"

"Amos Cadbury. Do you know him?"

"Oh, yes."

"Why don't you come to the house then? The rest of us are going. There'll be a brunch."

"And the reading of the will?"

The smile went, although his lips had trouble eclipsing his teeth. He was looking over Father Dowling's shoulder at the urn.

"I am going to miss Uncle Fielding. We knew he must go some time, and sooner rather than later, but still it's sad."

"How was his health?"

"You and I should be as healthy. He was old, of course, and no one lives forever. He did hope to see one hundred. The way he worked out with Bruno, his trainer, I'm surprised he didn't."

"What was the cause of death?"

An expression of total surprise. "I never asked. I assume it was old age."

"Regis invited me to the house," he said to Emily as they were leaving.

"Why?" she asked, searching for his hand, but Father Dowling gripped his books. "I meant why did he ask? But you must come."

The prospect of watching heirs learn that they were going to be even wealthier than they already were was not high on his list of things to do. But the image of that elderly man lying dead on the steps of St. Hilary's school, cast aside like rubbish deprived of his identity, moved him. He would find it difficult to rest until he knew what had happened and, if it had been made to happen, by whom.

★　★　★　★　★

Emily, thank God, was taken by the Folwells, so it was alone that Father Dowling once more drove up the long drive to the Potter mansion. He could not help but think how oddly a life can end. After more than eighty years, a moment came that was the last for Potter, and yet things went on; his relatives converged on his house to learn what his will for them was, a last word from beyond the grave.

Folwell and Earl and their wives fell upon the food as if they had just discovered their reason for being. After an unusual morning, here was something familiar. There was champagne cocktail, scrambled eggs, sausages, bacon, ham, French toast and ordinary toast, and coffee, extremely good coffee. Father Dowling took some French toast and coffee and followed the Folwells and Earls to the living room, but on the way he encountered Cadbury.

To say that Amos Cadbury, Fox River's premier lawyer, was surprised to see him there was an understatement, but his reaction was as nothing compared with that he gave Regis' account of the service at the mortuary. He could not wait to get Father Dowling aside, steering him into the kitchen where a cook and a burly man who seemed about to burst from his shirt stopped talking when they entered. Cadbury waved at them, urging them to go on doing whatever they were doing.

"Father, don't tell me that Fielding Potter is a convert of yours."

"Only posthumously."

Cadbury thought about it and decided it made no sense. "I don't understand."

"His body was found on the steps of St. Hilary's school."

"Really! The newspapers were vague. I gathered that he had been felled while out walking."

"The family thought he was in Florida."

"Regis?"

"No. Emily."

Cadbury permitted his eyes to flicker heavenward. "Fielding was not in the habit of keeping Emily well informed of his doings."

"You must tell me about Emily sometime."

"Such a story! Tragic love, thwarted elopement, decades spent writing unreadable verse."

"But surely she would have known whether her father was home or not?"

"That seems a reasonable assumption. But not with Emily."

Regis found them. "Conspiring with the lawyer? Amos, this man will have his parish benefit from events no matter what." The smile. "I am kidding, of course." The hand on his arm. "We are deeply indebted to Father Dowling."

"We are old friends," Amos said. "Shall we begin?"

"What was it Uncle Fielding used to say? 'Possums ain't caught till they're caught.' I'm ready."

Cadbury set up shop at one end of the dining room table, telling the Folwells and Earls to continue eating; this would not take long at all.

"There have been some recent changes," he said, moving his glasses to his forehead, then lowering them again. "But I doubt that anyone will be severely disappointed." A little bow of a smile, and then he began to read. Father Dowling did not follow the details. It was written in the jargon devised to make such documents crystal clear to anyone who had lost his sense of ordinary language. Intelligible to lawyers, that is. Regis was named president of the family corporation. Folwell and Earl were continued on the board, thanked for loyal service over the years, and given equal and ample amounts. Their spouses stopped chewing for a moment, and then resumed with vigor. Emily got the house they were in, Regis the one in Sarasota.

After the accounting and taxes, eighty percent of the net worth was to be divided between them, forty-five percent to Emily, thirty-five to Regis. Neither her powdered face nor his radiant smile altered as this was read. But the fifteen percent left to Bruno Armshlager, Fielding's trainer and masseur, caused a stir. Father Dowling had noticed Amos whisper to Bruno before they left the kitchen, and he had been standing unobtrusively next to the kitchen door.

"Did you say fifteen percent?" Regis asked.

"That's right."

"With all due respect for my uncle's soundness of mind, isn't that a little strange?"

"We discussed it before the change was made," Amos said. "He was adamant. And his mind was sound as a dollar."

"Oh? He thought that exercise would make him live to a hundred."

Bruno's face looked like a shadowgraph made with a fist. If he resented this discussion, he did not show it.

"Wasn't it the exercise that killed him?" Mrs. Folwell asked.

Cadbury let these interruptions subside and finished reading. People whom Father Dowling had assumed were staff and clerical help were provided for, though in a much more modest way than Bruno. As Amos was scooping up his papers, Father Dowling asked him, *sotto voce,* what fifteen percent of the net worth would be.

Amos did not hesitate. "At the least, twenty million dollars, at the most thirty."

He had not answered in a whisper. Mouths fell open all around the table.

"That's absurd," Regis said, and he wasn't smiling at all.

"There are other absurdities in the will," Emily informed the ceiling.

Amos Cadbury said, "There are of course legal steps you

could take. I do not recommend them. Indeed, I will defend this will to my dying breath."

Priest and lawyer left together, and on the driveway Father Dowling asked, "What was your reaction when Fielding Potter left that much to Bruno?"

"I thought he was crazy."

"You said his mind was sound as a dollar."

"Yes." The little bow of a smile. "A Confederate dollar. He wrote a column under the name Jeff Davis, you know."

"So I've heard."

Cadbury looked back at the house. "They were all treated better than they deserve. But I do not think they will let Bruno have his portion uncontested."

"Amos, have you spoken to the police about the way Potter died?"

"Captain Keegan has been trying to reach me. I mean to return his call when I get back to my office."

"Fielding Potter may have been killed, Amos."

"What?"

"Smothered. Smothered and then brought to St. Hilary's and left on the steps of the school without identification."

"Why haven't I been told this?"

"Talk to Captain Keegan."

Again Amos looked back at the house, this time with an expression of wonderment on his face. He turned to his companion. "I intend to, Father. Goodbye."

He slid into the backseat of the gleaming black car with gray upholstery that had been waiting for him, and it began to move soundlessly away.

During the rest of that week, the investigation of the death of Fielding Potter went discreetly on, all but fading from the newspapers, although Merlin of the *Fox River Tribune* was said to have written thousands of words that did not find their way into print. But then Regis Potter, true to Cadbury's prediction, began a court case to modify his uncle's will in the matter of Bruno Armshlager.

"Cadbury will fight it," Father Dowling told the reporter when he visited the rectory.

"Regis Potter has put the matter in Tuttle's hands."

"Tuttle! Surely you're not serious."

Tuttle was a particularly vivid example of what happens when the ranks of lawyers swell. He was an extraordinary choice for Regis to make.

"Maybe Cadbury recommended him." Merlin grinned. "I'm kidding. I think Regis figured Tuttle was just the lawyer he needed to shake the patrician loftiness of Amos Cadbury. They will suggest that Bruno twisted the old man's arm."

"Because Bruno is strong?"

"I can see him carrying Potter through the deserted night streets and dumping him on the school steps."

The task of getting Potter to where he had been found was, Father Dowling conceded, not negligible. He had the feeling that Bruno would not fare well in the stories Merlin would write. He decided to accompany the reporter to the school to shield Edna Hospers from the reporter, but she gave a crisp, accurate account, several times, and Merlin wrote it down. Father Dowling noticed that she did not mention any of the seniors who were there, not even Austin Beatty. He ran into Austin on his way back to the rectory.

"I understand you met the family, Father."

"What exactly did you do for Fielding Potter, Austin?"

"I made him rich." The solemn look gave way to a broad smile. "He certainly didn't make me rich. I was in charge of circulation."

"I thought his papers are given away."

"Yes. But they have to get to people's doorsteps. That may sound simple, but it isn't. Who will complain if he receives no copy of a paper to which he has not subscribed? It is a great temptation for carriers to simply dump their papers. My job was to police the carriers."

"Were they well paid?"

"They would have done better on welfare. Potter was not inclined to pay much for unskilled labor. There was an infinite supply of people willing to do it. But once they got the job, they resented the pay."

"You actually went around checking on carriers?"

"My man on the street was Bruno Armshlager."

"Well, well. He has come into his own, hasn't he?"

"He deserves every penny." Austin spoke with controlled evenness. "For once in his life, old Potter showed some gratitude."

It was good to hear someone who did not resent the silent masseur's good fortune. But of course Austin Beatty did not suffer from Bruno's gain.

When he returned to the rectory Emily Potter called to ask if Father Dowling could come to the house immediately.

"This is rather an emergency, Father. You must not think that I am determined to pester you because once you were kind."

"An emergency?"

"It has to do with Regis' legal action. Bruno is with me."

Father Dowling said he would come, and so twenty minutes later he turned for the third time into the Potter driveway, was invited by Emily's voice to enter, and proceeded to the house. The imposing figure of Bruno Armshlager awaited him on the steps.

"Miss Emily has gone to the gazebo. I'll take you there."

He turned and started across the lawn and Father Dowling

fell into step with him.

"I didn't get the chance to congratulate you on your good fortune."

Bruno shrugged.

"What will you do with all that money?"

"I don't want it!" he blurted out as they came round the house with the gazebo straight ahead.

And that was the emergency Emily had called him to discuss. Bruno, offended by the reaction to his good fortune, had decided to refuse the money. He was content to let Emily speak for him.

"Of course he must do nothing of the kind. Regis cannot possibly break the will. Amos Cadbury assures me of that."

"I don't want the money," Bruno said as urgently as before.

Emily ignored him. "Admittedly a transition from the modest salary he has been receiving to the life of a millionaire poses problems. I have been instructing him in the matter. I am a millionaire myself, for heaven's sake, or so I have always been told. Now it is a matter of public news. It really makes little difference." She patted her maroon turban, adjusted her dark glasses, and disturbed the chalky blankness of her face with a smile. "One of the options open to one with money is to live modestly."

"I don't need money to live the way I want," Bruno said.

Emily shooed him away. "I wanted you to know this, Father. You and Amos Cadbury are friends. Of course, Amos needs no inducement to defend my father's will. But your moral support may be appreciated."

"What is to prevent Bruno from refusing the money?"

"It will be his in any case. Making him keep it is another matter. I assured him that the Potter estate will not accept such a gift from Bruno Armshlager."

Late that afternoon, Phil Keegan called to say that Bruno Armshlager had been arrested.

"What on earth for?"

"The prosecutor's office is still working on the precise indictment. Failing to report a crime, for starters."

"What crime?"

"The murder of Fielding Potter."

"And Bruno was a witness?"

"At least. He must have known something. He was the one who put Potter's body where it was found."

"How did you learn that?"

"Potter's clothes have fibers from a flannel warm-up jacket of Bruno's. Which in turn has fibers of Potter's clothing. Suggesting that he carried the old man."

"Phil, even Tuttle could defend him against that. The two men worked out together daily."

"Potter was eighty-two years old."

"I know. But he had become an exercise freak. He ran a couple of miles a day."

"I'd have to see that to believe it."

"Why would he carry the old man anywhere, let alone here?"

"I was hoping you could enlighten me on that score."

Father Dowling had pondered that question. Why would someone leave the old man's body anywhere, let alone St. Hilary's? One answer was that it could have been anywhere but had to be somewhere and St. Hilary's had been it. But he was not satisfied with this. There seemed to be something significant, symbolic, in putting the old man there. What possible connection could there be between Fielding Potter and St. Hilary's school? If the old man had been a parishioner, if he had attended the parish school . . . And then he thought of Austin Beatty.

It was the only connection he knew between Potter and the school, tenuous as it was. He picked up the phone and rang

Edna Hospers.

"How often does Austin Beatty come to the center, Edna?"

"Oh, he's become one of the regulars. And tells others about it. There must be ten others who have come because of Austin's publicizing what we're doing."

Other former employees of Fielding Potter? Not a question he could put to Edna.

"Is he around today?"

"I saw him ten minutes ago."

"Would it be too much trouble to ask him to come see me?"

"Will do."

But Austin did not come to the rectory. Edna called back to say he must have left for the day. "A friend of his is in some kind of trouble, and he has gone to see him."

"What kind of trouble?"

"I was told Austin went downtown to the jail."

Amos Cadbury was furious. "I will defend the man myself, Father Dowling. This is all part of Regis' attempt to break his uncle's will and I won't have it. My clients have a right to my steadfast loyalty, in death as in life. I will not stand idly by while stunts like this are pulled."

"Regis didn't arrest Bruno, Amos. The police did."

"And where did they get the supposed evidence?"

"I understand there is proof that Bruno carried the old man, Amos."

"Of course he did. He carried him every day. Fielding had become a fanatic. He had actually put before himself the goal of a five-mile run. He pushed himself incredibly, to the point of exhaustion. Father Dowling, I myself have seen Bruno lift him up, support him, and, yes, carry him. It was because of that devotion that Fielding was so generous to the man."

"If that is testified to, there won't be much of a case."

"If I don't prevent it from going to trial, I won't be much of a lawyer. I promise you I will have Bruno out of jail within the hour."

Phil Keegan came to the noon Mass the following day and remained for lunch. Marie, who normally delighted in having someone at table with a more demanding palate than the pastor's, seemed uncharacteristically cool, so much so that Phil commented on it.

"I am sure you know what you are doing, Captain Keegan."

"That is a very broad statement, Mrs. Murkin."

She had been heading for the kitchen but turned in the doorway. "Why couldn't you arrest one of the others if you had to do something, the nephew or the daughter? Oh, no. It has to be someone else. Why do you always go after the little man?"

"The little man!" Phil laughed. "I hope you don't mean Bruno Armshlager."

"You know I do."

"Then you haven't seen him. He weighs as much as I do and is half my height. And what there is of him is all muscle. Including between his ears."

"Dumb enough to be arrested?"

"Marie, we brought him in for questioning. The account in the paper was inaccurate, as usual. He was released yesterday. And we are giving equal attention to the other heirs."

"So you're bringing Emily and Regis in for questioning?" Father Dowling asked.

"The missing identification of Fielding Potter showed up."

"Where was it found?"

"We got an anonymous call advising us to check Regis Potter's locker at the athletic club. There was a paper bag with a wallet, keys, handkerchief, pen, pencil, and change. The contents of his pockets, apparently."

"What is Regis' explanation?"

Phil looked at his watch. "I will know that in approximately one hour. He comes by my office at two."

Not exactly the way Bruno had been treated, but Father Dowling made no comment. Bruno in any case was now free.

"Gone back to Miss Emily?"

"I suppose."

But at that very moment, Bruno was waiting in the front parlor where Marie Murkin had put him. He had not had to convince her that he needed to see the pastor alone. She would not deliver him into the hands of the enemy. Not that her sense of solidarity was not strained when she saw Bruno Armshlager in the flesh. After Phil Keegan was gone, Marie told Father Dowling of his visitor and he came immediately into the parlor.

Bruno sat on the edge of a chair, cracking his knuckles, nervous as a cat. If this man were ever put in jail he would lose his mind within a week. He put out his hand and it was enclosed in a viselike grip.

"I want to give you the money," Bruno said.

"That's nonsense, Bruno. I appreciate the thought, but there are far more demanding causes than this parish if you want to give away the money."

"I don't want the money."

"I understand that. If I were you, I would discuss this with Mr. Cadbury. He would be happy to help you pick out worthy causes."

"I want you to have it."

"I'll speak to Mr. Cadbury for you."

"You take it."

"Bruno, why St. Hilary's?"

He did not get the point of the question. Father Dowling grew bold.

"Bruno, why did you put Mr. Potter's body on the school steps?"

Bruno did not answer, but something reminiscent of a smile disturbed his mouth. It looked like a healed wound in repose and now opened to reveal a row of very even lower teeth. He rose. Was it fanciful to take his reaction as an admission? But Bruno had done all the visiting he intended to do. At the door he said again, "You take the money."

"I will speak to Mr. Cadbury for you."

And then, as the masseur rolled down the walk, the priest called after him. "Austin Beatty comes here, you know. Would you like to see him?"

There was a hitch in his gait, as if he would stop, but he continued on to the van parked at the curb and in a moment drove away.

Roger Dowling left the rectory himself and went over to the school where he found Austin Beatty playing bridge. At the moment, he was dummy, and Father Dowling motioned him away from the table.

"It was nice of you to visit Bruno Armshlager the other day."

A frown, then anger. "Bruno is an idiot."

"Because he doesn't want the money?"

"The family wants to take it from him and he wants to give it away."

"He just offered it to me."

"Are you serious?"

"I refused, of course. I suggested that he have a lawyer set up a benevolent foundation if he wants to give it away."

Austin's face returned to its normal bland expression. "Not a bad idea."

"Why would Bruno bring the body of Fielding Potter here, Austin? It seems deliberate rather than accidental. Why St. Hilary's school?"

"What Bruno does need not make sense."

Father Dowling entered the rectory by the front door and a clearly disturbed Marie Murkin awaited him.

"I was just going to come looking for you."

"Is something wrong?"

"Miss Potter is waiting for you in the study."

Emily had lifted her dark glasses to her forehead and was peering at books. She dropped her glasses before she turned.

"So much poetry. But then you read Tennyson for Father, didn't you?"

"Please sit down."

"I have something on my conscience, Father, and I must discuss it. Am I right in thinking that you would accept death before revealing a confidence?"

"That is a strong statement of it, but you can feel free to speak."

"My cousin Regis has been questioned because the things missing from my father's pockets were found in his possession."

"In his locker at the athletic club."

"Yes. Regis is guilty of many things, but I cannot see him accused of killing my father."

"Has that accusation been made?"

"The assumption will be that he took those things from my father. This will invite the further assumption that he killed my father. He did not."

"You are very sure."

"Those items were put where they were found."

"How do you know that?"

She was silent for a while. "Because Bruno had them in his possession. Now you see why I want this to be confidential."

"No, I don't."

"I don't want Bruno accused of murdering my father any more than I want Regis to be."

"Emily, you yourself said it. The one who had those things could very well be the one who killed your father."

"You don't know Bruno."

"I don't know Regis either. Emily, your father was killed. Someone did it. Someone left him on the steps of the school here."

"That is what puzzles me. None of us knew you before these events. Do you think this was meant to bring us all together?"

"Not for a minute." He turned toward the window and caught a glimpse of Austin Beatty lunging for the shuttlecock in a game in progress behind the school.

"It has had that effect."

"Emily, do you know a man named Austin Beatty?"

She sat back. "Do you know everyone and everything?"

"Then you do?"

"He was one of my father's most valuable employees. Father often said that a significant fraction of his success was due to Mr. Beatty."

"Did they part amicably?"

"Father threw a magnificent banquet for him. Even I was forced to go who had never met Austin Beatty before in my life though I had heard his praises sung for years. Speeches, champagne, a great fete."

"A gold watch?"

"That was the only time I ever saw Austin Beatty."

"You can see him again from that window."

"Really."

"Better still, we can go over to the school and talk to him."

"Whatever for? But tell me, what am I to do about Regis?"

"Why not tell the police all you know?"

"And jeopardize Bruno?"

"Nothing will happen to Bruno."

"You seem very sure of that."

"I am," Father Dowling said, and he did not sound happy saying it. "Bruno did not kill your father."

After five, Father Dowling went back to the senior center, wanting to catch Austin before he might leave. He found Austin standing on the steps where the body of Fielding Potter had been found. He was lighting a cigarette with cupped hands as if a strong wind were blowing.

"We are part of a dwindling fraternity, Austin," the priest said, indicating his pipe.

"Do priests get nagged about tobacco as well?"

"I tell them the only nonsmoking area I aspire to is in the next world."

The two men started walking across the playground. "Are you having second thoughts about Bruno's offer, Father?"

"Not about accepting it, no."

"How so then?"

"I have been wondering why Fielding Potter didn't mention you in his will."

"Me?" He had been lifting his cigarette to his lips, but the motion stopped.

"Emily Potter told me how grateful her father was for all you had done for him."

"Oh, very grateful. He gave me a retirement banquet."

It was difficult to decipher the tone of voice, except that it was very much under control.

"Emily said that even she went to the banquet."

"That was the second time I saw her."

"A banquet doesn't seem much compared with twenty or thirty million dollars."

They had reached the far end of the playground, where it abutted an empty lot in which weeds grew high and luxuriantly. Austin started down the path kids had made. Father Dowling did not follow. Five yards into the field, Austin turned.

"Let's keep walking, Father."

"Fine. But not through there."

Austin shrugged and returned to the priest. Abruptly he grabbed Father Dowling's arm and began to pull him toward the path. His effort was unnecessary since the priest offered no resistance. When they were out of sight of the school, Austin turned and his usually calm face was distorted with rage.

"So Bruno told you everything."

"I would rather hear your version. You needn't grip my arm, Austin."

"It's why he brought the body of that old penny-pincher here. The idiot thought everyone would see the connection."

"With you?"

He ignored the question. "I heard he meant to leave money to Bruno. To Bruno! That ape did nothing but encourage the thought that age could be overcome with exercise, and he is left a king's ransom. Potter was only too glad to tell me I had heard correctly. He cackled about it. He thought it was funny."

"So you killed him?"

"Yes, I killed him!" His grip on Father Dowling's arm tightened. His expression was wild, reason clearly on holiday.

"Tell me about it."

Beatty was happy to describe his act of vengeance. Through Bruno, he had gained access to the grounds and confronted Potter in the gymnasium. The flaw in the plan was that Bruno knew who had been with the old man when he found him dead.

"That's why he brought the body here."

"I'm surprised he didn't do you physical injury."

"So am I."

"What has this gained you, Austin?"

The question seemed to penetrate to his clouded mind. "Satisfaction!"

"But you wanted money."

"I could have accepted not getting any, if he gave it only to his family. But Bruno!"

"And Bruno doesn't want the money."

A pained look came over Austin's face. "He's crazy."

"But is he? What if you had been given thirty million dollars, Austin? What would you really have?"

Beatty stared at the priest as if he had just remembered that the whole world was not worth the price of his soul.

"Come along to the rectory with me, Austin." And he started across the playground.

"Father, wait."

Austin's hand was briefly on his arm, but there was the thudding sound of someone approaching, the hand was withdrawn, and Austin cried out. The priest turned to see Austin Beatty in Bruno's bear grip, in an agony of pain, his feet high off the ground.

"I got him, Father," Bruno said. "He won't lay a hand on you."

Phil Keegan poured out the rest of his beer and crushed the can in his palm.

"You're as strong as Bruno," Father Dowling said dryly.

"How is the new physical fitness room working out?"

"Working out is the right word. The women take to it as readily as the men. Bruno has become a great favorite."

"As well as a great benefactor."

"A too-generous benefactor."

Bruno had underwritten the transformation of a room in the school into a physical fitness center. He had tried to press a new church on the parish; he wanted to knock down the school and replace it with a new building. As a trustee of the Bruno Armshlager Foundation, Father Dowling was able to channel

Bruno's generosity in other directions.

Austin Beatty had been represented by Tuttle. He had been allowed to plead guilty to a charge of manslaughter and got off relatively easily. Of course, he would be beyond the restorative powers of exercise when he was free again, but things could have gone worse for him. Father Dowling hoped they might go better. That was why he had relented and accepted Bruno's money for the shrine that had gone up along the pathway to the church, a granite plinth and a fine marble statue by Reed Armstrong.

"Who is it?" Phil Keegan asked. "Statues all look alike to me."

"St. Jude Thaddeus."

Phil Keegan thought a minute. "Isn't he the patron of lost causes?"

"Yes, he is."

THE FAT CAT

1

Father Dowling thought, as he often had before, how nice it would be if he could identify the flowers and trees and birds that made the walk from the church to the rectory so pleasant on a summer day.

"All you need is a book," Marie Murkin said. "Match the picture with a bush or bird, and that's all there is to it."

"That sounds easy enough."

"But what's the point of it? Would the birds sound better or the flowers smell sweeter just because you know their names?"

"A rose by any other name would smell as sweet?"

"I hate roses." Marie looked over her shoulder as if this heresy might be overheard by old Saunders, who spent the day puttering around the flower beds, leaving the mowing to Gerry Hospers. Not that Marie thought a lot of Saunders. She did not approve of Father Dowling's hiring ex-convicts to work on the parish grounds. But he had come with the highest recommendation from Father Klima, the prison chaplain. "He grew orchids in coffee cans, Roger."

"He has a green thumb?"

"In several senses." Saunders spent years in Joliet because as a bank teller he had thumbed too many dollars into his own pocket.

Father Dowling did talk to Saunders, and found him a fount of information on flora and fauna. "What's that plant, Bob?"

"Ah, that's an old friend. I've had him for years."

"When you were in Joliet?"

Saunders nodded. His expression suggested that Father Dowling had mentioned some far-off place he hardly remembered.

"It looks almost edible."

Saunders looked sharply at the pastor. "I wouldn't advise that."

"I realize it isn't a vegetable."

"Oh, there are lots of flowers and plants you can eat. A pretty good salad could be made up of the things in this bed."

"But not your old friend?"

Bob Saunders moved on to another bed and Father Dowling followed along. How satisfying work with living things must be when you had such skill.

"Bob says you could make a salad of the flowers out there."

Marie took umbrage at this. "I won't tell him how to garden if he doesn't tell me how to cook."

2

Father Dowling made a monthly day of recollection, preferring a religious house in which to do so. Dominicans, Jesuits, even the Franciscans, though he found it best not to tell Marie this. There was an enmity between her and the Franciscans that antedated Father Dowling's assignment to St. Hilary's parish in Fox River, Illinois. On the day he went to the former Franciscan house of studies where a few ancient priests lived, he was surprised and delighted to find that Klima was also there.

"How's Saunders doing?"

"He's exactly what I needed."

"How long you here for?"

"Through the afternoon."

"Care to have dinner?"

"Why don't we go to my rectory? You'll never have better cooking than Marie Murkin's."

That arranged, the two priests settled down to a day of meditation and devotions. The state of the grounds was a distraction—lawn in need of mowing, weeds and flowers fighting for primacy in the flower beds, hedges grown shapeless. Strange that Klima hadn't sent Saunders here to the house of the order to which he belonged. But Father Dowling drove out such thoughts and turned to the Imitation of Christ.

"I'm surprised you didn't hire Klima to take care of your house of studies," he said when they were on their way to the St. Hilary's rectory in Father Dowling's car. He had phoned Marie to tell her there would be a guest and she had responded with enthusiasm. She regarded the pastor as anorexic and the prospect of a priest with an appetite cheered her. Father Dowling saw no reason to tell Marie that Father Klima was a Franciscan.

"We couldn't afford him, Roger. Besides, we're thinking of selling the place."

"No!"

"A few more deaths, and there won't be any excuse for keeping it."

They observed a minute of silence. Many good things were happening in the Church again, but priests their age had seen the withering away of once mighty orders and institutions. For decades properties once devoted to the housing of nuns or seminarians had gone on the block and places that were the repositories of youthful dreams fell into alien hands. Now new seminaries were being built and the number of seminarians slowly rising, at least in some locales.

"The penitentiary reminds me of the old days."

From anyone other than Klima this would have been a damning criticism of the past. But all he meant was the regularity, the schedule, the absence of worldly concerns.

After Father Dowling parked the car and he and Klima approached the rectory, the aroma of dinner came to meet them. "Is that goulash?"

Goulash it was, as succulent as it can be. There was a green salad as well as fruit salad, but it was a simple meal, the main dish the main attraction.

"I remembered Father Dowling mentioning you were Hungarian."

This delighted Klima even more. He praised the salads as well.

"Does this one come from our garden?" Father Dowling asked, but Marie ignored him.

"It must be very difficult, living in a prison?" Marie said to Klima toward the end of the meal.

"Not while I'm there. Right now I'm thinking how pleasant it would be to have a little parish of my own."

"Is Bob Saunders around, Marie?"

"He should be."

She went out the kitchen door and was gone ten minutes before reappearing, shaking her head. "That's funny. He's gone off to a movie. I told him you were coming, Father Klima."

"Maybe he doesn't want to be reminded of the past."

The two priests repaired to the study and fell into the kind of clerical gossip that forms a strong fraternal bond among priests. The trouble was that Klima's stories mostly concerned members of his order and thus were of limited interest to the pastor of St. Hilary's. So the conversation drifted to the scene of Klima's priestly work.

He spoke with great affection of the lifers. Theirs was a death sentence as sure as those who were on death row, enjoying the moratorium on capital punishment the governor of Illinois had introduced. Klima had his own views on whether a life sentence was preferable to execution. "Some become reconciled and gentle. There is a kind of holiness even, I think. Others become evil. Saunders' cell mate was a lifer."

"He's still there?"

"No, he died before Saunders was released." Klima frowned. "An odd death."

"How so?"

"He poisoned himself. One of Saunders' plants was poisonous and when Ed Factor heard that he had his ticket out of Joliet."

3

The world is divided into those who love cats and those who can't stand them. Marie Murkin fell into the latter category. Her current *bête noire* was a large black cat with insolent eyes that had laid claim to a ledge on the back porch where sun was filtered through gently moving leaves and prolonged feline leisure could be enjoyed. The cat was brought each day to the parish center by Chester Fields, whom some called Smokes. Fields dismissed the idea that he should leave Felix at home.

"He gets lonely."

"He spends all day lurking around the rectory."

"It's the food."

"But I don't feed him."

Chester Fields smiled. "You will."

"I know what I'd like to feed him," Marie grumbled, but Fields was a prophet after all. Father Dowling noticed the housekeeper's attitude to the large cat drowsing on the ledge outside her kitchen slowly change. There was something flattering in the need Felix felt to spend his day in the proximity of Marie Murkin.

"I think he listens to the radio," Marie said, when Father

Dowling asked if she had put catnip on the porch ledge to keep Felix there.

Shortly after that, Marie began to set aside tidbits for Felix. "It would just be thrown out anyway."

"Maybe Chester would let you keep him."

"I hate cats!" But her tone was not as apodictic as before.

Marie concealed her change of attitude from all others, however much the pastor guessed her altered regard for Felix. On occasion, when Marie saw a need to deflect suspicion, Bob Saunders became the grateful recipient of morsels that might have gone to the cat. It was an odd thought that the gardener and the cat were rivals for Marie's largesse. And Chester continued to be told what a nuisance his cat was.

"He knows when people like him," Chester said smugly.

"I hate cats!"

Chester winked at Saunders and strolled off to the center, leaving Felix to arrange his own day. Within a minute, Felix had arranged himself on the warm ledge of the rectory's back porch.

It was going on four in the afternoon when Chester knocked on the kitchen door then shaded the screen with his hand as he peered in at Marie Murkin.

"Felix in there?"

"In my kitchen! Certainly not."

"Have you seen him?"

"Chester, if you think I am going to babysit your animal, you are mistaken."

"Ever since you started feeding him, you made a lifelong friend."

Marie came out onto the porch. "Feed him? Who said I feed him?"

"He's gained four pounds in as many weeks."

"How often do you weigh him?"

"Every morning. After my exercise."

"Why?"

"Actually I'm usually holding him when I get on the scale, so I have to subtract. I thought I was gaining weight. But it was Felix. And how would he gain weight if you didn't feed him?"

"What nonsense."

But she helped him look around the yard for the cat. Chester wondered if Felix was hiding. "So he could stay here with you."

"Ha."

Marie started back to the house and was halfway there when a wail went up behind her. She turned to see Chester backing away from the fence, a look of horror on his face. He turned to Marie. His expression changed.

"You!" Chester cried, and then he pushed through the gate and disappeared.

"What's wrong?" Bob Saunders said.

"I think something has happened to Chester Fields' cat."

She kept a pace or two behind Saunders as he shuffled toward the back fence. Felix lay as if asleep behind a stand of hollyhocks. But his eyes were open and his body was still. Marie fled to the house.

4

In the study, Father Dowling picked up the ringing phone to find Edna Hospers on the line.

"What happened to Chester Fields' cat?"

"Felix?"

"Chester is almost hysterical. He claims Marie Murkin killed his cat."

"Can I speak to him?"

"He's in no condition, Father."

"I'll talk to Marie."

When he hung up the phone and turned, Marie stood in the doorway, her face a mask of puzzled pain. She drifted into the room and sat, staring at Father Dowling.

"That was Edna, Marie."

Marie nodded. Father Dowling had never seen her so subdued.

"Has something happened to Chester's cat?"

A nod. "He's dead."

"What happened?"

"I don't know! Father, Chester thinks I harmed that animal."

"That's ridiculous. I'll go talk to him."

In the parish school, now used as a parish center where senior
citizens could spend their day at bridge, shuffleboard, checkers,
chess, or conversation, Father Dowling found Chester Fields
ringed by the sympathetic and curious. The old man was literally sobbing. When he saw Father Dowling, he rose like Lazarus
and came through the parted crowd to the pastor.

"Do cats have souls, Father Dowling?"

"Of course they do."

Chester stopped weeping and rubbed his eyes. There was a
sigh of relief from the others. No need to explain that according
to Aristotle every living thing had a soul, from weeds to your
mother-in-law, but of course there are kinds of soul. The human
soul is utterly different from those of plants and animals and is
our ticket to immortality.

"Let's go upstairs, Chester."

"Call me Smokes, Father."

In Edna's office, they continued the theological discussion
begun below, with Edna an interested onlooker. "He could
understand me, Father. Sometimes I thought he knew how to
talk but refrained for fear of embarrassing me."

"How so?"

"I think he was smarter than me."

"We'll never know."

"Is the cat dead?" Edna asked.

312

Father Dowling waited for Chester to answer. "She killed it."

"Chester, that's foolish. Marie was very good to that cat."

"She threatened to kill Felix! I heard her. You must have heard her."

How to defend Marie against the threatening remarks that increasingly had masked her affection for the cat?

"Chester, come back to the rectory with me."

The old man shuddered. "I couldn't look at him again." Chester had buried two wives and lived to tell of it, but the death of his cat had unmanned him. Finally, with cajoling and sternness, Father Dowling got Chester onto the walk leading to the rectory. Standing in the doorway of the school were a dozen old people, hesitant whether or not to follow the pastor and the bereaved Chester for possible further emotional fireworks.

Marie sat at the kitchen table, her hands twisted in her apron. She looked abjectly at Father Dowling when he came in, but when she saw that Chester was with him, she sprang to her feet.

"I did not harm that cat, Chester Fields. I watched over him. I fed him."

"The question is," Chester squeaked, "what did you feed him?"

"What is that supposed to mean?"

"You did what you said you'd do. You poisoned him!"

"Chester Fields, if you say that again I will sue you for libel. I will get on that phone and talk to Mr. Amos Cadbury and he will teach you a lesson about libeling people. I am sorry about your cat. Much sorrier than you know."

"Do they do autopsies on cats?" Father Dowling wondered aloud.

"That's the ticket!" Marie said.

She went to the back door and held the screen open so that Father Dowling and Chester would follow her. Then she marched out to the fence and the stand of hollyhocks. The distance between her and Father Dowling and Chester grew as her pace quickened. At the fence, she stopped. She parted the long stalked hollyhocks, bending to study the ground. She turned and looked openmouthed at the two men.

"It's not here."

5

Confusion followed the discovery that the dead cat was gone. Chester began once more his strident accusations of Marie. Marie stalked off to the house to call Amos Cadbury. While she was talking to the lawyer, Phil Keegan and Cy Horvath drove up. Keegan frowned at the sobbing Chester.

"What's wrong with him?"

"His cat's dead."

"Tough."

"He was killed! And now the body's been stolen. Marie Murkin killed my cat and now she's hidden the body."

"Marie?" Phil could not keep a malicious little smile from dimpling the corners of his mouth.

"I buried it."

They all turned to Bob Saunders, who stood there, spade in hand. "You don't want a dead animal lying around like that. So I buried it."

"You had no right!"

Cy took Chester's arm and led him across the lawn to a bench beneath an apple tree. The two men settled on the bench and Cy, like a father confessor, listened impassively through Chester's tale of woe. Marie came out of the house to announce that Amos Cadbury was on his way to protect her from libelous accusations.

"It's my punishment for feeding that beast."

"Bob Saunders buried the body."

"Well, he'll have to dig it up again. Mr. Cadbury insists that there be an autopsy."

"An autopsy!" Phil headed for the kitchen.

"You got any beer, Marie?"

Bob Saunders dug up the body of Felix the cat, Amos arrived with the veterinarian that looked after his Irish setters, and the body of Felix was taken away. Chester Fields, subdued by the consolation he had derived from Cy's mute and patient listening, had finally gotten a grip on himself. The imposing presence of Amos Cadbury was a check upon his tongue. Marie kept close to the lawyer. Phil leaned against the porch ledge, drinking a beer. Some yards away, the contingent from the center looked on from where they had come to a stop, just short of the rectory, at a point where they had been able to follow events.

"Why don't you join the others, Chester?" Father Dowling suggested.

Cy led the stricken Chester to the others, who surrounded him and convoyed him back to the school.

6

The autopsy was inconclusive. There were traces of what might have been poison in Felix, but the report was unable to identify it. The more likely cause of death was a heart attack.

"His cholesterol was at a deadly level."

"Why don't we just leave it at a heart attack?" Father Dowling suggested.

Chester listened calmly when told that Felix had been betrayed by his heart. His wives had died of heart attacks. This was a role he could handle. He nodded with dignity and then turned silently away. And that was that.

Father Dowling went for a walk, stopping by one of the flower beds. He studied it for some time. Bob Saunders' old friend seemed to be missing, replaced with an innocuous-looking pinkish flower. He could have looked it up in a book, but there seemed no point.

In the rectory, Marie Murkin walked with the burden of guilt. Had she fed Felix to death, giving him tasty and unhealthy foods that had stopped up his arteries and killed him?

"It just goes to show," she said.

"Show what?"

"No good deed goes unpunished."

"Now, Marie."

Chester Fields, after talking with Amos, decided to replace Felix with a magnificent Irish setter. But this animal could not be accommodated at the parish center during the day and Chester became an infrequent visitor.

"What happened to your old friend?" Father Dowling asked Bob Saunders some days later. He pointed to the flower bed.

"I got rid of it, Father. I think it was bad luck."

"How so?"

"My cell mate committed suicide by eating its leaves."

"It's that lethal?"

"He was dead in the morning."

"I wonder if Felix could have . . ."

Bob Saunders waited for Father Dowling to finish the sentence. But the pastor let it go. There was a strange vacancy in Bob Saunders' eyes, the look of a man who had seen, and done, more than he cared to remember. Had Bob been simply a spectator of the deaths associated with his old friend?

"Roger," Father Klima said when he telephoned the following week. "I want to talk to Bob Saunders, but not before I get your reaction. We're suddenly getting vocations again. How about if we take Bob off your hands and put him to work on the grounds of the old house of studies?"

This was arranged. Edna's son Gerry would expand his duties beyond mowing the lawns. One day Bob Saunders was driven away by Father Klima, to beautify the grounds of the

Franciscan house of studies.

"Franciscan!" Marie cried.

"Father Klima is a Franciscan."

"But you said he was a Hungarian."

"The two are not incompatible, Marie."

There were times during the following weeks when Father Dowling would be distracted from what he was doing, would look up from his book and stare across his study. Danger is all around us. Any of the four elements, fire, air, earth or water, can be an instrument of death. Food can kill you, if not because it's poisonous, because it fills the blood with obstacles to circulation. But such speculation soon gave way to the enigmatic countenance of Bob Saunders. Killing a cat may not be murder, but it is an injustice to its owner. As for a cell mate . . . But there are mysteries.

WINTER SCHEMES

1

For an hour or two soft wet flakes fluttered down from the lowering clouds, some clinging to bare branches of trees, some lying puffy and impermanent upon the parish lawn until the wind began to blow, the temperature dropped, and the blizzard began. An Illinois blizzard. A December blizzard. Looking out of her kitchen window in the St. Hilary rectory, Marie Murkin could believe that months and months of a snowy world stretched before her. Her mood was mildly melancholy. She remembered something her mother had told her, a remark of an old man to a young girl years and years ago, at just this season of the year. "I don't think I'll winter this year." A tear formed in Marie's eye at the memory. And then she made the mistake of telling the story when Phil Keegan was in the house, visiting Father Dowling.

"He meant he was going to Florida, Marie?"

"He meant he didn't think he'd last the winter!" Marie glared at Captain Keegan. Honestly, sometimes she believed that men didn't have a soft spot in their hearts.

"I think he must have been talking of a trip south."

"Did he last the winter, Marie?" Father Dowling asked gently.

"I don't know." Marie shut the study door after her when she left them, closing it harder than necessary, and retreated to her kitchen where she sat at the table and became once more mesmerized by the snow that swirled and eddied at the window.

Suddenly she lurched. There was a face pressed again the pane. Marie was on her feet. Undecided, she started toward the study, then stopped. When she looked again at the window the face was gone.

She leaned over the sink toward the window, rubbing it clear, but there was no face in sight. But how could anyone look in that window with the snow swirling and piling up? She hurried in to tell Father Dowling.

"The window over the sink?" he asked.

"I know. He'd have to be tall to look in that window."

The pastor had risen, but Phil remained comfortably seated.

"Maybe he decided to winter after all, Marie."

Before Marie could express her anger, Father Dowling intervened. "Come on, Phil. There might be someone freezing out there."

"Why doesn't he come to the door?" Phil groused, but he got up and followed the pastor.

Dressed in a great hooded jacket, Father Dowling opened the kitchen door. The roar of the blizzard rose and almost immediately the panes of the storm window steamed up. Father Dowling pushed outside, Phil following. Marie put on water for tea and kept busy. But the face she had seen in the window was still vividly present to her. An old man's face, with deep creases in his cheeks, the hair on his hatless head tossed about by the wind, staring at her with wide bloodshot eyes.

Five minutes later, Father Dowling and Phil came in, stamping their shoes free of snow.

"No sign of anyone, Marie."

"False alarm," Phil said, and Marie did not like the tone of his voice.

"But there must have been tracks."

"Then they've blown away, Marie. We went around to the front of the house but there was no sign of anyone." He seemed to be avoiding her eyes.

Marie did not see the face in the window again. No knock came at the door. The wind whined and howled about the rectory, and the thought of anyone out in that storm filled Marie's heart with pity. Marie thought seriously of bundling up and going outside herself. Neither Father Dowling nor Phil Keegan would have searched in the certainty that someone had looked in the kitchen window. But she did not go outside. Instead she continued preparing dinner, assuming Phil Keegan would be the pastor's guest, if someone who came so often could be called a guest.

The two men lingered at the table after Marie had taken away the dishes. She had been in and out of the dining room several times, but hurried right back to the kitchen. The first time, she remained at the door, listening to hear what they might be saying. But the idiotic conversation about the Chicago Bears went on.

"Still snowing?" Phil asked when she went in to freshen their coffee.

"Can't you hear it?"

They observed a moment of silence, listening. The blizzard went on.

"Maybe I'll winter here," Phil said.

Marie said nothing.

"Better looking out than looking in."

There were times when Marie was certain she would scoot right through Purgatory to total bliss. Holding her tongue in the face of such teasing might not seem to be in the same league as St. Sebastian being hit by all those arrows or Saint Cecilia hacked at the neck with a sword, but it took heroic virtue for Marie to get back into her kitchen without responding to Phil Keegan's taunting.

She went up to her apartment as soon as she had the dishes

in the washer. Phil Keegan's voice was audible from the study. The sound of the storm seemed to increase, but her rooms were cozy and warm. And she would have a wee glass of sherry as she read the new Monica Quill mystery. She found herself avoiding the windows, looking away even as she pulled the blinds. Could she have imagined that face? She could still see it as clearly as she had when she looked at the kitchen window. But if someone had looked in that window, they would have left signs of it, no matter how heavily the snow was falling and the wind was whipping it about. She decided that Father Dowling and Phil Keegan had not looked very closely. Nor had they taken a flashlight!

Marie settled down with her sherry, dismissing the thought that she had seen a ghost at the kitchen window, conjuring from memory the old man who had told her mother years ago that he did not think he would winter that year.

2

The body of the old man was found the following day, in midafternoon, by Gerry, one of Edna Hospers' sons, who had volunteered to run the snowblower over the sidewalks to make them passable after the heavy snowfall. From a clear cloudless sky the sun softened the wintry scene, and Gerry had been fascinated by the plume of snow the blower sent in a graceful arc away from the walk. And then he noticed the shoes emerging from the snow and the outline of a body beneath it. The boy stopped pushing and stared for half a minute, and then he ran to the school to tell his mother what he had found.

"It's Edna," Marie said, looking into the study. Father Dowling picked up the phone and received the grisly news. A minute later, having put on coat and hat, the pastor was hurrying in the direction of the school. The snowblower stood where Gerry had left it, as if to point to where the body lay. Edna, a scarf pulled over her head, clutching her unbuttoned coat about her, came hurrying from the school, followed by her son.

"I called nine-one-one, Father."

"Good."

Father Dowling stepped into the heavy snow and moved toward the body. The first thing he did was to pronounce the words of absolution, then he knelt and began to brush snow off the body.

"It's Jacob!" Edna cried. She had followed the pastor into the snow, despite the fact that she, like the priest, wore street shoes. "Oh, the poor man."

The next hour was hectic. In the rectory, Marie had called Phil and when he came, she managed not to say what she was surely thinking. So much for the skepticism with which they had met her claim to have seen a face at the kitchen window last night.

"We should have searched more carefully, Phil," Father Dowling said.

"Was this the man, Marie?"

The housekeeper nodded, but there was no triumph in her manner. "I should have recognized him." Her mind had been filled with memories of the old man her mother had told her of and she had not seen that it was Jacob Newby looking in her window, seeking a refuge that had been refused him.

The ambulance drove right across the snow to the body, its wheels straddling the half-hidden sidewalk. The official confirmation was made. Jacob was dead. Frozen to death.

"They say it's a painless death," Marie murmured.

"He was at the school yesterday," Edna said.

The body was put into the ambulance and taken away. Edna herded the old people who had been lured by the excitement back to the school that had become a center for seniors in the parish, and Father Dowling and Phil followed a shivering Marie back to the rectory.

"I'll make cocoa."

"Do you have marshmallows, Marie?" Phil asked.

"Of course."

In the study, Father Dowling told Phil who Jacob was.

"He had a crush on Marie."

Jacob Newby had been in the parish for half a century but it was only during the past month that he had come to the parish center. Father Dowling had seen the old man at Mass over the years, but did not really know him. Jacob's wife was long since dead, but a married and childless daughter had moved in with him: Carlotta Burke, and her husband, Will.

"She's after the house," Marie had said. "It's the camel and the tent."

"Push him out?"

"You know what they do with elderly parents nowadays." Marie had paused, but Father Dowling did not take up the theme. "Nursing homes!"

"Don't fret, Marie. You can stay here as long as I do."

This did not give her the reassurance he had intended. She looked him over appraisingly, as if this were the county fair and she was guessing not his weight but his longevity.

"Maybe you should encourage him to spend his days at the center."

"Good idea!"

And Marie had acted on the suggestion, giving the pastor a vivid account afterward of her visit to Jacob Newby's house.

"I talked with the daughter. Carlotta. She was nervous as a cat. Maybe she thought I'd ask her where she and her husband are Sundays when they should be at Mass."

"Did you ask her?"

"Not directly." But Marie shook off this distraction. "She didn't want to let me talk with her father."

"Did you tell her what you had in mind?"

"Is she his keeper? Does he need her permission?"

"You didn't tell her?"

"Only when I could see I'd get no place until I did."

"And that did the trick?"

"Of course she jumped at the idea. That way, she can be rid of him all day long."

"Did you see him?"

Marie firmed her mouth. "No. She said he wasn't presentable. Then she said he was napping. Honestly, I could imagine they had him locked up somewhere."

But two days later, Carlotta Burke drove her father to the senior center in the parish school. Marie, spying the old man emerging from the car, hurried over to the school. Little did she know how Jacob would regard her role in his rescue from his own house. For days, Marie and Jacob were inseparable while Marie debriefed the old man and passed on what she learned to Father Dowling.

"They did keep him in his room, with a portable radio whose batteries were dead. They fed him once a day."

It was difficult to believe what became, in Marie's telling, a horror story. Jacob's gratitude turned to something more. The falling leaves of autumn stirred a springtime urgency in him. They were sitting on a bench beside the sidewalk that ran from rectory to school when Jacob suddenly took Marie in his arms and tried to kiss her. Marie managed to unwind his arms, give him a scolding, and then hurry back to the rectory.

"I couldn't believe it, Father. A man that age."

"You can't blame him for being grateful to you."

"Grateful." Marie rolled her eyes. But her indignation did not prevent the story from getting around. Marie herself told Edna and then Phil Keegan.

"I'm not surprised," Phil said.

"What do you mean?"

"Marie, you put a starving man in front of full meal and what's he going to do?"

"I might have known you'd say something sarcastic."

"Do you want to bring charges?"

Jacob's visits to the senior center ceased, and Father Dowling expected Marie to show concern, given the account she had given of Jacob's living conditions in his own home.

"I think he exaggerated, Father."

"They didn't lock him in his room?"

"Why on earth would they do a thing like that?"

3

Father Dowling had to decide how much of what Marie had told him of Jacob Newby should be passed on to Phil. But when Phil asked if there was anyone who should have sounded the alarm when the old man was missing in a blizzard, Roger Dowling decided to tell him the whole story.

"Make of it what you will," he said when he had finished.

The task of telling Jacob's daughter fell to Father Dowling and he drove through the snowy streets to the address. The driveway was drifted closed with snow and there were no lights on in the house. He waded through the snow to the door anyway and pressed the bell. He pressed it twice more before he gave up and started back to his car.

"They're not home," someone called.

It was a man emerging from the house next door, pulling his parka hood over his head. Father Dowling went to meet him.

"They've gone to Florida, Father."

And then Father Dowling recognized him. "You shouldn't be out in this weather, Nick."

The hood nodded. "That's why I haven't been to the center."

"If his daughter went to Florida . . ."

Nick Cody made an impatient sound, sending a visible puff of breath into the frigid air. "They put him in Holy Cross Nursing." Another angry sound. "Like a kennel."

Father Dowling hesitated but then decided to tell Nick what had befallen Jacob Newby. Nick pushed back the hood of his parka and there was a bitter smile on his face.

"He must have escaped."

The nursing home, it emerged, had reported Jacob missing that morning. The night crew had not reacted to his absence because he was only a temporary. "They thought he had gone home."

Perhaps he had, but there were no house keys among the things that had been removed from the body. Had he confronted a locked house and then come to the rectory? Why hadn't he knocked? Why hadn't he rung the bell? But these questions seemed to put the blame on the old man, and Father Dowling felt a profound guilt over the whole affair. Marie, to her credit, did not question the thoroughness of the search he and Phil had made.

4

Marie was not impressed by the grief shown by Carlotta Burke and her husband, Will, hastily returned from Florida to preside at the wake for Jacob Newby. Carlotta had a marvelous tan and Will's nose was peeling from sunburn.

"We think we should sue," Carlotta said to Father Dowling. The rosary had been said, the open casket stood at the end of the viewing room in which mourners lingered. Edna had arranged for a bus from the center so parish seniors were well represented.

"The parish?"

She lay a hand on his arm with just a flicker of a smile. "The nursing home."

Father Dowling lifted his brows and widened his eyes.

"Our minds were at rest and then to find he was wandering around in a blizzard."

"I shouldn't think they'd have much money,"

"Insurance, Father. They must be insured. There's nothing personal about it."

Was she thinking of the nuns who had accepted the responsibility for Jacob while she herself went off to Florida? In an unwise moment, Father Dowling told Marie Murkin what Carlotta had said.

"Sue? I don't believe it. They are the ones who should be taken to court!"

Amos Cadbury, when consulted, made a long face. "It's a suit they could very well win."

"But that is so unfair," Marie wailed.

"Holy Cross Nursing is a client of mine," Amos said. Just a remark. But it might have been a promise that the Burkes would not easily extract money from the nursing home, insurance or no insurance.

"They shouldn't get a cent."

"Well, if they did it would be all they got from her father's death."

"They'll get the house," Marie said angrily.

"Not unless you give it to them."

"Unless I give it to them!"

"Let me tell you of a visit Jacob Newby made to my office a month ago."

A month ago, two men had shown up at the offices of Amos Cadbury and Associates in downtown Fox River. "Nicholas Cody and I were classmates at Notre Dame. He brought Jacob Newby to me, explaining that Jacob wanted to consult with a lawyer."

Jacob consulted with Amos and Amos was glad to help the

old man fulfill his wishes.

"I confess I was a bit surprised when I heard that you were the beneficiary, Marie. Obviously you made a profound impression on him."

For once in her life, Marie Murkin was speechless. She was Jacob Newby's heir.

5

In the end Carlotta and Will Burke sued Marie Murkin, claiming that her father could only have bequeathed all his worldly goods to her because he was no longer compos mentis. A grasping widow preying on a susceptible and senile man, that was the charge. But Amos was Marie's lawyer and the issue was never in doubt. The charge of the Burkes against Marie had implications for himself as the lawyer who had drawn up Jacob's new will, so Amos had double motivation to ensure that the Burkes returned to Florida with their financial status unchanged for the better. Of course, they were out travel expenses, whatever Tuttle the lawyer had charged them, and the bill at the motel to which they had moved when Amos decided that Marie's legal adversaries should not be the beneficiary of her largess while they sued her.

"Where are you thinking of settling down?" Phil Keegan asked some weeks later when the rectory had once more resumed an even tenor.

"What are you talking about?"

"Florida probably isn't large enough to hold both you and the Burkes. But there's always Arizona."

"Why don't you go to Arizona, Phil Keegan?"

"Is that a proposal?"

Father Dowling intervened. It was difficult for a celibate to interpret the half-coded exchanges of male and female. Who would have guessed the storm of passion Marie had stirred up in the breast of Jacob Newby? Who knew what the badinage of Marie and Phil could lead to? The prospect of losing both his friends to the salvific air of the southwest was not attractive to the pastor of St. Hilary's.

"Marie," he said, "why don't you get Phil a beer."

"He needs some antifreeze."

And she turned on her heel to leave.

"You're right, Marie."

I LOVE THE DEAR
SILVER . . .

1

It was on the playground of St. Hilary's parish school, half a century after he had played there as a boy, that Ward Ripley decided to die, and he asked Joe Walsh to be his collaborator. The decision was prompted, in a way, by the coming together again, after a half-century interval, of Joe, Ward Ripley, and the still lovely Peggy Schwartz.

"How strange to be called that again," Peggy cried, and her laughter ran up and down a scale that might have been Joe's heartstrings. "My married name is Fenster."

"I kept my maiden name," Ward Ripley said, and got a playful slap on the arm as his reward.

"Didn't you marry?"

"Marry! I married three times."

"Ward. How could you?"

"Do you know what the bigamist said when the judge asked how he could possibly keep two wives on opposite sides of town? 'I had a bicycle.' "

Another little slap, but Peggy was clearly fascinated by Ward's breezy charm. Joe did not recognize the historical facts in the account Ward gave of his marriages. The first wife had died, his second marriage had been annulled, and his third wife, thirty years his junior, was on what Ward called sabbatical.

"She's going to law school."

"Where?"

"In Minneapolis."

But how was that possible, Peggy wanted to know, if Ward was living here in Fox River? Joe Walsh had been marginalized by this turn in the conversation. He had unsettling memories of boyhood when Ward had similarly elbowed him out of competition. This improbable reunion at the school they had attended as kids but which was now a senior center brought it all back. After a long lifetime Joe seemed to have ended up where he had begun, the kind of person who gives the phrase "three's a crowd" its bite.

Joe Walsh had taken a position in the First Fox River Bank immediately upon graduating from DePaul, raised two grades to chief teller during the course of his career, and retired at the age of sixty-two, comfortably provided for. But his sense of satisfaction was short-lived.

"You worked thirty-five years as a teller?" Peggy asked and there was the ripple of suppressed laughter in her voice.

"In the First Fox River," Walsh replied.

"That's where I did all my banking," Ripley said, avoiding Walsh's eye. Of course Joe wouldn't mention the foreclosed mortgage and the two cars that had been repossessed.

How could more than fifty years seem so short a time? It was as if it were only yesterday that the three of them had been classmates at St. Hilary's school. Peggy's family had moved out of the state while she was in high school, but she had returned to attend Northwestern, where she met Ignatius Fenster—who had passed on to his eternal reward two years before. Ripley had discovered her, renewed their old acquaintance, and shamelessly misrepresented the course of his life to the susceptible Peggy. What could be more natural than that he should bring her back to the old school, now a center for senior citizens of

St. Hilary's parish?

"It seems like yesterday," Peggy had sighed as they drifted through the corridors of the school, climbed the broad staircases, and looked into the auditorium. "I played 'Country Gardens' on that stage. It was my first recital."

"I recited 'A Visit from St. Nicholas,' " Joe Walsh said, surprising himself that he remembered, but suddenly the occasion was fresh in his mind: he had stood out in front of the drawn curtain, the lights blinding him, going from line to line, from stanza to stanza, the whole thing ending in applause.

"I'll bet you could still play it," Ripley said and a moment later Peggy was at the piano, playing tentatively at first but then her fingers remembered and she was radiant with happiness. Ripley bent over and hugged her, the perfect gesture. How Walsh envied Ripley's ability to seize the moment.

Now in the playground, Walsh found his life in the bank the object of gentle mockery. He seemed to remember that he had had a crush on Peggy when they were children together. It had continued into high school when she refused his invitation to the junior prom. That had been a low moment. Thoughts of a monastic vocation came and went but Peggy would have neither known nor cared that he was throwing away his life for her. In a sense he had, however. He never married. He took a degree in business and worked in the bank and he might have been a monk after all. Not that he brooded. The brooding only began with retirement. It increased when he realized that in Peggy's eyes his life had been a boring waste. He couldn't help but think that if only Ward would get lost he might have a second chance with Peggy. Her interest in Ward seemed to flag, but of course the resourceful Ward could not accept that and decided to do something about it.

"I've got a terrific idea but I can't bring it off without your help."

"What is it?" Joe asked warily.

Ward was beside himself with excitement. But he calmed down and told Joe confidentially that he had been coming to the senior center for weeks now and the truth was it was pretty dull. Something was needed to liven the place up. "How much longer do you suppose Peggy is going to want to come here?"

"She seems to enjoy being here." Peggy was playing bridge at a table on the far side of the former gym and looked anything but bored.

"She's a good scout, is all."

"So what's the terrific idea?"

Ward looked around, then leaned toward Joe and whispered theatrically, "I am going to die."

"What!"

Ward grabbed his arm. "Take it easy. I don't mean really die. This is a gag."

Death was not exactly a punch line at the senior center. What had for most of their lives seemed some remote destination at which they would eventually arrive now seemed to lie around any corner. These men and women had lost spouses and children and some of them were being treated for serious complaints. No one needed a reminder that death might come at any moment. A little distracting game of shuffleboard or bridge was almost a necessity to get your mind off it.

"I think it will also help my chances with Peggy."

"Oh?"

"Do you remember when I broke my leg in sixth grade?"

"No, I don't." It was the sort of thing he should remember.

"Peggy does. I reminded her of it. Before that she hadn't known me from the next guy. But when I was laid up with that broken leg, she would come visit me and my mom would serve us cocoa. She even drew a heart on my cast with our initials in it."

"Why don't you just break a leg?" It would have been difficult to tell Ward how little inclined he was to help him in his
campaign with Peggy. "Your wife could sue the parish."

"My wife?"

"The one on sabbatical!"

Ward seemed to have to think back to see what he had or had
not said. He grew solemn. "I wouldn't tell this to anyone, Joe,
but I think we're washed up. Law school was just a symptom.
She wants a divorce."

"A divorce!"

"Look, it sounds worse than it is. How bad a Catholic do you
think I am? Why do you think I took the precaution not to
marry Susan in the church? In the eyes of the church we're not
really married, are we? So what does a divorce mean?"

"That's pretty cynical."

"Joe. I don't make the rules."

"You just break them?"

"Hey."

If Ward's success with Peggy repeated a triumph of his boyhood, Joe's inability not to be manipulated by Ward brought
back the time before his achievements and position had given
him a sense of self-reliance and autonomy. All that seemed to
have fled now, and they were two boys on the playground, the
one dominating the other and with the attention of Peggy at
stake. After some resistance, Joe agreed to take part in Ward's
practical joke. Maybe he found it attractive to imagine himself
bringing Peggy the news that Ward Ripley was no more.

The plan was simple enough. The following day, Joe would
show up at St. Hilary's with a sealed letter for Peggy. When she
opened it, she would read a farewell from Ward Ripley. He
would not bother her with the long tale of the ills that weighed
him down. Suffice it to say that they were more than he could
bear any longer. Farewell, sweet Peggy. This would have been so

much easier if you had not come back into my life.

They worked on the letter that afternoon, writing it on Joe's computer. Joe printed it out and watched Ward sign it. It might be a joke, but it was a solemn moment watching him put his signature to such a statement. Maybe a foreclosed mortgage and repossessed cars make documents seem unimportant. Joe realized that he could never sign such a letter even as a joke.

"I'll get an envelope, Ward."

When he came back, Ward slipped the folded letter into the envelope, sealed it, and handed it to Joe.

"How long do you plan to stay dead?"

"Twenty-four hours ought to do it."

The next morning when Joe arrived at St. Hilary's to pass on the letter to Peggy, he was surprised when a patrol car pulled into the parking lot with Ward Ripley in the backseat, and he found himself under arrest.

2

Father Dowling saw the police car pull into the parking lot behind the school and asked Marie Murkin what she thought was going on.

"That's a police car," she said.

"I think you're right."

"They seem to be arresting someone."

Father Dowling got up from the table and went to the door. When he saw an unmarked car pull in and Cy Horvath get out, Father Dowling left the rectory and went toward the scene of all the excitement.

"They've arrested Joe Walsh, Father," Mrs. Mackle chirped.

"Can they do that on church property?" Old Charlie Quirk had the look of a man about to quote the Constitution.

"What's going on, Cy?"

Joe Walsh was being led toward a patrol car but when he saw

Father Dowling he dug in his heels. "Stop them, Father. I haven't done anything."

"What is the charge?"

"A murder threat."

"It was a joke!" Joe cried and he threw his wide-eyed appeal beyond the pastor to the other seniors. But they shuffled their feet and turned away, embarrassed. A hand was put on Joe's head as he was pushed into the backseat of the patrol car.

Joke? Father Dowling went to the patrol car and tapped on the window. The cop sitting back there with Joe rolled down the window.

"Don't worry, Joe. I'll be down as soon as I can."

"I'm innocent!"

Difficult as it was to think of Joe Walsh as a potential murderer, the facts were even more difficult to dismiss. An anonymous call had led to the discovery of Ward Ripley locked in his car with the motor running and the garage doors shut. With reluctance, he told the rescuing police that it was Joe Walsh who had done this to him. On the seat beside him was a sealed envelope. In it was a letter that professed to be Ward's suicide note.

"I don't even own a computer," he said.

On the playground, when Joe wormed free of the police sufficiently to pull from his pocket the envelope he had brought to give to Peggy, a silence fell. This, it was recognized, was a dramatic moment. The envelope was opened and its contents unfolded. A blank sheet of paper. Joe had the look of someone for whom the fundamental unfairness of things had just struck.

That things are not so badly arranged after all became apparent the following morning. Joe was still being detained while conversations between Tuttle and the prosecutor went on.

"This is a lovers' quarrel," Tuttle insisted.

"Lovers!"

"Puppy love."

With such representation, Joe spent the night in custody. He was having his breakfast from a metal bowl when the news came. Ward Ripley had been found dead in his automobile, the motor running, the garage doors shut.

Readers of the *Fox River Tribune* had the feeling they were getting the previous day's news. It took attentive reading of the elementary prose, no sentence longer than six words, to realize that while yesterday there had been an alleged attempt on the life of Ward Ripley, this morning he had been found dead. The fact that the first failed and second successful attempt involved the same means added zest to the story. For Joe Walsh, the important thing was that he was exonerated. Free, he locked himself in his apartment and sat in utter and elected solitude, forming in the silence of his mind the resolution never again to go the St. Hilary's senior center. He was not sure he could look into Peggy Schwartz Fenster's sparkling eyes after the public humiliation that had been brought down on his head by Ward Ripley. Joe had still to realize that Ward was truly dead. That phoenix had risen too frequently from its ashes for him to be so soon at ease.

Marie Murkin was convinced that this reprise of the locked car, running motor, closed garage scene meant that, having feigned his death once, Ward Ripley had decided to do himself in.

"Why?"

Marie studied the pastor as if wondering whether he was ready for a deep insight into human nature. "It will seem odd if I say it was for love."

"It will seem odder if you don't explain what you mean."

Marie's explanation, fanciful and romantic as befitted her nature, was not without anchor in the world of the St. Hilary senior center. The phrase "second childhood" has lost its innocence in an age of Alzheimer's disease, but there is a benign form of the return to the simplicity that was ours before experience and Original Sin really made themselves felt. Elderly citizens have a way of taking on again the personae that were theirs before they made their mark in the world, or vice versa. Grandmothers put aside their wisdom and dignity and simper at toothless old men they remember as swains. Half-deaf men whose posture has become a permanent courtly bow do the septuagenarian equivalent of walking on their hands to attract the attention of trifocaled silver-haired grandmothers. If there is no fool like an old fool, it is because the old are mimicking the foolish young. Father Dowling could thus believe Marie's story that there had been a rivalry between Joe Walsh and Ward Ripley for the attention of Peggy Schwartz Fenster.

Not that Marie thought Peggy without fault.

"She has been vamping those two shamelessly for weeks."

"Vamping?"

"You know what I mean."

Peggy Schwartz Fenster seemed flustered but not devastated when Father Dowling spoke to her. She dismissed any suggestion of an interest in Ward Ripley that went beyond a little harmless nostalgia. "I suppose you could say we were childhood sweethearts, Father. But that was a very long time ago."

"Did Ward feel the same way?"

"Father, he is a married man."

Roger Dowling was surprised to hear this and somewhat dismayed that he was. It was the sort of thing he knew about the regulars at the senior center, if only because Edna Hospers kept him informed of her operation.

"She's a flirt, of course," Edna said. "I think she got a big kick out of making those two old hearts flutter."

"Two?"

"Joe Walsh was absolutely bedazzled by her. Ward did a lot of showing off and Peggy enjoyed that, but Joe just stood there worshipping her. And don't think she didn't know it."

"What do you make of Joe's story?"

Edna frowned. "If a man wasn't dead, I could believe it was some kind of practical joke."

The joke, as Joe Walsh described it, was for Ward to feign death in order to elicit from Peggy, and others, an outpouring of affection and eulogy. At a crucial point, he would appear and take his bow.

"But they would lynch him."

Joe shrugged. It was the effect Ward wanted, being the apple of every eye. He just didn't think too far beyond the next minute or two.

"Edna Hospers says he is married."

"Well, sort of. He told me he is getting a divorce."

"A divorce?"

"He's not married in the church. His wife is very young, a law student. He says she's on sabbatical."

"From law school?"

"No, from their marriage. But he spoke of it as if it were all over."

"He didn't intend to fake killing himself, did he?"

"He was just going to disappear. Read the letter."

The letter had been retrieved from Joe Walsh's computer, stored under "Peggy." This was the letter he had thought was sealed into the envelope he delivered into Peggy's hands after his arrest.

Computerized texts, laser printed, had a bogus authority about them. Maybe it was their uniformity. Pages emerged from word processors the way sausages emerged from a sausage processor:

Dear Peggy:

Seeing you again after all these years has convinced me of the futility of my life. Years ago, with someone like you, I might have become what my talents equip me for. Alas, I have squandered everything. Do not think less of me for departing in this fashion. I am told that only imitation courage is required to take one's own life. Somehow that seems to fit me to a tee. Farewell. And, may I say—with love. Ward.

"You printed this out for Ward?"

"I saw him fold it up. I went to get an envelope. He put a folded sheet in it and sealed it."

"So the joke was on you."

"Why am I not laughing?"

Silly as it was, the practical joke Joe Walsh attributed to Ward Ripley made some kind of sense. What didn't make sense was that he should go on and actually kill himself. Father Dowling wished he had come to know the man better. Marie thought that he had been so taken by the attention the practical joke brought him that he went on to commit suicide in an effort to hold his audience.

"That's pretty far-fetched, Marie."

Marie's eyes lifted. Don't hold her responsible for the folly of human beings. Father Dowling wondered if the second time hadn't been intended as a joke, too, a joke that had gotten out of hand. That was ruled out by the autopsy.

That Ward had been killed was now beyond doubt, thanks to the autopsy. The cord that bound his wrists had been cut from his NordicTrack. Only a Houdini could have bound himself that way. More decisively still, there was a contusion on Ward's head that indicated he had been dumped into his car unconscious. Dr. Pippen could not rule out the possibility that the blow rather than the carbon dioxide was the principal cause of death.

Who had killed Ward Ripley?

Phil Keegan said they were exploring various possibilities. "Abstract possibilities, Roger, that's all." Had someone attempted to rob Ward and been too vigorous in quieting him while valuables were sought? The trouble with this was that Ward had no valuables. Anyone who knew him realized that he was a glib charmer who had used up every avenue of trust and now subsisted on what he received from Social Security. He had no pension or other source of income, and any valuables he possessed had long since gone to pawnbrokers. A thief would have to be as inept as his victim to imagine there was profit to be had from ransacking Ward's apartment.

"Was it ransacked?"

"Either that or he was the sloppiest housekeeper in creation."

It was Marie Murkin who turned Phil Keegan's attention in another direction. The housekeeper had been following developments with uncharacteristic silence, absorbing what she heard, pondering it in her easy chair as she sat evenings in her apartment at the back of the house, not watching television, not reading the book open on her lap, simply holding in readiness the beads that dangled from her hand. Now the fruit of that meditation was placed at the disposal of the police.

"You are asking who benefited from Ward Ripley's death."

"You got any ideas, Marie?"

"You're looking in the wrong direction."

Marie was alluding to Peggy Schwartz Fenster and her son Maurice. Maurice, a tall, pudgy man whose expression told of his disappointment with the world, had recently lost a pile of money speculating on silver.

"Silver?"

"Peggy says Ward put him onto it, saying he had authoritative information from his banker."

"His banker?"

"He had suggested to Maurice that, while Joe Walsh was retired, he kept his old contacts in the world of finance and was privy to the coming boom in the silver market." Maurice, whose biography could rival Ward's own in terms of lost opportunities, failed hopes, and missed trains, saw a chance to recoup the losses of a lifetime. He put every nickel he had into silver. The price of silver reacted by dropping like a rock. Within a month, Maurice's assets were ten percent of what they had been.

"He blamed Ward of course."

It didn't help that Ward hinted to the son that there was a nuptial future for himself and Maurice's mother. This is where Marie's thoughts became byzantine.

"He has lost everything because of Ward?" Phil said.

"Not everything."

"Oh."

"He is his mother's heir."

Phil's mouth rounded in comprehension. Cy Horvath's eyebrows lifted a millimeter, the extent of his reaction to even the most surprising information.

"Ah," said Phil. "And she's loaded." Peggy's assets amounted to several million dollars. She had carefully kept her own finances out of her son's reach, so that while he plummeted with the price of silver, she rose even higher with a stock market gone mad.

"What if he saw Ward Ripley coming into control of all his mother's money?"

"I'll talk to him."

"I hate to be the one responsible for his misfortune," Marie said after Phil and Cy had left.

"Did you urge him into silver, too?"

She lifted her chin and lowered her lids. She knew grudging

admiration when she heard it. She sailed off to the kitchen as if she had just made a citizen's arrest.

3

Joe Walsh might never have returned to the St. Hilary's senior center if Edna Hospers had not made a special trip to convince him to come back.

"Everyone is asking about you."

"That's what I'm afraid of."

"Peggy just mopes around."

That did it, of course. The thought that Peggy might mope for him swept despondency from Joe Walsh's soul. He wore a new and rather gaudy sport shirt when he returned, and there was the suggestion of a peacock in the way he paraded along one side of the former gym, looking at the table where Peggy was playing bridge. Her triumphant production of a forgotten trump while he watched might not suggest a moping woman to the undiscerning eye, but Joe was in the grips of the certainty that longings that had been his since childhood were not far from being fulfilled.

"Some shirt." Charles Quirk smiled malevolently at him.

Joe bowed at the ironic compliment.

"That one of Ward's?"

Joe glared at Quirk and for a mad moment he felt like tearing off the garment.

"He couldn't have afforded it."

Peggy, dummy while her partner played their bid, looked across the room at Joe Walsh. He drifted toward her as if he were weightless in outer space and she an irresistible star. She held out her hand and silently he took it. It was the moment he had dreamt of as a boy and now, as an old man, could regard as the purpose of his life. But it was a moment that lasted for only a moment. Captain Phil Keegan appeared in the doorway and wanted to know where Mrs. Margaret Fenster was.

Joe remained at her side when Keegan led her out of the gym and told her of the arrest of her son Maurice. She tottered and Joe supported her. How fragile she seemed, hardly more than bones in her frilly dress. She let out a cry when she heard that her son was suspected of murdering Ward, and Joe slipped a supporting arm around her waist. How toil-worn the hand he held seemed, how furrowed with care her brow. A great tenderness swept over him.

"You should get a lawyer for him," Keegan advised.

"Not Tuttle," Joe said.

Amos Cadbury, who had known Ignatius Fenster, agreed to defend Maurice, though, given the evidence, there was little that any lawyer could do beyond ensuring that the law was fairly applied. Maurice's fingerprints were all over Ward's apartment; a wrench that proved to be the weapon with which Ward had been struck also bore the prints of Maurice Fenster. The motive?

"Because of him I put everything in silver! I lost my shirt."

Mr. Cadbury was astonished. "Why would you follow the advice of such a man?"

"He said he had a friend, a banker, with inside information."

When the price of silver began to drop, Ward assured Maurice that this was part of the prediction. That was meant to scare off the weak-hearted. But just wait. Maurice waited and the price dropped like a plumb line toward financial disaster. By the time he could sell, he had lost over ninety percent of his savings.

"He said he would make it good to me," Maurice said. His fat lower lip was moist and his lidded eyes tragic.

Mr. Cadbury sat back in surprise. "With what?"

"He said he was going to marry my mother. Once he got control of her money . . ."

He could not go on. He broke down. The thought that the

author of his ruin should marry his mother and interpose himself between Maurice and his hoped-for inheritance was too much. The faked death had given Maurice his inspiration.

"I felt that I was performing a public service." This was a thought that Father Dowling pursued with Maurice after his trial and conviction and the failure of the pro forma appeal.

"Father, if the public executioner is justified then so was I."

"Do you believe in capital punishment?"

"Of course!"

The belief seemed to focus on Ward Ripley rather than himself. In any case, with time came something like composure. Maurice recognized that he had acted wrongly and made a good confession. For the rest, he devoted his days to studying the market, unable not to keep an eye on the price of gold and silver.

4

"They make a lovely couple," Marie acknowledged when Peggy and Joe left the rectory and wandered up the path toward the school.

"A mature couple anyway."

Peggy and Joe had been with the pastor to arrange for their wedding. She favored a low-key affair, just a few friends, but Joe wanted a full-tilt church wedding.

"I want to see you in a bridal gown."

It took some time to convince him that this would not do. Father Dowling's reference to Miss Havisham went uncaught, which was probably just as well. The arrangements were made; all was in readiness.

"It's Joe Walsh," Marie said that evening, looking into the study. She added in a whisper, "I hope he isn't getting cold feet."

But Marie would never know what it was that brought Joe to

Father Dowling that night. He was troubled of mind and spirit and sought peace and pardon before approaching the altar with Peggy on his arm.

"I feel responsible, Father."

"For Ward's death?"

"Not the actual killing. You see, I did tell him about silver stock."

"You did!"

"I thought he might pass the tip on to Peggy and . . ."

"Aha." The dismay Maurice came to feel would have been felt by his mother, thus removing the obstacle of Ward Ripley from Joe's path.

"That doesn't make you guilty of murder."

"It was a malevolent intent, Father."

He made a good confession and bowed his head when Father Dowling pronounced the formula of absolution. He rose then, but he hesitated in the doorway.

"Thank you, Father."

"You're welcome."

"It is ironic though."

"What's that, Joe?"

"Have you seen what's happened to the price of silver?"

That precious metal, reversing a long-term trend, had suddenly skyrocketed in price. And in Joliet, Maurice realized that if he had only hung on to silver he would be the richest prisoner there.

ABOUT THE AUTHOR

Author and editor **Ralph McInerny** (1929–2010) was acknowledged as one of the most vital voices in lay Catholic activities in America. He was cofounder and copublisher of *Crisis*, a widely read journal of Catholic opinion; he also taught medieval studies at Notre Dame University and wrote several series of mystery novels, one of which, *The Father Dowling Mysteries*, ran on network television for several seasons and can still be seen on cable today. Scholars are rarely entertainers, but Ralph McInerny, both as himself and under his pseudonym Monica Quill, was both for many years.